271018

HIGHNESS IN HIDING

Highness in Hiding

Nigel Tranter

271018

Hodder & Stoughton

First published in Great Britain in 1995 by
Hodder and Stoughton
A division of Hodder Headline PLC

10 9 8 7 6 5 4 3 2 1

British Library Cataloguing in Publication Data

Tranter, Nigel
Highness in Hiding
I. Title
823.912 [F]

ISBN 0-340-62585-6

Typeset by Hewer Text Composition Services, Edinburgh
Printed and bound in Great Britain by Mackays of Chatham PLC

Hodder and Stoughton
A division of Hodder Headline PLC
338 Euston Road
London NW1 3BH

Principal Characters in order of appearance

Charles Edward Stuart: Elder son of The Old Pretender, or
 James the Eighth and Third
Young Clanranald: Son of that chief. Commander of the
 Clanranald regiment
Captain John William O'Sullivan: Adjutant-general of the
 Jacobite army
Captain Felix O'Neill: Officer of the French army. Aide-de-camp
Aeneas MacDonald of Borrodale: Tacksman.
Father Allan MacDonald: Chaplain
Donald MacLeod of Gualtergill: Merchant from Skye and
 expert pilot
Ned Burke: Former sedan chair bearer from Edinburgh
Clanranald: Ranald MacDonald, chief of that branch of Clan
 Donald
MacDonald of Boisdale: Step-brother of Clanranald
Donald Campbell: Tacksman of Isle of Scalpay
Hector Campbell: Son of above
Aileen Mackenzie of Kildun: Widow of a Lewis laird
Neil MacEachain: Former tutor of Young Clanranald
Hugh MacDonald of Baleshare: Tacksman thereof
Morag MacDonald: Crofter's widow, in Scarilode
Hugh MacDonald of Armadale: Captain of the Skye militia
Flora MacDonald: Step-daughter of MacDonald of Armadale
 above
Lady Clanranald: Wife of that chief
Alexander MacDonald of Kingsburgh: Factor to Sir Alexander
 MacDonald of Sleat
Captain Donald Roy MacDonald: Son of Hugh of Baleshare
 above
Captain Malcolm MacLeod of Brea: Officer of the Clanranald
 regiment
John MacLeod, Younger of Raasay: Officer of the Clanranald
 regiment
Murdoch MacLeod of Rona: Brother of above
Meg Mackinnon: Sister of MacLeod of Brea above

Captain John Mackinnon of Elgol: Husband of above
Mackinnon of Mackinnon: Chief of that small clan
John Macinnes
MacDonald of Morar: Clan Donald chieftain
Angus MacDonald of Borrodale: Another Clan Donald chieftain
Alexander MacDonald of Glenaladale: Nephew of above. Major in the Clanranald regiment
John MacDonald, Younger of Borrodale: Lieutenant
John MacDonald: Younger brother of Glenaladale
Angus MacEachain of Meoble: Son-in-law of Borrodale
Major Donald Cameron of Glenpean: Kinsman of Lochiel, the Cameron chief
Donald MacDonald
Seven Men of Glen Moriston: Former soldiers of the Glengarry regiment, led by Patrick Grant, three Chisholms, two MacDonalds, and a MacGregor. Later joined by a Macmillan
Donald MacDonell of Lochgarry: Captain in the Glengarry regiment
Cameron of Clunes: Captain in the Lochiel regiment
Dr Archibald Cameron: Brother of Lochiel
Ranald MacDonell of Aberarder: Kinsman of Lochgarry
Macpherson, Younger of Breakachie: Officer in the Macpherson regiment
Allan Cameron: Brother-in-law of Lochiel
Ewan Cameron of Lochiel: Chief of Clan Cameron
Ewan Macpherson of Cluny: Chief of Clan Macpherson
Colonel John Roy Stewart: Officer in the French army
Captain Michael Sheridan: Officer in the French army
Colonel Richard Warren: Emissary of the King of France

1

The talking died away in that overcrowded and untidy room of the humble cottage in the birch wood of Glenbeasdale as the young man at the head of the rough board which served as table raised head and hand. He had been silent for some time as men had discussed and argued, with so much in the balance. Now he spoke.

"I have decided," he declared. "We go. Or, *I* go. Whence I came. We dare not wait longer here. Every day, every hour, *ma foi*, endangers us, endangers all. That I will not have. You all, and so many others, endangered further. There has been a sufficiency of hurt, to over many. I go to France, God willing, to return hereafter. *Maintenant*, it is enough!"

His hearers gazed at him, expressions varying on their faces, mainly tired faces, few welcoming that statement, however much it expressed concern for them. It was Young Clanranald who spoke first, as he was entitled to do.

"But, Highness – no!" he protested. "To go now would be to lose all. To throw away all the great endeavour. All is not lost – not yet! But if you go, all will be. The Lord George, Cluny Macpherson, Keppoch and the rest, they will be assembling at Ruthven in Badenoch. Others elsewhere. Lochiel is gathering more of his Camerons. Clan Donald will rally again. To leave all now would be . . . disaster. You must see it, Highness."

"I see disaster, yes, my friend – but not in this of my going. And I bade you all to cease naming me Highness. I am Dumont, Monsieur Dumont, a French visitor. Disaster for *you*, and for so many another, is what I fear. Already too many have suffered on my behalf, *le bon Dieu* forgive me! I must not, I will not, have more to lose all, their freedom, their homes and families, their lives, for my father's cause. I came to bring freedom, justice, good for his realm, not hurt, pain, sorrow. It is enough."

The speaker rose, as though to indicate conclusion and, weary as he was, garbed all but in rags, he still bore an air of inborn authority. His were handsome features, pleasingly attractive rather than strong, however drawn now with fatigue, stress and disappointment, grief indeed. High of forehead, under uncombed fair hair, with expressive and sensitive brown eyes, cheek bruised from a fall, above a firm mouth and unshaven chin, he held himself, as always, gracefully, a well-made if slender young man of twenty-four years, Charles Edward Stuart.

One standing near, older, a solid, heavy man, John William O'Sullivan, lately adjutant-general of the Jacobite army, nodded.

"You choose aright, Charles." As the prince's close associate, he could and did so name him. "You say to go, yes. Go now. On the morrow, to be sure. That is best." He spoke with the tongue of Ireland overlaid with a French accent. "To France, yes. But . . . the going? That will not be easy, I fear."

It was another Irish voice which was raised, that of Captain Felix O'Neill, of the French service. "How to win to France from this wilderness of mountains and waters? We have reached the tide's edge here, have we not? After our travail of these last days. But – the English ships, which Borrodale tells us patrol these narrow seas to keep away French aid for us. How to reach France without a French ship to take us?"

"We must sail by night, my friend, in some small boat. Out from this loch, out to beyond where the English ships wait. To the Long Island, the Outer Isles. There we shall not be looked for, I think. In some harbour there we will find a vessel, no?" The prince spread his hands.

"Highness . . . Monsieur!" That was Aeneas MacDonald of Borrodale, their host, although this was not Borrodale House but a hidden cottage nearby in which the fugitives would be safer. "I beg of you, see it otherwise. Your place is still *here*, in Scotland, not in France. Your army has suffered defeat, yes, at that Culloden Moor. But the cause is not lost. Your people are only dispersed. But there are still thousands who will flock to your royal cause."

Young Clanranald supported that. "After Falkirk, sir, many of the clansmen made for their own glens after all the months of fighting and march. They are still your men, and would rally. There are others, who never rose, who delayed. Even, to my sorrow, in Clan Donald. Murray, Cluny and the rest, those who won free from Culloden, reassemble at Badenoch's Ruthven Castle. Go there, I say, and rejoin them. They will take up arms again. Go to them, sir, not to France." The speaker was a red-headed, vehement young man with a flashing eye, who had led the Clanranald regiment throughout; his elderly father, Clanranald, chief of one of the greatest Clan Donald septs, was dwelling these difficult days over on his properties in the Outer Isles.

"You say go to Badenoch, man," O'Sullivan charged him. "How? How many miles through your endless mountains? Hundreds. And Cumberland's troops everywhere. Searching for us. How far would we get?"

"We would guide the prince by little-known paths and passes which no Cumberland's men would know. Rest, after our weary passage here, a couple of days. Then south by east, by Sunart and Ardgour and Mamore to Glen Spean, and so up Laggan to the Spey and Ruthven. Four days, I will have you there."

"I agree with my kinsman, Monsieur." That was Father Allan MacDonald, a young priest and the prince's chaplain. "One defeat, even two, is not a war lost. You came to free your royal father's people from the English yoke, from the usurping Elector and his German brood. You can still do it. Free Scotland, at least. Later England, perchance. But Scotland, yes. A summer campaign of attrition and raid and sally from our trackless mountains, and then a winter offensive in force. Cumberland and his English and Lowland levies will not face a winter war in Scotland, nothing more sure. They will depart for kinder climes, I say. As will their ships in these Hebridean seas. One year hence and you could be sitting again in Holyroodhouse, King of Scots, secure! Or your father could." For a cleric, that one seemed to have a fair grasp of matters military and strategic.

Charles, eyeing him all but lovingly, bit his lip as though his resolve shaken. Then he shook his fair head.

"Father Allan, you say that I came to free my people, or my father's, from the usurper's yoke. That was my wish and aim, yes. But not to bring them pain and hurt and death. As I have done. The slaughter and bloodshed and savagery of Culloden Moor taught me the price that I was demanding for my cause. It was enough. More than enough. Every day that I remain in this land now more will suffer. Cumberland showed us back there what he could do. Shooting the prisoners. Slaying the wounded. Burning men alive. Torturing. Even flaying men's skins! It was beyond all belief! He

3

is worse than any animal! Now, while I remain, he will be wreaking the like inhumanities on all whom he thinks support me, shelter my men, recognise my father as king. Men, women, children. No – I will not have it, I say! I go. When they learn that I am gone, and the threat to their Elector over meantime, they will leave it, leave Scotland, return south. A man of God, you must see it so, Father?"

That silenced the priest, but not his MacDonald cousin. "Wait you here a day or two, Monsieur, until we know the true position. Learn what Cumberland does now. Where he is. Learn how many flock to the Lord George and the others. I will send out running gillies, scouts, north, east and south, to discover the situation. You . . . we are all weary after four days' travel through the mountains from the battle, unfed, dispirited. Give me two or three days, then decide. You are safe here, I swear, in Clanranald country. You could not leave, anyway, to the Outer Isles, until we have found a suitable craft and crew to take you. Give me, give Scotland, those days, sir!"

Sighing, Charles Stuart inclined his head. "As you will, meantime, my good friend."

"You will at least have a bed to sleep in this night! As will all. May I lead you to it, sir?"

They left that table with its broken meats and empty flagons having precious little consumable left therein, the first real meal they all had eaten for days, for the Borrodale maids to clear away, none seeking to linger. Young Clanranald had to go and issue orders for his running gillies to prepare.

In the morning of a showery late April day of scudding clouds and fitful burst of brilliant sunshine, rested, Charles was in more cheerful mood, although not enlarging upon his intentions as to the future. He was now wearing more suitable garb, provided from the Borrodale wardrobes, in place of the humble, ragged clothes the fugitives had picked up at the Lord Lovat's Gortuleg cot-houses after the battle to disguise their identities on their secret flight westwards. Bathed and shaved and hair combed, in fine tartan trews and doublet, he looked much more like the handsome representative of the ancient royal Stewart line who had landed nearby those nine months before, with the Seven Men of Moidart, to proceed to set up his standard and proclaim his father King

4

James the Eighth, at Glenfinnan, none so far off. Then to march southwards to the Lowlands, to take Edinburgh with acclaim, to win the Battle of Prestonpans and so to head on to enter England, victorious. As far as Derby he had won before he had turned back, persuaded against his will not to go on to London on the advice of his lieutenant-general the Lord George Murray, with the English failing to rise in his support and fears of government forces massing behind them, back to Scotland, a hungry, disappointed and dispersing army. Admittedly they had won a small victory at Falkirk, and then disaster at Culloden Moor.

After a late and hearty breakfast, Charles announced that he would like to go down to the loch shore, to revisit the spot where he had landed from the French vessel, the *Du Tellay*, with such high hopes those nine months ago with his seven companions, the Seven Men of Moidart, of whom only two were with him now, having survived the campaign, O'Sullivan and Aeneas MacDonald, the treasurer, brother of Kinlochmoidart.

It was not far down to the very lovely loch's indented coastline, with all its colourful weed-hung reefs and skerries and offshore islets, a feast for the eye however much of a hazard for navigation. Loch nan Uamh, the Loch of the Cave, opened out into the Sound of Arisaig, itself opening on to the great Inner Sound of the Sea of the Hebrides, with the large islands of Muck and Eigg blocking most of the horizon, and the jagged mountains of Rhum just appearing above the Arisaig headland to the west.

That stupendous vista brought a lump into Charles's throat, whatever it did for his companions. This had been his first introduction to mainland Scotland, his ancestral Stewart homeland – even if he did spell it now in the French way, Stuart – and a dramatic initiation it had been, such as he had never before viewed nor imagined. Beauty, grandeur, spectacle it presented – and challenge. Challenge to him who had come to meet a different challenge, to win back for his father his ancient kingdom and throne. And now, viewing it all again, having failed in that challenge, he knew a great and aching sorrow. And yet, and yet, the challenge still there, an urge, an exhortation, to come back one day and try again.

Young Clanranald pointed. "See, sir – there! Yonder, between us and the cliffs of Eigg. One of the English ships of war. See it? They wait. For you! And for the French. There are always one or two off this Moidart coast, my people tell me. A curse on them! They keep well offshore, as well they may, for this coast is a graveyard for shipping."

"They do not send men ashore, in boats? Searching for us?"

"Not yet here, sir. They *have* sent their longboats to land on various isles and headlands, but not here. There are over-many reefs and traps for their liking, their safety."

It was certainly a very wild coast, however beautiful. Charles counted eight islets immediately offshore within a mile or so, not to mention the innumerable rocks and skerries, great and small. With the mountains coming down so close, and only the mouth of Glenbeasdale opening inland, it was no welcoming haven for mariners. And yet, here the *Du Tellay* had brought him those months ago. He was recounting, somewhat ruefully, how the Marquis of Tullibardine, one of the original seven, elder brother of the Lord George and heir to Atholl, had seen an eagle hovering over that ship for almost an hour, perceiving this as an excellent augury for their endeavour, the king of birds come to welcome the prince to Scotland.

With dramatic suddenness, one of the rain-squalls blew up from the south-west, blotting out the seascape, and their host hurried them all into a quite large cave nearby, for shelter. This, he declared, he had haunted as a boy, convinced that he would eventually see the spirit of that ancient Celtic Church missionary, Saint Boisel, after whom some said Glenbeasdale was named, and whose retreat this cavern was said to be. Father Allan took the opportunity to offer up a prayer for St Boisel's intervention with the Almighty on behalf of the royal cause, and that the prince might be persuaded to remain in Scotland until victory was won, Charles wagging his head.

The rain-shower over, they returned to Borrodale House.

That evening the first of the running gillies arrived back from a visit to the Morar area to the north where, at Mallaig's haven, only five miles from the Isle of Skye across the Sound of Sleat, he had gained the word that the Campbell Earl of Loudoun, one of the enemy commanders, had reached Skye, searching for the fugitive prince on that island.

This was, of course, grievous news, coming from so comparatively near at hand, and indicating that Cumberland knew or suspected that Charles was somewhere on this area of the

6

west coast; and that they could therefore expect the search for him to narrow and intensify. Also the messenger brought the extraordinary story that the Skye fisherman who had told them about Loudoun, said that the Duke of Cumberland was offering the vast reward of thirty thousand pounds to anyone who would deliver up the prince to him.

Such a sum was almost beyond all Highland dreams of avarice, and greatly alarmed O'Sullivan, O'Neill and other non-Scottish members of the party, but not, strangely, the MacDonalds and other clansmen, who declared that no Highlander, however unsympathetic to the cause, would ever dream of selling the prince for English gold.

But it was a vivid indication as to the urgency of the government's determination to lay hands on Charles Stuart. It sent all to bed in thoughtful frame of mind.

The following day brought a significant development. One of Young Clanranald's scouts had met in Glen Spean two travellers and their escort heading westwards from Badenoch, Secretary John Hay and Lockhart, Younger of Carnwath, both prominent in the Jacobite cause, and now seeking the prince, being sent from Ruthven Castle. They were brought to Glenbeasdale. Lockhart, a Lowlander from Lanarkshire, of ancient line, because he felt that his place should be near to Charles; but Hay brought a letter from the Lord George Murray, lieutenant-general. And the letter was of consequence. As Charles read it, his features set.

It started well enough: "May it please Your Royal Highness . . ." But please him it did not, even though Murray went on to say that he was greatly concerned for the prince's safety and well-being, and sorely distressed over the disaster of the recent battle. Then he craved His Highness's pardon if he mentioned a few truths. And these truths were blunt, he declaring that he personally had ventured more frankly in the royal cause, and in his position had put more at stake, than all the others put together. He held, first of all, that the prince had been wrong to raise the standard as he had done without firm assurance of French major aid in men and moneys. Then he wrote that His Highness had burdened his cause with incompetent aides, in especial the man O'Sullivan, unfit for trust, and who had committed gross blunders and issued confused orders as to battle, which were no concern of his as adjutant-general. He should have been no more than in charge of the baggage-train! Then the secretary, John Hay, who would deliver this letter, was little better. He had served the cause ill, neglected his duties and caused the starvation of the army. If they had had a sufficiency of provisioning, as was his province and concern – for he had had moneys enough, five hundred gold pieces of which was still at Ruthven Castle – the outcome could well have been quite different, empty stomachs being no help in warfare. O'Sullivan's and Hay's names had become odious to all the army, and indeed had all but bred mutiny.

Charles Stuart, reading thus far, put his head in his hands, to the concern of the watchers.

But there was more. The Lord George went on to say that he had no desire to continue as lieutenant-general of the army. He had not resigned earlier because it could have prejudiced the cause at a critical time. But now he hoped that His Royal Highness would accept his demission, while being assured that he remained his loyal supporter and friend.

It took some time for the prince to compose himself. His was a sensitive and perceptive nature, and all this from his principal commander in the field and adviser on things military was a dire blow, with its implicit criticism of himself and his judgment.

At length, looking up, he asked John Hay if he knew of the contents of this letter. The other said that he did not, whereupon the prince folded up the paper and pocketed it in his doublet. Since he had to make some comment thereon, he said that the Lord George was reconsidering his position. What was the state of the assembly over there in Badenoch? What of its morale? Who was in fact in command? And what was the intention for the immediate future?

Hay said that spirits were scarcely high, but that all saw the fight as going on, the cause by no means lost. The Duke of Perth, the Lord Elcho and Cluny Macpherson were strong for a summer campaign, saying that large numbers of men could still be raised from the glens, Lockhart adding that few saw their recent defeat as more than a temporary setback. The royal cause would triumph yet.

Charles rose abruptly, and said that he would retire to his room for a space, leaving all wondering.

When, after a while, he returned to his host and companions, the prince was in control of himself and quietly resolved.

"I have made my decision, my friends," he said. "My final decision. It is as I said earlier. I go. To France. The Lord George's letter, what he says therein, confirms me in my judgment and conclusion. Here, meantime, I can do nothing to effect. In France I can, I hope and believe, raise the French aid in men and moneys which we need. And which, perchance, I should have ensured before I set out on this great venture. To return in due course. So – I go." He turned to Young Clanranald. "You, my friend, must seek out a suitable boat and crew to take me to the Outer Isles, where I shall seek to find a sea-going vessel to win me to France. How long will that take, think you?"

"Highness, I beg of you . . . !"

Charles held up his hand. "No more, I pray you. I see my course. How long, think you?"

"It will require a sturdy craft. These seas are strong, treacherous, with currents and down-draughts and undertows. No inshore fishing-boat will serve for the Outer Isles. A six- or eight-oared craft, with square sail, will be necessary. None such will I find nearer than Mallaig, I fear."

"Very well. Can you have one here by tomorrow night, then? Since it seems that we must sail in darkness, to avoid the English ships." The prince was all decision now, summoning up his inherent authority. He turned to Hay and Lockhart. "Meantime you, my friends, return to your Badenoch, and declare that I order the dispersal to their own places of all presently assembled there, conveying my most grateful thanks to one and all for their aid and service. But to be ready to muster again to my royal father's standard in due course, pray God before very long. I go – but to return. The stronger. Best thus, I swear. And none to be told whence I go, save eventually to France. And that for aid. It is understood?"

When the prince spoke thus, none would say him nay, even O'Sullivan.

"How long a voyage to these Outer Isles, Charles?" that man asked nevertheless. "When we came first, we landed first at Eriskay, did we not? That is one of the Outer Isles?"

Young Clanranald answered him. "Direct, it is some ninety miles, I would say. To the nearest of the isles, which would be Barra. But there will be no sailing direct, see you. It will be necessary to dodge and shift and hide amongst the Inner Isles, to

9

hide from the Englishmen. And that only by night. So the distance could be doubled, and more. And some pilot will be required, who well knows these seas and sounds."

"You will find one such, for me?" Charles asked.

"I can think of one, Highness. You have already met him. Donald MacLeod of Gualtergill in Skye. We saw him at Inverness when Your Highness was there, before the battle. He was there shipping barley to Skye, for his own purposes. We know that he knows these waters like the palm of his hand!" He mustered a smile. "He distils and delivers whisky to all who have not his art themselves! All along this coast. And Aeneas, here, says that he was at Kinlochmoidart when *he* left there. If he is still there, with my kinsman, he would be best. You have tasted some of his wares here!"

That at least met with approving nods.

The prince retired again. He too had a letter to write.

The letter was to the chiefs and chieftains of clans, and his lairdly supporters, active and otherwise. Charles pondered long before putting pen to paper, for this epistle and declaration was intended not only for those who had raised men for his cause but also for those who had, for one reason or another, failed to do so, usually because they feared for its success without major French involvement. His present failure would only confirm these in their reluctance; so it was necessary to try to convince all of betterment in the future, regrets and sorrow for present defeat and loss, yes, but as near to promise as he could make it of a better effort to come.

He headed it "For the Chiefs", and wrote that he had come to Scotland with the best of goodwill towards his father's ancient kingdom, meaning to bring it only benefit and weal. If he had failed them all, this on account of insufficient backing from the Auld Alliance with France, he accepted the blame, and laid it at the door of his inexperience in the field. But now he was wiser, having learned the sore and hard way, and at whatever cost to others. So he was for France again, this time to win the backing in men, ships and moneys, which was required, and which he was assured the King of France would provide as promised. It was necessary that he went in person to gain this, as they all would understand. Moreover there was little that he could do meantime

10

this side of the water. But he would, God willing, be back, and in better case.

He went on to suggest the formation of a Council of Chiefs, to prepare the way for his return, and to choose and appoint a new commander of the forces, on the advice and guidance of the Duke of Perth and the Lord George Murray, with the Lord Elcho, Master of Horse.

He ended by urging that his departure be kept secret meantime as far as was practicable, for the sake of all concerned. And might the Almighty bless and direct them, and himself.

He made out a number of copies of this writing, to be distributed as widely but as secretly as was possible.

With Young Clanranald gone north to Mallaig, on horseback, as could be possible here, and Aeneas MacDonald southwards to Kinlochmoidart to seek to enlist this Donald MacLeod, the remainder of the company had little to do but rest and eat and sample more of the recommended Skye whisky. But Charles himself was restless and chose to go walking alone, well aware that the course he had decided upon was less than popular with most of his companions. But he saw this as essential, his simple duty and personal responsibility. One day, God willing, he would be king of this people. He had to take the far-sighted course, the more so as it seemed that he had failed to do so hitherto.

Late that night Young Clanranald arrived back from Mallaig, a dozen miles away, with the news that he had persuaded a crew to bring their eight-oared craft round the coast to Loch nan Uamh this very night. It should be here by the dawn. The men were sworn to secrecy as to their passengers and destination. Two of the boatmen had, in fact, been with the army throughout the campaign, in his own Clanranald regiment.

When he arose next morning, Charles found the boat crew eating breakfast in the kitchen, seven of them, one having apparently called off at the last moment, youngish men all, and distinctly embarrassed when they found themselves being addressed and thanked by the prince himself, even though he was insisting on them addressing *him* as Monsieur Dumont, a visiting Frenchman. They said that they had clung as close to the shoreline on their way here as the reefs and rocks would let them. It had been too dark for them to have glimpsed any of the English warships out in the sound, but all had seen them patrolling previously.

11

It was mid-afternoon before Banker Aeneas arrived back from Kinlochmoidart and, thankfully, he had the distilling and piloting expert, Donald MacLeod, with him, an elderly, massively built man with strong features and a very direct gaze. He was respectful when presented to Charles, but far from subservient, indeed not being long in declaring that he strongly advised His Highness not to embark on this voyage to the Outer Isles, which he saw to be hazardous in the extreme, both in respect of avoiding the English warships and in the perils of the seas themselves, the most dangerous, he averred, of all the Scottish seaboard, in any small vessel. Moreover, he had a fair judgment of weather, and he feared that the next day or two would see poor conditions for open boating. There were none of the famed and usual captive clouds on the Isle of Rhum peaks, which was a bad sign, apt to presage high winds, even gales. He advised against the expedition.

Charles shook his head, not censoriously at being thus counselled by a mere stranger of no great standing, but making clear his determination to go ahead with his chosen course, and forthwith, that very night. Cumberland's troops were reported to be at Fort Augustus and heading in this direction, and Loudoun was in Skye, only a few miles away. It was time to be gone, for all their sakes. Tonight let them sail.

The other shrugged, but did not refuse to collaborate, their host shaking his head also.

They went down to inspect the boat drawn up on the shingle. It was of open construction, sturdily built with high prow and stern posts, some twenty-five feet in length with a central short mast and four oar-holes on each side but no decking, and indeed little room for passengers, scarcely a sea-going craft in appearance, although probably not unlike the ancient traditional birlinns of these parts. Presumably these boatmen knew what they were at.

MacLeod reckoned that, sailing only by night, even in favourable weather conditions, it would take them two days to reach Barra, so they would need something in the way of provisioning, for they certainly could not rely on picking up food at islands on the way. Oatmeal was best, which eaten uncooked and mixed with water, or indeed whisky, would sustain them sufficiently – scarcely princely fare, but then this was no princely journey, was it?

As to who should accompany the prince there was but little discussion, with room for few indeed in the boat, and no point anyway in those Scots-based heading off for France. The two Irishmen, O'Sullivan and O'Neill, Father Allan MacDonald, who was not to be parted from his spiritual charge, and Ned Burke, Charles's faithful body-servant throughout much of the campaign. These four would go, no more. It seemed that Donald MacLeod was going to man the eighth oar, elderly as he was.

So, as dusk fell, it was time for farewells in an emotional scene, as they all trooped down to the shore with four pecks of oatmeal and two kegs of water and whisky, Charles returning his borrowed tartans to Young Clanranald and resorting to his ragged garb and Ned Burke's old coat. They took a pile of plaids to wrap around them for warmth, Aeneas presenting the prince with a bag of tobacco brought from Kinlochmoidart, knowing Charles's weakness for the weed.

At the boat, Father Allan said a brief prayer for the welfare of all concerned, blessed them, and the passengers climbed aboard, after much kissing of the prince's hand and fervent good wishes, tears in those sensitive royal eyes as he seated himself at the stern, indeed forced to lean against MacLeod's knees, so little space was available, the four others huddled beside him.

Oars out, the craft was pushed off, for better or for worse. It was a fairly calm night, despite their pilot's forebodings.

2

They pulled almost due westwards at first, and as close to the indented shore as the thickly scattered projections and reefs would let them; they had to do this, if they were not going to venture out into mid-loch, because of the series of islets which dotted that coastline four or five hundred yards out. MacLeod declared that there were no fewer than thirteen of these, and a major hazard for navigation, not only because of their own complement of rocks and skerries, but on account of the swirls and currents they created in the tides, difficult enough as these were in all conscience without that, such much affecting any light craft even in a fairly calm sea. In fact, such eddies and drags and pulls would be one of their main problems on this voyage, the passengers were told, for nowhere was there a stretch of ocean like the Sea of the Hebrides, with over five hundred islands which might be termed major, and thousands of minor ones such as these. But at least this nearby screen did protect them meantime, both from seaward view – not that, in this half-dark, viewing them was likely against the background loom of the land – and also from the pressure of the prevailing south-west wind. But only for a short while, for, to be sure, most of their journey would be west by south.

They had over two miles of this shoreline-creeping to cover before they would have to head out into the Sound of Arisaig, and made much more than that by the continual turning, twisting and sidling, with backing of oars, to avoid skerries and sunken rock, indeed sometimes their oar-blades scraping obstacles and catching on floating weed, Donald MacLeod directing and warning the other rowers, at the same time as naming the islets on their left as they passed them: Eilean nan Cabar, the Isle of the Poles or Beams; An Fraoch Eilean, the Bracken Islet; An Garbh Eilean, the Rough Islet, and so on.

By the end of April the nights were never very dark in these latitudes, which was both advantageous and the reverse; but as

14

they passed the last of the islets, An Glas Eilean, conditions altered in more ways than one, and suddenly. They pulled round to head more southwards and, deprived of that screen, the wind and waves grew considerably stronger; and at the same time they realised that it was becoming quite noticeably darker, this causing Donald to point ahead and upwards.

"I feared it, aye. Weather, see you! Low cloud, just. It is going to be ill sailing, I reckon. Are you for turning back, Highness?"

"No, no," Charles said. "Not that, now that we are on our way. Never that."

"It might be wise, Charles," O'Sullivan said. "This boat is heaving sufficiently already! And . . . my God!" That was added as a shower of spray splashed on them from over the high curving bows-post.

Certainly the craft was now pitching and rearing, so much so that occasionally the forward oarsmen failed to make contact with the water, this not helping progress.

"Wait you!" the pilot advised. "This is just the start of it, whatever. Yonder cloud ahead, low as it is, will bring a gale, nothing more sure. And the seas will rise. This is nothing at all, I tell you, just usual for these waters. But a gale! I'm thinking that we should make for the lee side of Eigg, just."

"Aye," one of the other rowers agreed. "But that will have us beam-on, getting there."

"I know it, man. But we will just have to be tholing it. Shelter we will need, just."

"Is there not an English ship biding off Eigg?" another crewman asked.

"We saw it," Charles said. "At this end of the island. Against the cliffs."

"I am not after forgetting it," Donald told them. "With this weather working up, her master will move her into the Port nan Partan there, I'm thinking. At the south end of the isle, a sheltered bay. He would be a fool not to do so. Och, we will need to be sailing up to the north end. Naught else for it, whatever. That, or turning back."

"No!" the prince exclaimed. "We have set our hands to this venture. Let us hold to it, and trust in the good God! Father Allan will say a prayer for us."

His chaplain, covering his head and shoulders with a plaid

15

against the flying spray, mumbled something less eloquent than his usual.

"How far to this north end of the island?" O'Neill asked.

"From here, eight or nine miles," they were told. "Long rowing, in this weather. But, because we will be going north-west instead of this south-west, we will be able to use the sail to some small use. Beam seas, yes – but a sail to aid. For a time, leastways . . ."

So they swung round to the right, in a north-westerly direction, and immediately all changed in conditions. Instead of pitching and dipping, the craft was rolling direly, or more accurately rolling as well as pitching, with the waves hitting it half-beam on, the rolling so violent that the crests came pouring over. Hastily Donald shouted for a partial turn westwards again, the starboard oars pulling hard, the port ones backing. That helped. They rolled less direly, but this was not in the direction they desired. Ordering the passengers to bale out water with some battered metal jugs in the stern-sheets, dizzy and breathless as they were with being tossed about by the heaving and swaying, he then had two of the port rowers transfer their oars over to the other side, and to dip them in the water, to act as lee-boards, difficult as this was without obstructing the other oarsmen. But the device did help to steady the boat.

He said that they would try the sail, but only half-up. Ned Burke sought to hoist it partly, and swiftly they felt the effect, a heeling over again and pulling round, the rowers having to duck heads to avoid the swinging stay.

"Too much! Too much!" Donald cried, and Ned hurriedly halved the amount of canvas raised, to distinct improvement.

The boat now began to make a curious crab-like progress, urged on by various forces, the part beam-on wind and seas, the sail's pressure, and the strong starboard pulling of the four oars, with the countering thrust of the two remaining port ones, the other two merely serving as balance against rolling. It made for odd and complicated headway, requiring constant adjustment, but headway there was, and in the desired direction.

Charles asked himself whether he was to be forgiven for subjecting his companions to this ordeal by his stubborn determination to proceed.

How far they had progressed towards their immediate goal, the shelter of the north-east end of the Isle of Eigg, it was hard to

16

calculate in the darkness. Then the actual storm hit them. The passengers had thought that it had done so already, but now they learned otherwise. It struck them like the smashing of a mighty fist, all but capsizing the boat, water pouring in, a blast of wind that took away their breaths and jerked persons sidelong. Breathless or not, Donald yelled for Ned to down that sail, which now could completely overturn them; and followed it with gasped orders to the rowers to get back to normal positions, difficult as this might be while they were being tossed about, the long oars awkward indeed to transfer, one in fact almost lost overboard. The object now was to get the craft back, at all costs, to its original course, facing into the storm, wherever this led them. Only so could they survive.

If the waves had been great before, now abruptly they were enormous, vast white hills and valleys of water, their crests whipped off in blinding spray, so that, dark as it was, the air and the sea both were white as they climbed and dipped and plunged and climbed again, the passengers scooping out water desperately, the rowers much of the time with their oars in the spume-filled rushing air.

Time lost all meaning, only motion, noise, stress, fear prevailed – and labour, labour.

How long it was before there was a change in conditions they none of them knew. When it came, it was as sudden as had been the impact of that storm. One moment they were breasting a white-maned sea-horse in the face of a gale of spray, and the next they were dropping, dropping, and not into just one more great trough of the waves but seemingly into a different level of water, and the wind dropping with it. Not altogether, of course, but a distinct lessening apparent, just as the breakers had abruptly lessened. The boat was rolling again, rather than with the up and down heaving and diving. The passengers stared at each other, pausing from the baling.

Donald jerked out explanation. "Shelves!" he panted. "Under-the-sea shelves. Waterfalls! Ledges deep down. Must be near to Eigg. Island ledges form overfalls."

"Thank God!" Allan gasped. "He has brought us into the lee of the island. Thank God, I say!"

"Be not so fast . . . with your thanks, man!" he was told. "Lee, yes. But overfalls are a danger. Whirlpools. They can cause whirlpools. And great holes. And the down-draughts from the hills

17

and cliffs. Storm still there. Isle but blocking it. But gaps, corries, glens – openings. Can cause down-draughts. These scoop pits in the waters. Dangers."

"We are near the island, then?" Charles asked.

Donald turned to peer. "Must be, aye. Not seeing it, with yonder dark cloud. But . . ."

His words were cut off as, without warning, their bows rose steeply and all were pitched backwards, with a clashing of oars, in cursing confusion. The craft's head swung round and it started to heel over again, Donald finding his voice to yell to the rowers.

Somehow they recovered their positions and got their oars working again, bringing the boat under some control.

"Another ledge," Donald jerked. "The other way, just. Och, I think that we must be close. Must not get *too* close. Skerries. Under the cliffs. Reefs. Turn north. Hoist that sail. But down it when I say. If a down-draught strikes. But could be none. These high cliffs. Better than braes and valleys . . ."

Ned did as he was told, clinging to the mast.

Now, strangely, heading due north under the lee of the all but unbroken bulwark of cliffs of the eastern side of Eigg, which they were beginning to perceive dimly against what Donald declared must be a lightening sky, they made the best progress of the night, the sail able to be fully hoisted, and the wind, swinging round the large island, for the first time aiding them. That is, until one of Donald's down-draughts struck them, coming out of a vast fissure of the precipices. Fortunately they had a warning, brief but sufficient for Ned to bring down that sail, in the rushing sound and altered turbulence of the water ahead. The oarsmen had to work hard again for a little, and then conditions improved once more.

They did not know how far up the side of the seven-mile-long island they had reached, although one of the fishermen rowers said that there was a large corrie in the cliffs, with a waterfall, fully three-quarters of the way to the head, which might be what they had just passed. Donald announced that, if so, they were none so far from a possible haven that he knew of at the very tip of the isle. Once beyond that and they were out into the Sea of the Hebrides itself, the Minch as it was called, with almost fifty miles across it to Barra in the Outer Isles, open water. Folly to start on that.

None of his companions disagreed. Even Charles Stuart had had enough for one night. If daylight caught them out in the open

Minch, they would be easy prey for any English ship. Donald's haven called.

The last mile or so presented no dire hazards, but as they commenced the turn westwards at the northern cape they met with a new challenge, a tide-race, this caused by the seas, after striking the western shores, swirling round the headland under pressure. The force of this was enough to all but halt them, hard as the oarsmen pulled, the sail now having to be lowered. They only made a creeping, zigzag course. Not only that, but because of the horseshoe-shaped islet just off this north headland, which Donald had said would provide a sheltered haven, an added danger was the effect of the high wind gusts, no longer sparing them, funnelled down between the headland cliffs and the islet, striking the water of the narrow channel and sending up alarming spouts when hitting the tide-race, extraordinary columns a dozen to a score of feet high.

Nevertheless, into that channel they had to pull if they wanted to gain the shelter of the little bay. Frightening as these spouts looked, Donald declared them not to be dangerous. There was no way they could avoid them for they could spout up anywhere; but although they could soak them all, they were wet through already. Even as he spoke they were drenched by a near miss. This demanded more baling, but did not distract the rowers from their fight with that tide-race, Donald ordering the prince and his friends to look out for reefs.

At least it was lighter now, whether on account of the storm clouds lifting or the dawn beginning to develop, and they could dimly see the islet's outline on their right, quite low-lying as compared with the soaring heights of the headland on their left. And there was the gap of the little bay, the swirling tide all but drawing them into it. Thankful indeed, they felt the pressures of wind and current ease as, edging their way past skerries and waving seaweed, they ran their bows up on to the shingle shore of Eilean Thuilm, the Islet of the Hillock. Land, solid, firm, reliable land.

They clambered out, and as the oarsmen drew up their craft to a safe grounding, Father Allan sank to his knees to kiss the wet grass and thank their Maker.

It was strange but good to walk and feel steady ground beneath them after all the hours of heaving uncertainty and cramped closeness. They quickly realised that they were cold, however, as well as wet – they had not had time to think of this hitherto – and were glad to stretch their legs by climbing up the little gorse-clad knoll, which gave the islet its name, thankfulness not confined to Allan MacDonald.

Charles it was who came across the hut, in a cleft of the knowe, a mere humble shed, doorless and with a turf roof, but a shelter of a sort, hay-strewn within with sheep droppings. No animals were in evidence now but presumably they could pasture here in summer.

The prince's calls brought the others, and all expressed their satisfaction at finding this. A fire here and they could warm themselves and partly dry off clothing and plaids.

When O'Sullivan asked with what they could make a fire, Donald pointed to the whins, or gorse bushes. There would be no trees on such an exposed islet, but whins always produced dead growth, however prickly, which would burn well; and once a good blaze was going, even the greenery burned.

So they were all set to the uncomfortable, jagged business of finding and breaking off dead gorse twigs, some quite thick but all barbed and scratchy, to much grunting and cursing. A great heap was piled at the open doorway of the hut, and flint and steel, with some of the dry hay from the floor, soon produced a most satisfactory and welcome blaze.

It was rather extraordinary what heat and flame could do for already reviving spirits, even if smoke clouds did have them all coughing. The oatmeal was fetched from the boat, liberally seasoned with whisky, and eaten by the handful with as much relish as would have been any splendid feast. The oars were brought, to set up and form a sort of fence behind the fire, and the plaids draped thereon to dry and, presently, some of the clothing discarded, with the warmed plaiding used to enfold denuded bodies. The warmth and respite from urgent activity, as well as the hour, soon induced lethargy and drooping eyelids. It was agreed that they should sleep, with always two of the thirteen awake, to tend the fire rather than to keep watch, for there was little likelihood of any need for the last in present circumstances.

Huddled together under the plaiding for warmth, eleven of them were quickly in blessed slumber.

It was daylight when Charles awoke – his companions had been kind enough to spare him the fire-tending duties – and although it was a morning of scudding clouds, the gale had blown itself out and there were glimpses of sunshine. The noise of crashing breakers on the cliff-foots remained, however.

When he emerged from the hut, it was to gaze up at the tremendous cliffs of Sgorr Sgaileach rearing high above that narrow entrance channel, this a mere three hundred yards or so across. Up there was the lofty plateau which formed most of the Isle of Eigg, wheeling, screaming seabirds circling the tops. Some of his companions still slept, as well they might, for they had the whole day to fill in here before darkness would allow them to continue with their journey. But not Donald MacLeod, who Charles found down near the boat, gazing across the narrows. Greeting the prince, he pointed.

Visible from here, and hitherto hidden behind the western horn of the little bay, could be seen not so much a cleft as a large green hollow in the line of cliffs, with its own smaller bay, this a mere quarter-mile away. And in the floor of this hollow was a small house, a cottage, with smoke rising from its thatched roof, and a couple of cows grazing nearby. But that was not at which Donald pointed, but to the figure of a man standing down at its beach and staring across at them.

"We have company, whatever! I had not known that there was a croft here. He will have seen our fire and smoke."

"Is it important?"

"It could be, yes. Best to go see him, just. He might tell us much."

Three of the oarsmen were gathering more gorse fuel, and Donald called them down, and to bring oars with them. They would cross the channel and have a word with that watcher.

It felt strange to the prince to be in that boat again and sculling calmly across the narrows, with no pitching and tossing, although there was still a strong current to be coped with, requiring some zigzagging.

Oddly enough, as they approached the other beach, the watching man turned and walked away, back towards the cottage.

"Our welcome!" Donald commented. "Yon one is playing it safe, whatever."

When they landed, they left two of the men at the boat, and the trio made their way up to the house, in the doorway of which the

21

man, a woman and two children now stood, waiting. What would they be thinking, perhaps fearing, was anybody's guess.

"Friends!" Donald called out, in the Gaelic. "We are friends. Come in shelter from the storm."

That received no answer.

"This is a MacDonald isle," he went on. "We come from Clanranald."

Now there was at least a nod. The couple were youngish, the children small.

"We have been caught in the storm, just. Sailing out from Loch nan Uamh. We took shelter over yonder. A dozen of us. You would see our fire?"

Another nod. The woman took the children inside. These were cautious folk.

Charles spoke. "The English. We were seeking to avoid them." He had just enough Gaelic to make that intelligible. It made an impact. The man grimaced, and spat.

"You have them here on Eigg?" Donald said.

"Aye, we have, a curse on them!" That was vehement. "Their ships sail these waters. They harry us all. Ravage. Destroy all boats. They smashed and sank mine." He pointed out to the channel. "English swine. They insulted my wife."

"I am sorry," Charles said, spreading his hands. He understood more of the native tongue than he could speak.

"You have a ship based here at Eigg, I think," Donald added. "That is why we sailed by night. We make for the Outer Isles. Barra."

"Aye, there is a ship at Kildonan. Their longboats came here. But there are others, och others. Five of them, I have counted. They defile these seas, just." He shook his head. "One, forby, is based at Barra, I am told."

"You say so? That is bad! Five? Then where are the others?"

"At the other isles. Rhum. Skye, Islay. What they do here, what they seek for, the good God knows!"

Charles almost declared that it was himself that they sought, but thought better of it.

Donald nodded. "We must avoid Barra, then. And these other isles. What of the Long Island itself? The Uists? Harris? Lewis?"

"I do not know, at all. I do not know what they are at. Why do they damage and sink all our boats? They have done the same at

22

Laig and at Port nan Partan and Kildonan. We are fishers. They destroy our living."

"It is war," Donald said, and glanced warningly at the prince. Nothing was to be gained by informing this unfortunate as to who they were or why they were here. "Have you any food, friend, that we could buy from you? Meats, perhaps? Even though you will have no fish. You rear sheep, I think? On the islet, there."

The other looked doubtful, and then shrugged. "I can let you have some salt mutton. Not much. But a little. The English steal my sheep also."

"Have you any silver?" Charles asked, in English. "O'Neill has our money."

"What can such as he do with coin, here? But – very well." Donald reached into a pocket of his coat and produced a silver bawbee, and offered it.

The man eyed it, hesitated, and then accepted it. He turned to go indoors.

The callers eyed each other.

Presently the crofter emerged, and with the major part of a leg of mutton, gleaming with its salt-curing, more than they had hoped for. Thankfully they took it and, wishing him and his well, declared that they would wait over on the islet until darkness and then sail off, to avoid being seen by the English ships.

They returned to their boat.

That mutton was well received by their party, salty as it was, more substantial than uncooked oats.

After eating they kept the fire going, to dry their gear fully. Arranging to have the sentinels posted in turns to keep watch, up on the summit of the knoll, the others settled down to sleep, for they would have another wakeful night, no doubt.

At dusk again, Donald MacLeod pointed out that although the storm was gone, the wind was still quite strong, and had changed into due south. This would inevitably affect their journey, and their route. It would be best for them to go north, so that they could use the sail. If an enemy ship was based on Barra they would have to avoid that isle anyway. One of the Uists, then. Rhum lay immediately to the north. Although that crofter had said that there was another ship of war stationed there, overnight it would almost certainly, in this weather, anchor in the deep inlet of Loch Scresort,

23

the only sheltered haven this side of the mountainous isle. So, in the darkness they ought to be quite safe heading northwards up the east side of Rhum, aided by the south wind and protected by its bulk. It would be a round dozen miles to its northern tip. They should cover that easily before dawn, and then turn westwards for Canna, a smaller isle, where they might pass the day. Then over the Minch to the Outer Isles the following night.

This seemed wise thinking. They all were thankful that they had the experienced Donald MacLeod as guide and pilot, for even the Mallaig oarsmen did not know the Sea of the Hebrides as he did. He mentioned, incidentally, pointing, that the Rhum peaks had recovered their captive clouds, which was a good sign, weatherwise. This was a strange natural circumstance, all but unique, whereby the group of jagged mountains somehow produced or attracted a series of small, flat white clouds to cap them, even when there was no other cloud in the sky, why none knew. But it served as a guide for seafarers.

So, finishing the last of the mutton and most of the oats, they all moved down to the boat, dark settling on land and sea.

They rowed eastwards, back along that channel, the tide-race for them this time, and then, out of it, turned north, hoisting the sail, the wind steady, not gusty, although fairly strong. Why did it not blow those clouds off the Rhum peaks? Charles asked – and was vouchsafed no answer.

From Eigg to Rhum was almost six miles, they were informed, then the dozen more in the lee of the larger island. They would have to keep well offshore to avoid down-draughts from its mighty mountains, these the most spectacular of all the Hebridean features save for the Cuillins of Skye.

Compared with the previous night's passage, if such it could be called, this proved to be ease itself, the rowers having very little to do, with the sail and the southerly wind doing the work, although they did keep the oars out, to be ready to cope with the occasional overfall and whirlpool, which seemed to be a general feature of these waters, caused by the submerged hills, valleys and ledges. Donald kept them almost a mile offshore once they reached Rhum, concerned about down-draughts. Little spray came inboard in these conditions, so no baling was necessary, and the passengers could huddle in their plaids, cramped yes, but dry and reasonably warm.

Even so, almost a score of miles in a small, open boat, with a modest sail, took some hours. Donald was beginning to worry about timing when at length they came level with the final headland of Rhum, Rubha Shamhnan. Would they have time to reach Canna before daylight? Another six miles or so, he reckoned. And no longer with the wind behind them. Easier probably to reach Soay, off the southern tip of Skye, due north still, and the sail aiding them?

But his passengers were concerned at the mention of Skye. Loudoun and the enemy militia were on Skye, and although they might not be on this offshore Soay, the word might reach them that the fugitives were in the vicinity, and searching start. Better to keep well away from Skye.

So they sailed westwards, and immediately had to get the oars working, with currents against them, as they had been round the tip of Eigg. They could still use half-sail, but progress was slower, and Donald kept looking eastwards where the dawn was just beginning to lighten the sky.

The darkness was almost gone, indeed, when they saw Canna ahead of them, no large island and not mountainous, indeed with sufficient level ground to support quite a number of people, some four or five miles long by one across, producing good cattle pasture and arable to grow barley. So comparatively near to the south of Skye, all recognised that it might be unwise to publish their presence to the local folk; but Donald said that there was an offshore rocky islet called Sanday at this end, where they could land and, he judged, remain unobserved. He thought that it was used for summer sheiling only.

Thankfully they pulled in to a little bay on the south shore of this Sanday, and so far as they could see there were no inhabitants. They had done well, covering almost twenty-five miles, they were not wet, and the southerly wind was not cold. They would not risk lighting a fire here, indeed there seemed to be no fuel available, no gorse nor trees. But they could wrap themselves in dry plaids and sleep the day away, after a frugal helping of oats and whisky. After the previous night's experience, there were no complaints.

They had only the Minch to cross now, and they would be in the Outer Isles and, it was hoped and believed, safety. They prayed that the southerly wind would continue, even turn easterly.

*   *   *

25

Prayer unsung did not go so far as to turn the wind into the east, but it did continue a southerly airstream when they launched the boat once more with the dusk, and they were able to hoist half-sail, with the rowing normal. This would be, admittedly, the longest leg of their voyage, over thirty miles; but in the conditions prevailing it ought to be the least difficult and hazardous, open sea with no down-draughts and tide-races, at least not until they reached the Outer Isles themselves. Hunger was now their problem, but they were not going to risk seeking provisions on Canna.

In fact, as they left the isle behind them, they did find the going simpler than they had had to face hitherto, however long. This length was, to be sure, affected by the wind, for since they were no longer making for Barra, the nearest of the Outer Isles, it signified little which of the great chain of all but connected islands they reached. So, with the wind southerly, a north-westwards course was indicated, for even though it added to the mileage it would enable them to gain great advantage from the sail, the hungry rowers spared much effort, the oars having to be used only intermittently to counter currents and correct surges. In fact, they made good time, although the rollers were higher here than in the Inner Sound, their craft riding them in rhythmic fashion. As well, perhaps, for some, that stomachs were empty.

It was a memorable passage in more ways than the one, this because of the lightning. Due south winds were not common here, but when they came they not infrequently brought thunder and heavy rain. On this occasion there was little thunder and no rain until almost dawn; but the lightning flickered throughout the night in brilliant display, giving brief glimpses of distant coasts and mountains, dramatic in the extreme, even though the travellers were not seeking vistas and visibility but the reverse – not that enemy seamen would be likely to be keeping keen watch from sheltered havens by night.

All were, in fact, congratulating themselves on progress, with the dawn beginning to compete somewhat with the lightning, and land on their left becoming visible no great distance off, when a sudden downpour of heavy rain soaked them and thunder crashed. They could have done without this, but grumbles were only moderate, for clearly their voyage was almost over and they had reached the Outer Isles, whichever one they were nearing. It had been a major venture for a small boat, Donald reckoning

26

not far off one hundred miles of some of the most difficult waters in the world.

Now they had to seek a landing-place, with all the inevitable problems of reefs, skerries, tide-races and the rest. They were indeed thankful for the lightning and the dawn to provide visibility. Lowering sail they turned inshore, but not over-close, coasting along and gazing landwards.

There seemed to be innumerable islets hereabouts, and it was hard to distinguish these from their background of more substantial land, which now appeared to be almost continuous. Donald was not sure, but he guessed that it would be either South Uist or Benbecula, depending on how far the wind and sail had carried them. At any rate, it was certainly part of what they called the Long Island of the Outer Hebrides, although that was a somewhat ridiculous name, for it was not one island but hundreds. Long was apt enough, for from north to south the line of them stretched for one hundred and seventy miles.

Presently their pilot pointed. A lowish headland was projecting before them, and so far as they could see it was part of no islet but a point of the greater landmass. Pull in towards that.

It proved to be quite a peninsula, liberally provided with rocks and shallows, and since they were approaching it from the south much oar-work and vigilance was called for to avoid the dangers. They worked along, eyes busy.

In fact, it was the sight of a hut which provided them with what they sought; it was now light enough to make this out, on a grassy slope above an inlet, almost certainly, in that position, a fishermen's bothy. If so, the inlet would admit them. Into it they turned, and saw sand at its head. Up on to this the boat was driven, amidst cries of acclaim.

Stiff as they all were, Father Allan was first over the side to plunge ashore and repeat his ground-kissing gesture with exclamations of thankfulness. On this occasion Charles Stuart did the same. He it was who had decided on this perilous and formidable journey, he who was for the Outer Isles. Now he had reached them, for better or for worse. His sense of gratitude all but overwhelmed him, momentarily. He turned to clutch Donald MacLeod's arm and then those of the rowers in turn, speechless. As wordlessly he thanked his Maker also.

One other of their number was silently expressing his own

thankfulness to be standing on one of the Outer Isles again –
Ned Burke. For, although prior to joining the Jacobite army as
servant to Alexander MacLeod of Muiravonside, the prince's
aide-de-camp, he had been a sedan chair bearer in Edinburgh,
Ned had in fact been born and reared on North Uist. So he was
almost home.

3

The entire situation was now changed for the group. It was improbable that they would be in any danger from their English enemies, whose attention would almost certainly be confined to the inner sounds, islands and the mainland shores. Here they need no longer hide. So there was no call to sleep by day and travel by night. Nevertheless they had been awake all that night, and they were wet through again by the heavy rain shower. With one accord they moved up to the hut.

It proved to be better than the other they had used, indeed was more of a cottage, or a hovel rather, than any shed, a fishermen's bothy as had been guessed, with a door to it, no windows, but a hole in the turf roof for smoke to escape from a central hearth on the floor of earth. Not only this, but there was a heap of peats in one corner and some kindling sticks beside it, all most acceptable and welcoming. Unfortunately no food appeared to be available, although water was at hand from a burn running nearby.

It was not long before they had a good fire burning, not blazing for peats do not flame but glow, sending out adequate heat nevertheless. Soon clothing and plaids were steaming, nakedness no concern of any, even the heir of the royal line of Stewart.

They might have rested around that fire for long enough, but hunger was working on them all and was not to be ignored. Somehow they must find food.

Charles, with Donald, Father Allan and O'Neill, decided to climb to the summit of the nearest hillock; there were no major heights hereabouts nor any in sight, only water and bog and heather, lochans and inlets everywhere. There they hoped to gain prospects. This fishing bothy and its cut peats must mean that there would be habitation reasonably near.

On the ridge they were afforded wide vistas indeed, in every direction. Nowhere within five or so miles of them was anything but low hills, lochans innumerable, bogs and bays. But to the south, perhaps ten miles off, were major heights, all but mountains, many of them; and to the north one high peak, a similar distance away, with many smaller. This vista had Donald nodding.

"We must be on Benbecula," he decided. "Benbecula, just. Those mountains to the south are South Uist, to be sure. And that tall one to the north, by itself, is Eaval – och, I would know it anywhere, by the shape of it. At the south-east corner of *North* Uist. Benbecula lies between the two Uists, just. It is no very large island, whatever – eight miles by five, it may be. But, God be praised, Clanranald country!"

That brought forth thankfulness.

Father Allan was pointing, to produce more thankfulness. No great distance inland from their bay or inlet, smoke was rising. This surely implied an abode, or at least some activity of men, although one of the unnumbered swellings of the heathery ground hid from their sight what was lower than the smoke. And O'Neill was pointing also, further off to the south-west, a couple of miles perhaps, where could be seen a group of buildings large enough to be a farmery, with cot-houses and trees nearby. That was not all that they saw. Grazing, not far off, was a scattering of small black cattle.

"Food!" Donald exclaimed, pointing. "Beef!"

"We cannot just take one. Kill one?" Charles said; but that was more question than denial.

"Why not, at all? Hunger knows no niceties, Monsieur Dumont! And we can pay for it. If we are after finding the owners, whatever. Yonder smoke. Belike there will be a croft there. Let us be seeking it."

O'Neill touched the prince's arm, and pointed in the opposite direction, back seawards. Out there, well to the other side of the Minch, could be seen a large three-masted vessel sailing northwards. They eyed it grimly.

The smoke drew them. It was good to stretch their legs walking, after so much restriction. The terrain was rough, tussocky grass, heather and cranberries, with burns to be jumped and boggy patches to be avoided.

Sure enough, when they surmounted the swelling of ground ahead, a cottage, barn and cultivation strips came into view, a small farmery rather than a croft. Donald had guessed as much by the number of cattle they had passed.

30

Their approach was not unnoticed. Two men were burning farm rubbish outside the steading. These moved towards the newcomers enquiringly.

"A good day to you," Donald called in greeting. "I am MacLeod of Gualtergill. And these are friends from France."

"But *my* name is MacDonald. And I am a priest of Holy Church," Father Allan added.

"Is that so?" the older man replied. Obviously they were father and son. "So long as you are not the English, at all! From those ships outby. A plague on them!"

"Amen to that!" Charles said, in his rather doubtful and French-accented Gaelic. "We come from Borrodale, our boat seeking to avoid them, the ships. We now seek to purchase food, provision."

"Och, Borrodale is it? You will be after seeking Clanranald, then?"

"Yes. This is Benbecula, I think?" Donald took him up. "Clanranald is on Benbecula, yes? We come from his son. I have met with him at Borve Castle, ere this. But never from this side of the island. Always the west."

"To be sure, yes. Himself is at Borve. With his younger son. Are you making for Borve, then?"

"Not now. Later, no doubt. There are others of us, just. Our crew. We are over yonder, where the bothy is. A fishery. Nets."

"Och, yes – Rossinish, just."

"We landed there by night, avoiding the ships. We have been three nights sailing. And with little of food. We are hungered. We would buy a beast from you, if so you will. There are nine others of us."

"A beast, is it? Och, we might find you a heifer, just. I can let you have some meal . . ."

"That would be kind," Charles said. "We have French *louis d'or*. Or silver bawbees."

"Och, that is not of the concern, whatever. Clanranald would expect you to have hospitality, I'm thinking."

"We pay for what we receive," the prince asserted. "And all will be grateful."

"We passed the cattle back there," Donald mentioned. "Yours? One of those young beasts would serve us well."

"Aye, then. Sandy here will pick you a heifer. And kill it

31

for you, just. See you, come and I will get you a bag of meal."

"The silver or the gold?" Charles asked.

Clearly the talk of money embarrassed the farmer, Highland hospitality involved, especially with people having links with his chief concerned. "Och, Sandy can see to that," they were told.

At the house they were provided with a bag of meal and a slab of cheese by the farmer's friendly wife, not a great deal for thirteen men but some help. With these, they thanked their benefactors and departed whence they had come, with the son Sandy, a silent young man.

When they reached the little herd of cattle, their guide had no difficulty in selecting a young beast, one which it seemed had a faulty leg. He offered to slaughter it for them there and then, but Donald declared that folly. Why have to carry or drag the carcase, when it could walk to the bothy on its own feet, however lame, and do the killing there? So, with a rope round its neck, the unfortunate animal was led off. Oddly, the rest of the cattle, eight of them, followed on uninvited.

So it was quite a parade which arrived at the bothy, to the satisfaction of the hungry company. When Sandy, whom it transpired was also a MacDonald, drew a dirk to cut the heifer's throat, his namesake, Father Allan, protested, saying that surely they could shoot the poor creature, not knife it. They had a couple of pistols down in the boat.

Duly fetched, leaded and primed, Sandy took the weapon and efficiently shot the animal in the head. It was strange how almost guilty some of the party felt as they watched, Charles amongst them, considering how much bloodshed they had witnessed those last few months, human blood, especially recently on Culloden Moor.

The other cattle, grazing from nearby, took fright at the pistol's report, and trundled off, to turn and gaze again from a distance.

Barely had the heifer collapsed to the ground, and while limbs still twitched, Sandy MacDonald had his dirk out again, and kneeling, began to skin the creature's black hide. Obviously he was no tyro at the business. Flayed, he proceeded to cut up the carcase into its major portions, legs, haunches, ribs and back, declaring that the watchers could slice the meat into pieces for cooking, as required. Presently, wiping his dirk on the grass, he stood up, duty done.

O'Neill, the treasurer, brought the leather money-bag and offered the young man his reward from a handful of gold and silver coins. Shaking his head unhappily, their benefactor reluctantly extracted three bawbees in silver, and nodding head towards them all, turned around and headed off to shouted thanks.

Famished as they all were, there was no delay in making use of that provision, alive as it had been only minutes before, the meat still steaming slightly. Knives duly slashed off collops to cook. It was decided that to boil the beef would be quickest, and Ned Burke had seen a large iron pot at the back of the bothy. He went to fetch this, but when he took it to the burn to fill it, discovered that there was a hole in the base, the water dribbling out. Here was a dilemma. Could it be repaired? Various suggestions were made, but no one was doubtful as to immediate action – that meat must be roasted forthwith on spits over the fire, which had been kept burning. There was no lack of volunteers to attend to the grilling. Meanwhile, Ned tried to plug the hole in the pot with tightly wedged-in cloth, for they perhaps might still use it to make porridge from the oatmeal.

It is to be feared that, however tough and undercooked, that meat was consumed all too promptly and appreciatively, blackened without and red within, this accompanied by handfuls of oatmeal soaked in cold water, plus lumps of cheese to enhance it all. None thought to pass critical comment.

All this took time, and with Ned still working on his pot, most there were well content to wrap themselves in their plaids and sleep again, however early the hour, their late exertions and stresses telling. Donald, eyeing the sky and sniffing the air, declared that he feared that the weather was going to get worse again. He pointed back eastwards to distant Rhum; those jagged peaks had lost their captive clouds once more.

He was proved right in his forebodings. That night, with the wind battering the bothy, the rain lashing down and the breakers booming from the shore, those sufficiently wakeful piled more peats upon that friendly fire.

In the morning the rain had ceased but the wind still was strong and the seas rough. Charles said that, weather or none, they ought to go and see Clanranald, or at least *he* should. Donald, who knew the chief and his castle at Borve, where he had delivered many a keg of whisky, agreed. He had never crossed the island from this east side, and with all its lochans and bogs, it would be an ill place to walk, even though the distance was probably no more than five or six miles. But to attempt to go roundabout, by boat, was not to be recommended in these seas, and would come to perhaps a score of miles anyway. He suggested that they returned to the MacDonalds at Hakaidh, as Sandy had told them the farm was named, and seek directions there. Possibly the young man himself would guide them. Father Allan offered to accompany them, Ned Burke also.

The wind in their faces, and gusting, they made their muddy and difficult way to Hakaidh, and were wondering whether indeed to try to proceed further in these conditions, for the already waterlogged land was trackless and dire, at least thus far, when there was an unexpected development, the arrival at the farm of a well-made young man in tartans, on horseback, who proved to be Clanranald's younger son, Duncan. It seemed that Sandy's father had himself gone over to Borve, on a garron, to inform his chief of the newcomers' arrival after they had left him the day before, as was a good clansman's duty; and Clanranald had sent his son now to discover who the visitors were and what brought them to Benbecula.

Once Duncan MacDonald saw Charles Stuart, of course, the secret was out. For he had been, with his brother, leading the Clanranald regiment during the late campaign, and he had known the prince well. He had left the army, with a section of the regiment, after the Battle of Falkirk, like many others had done, not anticipating Cumberland's advance northwards into the Highlands after his defeat there, and intending to rejoin the prince later. Now, instantly recognising Charles, despite his extraordinary garb, he ran forward to bend the knee and kiss the royal hand, at a loss for words.

Presently, after explanations as to their presence on the island, and the young man's distress at the prince's predicament, Duncan found his tongue, and to some effect. Despite the remoteness of the island, it seemed that its inhabitants were not deprived of news of what went on elsewhere, the Hebrideans having their own methods of gaining and dispensing information. It seemed that the assembly of leaders and troops at Ruthven of Badenoch had dispersed, as ordered, all making for their own homes and glens until summoned to muster again for a renewal of the fight. Meantime, Cumberland and his lieutenants were savaging the Highlands, slaying and burning. It was said that he was based on Fort Augustus, at the head of Loch Ness, halfway across to the western seaboard. It was known that the prince had headed for the Isles, no doubt to seek a ship for France, and all his enemies were on the lookout for him. The Earl of Loudoun was making the Campbell name stink on Skye even more than it traditionally did. And more urgently still, his father had heard from his uncle, MacDonald of Boisdale on South Uist, that English sailors from the ships of war had landed on Barra, the next major island to the south, and were searching it. So it looked as though there were suspicions that the prince had reached the Outer Isles.

This was serious news. Barra was only some six miles from the foot of South Uist and thirty from Benbecula, and if the enemy were looking for Charles there, he was scarcely safe here. Not that seamen from the English vessels would find *this* watery island easy to search; Duncan MacDonald admitted that there were said to be over two hundred lochs and lochans, apart from as many probing inlets of the sea, in its fifty square but anything but regular miles. But it was probably unwise to linger here. Yet Donald MacLeod was reluctant to leave before seeking to discover whether any ships for or from France might be available at Loch Boisdale. For, next to Stornoway on Lewis, well to the north, this was perhaps the best and safest port of the Outer Isles, a wide and sheltered harbour which they ought to investigate, Charles agreeing. The English, to be sure, would know this also; and if they were investigating Barra, might well move to South Uist next.

Duncan, listening, said that his uncle would know of the situation at Daliburgh, its port there. He had brought the word of the Barra landings personally to Borve, and was with his brother Clanranald there now. He would advise.

Charles was for setting off for Borve Castle there and then, although the difficulties of their progress thus far were not encouraging for walkers, and there were at least five miles still to go. But Duncan said no. Horses, their sturdy, surefooted Highland garrons, used to these boggy conditions, were called for, not foot-trudging. His uncle and father would come to *them*, not the reverse; they would not have the heir to Scotland ploutering through any more mire and flood, that was certain. He would return to Borve, and tomorrow come to the bothy at Rossinish, with his elders, a-horse. The rough seas would hold the visitors there anyway – as they would hamper the English ships' boats.

This solution was accepted gratefully, and after some welcome refreshment from the Hakaidh family, they parted, the prince's group to head back eastwards, Duncan MacDonald to ride west by south for Borve, by tracks he knew.

More beef and oatmeal that evening were enhanced by a welcome addition of fish. For the oarsmen, who were themselves fishermen, had spent the interval trawling the nets they had found behind the bothy in a channel between skerries where the tide ran, sheltered from the breakers, and with heartening results. Ned's pot, plugged with the cloth, was not entirely mended, and the fish were more fried or baked than boiled, but edible.

There had been no sighting of ships that day, the weather but little improving.

They all spent a fair night, warm and not coughing so much with the peat smoke to which they were getting used, in that bothy.

It was the following noon when five horsemen arrived, for Clanranald had brought two henchmen with pack-garrons laden with supplies, salted mutton and venison, oats and oatcakes, cheese, fruit, even some of Donald's own Skye whisky, to be received with acclaim. The chief, elderly and spare where his brother was heavy made, dismounted from his garron stiffly, but got down on his knees thereafter nevertheless, to take Charles's hand between both of his, in the traditional gesture of fealty, and to kiss it.

"Your Royal Highness!" he exclaimed. "The good God keep and prosper you, and better than this. I am your devoted supporter and your royal father's humble servant. It greatly grieves me to welcome you to my land thus, in secret hiding and want. But I greet you from a full heart, Highness, whatever. Better days shall come."

When he rose, the prince raising him physically, his brother Boisdale knelt in turn, making similar assertions of loyalty and concern.

Charles, most touched, declared his joy at meeting them and his great appreciation of the Clanranald regiment which they had sent to aid his cause, with the services of Young Clanranald and this Duncan acknowledged. He would, in due course, inform King James, and duly praise them.

Clanranald was a major branch of the great Clan Donald, descended from Ranald, second son of the mighty Somerled, first Lord of the Isles, indeed styling himself king thereof. The eldest son had been Dougal, from whom the Clan MacDougall sprang; the third Angus. These three had divided up the West Highland seaboard and the Hebrides largely between them, Ranald being given Garmoran, Lorn and Kintyre on the mainland, with Islay and these Outer Isles. Oddly, the main stem had taken its name from Donald, son of Dougal; and there was a certain rivalry between the clans and their various septs of Glengarry, Keppoch, Lochalsh, Moidart and the rest, unfortunate for Somerled's great heritage since it allowed the acquisitive Campbells to move in and grasp sizeable portions. But Clanranald at least still held most of their territories.

Round the fire in the bothy, out of the wind, they sat on old sailcloth and plaids on the earthen floor, and pledged goodwill and service with the whisky brought, although the donors merely sipped a taste, not to deny the rest to the royal party. Charles recounted some of their adventures since leaving Borrodale, and made some mention of what had transpired after their minor victory at Falkirk and the later disaster of Culloden, to much wagging of heads and curses on the Elector's son, Cumberland. He would roast in hell for what he was doing to the Highlands, all agreed.

"And yet MacDonald himself is with the German fiend, at Kilchumein, that they are now naming Fort Augustus after the creature – MacDonald!" Boisdale declared. "The shame of it, the sorry shame! He and MacLeod." He glanced at Donald, almost apologetically, for MacLeod of MacLeod and Sir Alexander MacDonald of Sleat had failed the prince, refusing to support the Stuart cause allegedly because the promised military aid from France had not materialised; but more probably they had preferred not to incur the enmity of the Hanoverian authorities until they were assured of the prince's victory. The scorn and contempt of these Clanranald MacDonalds was vehement.

Donald MacLeod observed that his present chief was a disappointment indeed, but that many MacLeods had joined the rising.

On the vital matter of Charles getting to France meantime,

Boisdale said that there had been no French vessels in Loch Boisdale of recent weeks, no doubt because it was known that the English ships of war were operating in the Minches. If any were indeed venturing up this seaboard, it was likely that they would remain in the open seas beyond these Outer Isles and use the port of Stornoway, in Lewis to the north. However, he was not hopeful about this, and feared that His Highness might wait long enough for such rescue, and meantime be in considerable danger of capture if Cumberland learned that he had reached the Long Island, as almost certainly he would. He, Boisdale, recommended a different route to France. Let the prince go to Stornoway, yes, but in the guise of a shipwrecked trader from Glasgow, on the way to Norway, seek to hire or purchase a sea-going vessel at that port, and sail in it up around Cape Wrath and through the Pentland Firth, past Orkney and across the North Sea. From Norway it would not be difficult to take ship to France, and safety.

Charles was somewhat doubtful about this, but Donald MacLeod supported the idea, as did O'Sullivan and O'Neill, both eager to get away from Scotland at the earliest, with no waiting for any French ships which might or might not appear. The prince allowed himself to be persuaded.

Clanranald said that he did not think that His Highness should continue to have himself called Monsieur Dumont, in these circumstances, if the party were allegedly Glasgow merchants. Use some typical Scots name. He and O'Sullivan, the eldest there, could be father and son, with their crew. Sinclair, say, which if they were questioned would allow them to come from north or south, that family being strong in both Lothian and Caithness.

This was agreed. And the sooner that they were off northwards for Stornoway the better, with the English searchers so close. And best to go by night again, if the seas permitted; this very night.

Donald said that he did not greatly like the look of the weather, but it might be possible; and he acceded that it would be wise to be off sooner rather than later. Unless another storm blew up, then, they would sail with the darkness.

The Clanranald group took its leave with profound good wishes, and assurances that when the prince returned to Scotland in due course to renew his campaign, he would find their regiment ready and eager. They went, taking with them heartfelt thanks.

4

So it was pack up and go again – not that the travellers had much to pack, although this time they did have more food to take along, thankfully. With dusk the wind was strengthening, but, from the south-west, they did have the bulk of the Long Island to give them some shelter.

It called for careful rowing again and picking their way out through the reefs of that inlet, with the tide surging strongly. But once out into the Minch and able to turn north-eastwards, although the waves were large they were not breaking, and they could hoist half-sail and use the oars mainly for steering. They had to go thus eastwards at first, in order to round Ronay, a two-mile-long isle flanking the foot of North Uist. So they had the wind behind them for this start, at least.

Once they turned due north, however, conditions were less favourable, with side gusts coming off the hilly land, especially off North Uist's greatest mountain of Eaval, close to the eastern coast. Moreover, as so often with nightfall, the weather deteriorated, and squalls of rain buffeted and soaked them. The sail had to come down, and all were back to the conditions of those nights before, although scarcely so grim. The visitors asked if the Hebrides were always like this, to be assured that this was unusual in late April and May – which was scant comfort.

Donald was unsure how far they might get that night. It would be at least sixty miles more up to Stornoway, near the head of Lewis, the most northerly of the Outer Isles, past Berneray, Harris and Scalpay, and they certainly would not make anything like that before daybreak, with these northern nights getting ever shorter. They might get as far as South Harris, he guessed.

That was an over-optimistic estimate. With wind and rain worsening, and seas rising, it soon was evident that they had to make a landfall. In the mirk, it was difficult for even Donald to tell just where they were, so broken was the shoreline with sounds, lochs and inlets. They might be off South Harris, for they had felt, by the tide-surge, that they had crossed a widish gap in the landmass, which he thought might well be the Sound of Harris which separated the large island from the smaller Berneray.

They edged their way in between low headlands into calmer water, slowly indeed, with Ned Burke in the bows warning and directing the oarsmen. Even so they twice struck weed-hung skerries, but insufficiently to cause them upset. At length they grounded on a shingle beach, just as, behind them, dawn was breaking.

Pulling up the boat, they went exploring. It was the usual rocky, broken terrain, gorse and heather and broom, with apparently no major heights near at hand at least, which made Donald wonder whether it was indeed South Harris. As the light grew, they climbed to the closest higher ground, for a view.

Up on a small ridge, they did learn much. They were at the head of an inlet or narrow bay, with only a brief neck of land separating them from a larger, wider channel, beyond which, to the north, was much higher ground and a great deal of it. Donald thought that they must be on the medium-sized isle of Scalpay, and the channel would be East Loch Tarbert, which all but separated South and North Harris. If so, they would surely find friendship here, for although Scalpay was MacLeod territory, its tenant under MacLeod of MacLeod was one Donald Campbell, whom he knew and had lodged with over the years, a buyer and distributor of his whisky.

At the name of Campbell his hearers looked askance, alarmed. But Donald said not to judge all Campbells alike. This one indeed had had a son in the prince's army, in Clanranald's regiment he believed; whether he had survived the campaign remained to be seen. If they were where he thought they were, Campbell's house should be due west about a couple of miles. They should go and introduce themselves.

Not entirely reassured, leaving most of the party to return to the boat, Donald, with the prince, Father Allan and Ned Burke, set off westwards.

It was very similar terrain to that of Benbecula, indeed all these components of the Long Island were very much alike, save that some were more hilly than others. As the sun rose at their backs, on this the first morning of May, extending their vistas, Donald was confirmed in his judgment. They were on Scalpay, and could see the moderate heights of South Harris to their left and the higher hills, less than mountains, of North Harris at the other side, across East Loch Tarbert, and the West Loch, with its narrow tongue of land, the *tarbert*, linking them, this far ahead.

They came to a croft after about a mile, and told a surprised family there that they were seeking Donald Campbell, the tacksman. Clearly this was most unusual, for any visitors who came to Scalpay reached it from its north-western inlet and harbour, near which was the tacksman's house. They did not reveal identities, merely declaring that the storm had cast up their boat on the eastern shore. Donald did ask, however, whether the Campbell son had returned from the prince's army, which drew a strange look. They were told, not yet.

Another mile of bog-hopping and pond-circling, and they saw the harbour inlet ahead of them, and a quite large house on the slope behind it, two cottages and sundry barns and sheds nearby, cattle, sheep and garrons in evidence.

Their approach was observed, and a man of later middle years came some way to meet them enquiringly. As they neared, Donald raised an arm in greeting.

"MacLeod of Gualtergill," he called. "With friends."

The other paused, stared, then waved and came on. He was a tall, stern-looking man, but when he smiled, as he did when he took Donald's hand, his rather unwelcoming features were transformed.

"What brings you this-away, Gualtergill?" he demanded. "Across the island? Here's strange travel, just!"

"It is a long story, friend. These with me will explain it. We had to land on your eastern shore. Some of our folk still there. Your son – is he back from the prince's army? Yonder crofter back there thought not."

"Not yet, no. I have no word. Save that there has been a sore defeat. Near to Inverness, just. The sorrow of it! We hope . . ."

"He was with Clanranald's regiment, no?" That was Charles Stuart. "Most of that regiment escaped, we have heard. They made a fighting retiral. Well led. Were not scattered, as were so many."

The other eyed him keenly. "You, young man, speak as though you know something of it all? Yet with no Scots nor Highland voice, at all. Might *you* have been there, whatever?"

"I was there, yes, *mon Dieu*! I was there." He turned. "As were these. Father Allan MacDonald. And Edward Burke, my . . . attendant."

"You may trust Donald Campbell, Highness," MacLeod said. "That I swear! My friend, this is himself! Prince Charles Edward Stuart."

Campbell gazed at the handsome, fair-headed young man, needing a shave like them all, and clad in nondescript, all but ragged clothes. Swallowing, he bowed low. "Highness! Your Highness, I, I am your servant! Your devoted servant, just. I salute you!"

The prince stepped forward to clasp the elder man's shoulder. "Then well met, friend. A friend in need, *ma foi*!" he said.

"But . . . how? How? And *here*!" The tacksman looked from one to the other of his visitors.

"A long story, as I said," Donald told him. "A sorry tale, yet . . ."

"Yes. So it must be, yes. But come you in. To my poor house, Highness. Honour it, if you will."

He led them up to where three women stood watching from the house door, clearly a mother and two daughters. They smiled at MacLeod, but the young women considered the particularly good-looking youngest man there assessingly. They were both darkly personable and well built, in their early twenties, their elder motherly. She began to speak, but her husband interrupted her.

"Here, Mhairi, is the prince! The prince himself! His Highness, Prince Charles. The son of our king."

Incredulous, the women stared, with drawn breaths, disbelief barely hidden.

Charles, smiling, made something of a flourish of a bow. "Ladies," he said, "I greet you warmly. And congratulate Monsieur Campbell on his good fortune in having you, having you all!"

While the mother, blinking, sought to make scarcely a curtsy but a bobbing, stooping gesture, her daughters eyed each other and their father, and one giggled nervously – to that man's frown.

"Off with you," he ordered. "And prepare comfort, food, drink, for His Highness. And his friends. Begone!" That was to the girls. "Mhairi, the prince has come far. By small boat. In the storm, just. He requires our best."

Bobbing again, she fled within, after her daughters, Charles protesting that he desired no fuss, no display.

They were ushered indoors. It proved to be a well-built substantial house of stone, with a roof of slates, not thatch, the rooms sizeable, furnished simply but adequately, Mistress Campbell hastily tidying, and telling the young women to bring this and that to the table.

While the situation and something of the visitors' adventures were being retailed, there was a new arrival, a youth of perhaps seventeen years, a shepherd's crook in his hand, a younger son introduced as Hector. Unlike his sisters, he seemed to accept the prince's coming as unexceptional, and was not long in asking whether they had any news of his brother. When they could not give him any, he seemed to lose interest and wandered off.

While refreshment was being prepared, they told Campbell of Clanranald's and Boisdale's suggestion that they should go to Stornoway as shipwrecked merchants by name of Sinclair from Glasgow, seeking to hire a vessel to take them to Orkney and then Norway. Their host saw this as sensible, but thought that it would be best to tackle the project in two stages. There was word that an English warship was now stationed at North Lewis, Stornoway its obvious base, and there might well be danger for the prince there, with his striking appearance and French accent. But Donald MacLeod would be known there, with his whisky, and should attract no hostile attention. He could make the necessary enquiries and prepare the way, so that the prince, when he arrived, need not delay in the town.

This was agreed. Donald would go off in the morning, using Campbell's four-oared boat, and the others wait here on Scalpay until they got word to proceed on to Stornoway.

Meanwhile, the tacksman's house was Prince Charles's. He was conducted to a bedchamber, which one of the daughters had been sent to prepare for him, fresh sheets on the bed, hot water to wash in, Campbell even providing a razor to shave with and whisky to sip while this was being used, some of the missing son's clothing being provided for a change, if desired, this being *his* room. A worthy meal would be following in due course.

Such hospitality left the visitors at a loss for words.

Ned Burke and the youth Hector were sent back to the eastern shore to fetch the rest of the party.

*   *   *

43

So commenced an interlude of ease and relaxation and comfort, quite extraordinary after all the exertions, dangers and difficulties of the last days, their hosts assiduous for their unexpected guests' well-being, not only the prince's.

Donald MacLeod and three of the oarsmen set off in the morning, from the haven below, in a smaller but quite sea-going boat, to head north-eastwards out of the Kyles of Scalpay and up into the Sound of Shiant, flanking North Harris. The weather was much improved, more typical of early May, the wind still south-westerly but much dropped, so that they could use sail. If these conditions prevailed, they might well cover the fifty miles to Stornoway by nightfall. It was a fairly typical fishing-boat, and should attract no investigation from any passing English ships. Donald would either come back with word as to the situation or send the others while remaining at Stornoway to arrange matters further for the prince.

That first day of ease and leisure the visitors were well content just to laze about and do little or nothing, other than eat and enjoy the prospects. For the first time they could, in fact, appreciate the magnificent Hebridean vistas, with blue skies and sunshine to bring out all the colour, contrast and drama of land and sea, the infinity of islands, the gleam of silvery lochs, the distant purple mountains, the green hills and blazing gorse against the brown of old heather, the white cockleshell sands of every bay, and the multi-hued seaweeds growing on the skerries. Even those not normally much concerned with scenic beauty, such as O'Neill, could not but be impressed by all that surrounded them. Charles was ecstatic. What a kingdom this to win back for his father! Hitherto he had tended to think of the Hebrides as storm and problems and danger; now, a man with an eye for beauty, he all but embraced the loveliness.

There was only one rift in the lute. John O'Sullivan was not well. The eldest of the party, it might be that all the hardships had been too much for him, had taken their toll. He was sick, dizzy, could not eat, and wanted only to lie in the sun. This, needless to say, indicated problems for the future.

Donald Campbell made an attentive host, however stern-looking. Charles had not seen his like before, used to dealing with lords and chiefs and lairds. Campbell was a tacksman, the

44

tenant of a large landowner, but a major one. He rented this whole island of some five square miles from MacLeod of MacLeod, who lived at Dunvegan on Skye, farming it, more prosperous indeed than many small lairds who adopted the graces which he did not. A dozen crofters on Scalpay were his sub-tenants. Now his family vied with each other to provide kindnesses.

Needless to say, they were all much exercised over the elder son, and Charles was sorry indeed not to be able to inform them. He could well, hopefully, be safe and making for home. Clanranald's regiment had been well led throughout the campaign, and had made a more disciplined retiral from the final field than had most. Young Clanranald, its colonel, had reached home at Borrodale, as no doubt had others. That the Campbell son had not yet done so could merely mean that he had been finding difficulty in getting passage across to the Outer Isles, as would be quite probable. That was the best that he could say.

That evening Charles and the others gave their hosts some account of the campaign which had started so hopefully and ended so direly, telling how, despite the English Stuart sympathisers failing to rise in any numbers in support, the army had fought its way from the Highlands as far south as Derby, when the Lord George Murray, lieutenant-general, and other leaders, had urged a return to Scotland. The prince still believed that they should have gone on to London, with no great opposition before them, where the Elector, who was now calling himself King George, was said to have all his bags packed ready to flee back to his own Hanover; but there was word of forces massing behind them under Marshal Wade, and the English naval ships could represent menace which they could not counter. Only a French fleet could have done that, and such had not materialised. So, sadly, the retiral – it was not a retreat – had begun. And that had been bad for the morale of the army in general. But all still believed that they had Scotland. That, the ancient original kingdom, could be retained for King James. And, thereafter, they *had* won the minor Battle of Falkirk. But from then onwards it had been trouble. The army was so very largely a Highland one, and the Highlanders, although splendid fighters, had the tradition of returning to their homes and glens after spells of warfare, for temporary relief and the care for their families, their flocks and herds, understandable in a clan society. So, much of the force had dispersed once it had reached the Highland Line, all promising to reassemble in due course when called for. But all that did not apply to the enemy, and the mercenary soldiery paid to fight for the Hanoverians, now placed under the overall command of the Elector's son, the ruthless Duke of Cumberland. *They* retained full strength, and also gained some Lowland Scots reinforcements, Presbyterians who saw the Catholic Stuarts as menace; and of course the ships of war held the seas and could land men where they would. So, near Inverness, the Jacobites had had to turn and face the foe, now outnumbered, weary, hungry – disaster. They had hoped that the French support would have arrived, as promised by King Louis, but it had not. And certain Highland chiefs, who had not been ready with their clansmen at the start, had been expected to rally now but had not done so. It made a sorry tale, yes, but there was pride and honour in it too, much gallantry and devotion, with so much sheer heroism at Culloden Moor. If only they had not turned back at Derby . . .

In the circumstances, they did not dwell on the atrocities which followed Cumberland's victory, the slaying of the wounded and prisoners, the tortures, the burnings, the flayings. Without it being said, the assumption had to be that young Campbell had escaped this.

His father asked how much the failure of certain great chiefs to rise, MacDonald of Sleat, MacLeod of MacLeod, the Mackenzie Earl of Seaforth and others, had affected the issue? And he cursed the Campbell attitude, particularly that of the Earl of Loudoun, so militarily oppressive in Skye.

Next day, with O'Sullivan somewhat recovered, Campbell took his guests sea-fishing, trawling with nets between two boats, a rewarding activity new to the prince. But all the time they were wondering how Donald MacLeod was faring in Stornoway, if he had indeed managed to get there.

They had to wait two more days for news, pleasant, leisurely days which Charles enjoyed, he and Ned Burke going off with young Hector Campbell to try to shoot a deer, many of which were apparently to be found on Scalpay – although not so apparent it proved, for they saw only two, at a distance and got nowhere nearly within range for a kill. But they did shoot a pair of mallard ducks on one of the lochans, which entailed Hector stripping to go in to retrieve.

Unfortunately it was Father Allan's turn to fall sick, with much the same symptoms as O'Sullivan had developed. Probably it was some of the strange feeding that they had had to consume earlier having a delayed effect; or it might have been just the privations and stress which they had all undergone, physical strains and circumstances to which they were entirely unused. Happily, Charles himself remained unaffected, in as good health as he demonstrated his spirits, quite the most lively and cheerful of the refugees.

It was the following day, with Charles out again with Hector and Ned seeking deer to stalk, for the pot as well as for the sport, that they came back, again empty-handed, to learn of trouble, major trouble. While away, a fishing-boat had come into the haven from the north, nine or ten men aboard, and when Campbell had gone down to see who these were, he was alarmed to discover coming ashore the Reverend Aulay MacAulay, parish minister of South Uist, a strict Presbyterian divine. More surprised still, he saw that the cleric's companions were all armed after a fashion, one even with an old sword, the others with dirks, even a hatchet, and by no means hiding these. When asked the meaning of this extraordinary visit, the clergyman had announced that they had come to arrest the Pretender, the Catholic Charles Stuart, who, they were reliably informed, was presently on this isle of Scalpay, as required by the Earl of Seaforth and the government. Campbell, shaken, without admitting that the prince's party was there, demanded to know what such matters had to do with a minister of the gospel, to be told that it was the duty of all loyal subjects of the Protestant crown to apprehend the rebel invader.

Campbell had asked if Master MacAulay thought that he, Campbell in Scalpay, was a militant Jacobite? And what made them think that Prince Charles was on this isle anyway? Surely they had been misinformed. A party had landed from a small boat three days earlier, but they were identified as the captain, mate and bosun of a ship on its way to Orkney, wrecked on Benbecula in the recent storm. That was not what *they* had been informed, the divine asserted. They were assured that it was the prince himself, and some companions. One of the Boisdale fishermen had told some of their own fisherfolk of South Uist that Clanranald himself and MacDonald of Boisdale had crossed the isle in person to visit these people who had landed on Benbecula, and taken them provisions. Would such as these do that for any ordinary folk?

47

Their fisher informant swore that it was Charles Stuart. Campbell had reiterated that they were mistaken, and that the shipwrecked party were under a Glasgow merchant skipper named Sinclair, and his son. They would be leaving Scalpay shortly, and meantime he hoped that Master MacAulay and his friends, come to his isle in such hostile fashion, with weapons, would do the same, before he gathered his own crofters to see that they did – and he could double their number without difficulty! Sourly and less than convinced, the visitors had departed.

Much perturbed, needless to say, the prince and his companions recognised that they must not linger here.

Fortunately, that late afternoon, the boat arrived back from Stornoway, but minus Donald MacLeod. His messengers brought fairly good tidings however. Donald had managed to arrange for the hire of a small ship to take the prince to the Orkneys, and from there he would have no difficulty in winning a passage to Norway, for there was much commerce between. Meantime Donald was remaining at Stornoway, to finalise the arrangements and see a crew mustered. But the prince was warned to be very careful about approaching the town, indeed best to remain outside it. For the rumour was rife that he had reached the Outer Isles, and the Earl of Seaforth, dwelling nearby, was giving orders that no aid was to be offered to the fugitives, princely or otherwise. Also there was a warship in the port.

So it was time to be off, to leave Scalpay's kindnesses, hospitality and protection, and resume their travels and possible travails. Campbell said that his son Hector, and Murdo MacDonald, one of the crofters' sons, who knew North Harris and the south of Lewis well enough, would go with them to act as guides. He advised that they sail up the Minch only as far as the entrance to Loch Seaforth, less than ten miles, for Donald's messengers reported that longboats from the Stornoway-based warship were searching the seaways, bays and islands, their own craft having been approached for inspection. But Loch Seaforth was long, probing inland far north-westwards for almost twenty miles, and they should be safe therein, for it was too shallow for any large vessel, and overlong for the English small boats to penetrate; also scantily inhabited. If they landed at, say, Ardvourlie, about a dozen miles up, where the loch made a bend in the wrong direction for them, then they could walk on northwards, by Aline and Balallan, by passable tracks, towards Stornoway, the way he drove his cattle to the market there.

The Campbell family escorted them down to the haven then, where goodbyes were said and profound thanks voiced by Charles and the others, the prince assuring that the kindness received would never be forgotten, to be told, in return, that if anything went wrong with their planned progress, welcome, cheer and greeting would always be theirs at Scalpay. And when His Highness's royal father sat on his Scottish throne, these Campbells at least would shout their thanksgiving and praise the good God.

On that note the boat was pushed off and the oars dipped in.

5

Out into the Kyles, or narrows, of Scalpay they pulled, until they could turn north-eastwards and raise sail, with the wind behind them, on a bright, breezy morning. Father Allan was still feeling unwell, O'Sullivan not fully recovered either, which was a concern for the walking advised ahead of them. There was some discussion, indeed, as to whether a parting might be advantageous, those less well remaining with the boat, leaving the prince, O'Neill, Burke and their guides to do the walking. After all, it was Charles Stuart whom the authorities were mainly seeking to capture, and who must take the safer, inland route; the others might well escape trouble and arrest, as innocent travellers, especially if they feigned illness brought on by shipwreck in that storm. There was some sense in this, admittedly. If unfit for long walking, the invalids might well hamper and endanger the prince.

Decision was postponed meantime.

Out of the Kyles, they were able to turn northwards, to flank the North Harris coast. Out in the Minch here they all anxiously scanned the waters for enemy longboats or larger vessels. Two small craft, near together, did have them concerned for a little, and they turned in closer to the shore; but presently it became apparent that these were fishermen with a drag-net between the two boats.

After six or seven miles' sailing they were thankfully able to draw in towards the mouth of Loch Seaforth, the greatest of the sea lochs of that coast. The mouth itself was fairly wide, but thereafter, they were told, although very long it was fairly narrow, hills thronging it on each side.

Soon they had to lower the sail, direction now wrong and down-draughts from the steepening slopes unpredictable, the oarsmen prepared for a dozen miles of rowing. It appeared to be almost uninhabited country, only the occasional fisherman's bothy and croft-house nestling at the foot of bare rocky hills, this

50

causing Charles to wonder why the Mackenzie chief had chosen to give the earldom the name of Seaforth when he owned wide lands elsewhere in the Hebrides and on the mainland. None could answer him that, all damning him anyway as a turncoat, although some of his great clan had been with the prince's army.

They did pass one or two fishing-boats, and exchanged waves, but that was all. Hector's father had been right in advising this route for the fugitives to make for Stornoway.

Rivers entered the loch on either side, usually in the form of waterfalls cascading down off the steeps, and these provided currents as well as down-draughts from their upper valleys, so that the rowing was apt to be demanding of constant care, Ned in the bows seeking always to give warning where he could. As a consequence, although they had covered less than a score of miles since leaving Scalpay, the sun had sunk behind those western hills leaving the narrow waters in deep shadow, when they came to an unexpected development. Ahead of them the loch appeared to divide into two, narrow as it already was, Hector announcing that this was Seaforth Island, a strange feature, over a mile long and half that in width, a sort of half-sunken hill in mid-loch, the channels on either side now attenuated indeed, the waters forced into tidal races. The eastern one would be all but impassable in an outgoing tide, as now, but fortunately their immediate destination was off the western. Beyond this island the scene changed, it seemed, the upper loch swinging off almost at right angles for another seven miles or so, north-eastwards. But before that they would come to a widening, a bay, with a haven at its head, Ardvourlie, one of the few communities, however minor, on all this long waterway. There they would land.

The oarsmen had to work hard, against that tide, to head the boat round and into the bay. At the head of this was a scatter of croft-houses, although with the barren hills so close it was to be wondered at how much crofting would be available to support the folk.

Drawing up on the beach and landing, it at once became apparent that Father Allan was in no state for long walking, or any walking indeed, having great difficulty in climbing out of the boat and all but collapsing on the shingle thereafter. What, then? This was very much Mackenzie country, and the Mackenzie chief, Seaforth, had given orders that no aid was to be given to Jacobite fugitives in his eagerness to remain on good terms with the dynastic winners; so Allan could not be left here, any more than they all could seek shelter and help.

Charles decided. There was nothing for it but separation meantime. His faithful chaplain had to go back to Scalpay and the Campbells until he was sufficiently recovered to be able to make his way to the mainland, to Moidart. He was cousin to MacDonald of Moidart and would be safe with him. Anyway, with foot-travel ahead, the oarsmen would no longer be accompanying them, so they could take Allan to Scalpay before making their own return to Young Clanranald and their homes at Mallaig.

John O'Sullivan asserted that he was now recovered, and able to proceed afoot.

So it was parting, there on the shore. Not only with the priest but with the men who had so nobly brought them thus far, shared all the hazards, discomforts and privations with them, all uncomplaining. They now refused O'Neill's offer of gold pieces in recognition, but when the prince made it a royal command, they had to accept, however unwillingly.

Father Allan's farewell was grievous for all, he in that he was failing his beloved spiritual charge and friend, leaving him while still he was so far from safety and succour; and they, concerned for the priest's health and well-being and the loss of a good companion. Allan, on his knees, said a prayer for them all, and then, tears in his eyes, was helped back into the boat. As the rowers joined him, and began to pull the craft's bows round, the six men left standing on the beach held up hands in parting, only Charles, O'Sullivan, O'Neill and Ned Burke, with the two guides, feelings and emotions various but intense.

They did not linger there. Even in the dusk their arrival would not have gone unnoticed from the nearer croft-houses, but no one had come down to greet them. In these dangerous and unsettled times, folk would be wise to be cautious, and who knew who such belated callers might be, wherever bound and on what bent? The newcomers were not eager to announce themselves, either. So, with the boat disappearing out of the bay – it at least would have the tide-run with it now – the six turned and set off northwards, by a clearly defined track, the first smirr of rain not encouraging them.

Both Hector and Murdo MacDonald, the other crofter's son,

had walked this way before, droving cattle to the market, but admittedly never in darkness. The track persisted, they said, by Aline and Balallan and Laxay into the lower moorlands of Lewis, eventually to Arnish and then Stornoway, perhaps four hours' walking. Would O'Sullivan be fit for that? He said that he would.

Unfortunately the rain became heavy and maintained, by no means assisting, for as well as soaking and chilling them it much restricted sight and vision, which was important to them, the half-dark becoming wholly dark. And their cattle track degenerated into a succession of muddy pools.

According to their guides they would follow roughly the side of upper Loch Seaforth for some five miles, then swing off left-handed by the crofting communities of Aline and Kintaraway and Balallan to Laxay, and then the moors and bogs of Arnish. They made it all sound fairly simple and straightforward, however unpleasant present conditions, Ned shaking his head.

It proved to be otherwise indeed, particularly for the prince and the Irishmen, unused to walking in the dark on muddy tracks, and nowise shod for it. All along, their footwear had been inadequate for present needs; now their shoes failed them badly, Charles's all but in shreds, O'Sullivan limping. They did pull boughs from wayside bushes to serve as walking-sticks, which helped, but only moderately. Those miles in the wet and windy mirk seemed long indeed, endless for three of them, although the two young Highlandmen and Ned strode out stoutly, the former in their rawhide brogans often having to pause and wait for their companions.

As guides they were patient, and sure enough of their direction for the first hour or two. But once their track turned away from the valley-side above the upper loch and into the higher and broken hilly ground, heather and marsh, they became less sure of themselves, the path twisting and turning necessarily to avoid lochans, outcrops of rock, scrub, bushes and the like. It was no very well-defined road in the first place, a cattle path used only occasionally; in these conditions, with surface water everywhere and visibility reduced to a few yards, it demanded not so much sight and memory as sheer instinct.

They blundered and splashed and stumbled their way along, back-tracking becoming ever more frequent, and the party tending to straggle, individuals often having to call out to keep in touch and to wait for one another, usually the last being O'Sullivan, the oldest. This dozen miles, Charles recognised, was going to take more than any four hours. Despite his damaged footwear, he was managing better than at least two of his friends. Always he had been a good walker, for which he had to thank his former tutor, who in his boyhood had taken him on lengthy trampings.

At length, it was when all found themselves almost knee-deep in water and, splashing about, they realised that this was more than any large puddle on the track, that Hector and Murdo were forced to admit that they were lost. They *thought* that they had been on the road up until a short distance back, but they might have strayed on to a deer path. They seemed to be into the edge of a lochan here, which was not what they looked for.

All agreed that to go on in these circumstances would be folly. They must find somewhere to shelter, if they could, and wait until dawn to discover where they were. But wet and cold as they had become, the thought of settling down, inactive, was less than appealing. And what shelter were they likely to find in this empty wilderness?

Getting out of that water, they cast about but could discover nothing which would protect them from the rain and wind. They had their plaids, of course, essential equipment for all travellers in the Highlands. These were wet, but draped over the sticks they had been using, three of them were used to form a sort of tent, and give them a little cover from the elements in the lee of a rocky outcrop; and pulling up armfuls of heather to form a springy couch, however damp, they lay down under the remaining three plaids, huddled together for an illusion of warmth.

Whether it was a relief to exchange their ploutering misery for this chilly alleged resting was debatable.

None managing to sleep, Charles sought to keep spirits up by recounting some of the stories he had grown up with about the previous Jacobite endeavour of thirty years before, the Fifteen Rising, although its non-success likewise was perhaps scant encouragement for the present situation.

Fortunately the May nights are short in these parts, and their waiting, although it seemed long enough in all conscience, did not last more than perhaps three hours. It helped that the rain had stopped, helped visibility as well as their spirits. Climbing a modest nearby height, the guides thought that they could make out approximately where they were, and where they had gone wrong. A lengthy loch which they could see to the west was almost certainly that of Langavat, by its Y-shape, which meant that they had strayed too far in that direction, much too far. So eastwards, towards the lightening sky for them, to rediscover the track.

They found it in due course, although they did not ascertain just where they had gone wrong and left it. But that was scarcely vital now, for this was North Harris which in daylight even Ned knew fairly well, and they could see the crofts of Kintaraway beyond a rocky escarpment ahead. It should not be difficult to find a track leading thereto, and their main route thereafter.

This proved to be correct, and after some ploutering they were back on course. A dozen miles, their guides agreed, and they would be into the Arnish area, south of Stornoway.

After the Reverend MacAulay incident, it was thought wise to avoid crofting houses; not that they would be likely to meet with trouble there, for although this was Mackenzie territory most of the people were Catholics, and would not take the attitude of the Presbyterian minister. This was one of the follies and injustices of the government system. The West Highlands and Isles were predominantly Catholic; yet they, like the rest of Scotland, had been divided up into parishes, and Protestant clergy appointed thereto, many of whom could not even speak the native tongue, the Gaelic. Priests there were also, of course, but these had to operate not exactly covertly but without showing too high a profile. The Reformation had reached these parts only officially.

They saw some crofters at a distance, out even that early in the morning, but none near enough for speech; in present circumstances, groups of strangers were apt to be avoided anyway.

Walking even in daylight was less than easy for ill-shod travellers but, unable to hurry, they nevertheless covered the muddy, roundabout miles past Loch Strandavat and Balallan and on to Laxay on the long sea loch of Erisort. And now they were entering different country, the hills receding and replaced by mainly moorland, still lochan-strewn and heathery and with much bog, peat-bog, indeed peat-stacks became ever more evident the nearer they got to Stornoway, clearly where much of the town's fuel came from. Some men and women they saw cutting and stacking peats.

They did not want to get too close to Stornoway at this stage.

Campbell had told them of what he considered to be a secure house which they might visit, to hide in, the small laird's establishment of Kildun, in Arnish. It was a Mackenzie place, but the laird was dead and his widow was known to be a good Jacobite. They ought to be safe with her while they made enquiries as to Donald MacLeod and his ship.

Hector and Murdo did not actually know this house, but they asked some track-side peat-cutters, and although three of the party were eyed warily, they were directed inland from the community of Orasay a good mile, and there they would find Kildun. By this time it was almost noon.

Presently they could see their destination, a fair-sized white-washed hall-house of two storeys and an attic, long, and larger than the Scalpay house, with a range of barns and outbuildings attached, cattle court and steading.

What, they wondered, awaited them here?

In fact, when they approached the central doorway of the house, they saw a tall, elderly woman was standing watching – folk did not approach dwellings these days unobserved – no smile of welcome greeting them. A man and another woman stood behind her, obviously servants.

Ned Burke, with his Highland voice, spoke up. "Is it Mistress Mackenzie of Kildun, just?" he asked. "She it is we seek, whatever."

A brief nod was his answer.

"Aye, well, here is Hector Campbell from Scalpay. And Murdo MacDonald. We were told to be bringing these friends to yourself, mistress. By Donald Campbell, see you."

"Indeed! Donald Campbell I know as an honest enough man, and married to a good MacDonald." The lady was a MacDonald herself, of the Clanranald line. "What can *I* do for these . . . friends?"

It was Charles who answered her now. "You, lady, are, we understand, not against the cause of King James? Say, I pray, if you are?"

She had a keen and direct gaze, that one, and used it now, scanning the speaker intently. "I wonder why you ask that?" she said carefully.

"Because it is important. To me. Very."

"You are, I think, French? By your voice?"

"Only my voice, madam. I am sufficiently Scots. My name is Stuart."

Now she stared indeed, and her lips parted. "Not . . . not?" She took a step forward. "Dear God, not . . . himself!"

"Himself, I think, would be King James. You have not answered my question, lady!"

"Can it be? In truth? Your looks! I heard tell that, that . . ." She shook her greying head. "To be sure, I favour – despite my late husband's name!"

O'Sullivan joined in. "This, madam, is Prince Charles Edward, yes. We seek your help."

The lady drew a deep breath, and then curtsied low. "Highness, your devoted . . . servant!" she got out.

Charles went to her, to take and kiss her hand.

"This is so good, so good!" she said. "But oh, Highness, you are in danger here. They search for you. From Stornoway. The miscreants, the traitors! You should not be here. There is great reward, filthy money, offered for your capture. The shame of it!"

"We know of that, madam. But we have a friend here, come here. At Stornoway. Who seeks to better our case. We look for him."

"What can I do, Highness? Anything! Anything I can I will do. But come you inside." She looked down at the prince's tattered footwear and mud-covered ragged clothing. "The state you are in! Dear God, this is most terrible!"

"We have walked far. And by night."

"Come, we must better this, at least."

"You are kind, lady."

In the house Mistress Mackenzie was as effective as she was urgent and concerned. Two women were sent to prepare and fetch food and drink, while she herself went upstairs to bring down a selection of her late husband's clothing which, although it might not fit exactly, was clean and dry and a deal more presentable than that worn by three of her guests. Plaids were taken to hang before the kitchen fire to dry, and the visitors shown into an upper room to change.

Presently, at the table eating and drinking, they explained to their hostess about Donald MacLeod of Gualtergill, of whom she knew, and his quest in Stornoway for the ship. She looked doubtful

57

about this. She declared that they must on no account enter the town, two miles off. She would go personally and seek to contact MacLeod and bring him back, trusting none other with the errand. The town was full of English sailors as well as Seaforth's men.

Solicitous for their comfort, Aileen Mackenzie thereafter mounted a garron and set off for Stornoway town. The visitors were glad to sleep.

All too soon for the sleepers, it seemed, the lady came back, although it transpired that she had been gone over three hours. And her news was not good. It seemed that Seaforth had sent his son and heir, Lord Fortrose, to marshal his men to search for the prince, who was suspected to be in the vicinity. Apparently the Reverend Aulay MacAulay, in South Uist, who was the Reverend John MacAulay's father, had sent word to his son that Charles Edward had landed in the Outer Isles with a large body of men, some were saying five hundred, and was bent on taking Stornoway as a base for French aid and reassembly of his army. The place was in an uproar. A Colonel Campbell, presumably one of Loudoun's force, had been sent from Skye with reinforcements. But their hostess had managed to find MacLeod of Gualtergill in a dockside tavern. He was coming on to Kildun by himself, on foot.

Heads ashake over these tidings, astonished over the follies of men, the party awaited Donald MacLeod.

When he arrived, glad as they were to see him, he did little to cheer them. All would have to be changed, he announced, their plans no longer practicable. He had indeed found and hired a small ship to take the prince to the Orkneys; but no one in Stornoway was prepared to skipper and crew it. Indeed it probably would not be allowed to leave the harbour. The whole town was in a state of panic, armed men everywhere, fearing attack from a Jacobite army. Those MacAulays had excelled themselves! If this was an example of Presbyterian thinking, God spare them from it, Donald added. So they had to abandon any hope of sailing from Stornoway.

"What, then?" Charles asked. "What are we to do now, *mon Dieu*? We cannot remain here, endangering this good lady."

"Nothing for it, at all, Highness, but to go back, as Donald Campbell told us if aught went wrong. Back to Scalpay. Or, better still, to Benbecula and Clanranald. Hope for a vessel from

Loch Boisdale. Or else sail back to the mainland, where they will no longer be searching for Your Highness."

They gazed at each other, helplessly. All this way, for nothing!

"Is there nowhere else on this Lewis where we could get a ship but Stornoway?" O'Sullivan demanded.

"It is the only port used by shipping, other than small boats. It and Loch Boisdale on Benbecula. And even to gain an oar-boat here would be difficult, dangerous now, with word abroad, see you. And the English warships will be the more searching. No, we must go south by land."

Mistress Mackenzie declared that, as it was now almost evening, they were safe enough at Kildun for the night. Rest they must have, and feeding. Actually, she did not think that the Stornoway folk were themselves eager to have the prince captured, only to be spared the threat of his alleged force of supporters descending upon them, which the MacAulays had invented. Donald agreed with this. But once this Colonel Campbell arrived from Skye with his soldiers, the situation would be different.

So it was arranged. A good night's rest, and they would be off early in the morning, before the peat-cutters were out, back whence they had so recently and painfully come. Meanwhile, Donald would borrow Mistress Mackenzie's garron and return to the town, and try to purchase shoes, the local rawhide brogans, for the four fugitives. Fortunately these were made to be adapted to fit almost any normal foot size, with lacing. His whisky trade made him well known in the town, and he would claim that they were for himself and a companion.

So it was more eating and sleeping for the others. Aileen Mackenzie, an attentive hostess if ever there was one, arranged that a couple of her servants, and herself, would be awake throughout the night, in turns, to watch for any possible nocturnal searchers – which she judged most unlikely – and a route of escape shown, by back door, cow byres and sheds, just in case. She also said that she would have a calf killed and cut up, so that they could carry some meat with them on their travels.

They passed an undisturbed night.

Before sun-up, after a hearty breakfast, they took their leave of that kind woman and her servants. Donald had been successful in finding them brogues, which could be laced up tightly or loosely to fit feet as required, these much appreciated by the four recipients.

Bags of raw beef were ready for them to carry, but there was an argument about payment, Aileen Mackenzie refusing O'Neill's coin; but when Charles insisted, she handed over, as compensation, a flask of brandy, bread, butter, meal, even a cooking utensil, such was her goodness.

They left Kildun with hearts and hands full, whatever their misgivings as to the future.

6

In the event, well shod, well fed and rested, they made very considerably better time and progress on their southwards journey, the weather being kind, and met with no opposition or problems other than the rough terrain presented, lighting a fire and eating a partially cooked meal at noon, by which time they were near to Balallan, ten miles on their way. The new footwear, being of rawhide, demanded no wearing in, and made their walking infinitely easier.

They halted for the night near the head of Loch Seaforth, when they found one more fisherman's bothy, with drying nets. With their supply of meat, meal and brandy, they made themselves comfortable, and blessed Aileen Mackenzie.

By noontide next day they were down at Ardvourlie, where Donald managed to persuade two fishermen to hire them a small four-oared boat, and their services to help row it, no identities revealed, whatever the men suspected, silver bawbees sufficiently eloquent introduction. This was to take them to Scalpay, where it was hoped that their original boat might well still be berthed.

Down the long loch they rowed, all save O'Sullivan, breathless, taking a hand at the oars, Charles having become quite expert at this.

Going almost due southwards they could not use the sail, so it took them some time to cover the eight miles or so to the open water of the Minch. However, thereafter it was only a roughly similar distance to Scalpay, so they did not grumble.

Not at first, that is. But they were barely out of the loch mouth when, none so far off to the south, indeed near Scalpay, they saw a three-masted ship, clearly one of the English frigates. It was not lying at anchor, either, for its sails were visible perhaps four or five miles away as it would be.

What to do? When they were spotted, as they would be, they might not be subject to investigation, but could they chance it?

They decided that they could not. To sail on their present course would bring them ever nearer to the ship. So, Scalpay not yet. Best to turn in the other direction, northwards, and seek to find a hiding place amongst the North Harris inlets and islets. Either that, or put back into Loch Seaforth. The two boat owners may have wondered why there was so much concern over the frigate; but all the fisherfolk of this seaboard had reason to fear and hate the English, who were ravaging, terrorising and destroying boats.

So they changed course completely. Out here the wind was quite strong, south-westerly, which meant that going north they could hoist sail, which would give them speed if the ship was coming this way; whereas entering the loch again, the wind would not serve them because of the hills. They would head north by east, and seek somewhere to give them cover up the Sound of Shiant.

Soon it was all too apparent that the frigate was coming north, whether deliberately following them or not. And, of course, however much help their sail was, the larger vessel, wind behind it also, would move more than twice as fast as they would. Those miles between would soon be eaten up.

Anxiously they watched the gap between shortening. Unfortunately the coastline they were off here was fairly flat and unsuitable for hiding. There were inlets, small bays and sea lochs, but open and bare; and if the enemy saw them heading into one of these it would look suspicious and a longboat might well be sent after them. So on further up the sound, eyes on the following ship.

Most of them, like those on the oars, were facing sternwards, but fortunately O'Sullivan was not. He it was who shouted and pointed. There, ahead of them, appearing round a headland perhaps another four miles away, was a similar tall ship, three-masted, almost certainly English.

Crisis. Caught between two enemy vessels.

Donald made quick decision. Shallow water, he exclaimed. Where these large vessels would not dare enter. They could launch longboats, yes, but these would be slower. The nearest shallows? Eilean Iubhard, a large, level, barren isle some way ahead, two miles perhaps. Half-left. Narrow channels round it. Could they make it in time? If that second ship turned in towards them, it could cut them off. But it was well out towards the centre of the Minch. Would it see them, bear down on them? Or more likely assume that they were just local fishermen, and move on to exchange salutations with the other frigate?

Desperately they rowed, almost due westwards now. It was difficult to distinguish this Iubhard island against the background of low rocky coast and channels, for it was, it seemed, no more than just a detached part of the same. A blessing indeed that Donald knew this seaboard so well; even the two boat owners had never had occasion to land on Iubhard, an uninhabited place at the narrow mouth of Loch Shell.

It was with major relief that they saw no altering of course towards them of the northern ship. If the two vessels were going to meet, rendezvous, then that might allow them to get into Loch Shell and behind this Iubhard, out of sight.

That indeed was what transpired, to their thankfulness. The warships seemed more interested in coming together than in investigating the odd fishing-boat. With profound relief the fugitives won into the inlet which proved to be the very inconspicuous and twisting entrance to Loch Shell. Donald said that they did not want to get far into this waterway, which penetrated quite far inland apparently, for thereon were the communities of Pairc and Eishken. The less they saw of their fellow-men meantime, the better. So they worked their way into a narrow passage on their right, hidden behind rocks and low spurs, to where they could beach the boat. This was Eilean Iubhard apparently, as featureless a tract as they were likely to find on all this barren coast, which was what they were in need of, Donald asserted, in this pass, somewhere to lie low and where they were unlikely to be looked for, until they could resume their journey to Scalpay.

Disembarking, they were all glad to stretch their legs, but careful not to show themselves up on any of the very modest higher ground, in case those ships came closer, scanning the shoreline, which admittedly seemed unlikely.

The Ardvourlie boatmen said that they had heard that some of the Lewis fishermen, and merchants who sold their fish, used this uninhabited and otherwise useless isle, which did not seem to belong to anyone, to wind-dry their cod and haddock, which could then be sent away for sale. Whether this was true or not they did not know; but if so, and it certainly was a windy enough spot, then they might find some sort of sheds or roofed shelters where the fish could be kept dry but aired. So they went exploring; and sure enough, in one of the innumerable hollows amongst the rocks, they discovered two strange erections on stilts, as it were, with roofs of thatch-reeds but no walls. Over another stony rise, they found a third, and while the first two had been empty, this one was half full of dried fish. Much cheered, they selected the best-roofed of the three to make into as fair a shelter as was possible, in case they had to remain here for some time, using plaids to represent walling, weighed down with stones, and finding the bags in which their meat had been carried of use in this.

All set to work to try to find fuel for a fire. Driftwood was scarce on this all but treeless coast, but they did discover some hardy gorse bushes in sheltered corners, some dead, and the roots of these would be substantial enough to burn as more than just a quick blaze like the prickly branches. They soon had a fire going, and Aileen Mackenzie's pot stewing purloined cod and meal soup, with a little beef added for flavour. They hoped that the smoke would not attract attention from seawards, although the wind was dispersing it.

That wind was worrying Donald and the two boatmen, gusting ever stronger, and presently bringing rain-squalls with it. They had hoped to be able to leave this place with darkness, to make their unobserved way to Scalpay; but in the conditions of this rock-bound shoreline of islets and channels, stormy weather could whip up dangerous seas in a short time, dangerous enough for a small boat at any time but in darkness the more so. It was very much feared that they would have to spend the night here, and therefore probably the following day also.

Well before an early dusk came down, hastened by heavy cloud and rain, it was apparent by the noise, not only of the wind but of breaking seas on rocks and reefs, that this was no night to be afloat. So it was down for sleep in their makeshift shelter, huddled together, amidst a strong smell of fish.

They passed a somewhat disturbed night, for the gusts wrenched loose their plaid walling, and this had to be secured again and again, weighed down with heavier stones. They took turns in dealing with this, Charles included. Throughout all their travels and trials he had insisted on being treated no differently from the others, taking his share in all the tasks, in fact doing more than the older O'Sullivan and O'Neill.

They were in no hurry to rise in the morning, wet and blustery as it was, and with showers of wave-spray drifting over the island. Ned Burke did make valiant efforts to get a fire going, but without success. So cold and uncooked food had to suffice; and lying under plaiding was as good a way of passing the time as any, in the circumstances. Unfortunately, presumably from strange and irregular feeding, some form of dysentery was apt to attack them, the prince included; unpleasant as this was, and inconvenient to say the least, it was more appropriately dealt with ashore than afloat.

Donald declared that these storms were unusual for late April and May on this seaboard, scant consolation; but at least they would have the effect of hampering the enemy warships, forcing them to find sheltered waters to anchor in, and so prevent searching, for the reefs and skerries and tide-races could be dangerous for larger vessels as well as small. A pity that Father Allan was not with them to inform whether it would be a sin to pray that some of the foemen might be wrecked?

The day seemed a long one, especially as it was obvious by the roaring seas that they were not going to be able to risk sailing again that night. It would take some time for these waves to subside.

They whiled away the time, since they could not sleep all day and all night, even the best slumberers of them, in recounting incidents, events of the campaign, and telling stories, Donald particularly good with tales of the Highlands and Islands, many supernatural and legendary, even dating back to pre-Christian, Pictish and Norse times, Charles learning more about some aspects of his nation's story than he had dreamed of or even could have imagined, perhaps good for him. For his part, he contributed royal family reminiscences and anecdotes, especially some relating to his extraordinary great-great-grandfather, James the Sixth and First, some of whose exploits, utterances and assertions would have been scarcely believable coming from a less authoritative source than his direct descendant.

Somehow the time passed.

The second night saw little improvement in the weather, although the rain was not so heavy. But the seas remained as high, and not for small craft. Somehow they had to get a good fire going, to cook and to dry gear. Hector and Ned, battling against the wind, found another of these fish-airing shelters, and since it was semi-broken-down anyway, they demolished it and brought its wooden poles and rafters to provide more substantial fuel than gorse roots and twigs, using its compacted reed roofing to make their plaid walling more effective. The others, at Murdo MacDonald's suggestion, spent much time hunting for shellfish, cockles, mussels and oysters, cast up by the breakers, and these, boiled on the improved fire, made, with beef stock, a sort of soup, edible if not to everyone's taste.

It became evident that still another night would have to be passed on this Iubhard, seas still high.

But in the morning, with the wind changed into the north-east, and colder, Donald declared that they might risk setting off, and in daylight, the landmass providing some cover and the waves not breaking whitely, although there was still a heavy swell. And there was no sign of any warships in the sound. All were only too thankful to leave that barren spot, refuge as it had been, so there was no controversy. Scalpay for them, then.

The breeze behind them now, they could use sail. It was reckoned that, having come thus far north to avoid the frigate, they had about a score of miles to cover, as they would be wise to remain fairly close inshore not to be obvious to possible shipping, although that meant having to watch for rocks and reefs instead. But it was good to be on the move again.

In fact, apart from queasy stomachs caused by the rolling, sidelong swell, and not helped perhaps by shellfish soup, they made good time of it, with no alarms, and entered the Kyles of Scalpay soon after noon, thankful to see that bay and haven opening before them, and the Campbell house up on its slope, a welcome sight.

But no one today coming down to welcome them, they were surprised. And on arrival up at the house, it was to receive ill tidings. Mistress Campbell and her daughters were still there, unhappy, but husband and father had departed meantime. Apparently, two days before, the Reverend MacAulay had come back again from South Uist with a dozen men, asserting that there were reports that the prince could be on Scalpay and being given shelter by Campbell. This being denied, they had set out to search the island, and prudently that man had betaken himself off, just where to it was better for his womenfolk not to know, but they guessed it would be to Benbecula and Clanranald's castle of Borve, a fairly secure retreat save for cannon-bearing warship attack. He had taken the ailing Father Allan with him.

The newcomers were much concerned, especially Hector naturally. Hasty discussion convinced them that they too should depart, and to Benbecula, although not necessarily to Borve which might bring down trouble on Clanranald; and this resolution was confirmed and action expedited by the sight of four men appearing over a ridge about half a mile off, presumably some of MacAulay's group. Hector decided that he also would be better away from Scalpay meantime, as did Murdo, and with Charles feeling guilty over his presence thus causing added trouble and upset for his companions, they hurriedly left the distracted womenfolk and returned to the boat, to push off before those four could come up with them.

Donald said that it was over twenty-five miles to North Uist and almost as far again to Benbecula, so they could not hope to get there that day, although, with this northerly wind, if they continued to sail all night, they just might make it. They had not had time or opportunity to stock up with more food at the Campbell house, so that problem loomed again.

It was late afternoon and they were more than halfway down the eastern shore of South Harris when ahead of them, appearing round the broken headlands of adjacent North Uist, they saw the three masts of a frigate, to general dismay. As ever, Donald acted swiftly, changing course eastwards, towards the mainland. The nearer the shoreline the less readily spotted would be their boat. If they could reach Rodel Point, the southern tip of this South Harris, they might hide behind that. Three miles perhaps . . .

But soon, by the direction of the ship's course, fully in sight now, it looked as though they had been seen. If they had, Donald said that Rodel was of little use to them, for there were cliffs there and deep water where the warship could approach close. Better, even though they were seen, to head across this Sound of Harris and into the multitude of islets off the North Uist shore, all shallows and skerries where no large vessel could penetrate. Then, if they were pursued, it would be by longboat, which would improve their chances of escape.

So they struck out into the sound, due southwards now and glad of the wind behind them; but they were, of course, thereby coming the nearer to the frigate, however diagonally. To be sure, they might be taken for innocent fishermen, and this course perhaps favourable to that presumption.

67

However, the ship soon was seen to be turning into the sound towards them, Donald reckoned a mere two miles off now. They headed a little more to the west. These islets, which Donald called Gilsay, Groay, Lingay and Scaraway, with all their reefs, would provide their needed refuge. That ship would not dare venture amongst them.

It became something of a race, with the passengers irked that they could do nothing to help. But the wind was in their favour, God be praised for that north-westerly, which the frigate was having to tack against.

Thankfully, at last they pulled in between Gilsay and Lingay, and immediately had to start to veer and backwater to avoid rocks and tide-races, sail lowered. They were safe from any large ship here. Would a longboat be lowered and sent after them?

Hiding behind a little promontory, they peered over, and thereafter sighed with relief and gratitude. They saw the ship turn and tack off north-westwards.

They landed, then, on this islet, Lingay, where at least they found a spring of fresh water to drink. But it was otherwise barren rock, and no place to spend the night if they could help it. Donald thought that once the ship was out of sight they ought to go on, make for somewhere on North Uist where they could get food, somewhere near Lochmaddy perhaps, none so far south of this, the second largest port of the Outer Isles, where they might even learn of a vessel on which the prince could embark.

Their frigate safely gone, then, it was back to oars and sail, with the sun beginning to sink.

It proved to be only some seven or eight miles southwards to Lochmaddy, by which time the dusk was settling on land and sea, for which they had reason to be thankful again, for there, in the sheltered mouth of the loch, was another frigate at anchor. Hastily they pulled on, southwards, hunger less important than safety, all concurred.

With the seas sinking and the breeze behind them, they in fact sailed on all night, rowing at a minimum, most able to sleep. Dawn saw them off the quite large isle of Ronay, not far north of Benbecula, and that channel between it and North Uist wherein lay Rossinish where first they had landed on the Outer Isles, a month ago, a month of continual and ineffective travel and hardships, but also of the receipt of much care and kindness. Charles never forgot that there was a price on his head, a reward of thirty thousand pounds, a fortune indeed, for the apprehension of his person, and only the MacAulays, father and son, had so far tried to earn it – although quite possibly their efforts were more in the cause of their stern religious dogma than for worldly gain.

With daylight burgeoning they had to be on the watch for warships, for clearly this area was being the more intensively patrolled. Donald said that he knew of a suitable hiding-place not far south of there, a crescent-shaped islet in the mouth of Loch Uskavagh, with small communities on the Benbecula shores nearby from which they might obtain food, three more miles perhaps. Meantime scan the sound for shipping.

They scarcely needed to be told that. Charles for one was ever eagerly watching, and not only for the enemy. He always was hoping that one time they might spot a ship flying the Lilies of France instead of the Union flag, and his wanderings might be over. King Louis *had* promised aid, even though Britain and France were not actually at war.

Avoiding numerous islets south of Ronay, they duly came to the wide entrance to this Loch Uskavagh, and half a mile in was Donald's isle of Bearran, which was so formed, he said, as to offer them hiding from almost every quarter. Once, long ago, caught in a storm with a boat-load of whisky, he had sheltered there, and remembered a fisher's bothy. If he recollected aright, there was a crofting community called Meanish not far across the loch, and another on the other side, of which he had forgotten the name.

This Bearran isle, they found, was indeed ideal for their purposes, so irregularly shaped, with inlets and coves, as to offer them comprehensive protection. But the bothy, they discovered, was less satisfactory, having evidently deteriorated over the years, so much so that the roof, over the doorway, had fallen in, and they could not get inside without digging. But by now they had become expert in making temporary repair of bothies, and soon they had it in some sort of order. With plenty of bushes around, they got a fire going. Meantime, Donald and the two Ardvourlie boatmen took the boat across the loch to the crofts of Meanish, just visible, with some coin from O'Neill, to try to purchase provisions. This was Benbecula, Clanranald's country, and even though the identity of the party might be suspected, there was little likelihood of any betrayal.

This food errand was successful, even though it took a little time, salt fish and oatmeal the main yield. The Meanish crofters had been civil and had not asked awkward questions, but significantly had volunteered that the English ships and their piratical crews were a menace and to be avoided at all costs, which probably implied some fairly accurate guesswork as to identity.

Thankfully the fugitives fed. It was good to eat oatmeal, cooked with fresh not salt sea water, *drammach* as Donald called that less than delectable fare; they had more than sufficient salt with the fish.

Now to inform Clanranald of their presence, and to seek his help. Donald said that, as the eagle might fly, he guessed they were approximately level with Borve Castle, at the other side of Benbecula – perhaps seven miles. But they were scarcely eagles, and with the lochan-dotted nature of the terrain between, literally hundreds of lochs, the journey there could be double that distance.

It was decided to send the two young men from Scalpay to try to reach Borve, Hector Campbell and his friend Murdo. The former thought that his father might well have gone to Clanranald for safety, and naturally wished to see him; and they were young and used to covering this sort of ground. The boatmen would take them right to the head of this Loch Uskavagh, which would save them almost three miles of difficult walking, and thereafter they must make their way due westwards as best they could. There was the quite large inland Loch Olaval to be got past on their route, which would add to their problems, best going north-about probably; but once past that they would be into better, clearer moorland, the Torlum district, with Borve near the coast. With the good wishes of their companions, the pair set off, by boat. It would be a full and testing day's walking.

Meanwhile it was minor exploration and rest for the remainder. Charles and Ned went seeking crabs and shellfish.

The following day, soon after noon, there was much satisfaction at the arrival of Clanranald himself. He came on horseback with three others, to the shore opposite, with waves and halloos requiring the boat to be sent for them. There were two pack-garrons with them also, and these had to be unloaded and their burdens transferred to the boat, and tethered there. The newcomers arrived therefore laden with food, drink, clothing and more plaids. Hector had not returned with them, for it seemed that his father was presently lodging with his brother-in-law, MacDonald of Balleshare, at the south-western tip of North Uist, and he had gone to join him. But as well as Murdo, Clanranald had brought a handsome, youngish man of genial character whom he introduced to Charles as Neil MacEachain, a far-out kinsman who had been Young Clanranald's tutor, and who, it seemed, was to be attached to the prince's party hereafter as guide and assistant, more or less as the chief's deputy.

After greetings and the obvious comments on the situation, Clanranald shook his greying head. "You are going to have to lie very low, Highness, I fear," he said. "And in more secure hiding than this. The search for you grows closer daily. It is suspected that you are somewhere in these parts of the Long Island, and all government forces are being brought in to find you. There are now no fewer than fifteen warships combing the isles, and they are sending landing-parties ashore to seek and question. Captain Fergusson of the *Furnace*, who commands, has twice called on me at Borve, making enquiries, giving warnings, scarcely hiding his suspicions. And General Campbell of Mamore is on Barra, to the south, with a regiment, sending detachments out with the ships. They are determined to capture Your Highness."

"*Mon Dieu*, all that! I regret, my friend, you being thus troubled. And here I am troubling, endangering you further! It is my sorrow to have brought hurt and trouble on these islands, when I came to bring betterment, freedom from the German yoke. I am sorry indeed."

"At least, Highness, it means that they still greatly fear you!" MacEachain said. "They would not be pursuing you thus if they judged you to be of no danger, your royal cause vanquished."

"*Voilà!* There speaks a true champion!" Charles commended. "That is how I tell myself to see it, also. We shall triumph yet!"

"But meantime, sir, you must be preserved from them," Clanranald declared. "With so many ships available, and with these landing-parties, every sea loch and hospitable isle will be searched, this Bearran and Loch Uskavagh amongst them, I judge. We must get you away from here. Fifteen ships and a regiment of troops!"

"Where? To go where? To the mainland again?"

"Not that, I fear. Every boat sailing the Minch will be watched for, investigated. No – I have somewhere on my property, not on Benbecula but on South Uist, where I think that Your Highness will be safe. Neil will take you there. It is on this east coast, yes, Corradale Bay. But secure, if anywhere is secure. That area has already been searched, I am told. But Corradale is especial. A long stretch of rock-bound coast. Cliffs. No road anywhere near. One empty cottage only, hidden from the Minch, for a summer sheiling shepherd. High mountains enclosing it. Deer to be stalked, many, on the hills. Your Highness will hide well there, until . . ." He left the rest unsaid.

"Until, yes!" Charles shrugged. "A ship. To take me to France. I have looked for that these long weeks. King Louis promised aid. It will come."

The other cleared his throat and eyed him, head ashake. "Prince Charles, I fear that it *has* come. And gone! So I have heard. I am sorry. My brother, Boisdale, got word from Moidart. Two weeks past, two French vessels came to Loch nan Uamh, to my son's house at Borrodale. After you had left. They brought much treasure, in gold. Aid for you. Too late! Gold pieces by the thousand. But they are gone! Back to France!"

"*Mon Dieu!* It came! The aid. Late. Too late!" The prince stared. "And they are gone away? Back to France?"

"That was the word, Highness. The sorrow of it! If you had but waited at Borrodale!"

"We feared capture. Or *I* did. *Ma foi*, I blame myself! I it was who insisted that we leave. Your son would have had me stay." He turned to look at Donald, who was listening, and who also had counselled waiting. "Here is fault, failing. I believed it for the best. But now I pay for my fault. And make others pay! *Le bon Dieu* forgive me!"

"Do not blame yourself, Highness. You could not know . . ."

O'Sullivan joined in. "The blame, Charles, was King Louis's. If he had sent his ships earlier, as promised."

O'Neill, treasurer, picked on that other aspect of the news. "This money? The gold brought. What of that? Who has it now?"

Clanranald wagged his head. "I know not. All that my brother was told was that it was sent by my son to Murray of Broughton, the secretary, who was with Cameron of Lochiel at Loch Arkaig. For the army. Then the ships sailed back to France."

There was silence for a space as his hearers considered the implications of all this. Then Charles spread his hands, French fashion. "They say that milk which is spilled should not be grieved over! I take the blame. But we can still look for a ship to take us. Or, perhaps go back? Back to the mainland. Rejoin the others. Your son, Clanranald. Lochiel. Murray. Elcho. Sheridan. Now that this gold is come. Money to pay for men, for the regiments. Muster forces anew?" He looked round them all.

Only doubtful glances met his.

Pursing lips, he nodded. "We shall consider," he told them, "what is best. Meantime . . . we go to this Corradale, yes?"

"That would be wise, Highness. Neil will take you there. He knows it," the chief said. "On the morrow, belike. He will come back to Borve with me now, and tomorrow bring more of what you will need. Decide what is required. A musket or two, see you, with shot. For stalking the deer. Many at Corradale. Better gear. Spirits, some of Gualtergill's whisky. Brandy. More than we have brought today."

"I thank you, from the bottom of my heart!" the prince said. "But, tell me, my friend, have you heard aught of Father Allan? My chaplain. Kinsman to MacDonald of Moidart. He fell sick. We sent him back to Scalpay, when on our way to Stornoway, to Campbell there. But they had fled, we learned, when we returned to that isle, to escape the Reformist minister and his people. Now we know that Campbell is at this – I forget the name of the isle. Do you know if Father Allan is still with him?"

"I do not know. Campbell is on Baleshare, yes, off North Uist, but none so far from here. Less than ten miles north of Borve. I will send to find out."

"That would be a kindness. One more kindness . . ."

Clanranald and MacEachain went off, ferried across to their garrons, the latter promising to return the following day. It would probably be evening before he got back, if he had to learn news of this priest, Allan MacDonald.

They went, with blessings.

It was indeed dusk the following evening before a horn, blowing from across the water, intimated that Neil MacEachain had returned and required the boat to be sent for him. And as well as men, with two more pack-horses, bearing the promised

73

supplies, he brought none other than Father Allan MacDonald, to a glad reunion.

The priest was looking frail, by no means fully recovered, but was cheerful and delighted to be back with the prince, whom he seemed to feel that he had deserted. He was full of the kindness shown to him by Donald Campbell and his brother-in-law, MacDonald of Baleshare. His son Hector was now reunited with his father.

Neil said that Clanranald had been urgent that they should lose no more time in setting off for his Corradale. Troops had landed on the south of Benbecula, and it might not be long before they reached this area. Somebody on Meanish might give away their secret. Off with full darkness, then. The north-west breeze maintained, and would help them on their way southwards.

So they left Loch Uskavagh, which had provided them with respite and much caring attention, and with a new guide, the same number in the boat, with Hector and Murdo replaced by Father Allan and MacEachain. The latter did not think that they could reach Corradale before daylight, even with a favourable wind, for the nights were growing ever shorter, and it would be fully twenty miles. Skiport, a quite major sea loch, with its scattering of islets, was approximately halfway, and they could hide therein over the next day.

Neil MacEachain was a fine singer, and whiled away their passage with traditional songs of the isles, as well as some classical ballads and even hymns, for he was a man of education, having been trained for the priesthood although never taking up the vocation. They all joined in the choruses, Charles, who himself had a fine voice, foremost in support, and Father Allan contributing.

They had to head quite some distance eastwards, out into the Minch, to avoid a plethora of islets; and then it was the larger Wiay to be rounded. The tide-races and overfalls made the sailing difficult, despite the favourable breeze, delaying their progress. Neil and Donald reckoned that they had less than six hours of real darkness; and with Wiay past, a more westerly course was necessary, over four miles of it before they could reach Loch Skiport. Their guides began to grow anxious about timing and daylight. Oars were used to increase speed.

The eastern sky was indeed lightening significantly when they did reach Skiport; and there concern over visibility changed into something much more urgent, when, in the loch mouth, they saw

74

anchored a sheltering frigate. At least the dawn enabled them to see it in good time. Hastily they pulled off south by west again, hoping that no especial watch was being kept on the vessel at that hour of the morning to spot them. Even if they were seen, of course, it would take time for the large ship to up anchor, raise sail, and come after them.

So now they were faced with another ten miles of sailing, in ever-brightening light; for according to Neil, the coast now, all the way to Corradale, was fierce and devoid of shelter, with the mountains coming down close to the shore in cliffs, the Usinish peninsula a menace in itself and to be heedfully avoided.

The passengers did not fail to perceive the dangers of the sea-board they were flanking now, savage in the extreme, such as they had not come across previously, high cliffs soaring above the white spray of breakers, and behind, as the sun rose to floodlight them, great mountains dominated by the mighty peaks of Ben More and Hekla. If this was the run-up to Corradale, then it was small wonder that Clanranald thought that they ought to be secure there from search, once they had found the landing-place, well hidden. When they were not looking back to ensure that the frigate was not following them, they were eyeing that hostile coast apprehensively.

It got worse, indeed, as they went southwards, the cliffs higher and the spouting waves likewise. What that shoreline would be like in a storm defied conception. Donald conceded that it was as bad as anything that he knew, not that he knew this part well, for he had always kept his distance from it on his travels.

Neil seemed untroubled, however, saying not to fear, that he knew of a fair hidden landing, although for small boats only. These mountains were the best place for deerstalking on all the Long Island, and Clanranald and he used it often for their favourite sport.

No ships appeared.

Past the Usinish peninsula's menace a couple of miles, turning westwards, landwards, they saw a narrow bay opening, but no evident improvement for a landing. Indeed, with the shallower waters they were moving into, the waves and turbulence grew the worse, with overfalls. But Neil, in the bows, seemed entirely confident, whatever his companions' reaction. The sail down, he guided the oarsmen exactly, heading it seemed for a great thrusting buttress of the cliffs, at the foot of which spray soared. Almost at it, the boat rising and falling alarmingly, he shouted, against the noise of breaking water, for a swift turn right-handed, then left again, and they swirled round the side of that projecting abutment only yards from it, and so into a tiny creek of calmer water with, at the head of it, a pebbly beach. The sudden lessening of their craft's motion was extraordinary.

Up to that little beach, and on to it, they ran the boat's prow, amid cries of acclaim and relief, their hidden haven.

"I defy anyone who does not know this entry to guess of it, or to find it," Neil declared, as they climbed over the side on to dry land.

But, thankful as they were, the newcomers stared upwards. For the cliffs soared abruptly high above them, seemingly unsurmountable. Perceiving their incomprehension, Neil pointed to their left to where, a short distance off, a post was driven into the ground to mark the start of a zigzag climbing track, scarcely to be distinguished, heading slantwise up, indeed the higher reaches of it indiscernible.

"Yonder is our stairway!" he said. "None so ill, taken with a little care."

Even Donald eyed him doubtfully.

Unloading the boat, most of the company were even more doubtful. They had, thanks to Clanranald, accumulated quite a lot of gear, food, clothing, cooking utensils, plaiding, flasks of brandy and whisky, the two muskets and bags of powder and shot. All this, presumably, had to be got to the top of these cliffs. How?

Neil took the muskets, weighty enough, and the even heavier bags of shot, hoisting them on to and over his shoulders, by way of demonstration, and gestured towards the rest of the baggage, grinning encouragingly. Less than eagerly the others went to pick up various burdens, some selectivity evinced. Charles shouldered a leg of beef in a sack, with a bundle of plaiding over an arm, and moved to follow their guide to that track-foot.

However lacking in prominence, the path was clear enough once they were on it, twisting and turning its way upwards but trending ever towards the left as they climbed. There were even footmarks on it, in muddy patches, pointed deer tracks. Observing these, the prince asked what they were. Sheep? Goats? What would bring such animals down to this barren shore?

"Deer," Neil said. "Roe-deer. Stags, the large red deer, would not come down here. But roe visit beaches. Why, I am not sure.

Perhaps they eat the seaweeds. There are many roe here, but no sheep nor goats. Good eating. This track is really of *their* making. We men have only adapted it. They have picked an effective way down and up."

"Clever . . . brutes. And sure- . . . footed. We need . . . to be . . . liker them!" Charles was already beginning to pant, with the steepness and the weight he was carrying. There was no chatter from behind them, either.

That was an alarming ascent, as they negotiated right-angled bends every two or three yards, to give them height and to avoid projections of rock and overhangs. Sometimes they edged along dizzy ledges and up wet and slippery tiny gullies running with water. Charles frequently heard panted curses from behind him, but these were brief, however heartfelt, lungs otherwise preoccupied. He did not suffer from vertigo, but even so he kept his eyes very much on the track, such as it was, following exactly in Neil's footsteps, the more so as they worked higher, for the sheer drop below was off-putting to say the least.

That climbing column became notably strung out, each man taking his own cautious time, Father Allan well to the rear. The prince worried about him and O'Sullivan. This was scarcely activity for the unfit. But, at least, it did emphasise Clanranald's assertion that they ought to be safe, wherever they were going, from searchers based on ships.

How high these cliffs soared was as difficult to estimate as to mount, between two and three hundred feet perhaps, although that might sound a very modest measurement as set against the toil, labour and time of the ascent – and the length of it indeed, for as well as all the zigzags and detours, their route took them a long way southwards, or what seemed a long way.

But at last they were up, or some of them, for, gasping for breath and lowering their burdens for a rest, they had to await the stragglers, Father Allan very much the last, and in a dire state. Indeed, Charles went back down the last few bends in the track to relieve his friend of the bundle he was carrying, and to praise his efforts and determination. The priest could not speak.

Thereafter, recovering, they turned to face inland, from that cliff-top. And the change in prospect was in itself breathtaking. Instead of overhanging, threatening rock and fearsome drops was wide immensity, far-flung vistas of hills and valleys, heather ridges

77

and grassy hollows, culminating in majestic peaks, lochans, even some stunted trees, a different world from anything that they had seen for long.

Neil pointed. "See you that ridge with the three bent hawthorn trees? Just behind that lies the cottage which we make for. We keep it in fair order, for this is a long way from Borve to come for our sport, overland, and we usually stay for two or three nights. It was built as summer sheiling for Boisdale's cattle, but he no longer sends beasts here. Come."

Picking up their baggage, they set off over the heather, occasionally able to make use of deer paths.

Perhaps halfway, Neil pointed again, westwards. There, on the flank of a braeside, a quarter-mile off, was a herd of red deer. At first few of the group could pick them out, so well did their colouring blend with the dark brown of old heather; but when, no doubt alarmed by the sight of the humans, they began to move off over the hill, almost like drifting cloud-shadows, they were to be seen more as movement than as individual animals, a score of them at least, their guide said. The company ought not to lack venison as food while here.

When, presently, they reached those gnarled, bent and stunted hawthorns crowning their ridge, it was to see in the hollow beyond what they had travelled so far to seek, a cottage, not large but no mere bothy or shed, low-set, thatched-roofed, with an outbuilding attached and a peat-stack nearby. Down there it was hidden from any distant view, especially from seawards, and to some extent sheltered from storms. Moreover, as Neil mentioned, smoke from its fire would not be evident either, even to the keenest-sighted, amongst those hills and breezes. Appreciatively, they trudged down to it.

That cottage had two doors but no windows, and proved to be divided into three apartments by rough partitions, two of these having wooden shelf-like beds against the walling, the central one with a stone circular hearth in mid-floor for a fire, and the thatching provided with a rudimentary flue above to draw up the smoke. Adjoining was a lean-to for use as a stable for the sportsmen's garrons. A stream ran close by, providing drinking water, and widened to an artificial pool for washing in.

Here was almost luxury compared with so much that they had had to put up in and with. Greatly cheered, the fugitives dumped their burdens.

7

They settled in, as they had not done before, as for a more prolonged stay. For, as well as savouring the feeling of security promised by this Corradale, there were plans forming which involved quite lengthy waiting. It was the news of that French gold which had instigated these. Charles was concerned to know what the effect this, over-late in coming as it was, would have on his affairs, where it was now, what impact it might have on his cause. It had been sent for him, and, if indeed it was as much as reported, then it might alter the situation very considerably. Money, the sinews of war! If it could be used to pay for the recruiting of forces, larger forces, from the chiefs and lairds, then he might not have to return to France, after all. So – information.

As well as this need, there was another. Father Allan should be in the hands of a physician, and none such was available on South Uist or Benbecula, indeed nowhere in the Outer Isles safe from enemy searching. The mainland for him, then, with whoever went for news, if that was possible. Donald MacLeod was the obvious choice. Not only did he know where and how to go, but he was known and accepted all over the Isles and the mainland coasts as a trader in whisky. No naval searchers could mistake him for anything other than a local islesman. If he and the Mallaig boatmen were intercepted, they ought not to be suspected of being linked with the prince. Father Allan would have to lie low, a sick man, not raise voice.

So, a day or two's rest, and they would be off, for Loch nan Uamh or Moidart, leaving O'Sullivan, O'Neill, with Ned Burke, the prince and MacEachain. For how long they would be gone was problematical; but two weeks it was calculated, at the least.

Meanwhile, it was settling in and exploring. All were delighted with their premises and surroundings, comparative comfort and a sense of freedom and relief from being hunted, that and hope, hope for the future. They had ample food and the prospect of more, venison, wildfowl, the eggs of mallard, teal and widgeon from the lochans. There was ample fuel also for the fire, peat and hawthorn wood, for cooking – it was scarcely necessary for keeping them warm now, but cheerful to sit round of an evening. And Charles kept looking towards those great mountains of Ben More and Hekla. He had an urge to climb them, or one of them, some feeling of challenge, a different aspect of the challenge his late campaign had presented to something within him, even though the others were not so keen. Neil said that he would accompany him one day, although their hill-climbing energies would be more profitably utilised in stalking red deer.

On the third evening at Corradale, Donald and the others took their leave, deciding to try to cross the Minch by night, there being no point in taking unnecessary risks. With a south-west wind they ought to be able to reach Canna by daylight, where they could rest for a while. Whether the Inner Sound was still being patrolled they did not know; but with the prince believed to be in the Outer Isles, possibly not. They could ask their friends on Canna perhaps. Then over to Young Clanranald at Loch nan Uamh.

The parting with Father Allan was affecting, since almost certainly he would not be back. Charles, with Neil and Ned Burke, insisted on accompanying the travellers down to the beach, despite the cliff's obstacle course, the priest glad to be assisted down in the dusk. Farewells were exchanged and a blessing bestowed. Then, amidst head-shakings and tightened lips, they pushed off, and in only moments the boat disappeared round that thrusting buttress of rock, gone. Charles, feeling strangely bereft, turned to face that daunting ascent again.

Next morning, Neil introduced the prince to the art of deer-stalking – for it proved to be an art, unlike Charles's previous and less than successful efforts at hunting the creatures, with Ned. It was emphasised to him that these red deer of the mountains had, as well as sharp eyes and ears, the keenest sense of smell in the animal kingdom, to add to their other attributes of alertness and speed. So they were highly difficult to get near enough to shoot, apart altogether from being hard to spot in the first place, with their protective colouring and ability to hide themselves in corries and hollows. Wind direction was all-important for any approach, therefore, so that their scent was not carried to the deer; and in the hills wind currents tended to swirl and eddy, which complicated any approach. In fact, in this chase, the odds were all in favour of the deer which, to be sure, added to the challenge and the satisfaction of possible success. So the prince must not be downcast if they failed to return with a kill.

Ned was eager to come along also, and although they had only the two muskets, he optimistically declared that he would be useful in helping to carry back the spoil. The two Irishmen were well content to stay behind.

They set off to the north-west, and were not long in spotting a small herd on the further side of a steep ridge. But undoubtedly they themselves had been spotted, or scented, first, by the head-high and watchful stance of the animals, and in only moments thereafter they were on the move away, in the graceful, almost floating motion with hooves seeming barely to touch the ground.

Neil said that, in fact, groups, herds, were not the most hopeful quarry, the more of them to be on the alert the less chance of successful approach. The best hope was in the lone beast or couple. Mature stags tended often, save in the breeding season, to absent themselves from the groups of hinds and calves, and were quite frequently to be found alone.

They saw another and larger herd a mile or so further, but these were already moving when observed and could be ignored. There was no point in following such, it seemed, for they could drift over miles of hill without halting, and usually did when alarmed. Clearly this terrain was highly populated with the creatures.

The land rose ever higher the further they went inland, the hills steepening into mountains. They had gone almost three miles before, circling an escarpment, Neil jerked a command to halt, to drop to their knees. He pointed.

At first Charles could see nothing to account for this. Then just a hint of movement made itself evident, and there, against a backdrop of old heather and outcropping rock, was a single stag, that obvious by its branching antlers, these just discernible at perhaps three hundred yards, although head down, grazing.

Neil signed for them to flatten themselves and to wriggle a little way backwards, out of possible sight.

"A chance here," he whispered, although that surely was not necessary. "He has not seen us." Then, oddly, he licked a forefinger and held it up. It was not a windy day, and this was to ascertain the air current direction. It was, as so often, from the south-west. He shook his head. "Back," he said. "We will have to work round. To the right. Eastwards. Round yonder hillock. Approach from the other side. Hope that there is no eddy from the larger hill."

They backed a little further until they could rise, well hidden now. They loaded and primed the muskets, then started to work their way round the back of a small, knobbly hill.

Cautiously, at the far side of this, they crept up to a minor ridge, to peer over, on hands and knees again. This was no sport for fine clothing.

Neither Charles nor Ned could identify the place where they had seen the stag, far less the animal itself. But the experienced Neil could.

"Beside that pulpit-shaped outcrop," he directed. "See, his tail towards us. The white of it. Still feeding."

"I see it now. Too far to shoot?"

"Much. To kill, no more than seventy yards. He is over double that, there." Neil eyed the ground between, and shook his head. "It will not serve. We could not cross that without being seen. Even on our bellies. But he is a good beast, worth our taking. Nothing for it but to go round. Again. That next ridge – round that. Then we will have that outcrop between him and us. If the wind does not betray us."

So they edged back, until they could stand again, out of sight, and begin to circle round a spur of a larger hill, Neil continually testing the breeze, and eyeing every dip and fold of the land. At length he pointed.

"Up there, I think. It should give us a view. Further west than I would like, for the wind. But . . ."

They climbed to another small ridge, went flat, and gazed over.

It took Charles a little while to ascertain that they were looking at the same area but from a different angle, and somewhat further away. But following Neil's glance, he perceived, not the stag but the pulpit-like projection of rock.

"The deer? Has it gone?" he wondered. "I cannot see it."

"We cannot tell, from here. But if we can follow that burn-channel down, and past those reeds of bog, then we ought to have a view. Come."

More crawling, and wet crawling now, the muskets having

to be carried carefully, not dragged over catching heather and obstructions. At a further little crest, Neil edged forward, to stare. Then he waved them on, and pointed once more.

The stag was still there, behind the rise, moving along slowly as it grazed.

"Wait until it gets behind that little spur. Then we ought to be able to get down nearer. Within range."

This time, cresting the next lift of ground warily, they could see their quarry clearly, apparently nowise alarmed, head down.

Lying flat, Neil whispered, "Just within range, I'd say. But tail-on. If he turned side-on, can you take him?"

"*You* shoot," the prince said. "More sure."

"No, Highness – you! Your first stalk. Aim a hand's breadth behind the shoulder. If you can . . ."

Cautiously Charles brought forward the musket, to cock its hammer. He had never shot from flat on the ground before. He raised shoulders somewhat, but Neil pressed him down again, head ashake, and cocked his own weapon.

It was difficult to take aim there amongst heather, and with his deep breathing, keeping his sights on the slowly moving deer. The animal kept on grazing, but its rear remained towards them. Would it move so right out of range?

Then it did turn, partially, head up suddenly. Neil let out a curse. But as the creature gazed back, Charles held breath, closed one eye, lining up his fore-sight on the creature's shoulder, and pressed the trigger.

The bang of the shot seemed deafening after all the silence. The stag leapt high, and swung round and away, as the prince gasped a malediction. But this was drowned by another bang, as Neil fired his musket also. And the deer, after a few stumbling yards, toppled and fell.

Ned Burke gave a whoop of triumph.

They got to their feet. "Did I miss?" Charles asked. "I am sorry."

"No. It is *I* who am sorry," Neil said. "Sorry to spoil your sport. You did not miss – but did not get the heart. Just behind it, I think. He could have run for miles, wounded, before dropping. So I shot. Through the head. Took a chance . . ."

"It moved. As I fired . . ."

They found the stag, legs twitching slightly, but dead.

"Your first stag, Highness," Neil said. "It is a fair sport, is it not? Less than simple, easy."

"Yours, not mine," Charles pointed. Just behind the ear was a bloody hole.

"A joint kill." The other pointed also. There was a second hole between shoulder and spine. "And a fine beast. Ten points." He was referring to the tines of the antlers, dark brown but white-tipped. "Sixteen stones, if a pound!"

"It is big, yes, much bigger than any deer I have seen. Sixteen stones? How much weight is that? How shall we carry it? Get the meat down to the house?"

"Garrons would take it, but we have none. We will have to cut it up, just. Take what is best of it. Haunches. Shoulders. I have never stalked without garrons to carry the kill."

Ned Burke had his dirk out promptly, and made no bones about the butchering, warm as the creature was, skilfully doing *his* part, skinning and severing. To carry those parcels of meat meant that their clothing would be bloodstained; but they were already wet and mud-stained, so it mattered not.

Swallowing something of revulsion, the prince took up a shoulder over *his* shoulder, with his musket over the other, Neil taking a similar burden, and Ned two front legs.

Thus laden, they turned for the quite long walk back to the Glen Corradale cottage, Charles going over the details of the stalk as they trudged, moderately pleased with himself. Something to tell those stay-at-home Irishry. How he wished, though, that he had aimed just a little more to the left!

It was wet over the next two days, and although they did not huddle all the time indoors, they did not venture far from the cottage. At least they had plenty of meat to eat, Ned quite expert at the cookery, roasting, stewing, braising, fuel no problem here.

Then, on the third day, they had a surprise, a visit from Clanranald himself, come overland on horseback with two of his men. It seemed that he had gone to stay with his brother at Loch Boisdale, and had been able to ride north from there the fifteen round-about rough miles, crossing over the pass of the Beallach Crosgard to the south of the towering Ben More, and into Glen Corradale.

The unexpected arrival of the elderly chief aroused great enthusiasm from the prince, especially as he came so well laden with gifts on the garrons.

He brought food and drink, brandy in abundance as well as whisky, a variety of clothing and more plaiding, which was always useful, extra footwear, tobacco and two clay pipes, even a little silver drinking-vessel with lid, fit for princely lips.

Amongst the miscellaneous clothing was a complete set of Highland dress for Charles, not only as suitable garb but as a sort of disguise, in case the enemy somehow managed to catch up with him, and he could then be seen to be a local laird rather than any suspect stranger. There was a philabeg or short kilt, stockings of check, and a tartan coat and vest, with more brogues. Nothing would do but for the prince to go and change into this outfit there and then, to emerge duly transformed, all exclaiming at the sight. Making a flourish of a bow to Clanranald, he declared, "*Voilà!* I only want the itch, now, to be a complete Highlander!" And he scratched himself dramatically.

The chief shook his head. "So long as Your Highness does not open your mouth! Then none would take you for one, I fear!"

There was laughter.

Clanranald stayed with them overnight, for the journey over the mountains and round all the lochs back to Loch Boisdale was not to be taken lightly. That evening they discussed the Culloden débâcle, Charles acknowledging the unfortunate displacing of the MacDonald contingent, including the Clanranald regiment, at that battle, from the prestigious right of the line, when his lieutenant-general, the Lord George Murray, insisted that his Atholl brigade should have that honour. There was no suggestion that the MacDonalds had flagged in their support as a consequence; but the general opinion was that matters might have turned out for the better had the prince not reluctantly agreed to it. They also wondered what news Donald MacLeod would bring from the mainland; the reported arrival of all that French gold could make a major difference to the entire situation, Clanranald admitted.

Neil described the prince's introduction to the sport of deer-stalking, praising his enthusiasm and how quickly he had picked up the essentials of it all, the need for care in approach, however uncomfortable and taxing, not only from sight but from scent and hearing, these almost more important, the patience required and something of respect for the quarry. He acclaimed him an apt pupil.

"My chasing of deer hitherto has been done on horseback," Charles explained. "Hunting, with hounds, not this stalking afoot. Usually in woodlands, with many men, the blowing of horns, much dash and, and *élan, grande parure*! But here is much the finer sport."

"His Highness now wishes to climb one of the mountains," Neil added. "I say that, if we are going up to the high ground, we should take the muskets with us, and see if we may shoot a grouse or two. On the wing. *There* is a difficult sport, also."

"Prince Charles will have to have a good eye and aim for that! I used to be fairish at it, but no longer. But, yes – try it. Ben More would be better than Hekla. And nearer. Up the Beallach Crosgard, as I go, then climb northwards to the Buail a' Ghaill ridge, that long scarp, the best ascent. At this season you will see much muirfowl there . . ."

In the morning, the skies clear, the climbers decided that they might as well take the opportunity of getting assistance on their way by accompanying Clanranald so far on his return journey, and thus be able to save themselves some three miles of preliminary walking by riding behind the two packhorse-men as far as the pass, this Beallach Crosgard. When this meant that Ned Burke could not go with them, to his disappointment, nothing would do but that Clanranald would take the prince behind himself, so that all three could ride.

So the six set off, muskets slung behind two of them, on the long and twisting ascent. They had not gone far when they saw, out in the Minch, two warships heading south. Fists were shaken at them.

Up in the jaws of the beallach, which, it was explained to Charles, meant pass, the climbers dismounted and bade farewell to Clanranald, thanking him for all his kindnesses, he for his part promising to send them another musket and considerably more ammunition. Then they faced the steep lift out of the deep and rocky defile.

This was as bad as climbing that Corradale cliff, and longer. But once up it, panting, they were rewarded by a splendid ridge-walk, well over a mile of it, gradually heightening all the way, but only difficult in outcropping sections, and providing magnificent views

86

in all directions, eastwards to the Inner Isles and even the mainland mountains, southwards to Eriskay, Barra, Pabbay and Mingulay, northwards with the Uists and Harris somewhat blocked by the mass of Hekla, and westwards, oceanwards, to infinity.

The prince was exclaiming over all this when he was interrupted. A whirring sound and a shout from Neil brought his gaze abruptly to much nearer at hand where, a mere score of yards off, five large brown birds had risen out of short heather and blaeberries and sailed off on down-bent wings, skimming the ground, and then over and down, out of sight.

"*Dia!* We should have been ready with the muskets," Neil exclaimed. "But, heed not – there will be more. Even ptarmigan when we get up on to the ben itself."

They promptly primed the muskets, and carried them at the ready thereafter, as they trudged.

They had not far to go before, a little way to the left, another and larger covey rose and went whirring off, with chuck-chucking cries. Up the two muskets rose to shoulders, aiming having to be swift, the two reports thereafter being almost simultaneous. The birds were still close together, so that it was not difficult to make hits, and amidst puffs of feathers, a pair fell.

"Ha! More easy than stalking deer!" the prince cried.

"Wait, you!" his friend advised. "They do not always rise in tight groups like that, hard to miss. More often in ones and twos, and keen aiming required."

Ned collected the birds. Advisedly he had brought a shoulder-bag for the carrying.

They had to go some considerable distance along that ridge before they got another opportunity for marksmanship; perhaps the sound of the gunshots had forewarned the grouse. When, at length, they did raise a target, it was only a single pair, and these flew off separately, on different courses.

"I take left!" Neil cried, aimed, and fired swiftly. The bird flew on, clucking.

Charles sighted, swinging his weapon to match the arc of flight, and pressed trigger. The feathers flew and the grouse dropped to the ground.

"Good! Good! You are a better shot than I am," Neil asserted. "I should have got that one."

They were reloading when, to their surprise, the missed grouse came circling back, possibly looking for its missing mate. Quick as thought, Charles pulled back the hammer, threw up the gun, swung it round after the bird flying just within rage, and pressed the trigger. His quarry plummeted into the heather.

"Lord!" Neil jerked. "That was notable shooting. Brilliant! You have a sure eye and aim, Highness."

"I have shot many birds in France. Not such as these, but duck, pigeons, quail, even larks. Now, there is difficult shooting, a small mark indeed. If one can shoot a soaring lark, one can shoot anything!"

"You shoot *larks*? Why?"

"I think it scarcely worthy sport, however difficult. Not worth the powder and shot. But others, many, think otherwise. Lark pie is a favoured dish."

Soon thereafter they came to the end of the long crest-like escarpment, the sides of which had now developed into cliffs, rock predominating everywhere, so that there were no more grouse. Now they had a short but sharp climb towards the southernmost of the twin summits of Ben More ahead of them. Since they would have to come back this way, Neil said that they should leave the muskets and the bag containing the four grouse on a recognisable outcrop – no need to burden themselves unnecessarily for this final ascent. It meant that they could not shoot ptarmigan, if they saw any; but these were not to be compared with the grouse, smaller, less eating, and they tended to scuttle off rather than fly when disturbed, providing little sport.

So, glad to leave the weight behind, they clambered on, and up on to an ever-narrowing rocky spine, demanding not only on their breathing and lungs but on their footwork, for it was almost entirely slantwise bare stone, and slippery in the extreme, Neil pointing out that it would be practically impossible to mount in icy winter conditions. The views grew more exciting and dramatic by the minute, although having to watch each step of the way, frequently balancing precariously and sometimes having to bend and use hands to steady themselves, they did less gazing than they might have done.

Ben More was an unusual mountain. Its two summit peaks were almost a mile apart, and the linking ridge attenuated, the drops on either side fierce. The wind up here was strong; it would be no place to visit in a gale, any more than in icy conditions. But it certainly represented a major challenge.

They did see two or three scrambling ptarmigan, not much larger than quail, Charles said, grey-brown with white patches, and wholly white in winter seemingly, with strange, almost furry-looking legs and feet, possibly useful in soft snow. Why these creatures chose to inhabit only these inhospitable heights, where so little but lichens grew, was a mystery.

Reaching the second, northern summit, they did sit, crouching, to savour that tremendous prospect to the full, the prince admitting that he had never seen anything like it, for extent and variety. He said that it made mankind seem all but insignificant.

They did not linger long there, nevertheless, in that battering wind, with all those difficult steps to retrace. Apart altogether from picking up the muskets and game, there was really no other way off that mountain, to reach the Corradale area, than by the route that they had come. They saw no more grouse near enough to shoot; and, although they did spot a small herd of deer on the western slopes of the beallach, this was no time to commence the task of stalking.

Physically tired but well pleased with their day, they returned to inform the two sceptical Irishmen of what they had missed.

Two days later they had another visitor, Hugh MacDonald of Baleshare, Donald Campbell's brother-in-law, who came with one of his men and a couple of laden pack-garrons. He had travelled a long way to bring them succour, food, bread, sacks of meal, honey, even flagons of goats' milk; not only this, but warning that his island had been searched by troops from this General Campbell's force, who were working their way southwards, very thoroughly searching for the prince, and seeming to know that he was somewhere on South Uist. He came advising a move; for there was word that the enemy were probing northwards from the foot of the island, also.

It fell to be explained to him that a move was scarcely possible meantime. They had no boat, and would have to wait until Donald MacLeod got back from the mainland with their craft and his information. They could, if necessary, go and hide in the high hills temporarily, under Neil MacEachain's guidance, but they could hardly leave the Corradale area. Anyway, would not the troops find this vicinity very hard to reach and search?

Baleshare conceded this last but pointed out that *he* had made it, admittedly on horseback, whereas the troops would be afoot. He had not known that their boat was amissing. He also agreed with Clanranald that the nearest occupied house was almost certainly Howmore, at least ten difficult miles to the north-east, with only deer tracks between.

Baleshare was a strange, argumentative sort of man, not exactly aggressive but opinionated and very outspoken, to the prince as to the others; yet he had come all this way at much trouble to himself, and possible danger. Charles was nowise offended, even when the other broached the subject of religion. Evidently a strong Protestant, he asserted that the prince's and his father's papistry, as he called it, was a serious handicap to hopes of a restoration of the Stewart monarchy in Scotland, whatever was the English position; also that no autocratic rule could be tolerated. Charles, whilst not meekly accepting this, assured that his devotional attitudes were not dogmatic nor narrow, any more than were his father's; and that he accepted that religion and government should be kept separate. O'Sullivan was less prepared to accept the MacDonald's strictures, and the prince found himself in the odd position of seeking to keep the peace between these two supporters.

Baleshare informed that Donald Campbell and his son, with Murdo, had now gone back to Scalpay, having heard that that island had been searched, and, with nothing found, was unlikely to be gone over again. Campbell had told him to assure the prince, if he managed to see him, that he would ever be welcome on his isle, but strongly urged him to get back to the mainland if at all possible.

This difficult advice was reinforced by another visitor next day, MacDonald of Boisdale himself. He came, also on horseback, at Clanranald's bidding, with the offer of a boat, reporting that General Campbell's searchings were proving very thorough, working up mile by mile from the Sound of Eriskay, and had now almost reached his own Loch Boisdale; he feared that it was only a question of time before they reached Corradale. Charles repeated that they must wait for Donald MacLeod, with his news as to the situation on the mainland; and Neil supported him, saying that the enemy would have great difficulty in tracing and finding them here, by land as well as by sea. He saw the boat journey across the Minch as much the more dangerous, meantime.

Boisdale had brought more supplies, including a considerable amount of brandy, to which he was very partial, it seemed; Charles had heard that he was a notable drinker. And he proved it that night, himself quaffing great quantities of his largesse and calling on the others to drink up, to drown their problems and trials while they might. Nothing loth, this urging was taken up especially by O'Sullivan and Baleshare, to the prolonged chanting of songs and telling of tales, Charles and Neil the least bibulous, however vocal. Indeed, the prince ended up the evening by a solo rendering of *De Profundis* over the all but prostrate persons of Boisdale and most of his companions, Neil beating time. Life had to have its lighter moments.

In the morning, none too early, Boisdale and his men departed, seemingly none the worse for the night's indulgence. He repeated his offer of providing a boat, strongly advising a move before many more days. Baleshare decided to stay with them a little longer, in order to try his hand at deerstalking. It seemed that they did not enjoy this on his flattish isle.

In the event, they did much stalking but no killing, possibly partly as a result of the previous evening's imbibings.

Next day, then, Baleshare was off, argumentative to the end, and declaring that deerstalking was a much over-rated sport.

The others were to prove him wrong in the days which followed, as they waited for Donald MacLeod. They saw considerable shipping activity, at a distance, but no sign of searching troops.

8

It was eighteen days after he had left Corradale before Donald got back, with a different boat crew, on the second day of June. He brought much less cheering news than Charles had hoped for. He had managed to reach the mainland at Loch nan Uamh, and Young Clanranald at Borrodale, without interception, to learn that the barbarian Duke of Cumberland had returned to England, and had been succeeded as commander in Scotland by his lieutenant-general, the Keppel Earl of Albemarle, reputed to be a less severe individual. Whether this would be proved by his behaviour now remained to be seen.

Young Clanranald accompanying him, Donald had gone south to deposit Father Allan with his kinsman at Moidart, where there was known to be a physician available, Donald shaking his head over the good priest's state. Then they had turned eastwards, by long Loch Sheil and Glenfinnan, where the prince's standard had been raised a year before, amidst such high hopes, and so by Glen Pean to Loch Arkaig, the word being that, although the Jacobite leadership had now mainly dispersed, Murray of Broughton, the secretary of the cause, a Lowlander and no connection of the Lord George Murray, was still with Lochiel, the Cameron chief, somewhere in Arkaig, Cameron country. So they had gone seeking these two.

"And the gold?" Charles demanded. "What of the French gold? The moneys which could so aid my cause?"

The other shook his head. "It is gone, Highness. A sorry story, whatever. Like the chiefs, just – dispersed! Or so it seems. Forty thousand gold *louis*, they say. Come on two French ships, frigates, *Bellona* and *Mars*. With arms and ammunition also . . ."

"Gone! How gone, man? Forty thousand gold pieces – that is a vast sum. Sacks of gold! It cannot just have gone, disappeared!"

"It seems that it has done, Highness. It came too late for useful purpose; and such leaders as were within reach of it took it, just.

Or most of it. Some was buried, it was said. Where, the good Lord knows! Somewhere by Loch Arkaig. It all caused much trouble, quarrel, whatever, chiefs and lairds grasping what they could – to pay their men, they said! That Murray said that *he* had very little, none to send to Your Highness! Whether he spoke truth, just, I know not. Lochiel – now, there is a better man, a fine man – he sent some of his own coin, not the French gold, for you. I have it here. But where the rest is now, none can tell."

"But, but . . . this is beyond all belief!" Charles gazed at his friends. "King Louis's promised aid gone! Lost! A vast sum. Enough to revive my army. Taken! Stolen!"

"Scarce stolen, Highness. These chiefs and lords all had brought men to your cause. They had not been paid for long, Murray said. So they took what they could, when it came. Och, I can see it all, mind. Yourself gone, themselves hunted, their folk afflicted by the enemy, their glens ravaged. Then, gold beyond belief coming! Who to have it? Yourself making back for France, belike. I can see it all, ill as it is . . ."

"To think that none of our Long Island folk have betrayed Your Highness for Cumberland's promised thirty thousand pounds! And here your own leaders grasp and fight over still greater moneys, much greater! It beggars belief!" That was Neil MacEachain.

The prince turned away, to stare and stare, a man shaken to the core.

Some found words to try to comfort him. Presently Donald came to hand over to him a leather bag of coins.

"Lochiel's moneys, Highness. All that he had by him. The Cameron is a true man. And he did say that some of the French gold was buried. He may know where . . ."

"If someone has not dug it up and taken it also, by now," O'Sullivan put in. "A plague on them all!"

Thereafter Charles Stuart was more depressed for a while than they had seen him hitherto, even after the last battle. Clearly he had been building up his hopes of a revival of his campaign, with the wherewithal to fund it, and no need to return to France. Now such hopes were dispersed, and in such shameful fashion. It was not only the loss of the money, indeed; it was the thought of all those men, his lieutenants and officers, who had risked their lives for his cause, fought their way almost down to London for him, and then to do this, to trade their honour, as he saw it, for easy money, to grab and quarrel over it, and then disperse, proud chieftains and lairds. Was this another aspect of defeat? And the fact that it was *French* gold, belated but earned?

Charles was not given long to brood over all this, for the very next day a messenger arrived, from Boisdale, to warn them that General Campbell's troops were getting dangerously near to Corradale from the south, and being supported by landing-parties from the ships. They had been reported as near as Loch Eynort, less than five miles away, although admittedly very difficult miles. His advice was to leave their sanctuary meantime, whether MacLeod had returned or not, and make by night for one of the uninhabited isles in the area already searched, to the north, possibly Wiay. He would send a boat to them, again by night. They might be able to come back to Corradale later, once the search-parties from north and south had met up, discovered nothing, and left the vicinity.

They sent the messenger back with the word that Donald had returned, and that they had no need for another boat. They would go to Wiay, yes, in a day or two. Meanwhile Neil MacEachain would keep a scouting watch from surrounding heights, and along the cliff-bound coast. It seemed improbable that there could be any effective landing from ships, however, hereabouts, certainly not to take them by surprise before the great hills could swallow them up.

With Neil and Ned, Charles was up on the southern slopes of Ben More next day, shooting grouse, when, mounting a lesser ridge, they saw in the isle-dotted waters of Loch Eynort, a mere two miles away, a couple of large ships, almost certainly English. More than that, Neil pointed down to a corrie in the hillside nearer still, where a long line of men could be seen, strung out, clearly searching. Hastily, they dropped below their skyline. This was indeed getting too close for safety, barely four miles from their cottage, and working nearer. It was undoubtedly time to move. They would leave that very night.

It was sad to depart from Corradale, where they had had three weeks of comparative comfort, relaxation, refuge, even sport, and so much kind assistance. But they might be able to come back. They sought to clean up and make that cottage and its vicinity seem as though it had not been occupied, not entirely successfully perhaps, getting rid of ashes from the fire and ensuring that bones of deer and the wings and feathers of grouse and duck were hidden, and the like. As dusk settled, they went, reluctantly leaving, with their increased baggage, muskets, shot, extra clothing and food, to descend that daunting cliff track to the boat.

Neil and Donald reckoned that it was about fourteen miles north to Wiay; and with the wind in its normal south-west they ought to be able to make that even in the short hours of June darkness. Not that it was ever really dark, but sufficiently so for a small boat, if it kept reasonably close inshore along such a broken coastline, not to be observed from any patrolling ship, which of course would have to keep much further out in the Minch to avoid reefs and shallows.

So, sail up, north-east they went, to round the great point of Usinish, and then due north, past the mouth of Loch Skiport and the Sound of Faoileann, which separated South Uist from Benbecula, and on to Wiay. They were getting to know this indented and unoccupied coast. Charles did remark on the difficulties it providentially must present to the search-parties.

They landed on Wiay just as the dawn was beginning to lighten the eastern sky, entering a narrow creek which opened out into a hidden bay, this dotted with islets. Neil said it ought to serve them well enough. Unfortunately there were no bothies nor sheds on this uninhabited isle, two miles long and half that in width; so they must just seek to build some sort of shelter of stones and turf and heather. A come-down as this was after their fine cottage, they set to work, finding a cleft between two outcrops where they were able to erect a reasonable refuge, plaids helping. After all, they were experienced in this by now.

Sadly there was little in the way of fuel to be had on this island; and anyway, smoke from a fire could be a signal to enemy ships. More unfortunate still, the weather deteriorated, with squalls of heavy rain developing, forcing them to huddle together in their retreat, and to put up with drips from the improvised roofing. The four new boatmen, whom Donald had brought from the mainland to replace the Mallaig men, were less than appreciative.

The prince, fond of smoking, was in the position of having a good supply of Clanranald's tobacco; but sadly the two clay pipes sent with it had snapped off at base in transit, so were unusable. He hit on the ingenious idea of fitting quills of some seabirds' feathers into the holes in the bowls, a bright notion but which demanded much searching for suitable feathers with quills which would fit and were wide enough to draw the smoke through. Whether this hunt was worth the trouble was open to question, since the process involved Charles getting soaked, and the resultant puffing requiring some special techniques; but it did provide amusement for the others not thus addicted.

They frequently saw warships, but none came near. And no boats approached with landing-parties.

A miserable two days were passed thus, the weather not improving, and sleep not possible all the time. Eventually it was agreed that this Wiay was not the answer to their problems. Fairly safe it might be, but it provided little or nothing that they required, shelter, food, fuel. Small wonder that it was uninhabited. It was decided that the restless prince, with Neil and Ned and O'Neill, should set off northwards, overland, for Rossinish, their original landing-place on Benbecula, where at least they had been better placed than here, to see whether they could get in touch with Clanranald at Borve. It was only six or seven miles off, Neil calculated, and he could guide them there, he was sure. Donald would ferry them across the narrow kyle to the Benbecula shore. If they did not return within two days, say, let him, O'Sullivan and the four boatmen come on to join them at Rossinish. They would take two of the muskets with them in the hope of shooting something, for the food situation was becoming serious again.

They made a difficult and circuitous walk of it in blustery showers, but to Charles at least it was better than sitting endlessly in that leaking and draughty shelter, doing nothing. Six or seven miles it may have been, but they had to trudge all but double that distance to avoid all the bays and inlets, the lochans and bogs, and around the great bight of Loch Uskavagh, before they reached their fishermen's bothy. They did manage to shoot a couple of duck on the way, from the lochans; but there were no grouse here, nor deer. They did not think that they could have been seen, from ships out in the Minch, against all that so rugged background.

At least they passed a more comfortable night than on Wiay. If this area had been searched, the bothy showed no signs of it.

In the morning they set off for the croft of Hakaidh where they had made their first call in the Outer Hebrides and bought their heifer. And there, welcomed kindly, they learned that Benbecula was also presently alive with troops hunting for the prince, three hundred of Sir Alexander MacDonald of Sleat's clansmen, under MacDonald of Armadale, come from Skye for the purpose, to the anger of Clanranald whose territory this was. The Clan Donald was sorely split in its loyalties. Their crofter in Hakaidh swore as he named Sir Alexander. He understood that MacLeod of MacLeod was also sending a force, from Dunvegan in Skye, to aid in the search – another turncoat!

They asked for Clanranald, and whether he was still at Borve, to be told that the word was that he had prudently disappeared meantime, whether to Loch Boisdale or one of his lesser properties was not known; but the Lady Clanranald was still at Borve, it was understood.

Neil decided that he should go on alone, to Borve, borrowing a Hakaidh garron, to collect supplies and gain news. If he was intercepted, he ought not to be suspected as a companion of the prince; he was known as Clanranald's friend and a former tutor of his son; also he knew MacDonald of Armadale quite well, who appeared to be in charge here, indeed they were on friendly terms, he having in fact long been an admirer of that laird's step-daughter. So he should be safe enough – but the others should return to the bothy.

This was agreed, and they parted. The crofter said that this Hakaidh–Rossinish area had indeed already been searched.

They collected some oatmeal and honey, but when they sought to purchase eggs and milk to improve and vary their diet from its preponderance of meat, venison and wildfowl, regretfully it was admitted that the croft was presently lacking in such. It was suggested, however, that if, instead of going straight back to the Rossinish bothy, they took a southerly roundabout route, only two or three extra miles, they could call at another croft, that of Scarilode, on a horn of Loch Uskavagh, tenanted by an elderly cousin of the crofters, a woman and her two daughters. They kept a herd of goats there, and were renowned for making butter and cheese with the milk. Morag would surely give them supplies.

So, while Neil rode off westwards, the others, given instructions as to how to get to this Scarilode, thanking the crofter and his wife and son, headed southwards towards Loch Uskavagh, O'Neill hoping that it would not entail any lengthy detour, for he was already feeling weary. He was the poorest walker of the party always.

As ever in this country, although the distance between the two crofts was not much more than a mile, the getting there more than doubled that, lochans and bogs having to be circled and hills avoided. And it grew the more hilly the further they went, quite steep braes and rocky spurs, to O'Neill's groans, goat-country indeed as Ned pointed out. That folk were able to dwell and make some sort of living in these conditions said a deal for their hardihood and initiative.

Perhaps, in their devious going, the trio took a wrong turning or two, for it seemed more than any three miles to Loch Uskavagh, not that Charles was over-concerned, for the day was theirs to fill in, and they were as well walking as sitting in that bothy, whatever O'Neill felt – that is, so long as no search-parties came their way. He was caring about Felix O'Neill's lack of physical energy, however, as he had been ere this, and did what he could to lighten their walking by singing ballads and ditties, in which Ned Burke at least joined.

At length, cresting a rise, they did see a long, narrow arm of a greater loch ahead of them, and down on its northern shore, the white walls of a croft-house.

Although scenically it was a very lovely situation amongst its lochside hills, it seemed a strange place for three women to live alone. They must be very strong-minded and adequate characters, Charles declared. Of course, by boat they would not be so isolated as it seemed to visitors coming thus by land. And if they were famed locally for goats' milk, cheese and butter, they must have the means of distributing it.

When they got down to the croft they did see two boats drawn up on the beach. There were a couple of sheds nearby. Also a woman watching them from one of these. She was of later middle years but sturdily built and presenting no signs of fear at their approach.

Charles greeted her with something of a flourish. "A good day to you, lady," he called. "We come to you on the word of Ewan MacDonald, Hakaidh. He says that you might provide us with cheese, eggs and butter. We would be grateful if you can do so. We will pay whatever you ask."

"Indeed and indeed!" he was answered, in a lilting voice. "If my cousin sends you, I think that you cannot be of those wretches who defile the land, just!" She was considering them keenly.

"Whether or no we defile the land, lady, I do not know. But we are not from the English ships nor the militia."

"Nor Skiachs, at all?"

"Skiachs . . . ?"

"From Skye, just. That wretched disgrace to the name of MacDonald! Sleat! And the MacLeod, whatever!"

"Ha! I think that you judge as we do, friend!"

"And I think, sir, that I know who *you* are! By your talk and looks and all. Do I speak with our prince, himself?"

"You do, lady. Come begging!"

She did not exactly curtsy but bowed after a fashion. "Here is honour, sir. Great honour. To come to the poor house of Morag MacDonald. The shame of men who would betray you, seek your hurt. Men of my own name."

"They have their own reasons, no doubt."

"What can I do for you, sir? Eggs and cheese and butter, you said? We have these, yes. But . . . see you, they are hidden. We have had these English in their boats. From the ships. They take anything they want. Steal it. Insult my daughters. So we hide all. Or the daughters do."

"I am sorry. Others suffer for my failure to win my father's throne for him. It grieves me." He shook his head. "But can we go to where these, these provisions are hidden?"

"You must see my daughters, sir. *They* have hidden them all. Up the hill somewhere, just. I have a bad leg, to my sorrow, and do not climb hills now. If you go see my daughters they will give you what you need. They are up yonder." She pointed. "Up behind that bit hill, there. At the milking. Go to them and they will aid you, sir."

"I thank you. We will do that. They will not fear our approach?"

"Shout you Clanranald when you hear them and they will accept you, for sure. Then tell them who you are, and they will give you all honour, sir. That I know."

"So be it. We will go. And see you again, lady, when we come down." They turned to mount that hill, O'Neill muttering.

There was a track, winding as it rose but clear enough, and no great ascent however slowly the Irishman tackled it, the prince unhappy at his obvious breathless labouring. Charles, halfway up, suggested that his treasurer and friend should perhaps just wait there, and they would pick him up on their way down. But O'Neill had not reached that stage yet, and struggled on.

At the crest, they looked down into a little hanging valley, a green hollow, grassy and hidden, with a higher hill rising beyond. And in the dip were many goats, scattered, with, at the centre, a roofed open shelter within a walled-off space, where two young women were working, and a dog crouched, the last staring towards them. It did more than stare, rising and beginning to bark.

The women, sitting on stools at the milking, rose to gaze.

Charles waved then, and feeling rather foolish, started to shout "Clanranald! Clanranald!" They moved on, down.

The young women waited where they were, but called in the advancing, growling dog.

"We hail you, ladies," Charles called. "Your mother sent us up to you. We seek your cheese and butter, lacking such food."

One of the girls, both in their early twenties, strapping and well built, spoke. "You are not Clanranald himself. We know him."

"No. It was your good mother who told me to cry the name. To assure you that we were of no danger to you. Clanranald is our friend indeed, our good friend. I am Charles Edward Stuart."

They stared, at him and then at each other.

"She said to tell you. That you might give us of your hidden store of cheese and butter. We need the like. Eating mainly meat and oats, living on what we can shoot and bag," he explained.

"You, you are the prince!" That was faltering. "Whom they seek, just. And come . . . to us!"

"In hope, yes."

These two had not their mother's self-possession and assurance. Clearly at a loss, they found no words.

"We heard that you have been troubled by the men from the ships. The English. So you hide your provender. We will pay, if you will sell us some of it, ladies."

"It is up there." The other girl pointed to the second and higher hillock. "Amongst rocks, sir. Where they would not find it. Twice we have had much taken, and, and . . ."

"I understand. Shame on them!"

"We have but simple cheeses, sir. And butter, from goat's milk. No fare for such as you! But, if you want them, come you . . ."

The pair turned to lead the way up the quite steep ascent. Charles looked at O'Neill, indicating that he should stay where he was meantime; but the other shook his head, frowning, and started to follow.

The prince was soon looking elsewhere, for the young women, climbing just ahead, had kilted up their skirts high in the process, and much shapely white leg was on view to those behind. It came then to Charles Stuart how little of his fondness and appreciation for the other sex had been his lot for long months now, and how indeed he had missed it. When had he last been able to savour what kind and attractive female company had to offer? Not since the notable Clementina Walkingshaw at Bannockburn House . . .

Whether Ned was as appreciative as was his master was not to be known, but certainly Felix was otherwise concerned.

Panting, they reached a sort of shelf of the hillside, with a rocky escarpment rising behind. The girls' panting had the advantage of evidencing the more their heaving bosoms. One of them gestured.

"Up there, sir. Not a cave. But between the rocks. Hidden. Stones. None will find it there."

It was only another very small climb, but O'Neill had had enough. He sank down where he had reached, lay on his back, and shut his eyes.

Charles, after a worried glance at him, went up with Ned after their pleasing guides.

They were led to a cleft between large rocks where, amongst much fallen stone, a larder of sorts had been contrived out of flattish slates and boulders, almost indistinguishable from its natural surroundings. And, stooping to remove a heavy covering stone, the young women revealed heaps of round cheeses, and large slabs of butter wrapped in some sort of light canvas material.

"*Ma foi*, you have much here!" Charles exclaimed. "A great store."

"We supply many with it," he was told. "None other keep goats round Loch Uskavagh as we do. We take it in the boat to them. Or they come for it, to us. It is our living, just."

"Then fortunate we are! What can we have?"

"Take what you want, sir. Or what you may carry."

"Excellent! Ned, as well that you have your bag." Burke's shoulder-satchel he always carried, useful indeed, although the worse for wear as it had become.

They took three cheeses and two packs of butter.

101

Heading back down the slope, thus laden, the prince happened to slip on a wet patch, and might have fallen had not a strong female hand and arm grabbed and encircled him. Almost automatically his own free arm went round the girl's helpful person, and satisfactorily reliable, however softly rounded, it felt, he in no hurry to withdraw, she giggling. The feel of her actually gave him an idea. That cheese had to be clutched tightly too, of course.

Down amongst the goats again, Charles shook his head over the still recumbent O'Neill. "He is less than well," he told their new friends. "Wearies easily. We have walked far. From Rossinish and Hakaidh and then here."

"A drink of goat's milk?" one of the sisters suggested. "It might help him. It is more strong, with more fat to it, than the cow's. You also, sir? All have some."

"Ah, gladly. You are kind."

Ladlefuls from a pail of milk were quaffed, O'Neill doubtfully whilst remaining seated.

The prince, looking from his depressed and jaded friend to the young women, decided to put his notion into practice. It might help, as well as affording some stimulation, and mark of his appreciation of the situation. He sketched a bow to the girls.

"Come, my kind ladies, what would you think to dance a Highland reel with me? Here and now? I fear that we cannot have bagpipes, but I shall sing you a strathspey reel. How say you?"

They stared at him, astonished, disbelieving. So he capered lightly there on the grass, heel and toe, just to show them that he meant it. And he hummed a stave or two, snapping his fingers to the beat of it.

Giggling again, the sisters nodded, looking at each other, somewhat embarrassed, but coming forward.

Charles looked at O'Neill, who shook a wondering head but did not rise. Then he glanced at Ned who, thus invited, grinned and stepped over.

So, the men bowing to the women, Charles raised his fine singing voice to *Macpherson's Rig*, the girls hoisting up skirts again to tuck into girdles, laughing a little nervously, and they all swung into a foursome reel, hesitantly at first but soon getting into the rhythm of it, swirling and circling, skipping and flouncing, linking arms and passing on, in lively dance, Charles snapping fingers and clapping hands when he was not holding tumultuous femininity, the others seeking to accompany his increasingly breathless singing with hummings, punctuated by girlish squeals of laughter. There was some shouting inevitably, for the uneven turf made but a doubtful dance-floor, but such staggers only served to call for further clutchings and bodily support. It all made for a notable and vivacious occasion.

That is, until the prince quite ran out of breath and the singing ended in gasps to which it was difficult to dance, especially with the girls' skirling laughter taking over instead. The footwork deteriorated even if the clasping did not. Indeed Charles was not so devoid of breath as to be unable to plant smacking kisses upon the female partners, these being received with the reverse of protest, indeed returned.

Whether shamed into it or not, O'Neill was now on his feet, and even clapped hands briefly. The panting women offered more goat's milk to drink.

The sisters, awe of royalty now evaporated, declared that they were almost finished with their milking, and if the visitors would like to take some down to the cottage with them, for future drinking, they would find some flagon or the like to carry it in. So they waited a little, while the last two nannies were milked, and then they all set off downhill together, Charles gallantly insisting on carrying the pail of milk, O'Neill, less than surefooted, being given a hand or two. He admitted that he had not been feeling himself for the last two or three days, but had not wanted to concern the prince with it.

A deal of friendly steadying was accorded Charles also, with his pail which must not spill, as they descended.

It was down at the house that the girls' mother, being informed of the dancing and the princely singing, and the other gentleman's poorly-seeming, had a suggestion to make. It was quite a long walk back to Rossinish, although no great distance off; but if they were to be taken in a Scarilode boat, up a long, narrow arm of Loch Uskavagh, they could be put ashore less than a mile from their destination. That would save the gentleman considerable walking.

Charles, protesting that this was not necessary, however kind, did not protest too much when Morag MacDonald insisted, in his concern for O'Neill. The older woman declared that although she had a bad leg, there was nothing wrong with her arms, and that she could row as well as her daughters, and did so frequently. There would be little or no risk from English seamen, for this inlet, really only a mile-long dead-end creek called Neavag Bay, was just round the corner from their shore here; and there was no sign of any warship in the main loch at present.

So, without more ado, with a bottle of goat's milk to add to their baggage, they all went down to the beach, to push off the larger of the two boats, and climbed aboard, dog and all, Charles helping the mother in, and offering to handle one of the oars, of which there were four. But they would have none of princely rowing, the women each taking an oar and Ned the fourth one. So Charles had another new experience in being rowed by the other sex. He played his part by chanting in time and tune to the regular rhythm of the pulling.

Sure enough, just round the headland of Scarilode Bay there branched off northwards a narrow fjord, barely two hundred yards wide, the mouth half blocked by an islet. Once past this they were hidden from all the rest of Loch Uskavagh, and they could see it stretching ahead, steep-sided, rock-bound, for over a mile. This was the Neavag creek.

The prince's singing continued as they pulled up this, the oarswomen clearly expert. At the head of it, they grounded the boat on shingle, and the men disembarked. Nothing would do, however, but that the girls should climb the slope ahead with them, to show them just where they were in relation to the bothy at Rossinish, their mother having to remain at the boat.

Charles, in his profound thanks, kissed her hand, assuring her that her help and kindness would never be forgotten – and reminding her that she could become a very rich woman by reporting his whereabouts to the Elector's forces. Meantime, here was a very small token of esteem and gratitude. And he held out one of O'Neill's silver coins, well aware that he risked giving some offence in so doing.

She raised hand, not to receive the money but to point to heaven, in fierce denunciation over the first and rejection of the second. God forgive those who valued gold and silver above honour and loyal faith, she declared.

He could only bow, and pocket that coin.

Thereafter, accompanied by the dog, they climbed the hill very slowly, in the interests of O'Neill. When they crested the ridge,

104

they had pointed out to them, less than a mile to the north-east, beyond some more small inlets, the approximate site of the bothy. Apparently this had been used at times by the girls' father, long dead. There goodbyes were said, the young women's kisses being on the lips, and being frankly returned. Charles had noticed a pocket in the apron that one of the sisters was wearing over her skirt. Into this he managed to slip that silver coin, unnoticed.

Waving down towards the boat, the men set off with their cheeses, butter and milk, much heartened by their experiences at Scarilode.

Nevertheless, O'Neill was near to collapse by the time they reached their bothy, a worrying development this.

When, late in the evening, Neil MacEachain arrived back, he brought, as well as more supplies and some brandy, extraordinary news. At Borve Castle he had found, with Lady Clanranald, none other than Hugh MacDonald of Armadale, the captain of Sir Alexander MacDonald's Skye contingent of searchers. And, far from being the disaster this might have represented, it had proved to be a very rewarding and hopeful meeting. For Armadale was his friend, to be sure, and had confessed to him that he was most unhappy over his present assignment. He had no wish to see Charles Edward captured, and had sought to persuade his chief not to put this duty upon him. But Sleat had insisted, and he could not refuse; he was only a *duin' uasal*, a tenant-in-chief, and not in any position to disobey. He had told Lady Clanranald so, and she had indicated that Neil MacEachain was apt to be in touch with those close to the prince.

Armadale had then proved that his heart was indeed in the right place. He had suggested that Charles should leave these Outer Isles, so dangerously infested with searchers, and make for the *Inner* Isles, for his own Skye indeed. After all, none would look for him there, on Sleat's and the MacLeod's territory; and with all his own men, and MacLeod's – that chief was presently searching South Uist, in co-operation with General Campbell – there would be few on Skye to look for the fugitives. And Lady MacDonald, Sir Alexander's wife, was strongly for the prince.

Neil had agreed with all that, but had pointed out that getting over to Skye was not going to be so simple, with all those warships patrolling, fifteen of them he had heard. Armadale had thought of that also, and come up with a quite remarkable suggestion. He had a step-daughter, Fionnghal, or Flora, who normally lived with him at Armadale, her mother his second wife, but who happened to be visiting her brother on South Uist at the moment. She was the daughter of MacDonald of Milton, a tacksman of Clanranald, now dead, and her brother inheriting Milton near to Ormaclett. She often came across from Skye, in summer, to aid him with his cattle-sheiling, for he was unmarried. Flora, if she would, could aid the prince to escape to Skye. Armadale had said that he understood Charles Edward to be fairly slightly built and somewhat fair of visage. If he was to dress in woman's clothing and travel as Flora's maid, then she could take him back to Skye with her.

Astonished, the others gazed at Neil, scarcely believing their ears.

But the other went on to say that Armadale thought it quite practicable. He would give his step-daughter a written pass to show if she was halted; and having a maid with her would not arouse suspicions. Lady Clanranald had supported the notion. If the young woman, Flora, would agree to do it . . .

After considerable debate, they all went to sleep on the idea.

9

They were awakened early, at dawn indeed, by callers at the bothy, none other than Donald MacLeod, O'Sullivan and their boatmen. They had come from Wiay, by night, to collect the prince and friends, for they had sure word from Boisdale that this whole coastline was to be inspected and probed, as with a toothcomb, by a large force in longboats, under the dreaded Captain Fergusson, and indeed some of these had landed just opposite Wiay, less than a mile across the kyle, their camp-fires plainly visible. So they had left that isle in a hurry, and here they were.

What now, then? This area of Benbecula was likewise swarming with militia, and despite Armadale's sympathies, they dared not linger here, for if apprehended, he could not save the prince's party.

Donald said that the only thing to be done, meantime, was to go back, closely skirting the coast, to the area which had already been searched, South Uist that was, and the Corradale vicinity, and from there seek to get in touch with Boisdale again. The newcomers listened to the Armadale step-daughter proposal distinctly doubtfully, but said that, if that was conceivable, it would not affect this of going south immediately, for that young woman was apparently on South Uist. So it was agreed, they would leave here with the darkness, making for Corradale and that cliff-girt refuge again. Let there be no searching of Rossinish at least, this day.

They lay low in the bothy, ready to bolt for the boat at a moment's notice, but no alarm developed. Unfortunately the weather seemed to be deteriorating again, with Donald shaking his head over the signs; but all acceded that they must not delay leaving, on this account. So, in a windy dusk, they embarked, to row southwards.

Three times on that short voyage they saw the gleam of fires on shores where no habitations were sited, undoubtedly enemy camps. But although these were alarming signs, it was rising wind and driving rain which tended to preoccupy them, and this sufficiently for Donald, in the small hours, with wave tops coming inboard, to declare that, although they were nowhere near Corradale, indeed just past Wiay, they should seek shelter. The loom of the great Usinish peninsula was just ahead of them, and with this south-westerly gale they could gain some protection within its north-east bight. With mighty breakers spouting white in the gloom on that rock-bound coast, none contested his advice.

They managed to pull in to some sort of cove and make a difficult landing, grazing semi-submerged rocks as they went. Soaking wet but thankful to be on firm land, dry or otherwise, they searched about for some corner amongst the small cliffs and crags where they might hide and gain some cover from the elements. At least they had the food Lady Clanranald had provided; and this weather should hamper the enemy equally with themselves.

All that next day, then, they huddled at this desolate spot, which Donald named as Acarsaid Falaich, or the concealed haven, however little of a haven it seemed, while rain and wind continued. They saw no sign of ships nor men, not surprisingly. With darkness, and the gale subsiding somewhat, they pushed off again, less than confidently.

Charles was beginning to feel that he had more than enough of this Outer Hebridean coast. The thought of a change, to Skye, was commending itself.

They were heading south-westwards now, and with the wind in that airt progress was slow and no sail to be hoisted. Donald now suggested that, instead of trying to land at those fearsome cliffs at Corradale, in these conditions, they might row on nearer to Loch Boisdale, seeking somewhere from which they might more readily contact MacDonald of Boisdale himself. That could be another ten miles or so, admittedly, but he was worried at the thought of trying to land in a half-gale at Corradale. Perhaps they might slip into the major loch of Eynort, some four miles or so ahead.

They pulled on, and within an hour were heading into the wide mouth of Eynort when, there just ahead of them in the gloom, loomed the bulks of two warships anchored only a few hundred yards off. Hastily the oarsmen backed water, and they turned to head off southwards.

With a ragged dawn breaking to the east, they soon had to make a landing. Donald informed that he knew of a sheltered haven behind the isle of Stuley. There had been crofts there once, no longer inhabited, under the shadow of high Stulaval, from which a track led over a pass towards the head of Loch Boisdale. They might get word of and to Boisdale thereabouts, and of the situation around that great loch and harbourage.

They sighted a couple of ships out in the Minch, but in that early and slanting light they themselves would not be obvious against the loom of the land; and seeing the mountain of Stulaval half-right ahead, they were able to enter a very narrow passage, which proved to be the kyle, or channel, between Stuley isle and the Uist shore, shallow and reef-dotted, no place for large vessels. A little way along this they came to a small haven, with two ruined croft-houses above it; and here, thankfully, they beached their boat. There were stunted bushes and even the scattered remains of a peat-stack nearby. They could have a fire, that blessing.

Rested and fed, Neil MacEachain said that he would make a reconnaissance over the climbing track which led south-westwards from here, over what Donald named the Beallach a' Chaolais, the pass to the kyle, to try to discover if Boisdale was at his main house, which lay no more than four miles from here. He would go alone, as less likely to attract attention.

Donald said that there were crofts on the way, occupied these, at Eligor and Clett.

The others settled in, seeking to make the sagging and leaking turf roof of the better of the houses more weatherproof.

Neil came back sooner than expected, and with most worrying news. He had had to go no further than the first croft, Eligor, where he had learned from its shocked and angry tenant that his own chieftain, Boisdale himself, had been arrested. If this was true, then it represented a major worsening of the situation, for themselves as well as for their good friend. It was quite unexpected, for Boisdale was known to have been against this Jacobite campaign, unlike his brother Clanranald; and if he was now imprisoned, it signified a hardening of attitudes by the government forces, and presumably their belief that the prince they sought was somewhere nearby, and Boisdale knew of it. Their searching would be the more concentrated, therefore.

What should be done, then? And how to get to Milton of Kildonan, to reach this young Flora MacDonald?

It was decided that Neil should go on again, over the pass and down to Boisdale House, to seek speech with Lady Boisdale, and discover from her what he could of conditions in the area, the best method of getting to this Milton on the west coast, and of course where and how her husband was. The others had to wait there at Kyle Stuley anyway, hidden, until darkness.

Somehow Boisdale's arrest had the effect of making them all the more apprehensive and aware of the need to get away from these Outer Isles. Was it worth risking their making their own way across the Minch and the Inner Sound beyond, either to Skye or to the mainland itself? If that was possible it would greatly improve the prince's situation. But reluctantly, all came to the conclusion that this was not to be attempted. With at least fifteen warships watching these waters, and with some fifty miles to Skye, and more than twice that to the mainland, with no cover from view, well beyond night-time crossing, they could hardly expect to escape detection and interception.

Neil returned again in the evening. He had managed to see Lady Boisdale and her daughter, greatly worried women. Boisdale himself was thought to be on Captain Fergusson's ship *Furness*, suspected of assisting the prince. How long he would be held they knew not. The idea of Charles making for Skye was strongly supported – if it could be effected. The ladies' advice was to go to the very head of Loch Boisdale, some miles up, leave their boat there, and cross over to the community of Daliburgh, from which it was less than another four miles up the coast to Milton of Kildonan. But they were urgent that an overland crossing, and onwards, should not be attempted by a party of almost a dozen. Two or three might escape notice; but more would almost certainly attract attention, for even though the shipmen or the militia did not spot them, the local folk would, and there would be talk, and someone might tell, for the entire area was being questioned and threatened. When even their chieftain was arrested, someone might well weaken and divulge. It seemed sound advice.

Lady Boisdale had not been so upset by her husband's plight as to fail to give Neil some brandy for His Highness's comfort.

Much discussion followed. It looked as though a break-up of the party was indeed necessary, for the sake of all, not only the prince. They could decide on that when they got to the head of Loch Boisdale in the boat. Meanwhile, it was to sea again, with the darkness, and southwards down into that great loch, no lengthy row – as well with these short June nights.

They had turned into the loch, passing the small isle of Calvay on their left, with its ruined castle of the ancient Lords of the Isles, when there, ahead of them, they made out two more ships anchored, more or less blocking their way. It was perhaps not to be wondered at; in this windy weather the seamen would undoubtedly prefer to pass the nights in the shelter of loch mouths than out on the stormy Minch. Cursing, they turned back.

Debating as they went, they decided that probably the warships would leave at daylight to resume their patrolling, leaving the way clear for their own boat to proceed up-loch. If they could hide until then. Donald, who knew Loch Boisdale well, second greatest port of the Outer Isles, said that there was a narrow kyle or strait at the outer, south, side of the Calvay isle. They could hide somewhere in there, possibly pass the rest of the night and early day on Calvay itself. They could perhaps, if those ships did depart with daylight, then head on up the loch as desired.

So they rowed back, and found their way in between the isle and the south shore. There was some question as to whether to land on that shore or the island, but Donald thought that the ruins of the castle on the latter would offer them shelter from rain and wind within its vaulted basements, also better hiding.

They found a cove to pull into and disembarked. But it occurred to Neil that if, with daylight, those ships put out longboats on their searches, the sight of their little craft lying beached there would give away the fact that there was somebody on this uninhabited isle. So it was decided that their oarsmen should take the boat over the kyle, and hide it there, and themselves, only a short distance away as it was, and be ready to come back for them when signalled to do so.

Charles was interested to see the castle ruins, and to ask about the renowned Lordship of the Isles, with Neil explaining that the famous Somerled and his successors were reputed to have had fifty castles dotted over the West Highland and Hebridean coasts, of which this would be a comparatively minor one. Clan Donald, of which MacEachain was a small sept, were of course descended from the lords, as was Clanranald, Sleat, Keppoch, Moidart,

111

MacDonnell of Glengarry, MacDougall and other branch clans. The Stewarts, Charles's ancestors, had intermarried with these Isles lords, so he was interested to hear more of them.

They did not risk a fire within the ruin, in case its gleam might be seen from the ships; but they warmed themselves with some of Lady Boisdale's brandy.

Neil, awake early and out on the watch, presently came to report that the warships had just passed the isle on their way out into the Minch. So far as he could see, they had left no longboats behind.

Breakfast over, such as it was, dared they embark and proceed up-loch? Donald said, it being something of a port, Loch Boisdale was apt to have much toing-and-froing of craft, although few of its rowing-boats would have as many as eleven men in them, other than the English longboats themselves. And, of course, there might be other enemy vessels based further up. But he thought that they might risk it, being ready to pull in to the shore and land at short notice, if necessary. For if they waited again all day here, the warships might well return to anchor as before, and they would be no better off.

This was accepted, and they went down to the kyle, to gaze across, looking for their boatmen. At first they could not see either boat nor men; but Neil, mounting a knoll, spied their craft not far off, seawards, beached in an inlet, but no sign of its crew. Presumably they were hidden somewhere nearby. If so, they were evidently not keenly on the watch, for no amount of waving, even a halloo or two, produced any result. There was a croft-house not far away, up the hill beyond; it was possible that they had gone up there.

Neil summoned the rest of the party to come and add their voices to the calling, these producing quite major hallooing, which some feared might be less than wise and draw more than their own men's attention to them. But they had to have their boat, so they kept up the calling.

At length the four figures did appear from behind a hummock and came down to the beach. Presumably they had been asleep.

When they had rowed over, they admitted that they had been up at that croft to seek some food. And the family there had told them that the word was that Lady Boisdale, her step-daughter and servants, had been assaulted, tied up, wrists and ankles, in their own house, on the orders of that evil and barbarous Captain Scott,

112

until they should reveal the whereabouts of Prince Charles, which it was assumed that they knew.

Appalled, the others heard this, the prince beating fist on thigh and declaring that it was too much. Better that he should yield himself up to these savages than that others, women in especial, should so suffer for his sake. His friends asserted that was foolish thinking; would he thus throw away all the sufferings and sacrifices that others were making on behalf of himself and his cause? Never let that be said.

While they were so declaring, their attention was diverted. Coming running down the hill from the direction of the croft was a man, waving his arms, obviously in signal to themselves. They must be as clearly seen by him as he was to them, not more than three hundred yards separating them. Reaching the beach he stood, shouting something which they could not hear.

Presumably this must be important, so Neil and two of the boatmen embarked, and rowed across to him.

They came back quickly indeed, grim-faced. The crofter had come to tell them that hundreds of militiamen were combing the hillsides over the ridge from his croft and coming this way. They could be up there, within sight, before long, within the house. They must flee, while they might. The man presumably realised that it would be the prince's party.

Flee, yes – but where to? They could not dare to remain on this islet, so near to the other shore. Hastily they had to make decision. These troops were coming overland. They would not have boats, not hereabouts anyway. Therefore, flee by water. With no ships now in the loch mouth, row across it to the north shore, and then set off over the hills westwards. At least, some of them. Not as a party, in this dangerous and comparatively populous area. Parting – nothing else for it. Get into the boat, now, and away, east-about round this Calvay and across the loch, before the troops came in sight of them. All haste!

At the castle ruins, grabbing their gear, muskets and plaiding, they were about to leave their provender behind when Charles cried that this was madness.

"*Mon Dieu!* They shall never say that we were so pressed that we abandoned our meat!" he declared, and picked up some of their store, insisting that others did the same. Thus burdened,

113

they hurried down to the boat, glancing upwards as they went. No sign of the enemy on the skyline yet.

All piling aboard, the prince waved his thanks to the crofter, still standing on the opposite shore, watching. With all speed the oarsmen pulled away eastwards up the kyle.

Still no militia appeared on the skyline behind them as they rounded the tip of Calvay. Now there was half a mile of open water to cross. Could they make it before the enemy were in a position to see them? A pity that they could not take advantage of the wind and hoist sail, to hasten them – but that would make them the more conspicuous.

Whether or not they had been spotted they could not tell when they reached the northern shore and pulled into one of the innumerable inlets there, the bends in this suitably hiding them thereafter. Up at the head of this creek they beached their boat and landed, the need for immediate haste over.

But now, the dire business of parting, none contesting that this was necessary, however grievous. Charles had long considered this situation and come to his own conclusions. He would have to take Neil MacEachain and Felix O'Neill with him, Donald remaining with O'Sullivan and Ned Burke, the boatmen choosing their own way. O'Neill had been the problem, since MacEachain was essential as guide and counsellor. No more than three to each party. O'Sullivan was the least fit, older, and best to remain with Donald and the boat, the faithful Ned aiding with him. But O'Neill, although he would almost certainly hold them back, Charles felt the greater responsibility for. Fortunately he was improving in health somewhat, and he was the youngest of the refugees next to the prince himself. And he was in an especial position *vis-à-vis* the entire situation, quite apart from being the treasurer. He had in fact been seconded to Charles by King Louis, an officer of the French Dauphin's regiment, to act as official link as well as bringing with him all the financial contribution. The prince felt that he had to keep him with him, if at all possible, for, when they got back to France, he was going to need much more support from King Louis if the campaign was to be renewed, and O'Neill would be important in that.

So, three parties, although Donald and his two others might elect to stay with the boatmen for a time.

Distressed as all were at this separation after all that they had been through together, none doubted the need for it, nor the grouping of identities. Charles got a scrap of paper from O'Neill, who as treasurer kept a record of payments, and wrote out a note-of-hand promising to pay sixty pistoles, about one thousand pounds Scots, and handed it to Donald as mere token of his indebtedness for all his devoted services, that man refusing to accept it at first, but on it being made a royal command, declared that he would keep it as a treasured memento of a never-to-be-forgotten and privileged part of his life.

To each of the boatmen the prince presented a silver shilling, all that could be spared from O'Neill's dwindling purse, but probably something which none of these characters had ever had in their hands before, silver coin being but little known amongst the common folk of the Highlands and Isles.

Then it was time for farewell, dire and moving indeed after all the shared experiences, trials and dangers – and who knew when, if ever, they would all see each other again. Clasping O'Sullivan, Ned and Donald to him, amidst all the incoherences, Charles shook his head as well as their persons, words totally inadequate to the occasion, especially as, in his state of emotion, those words tended to be in French. The others were scarcely less affected, Ned Burke indeed breaking down in tears.

It was those tears, after the prince had given the one-time sedan chair man a keepsake of the broken bowl of a clay pipe, which somehow forced the actual departure, this ordeal not to be prolonged. Donald and the others would wait there by the boat, hidden, until darkness, if they were allowed to; but Charles and his two companions should set off right away, needing daylight in crossing the hills and trackless wilderness on their stumbling lengthy walking north-westwards. How long it would be before they reached this Milton of Kildonan and the young woman, Flora, they did not know. But a start should be made . . .

They went warily, to be sure, very much aware that they would hereafter be passing through an area abounding in their enemies, whose whole object and endeavour was to find them. Admittedly they were fortunate in that the said area was ideal for hiding in, small, stony hills and lochans innumerable, corries and hollows, bogs and burns everywhere, perhaps ten miles of this until they reached their west coast goal at Kildonan. The greatest danger was that they might suddenly come face to face with searchers for them in any hidden glen or round some shoulder of hill, long-distance sighting being all but impossible on both sides.

It was this need for prospects and viewing which caused Neil to suggest that really their best course was to climb to the summit of the nearest major height where they might gain some overall vista, even though this was due north rather than in the north-west direction they wished to go, little as O'Neill favoured the proposal. But Charles supported it, recognising the hazards of the lower ground. Neil was their guide, and they must accept his guidance.

So it was a long up-and-down, but mainly up, trudge to their hill, which stood out amongst all the lesser summits and which Neil called Truire Ben, more than one thousand feet up from the shoreline. And before they were halfway up it they began to perceive the wisdom of Neil's thinking. Smoke they saw to north and west, and not just one cloud of it. Four they counted, and from no minor fires. Those were crofts burning, the crofts of Boisdale's tenants. Devastation was going on over a wide area, wreaked by General Campbell's militia, Captain Fergusson's sailors or MacLeod of MacLeod's clansmen they knew not, but savagery on a major scale. Even as they gazed, new smoke arose nearer at hand. What the point of this burning was they could not comprehend, other than mere oppression and threat to others. But men who could shackle Lady Boisdale and daughter in their own house, in their efforts to gain information about the prince in hiding, and show the power of their hostility, could do this burning in the process.

They had to climb slowly, for O'Neill's sake, and even so he was labouring sorely before they reached the rocky broken summit of the ben. Certainly the views from here, all around, were widespread, spectacular, over land and sea, the latter on both sides, the Minch and the infinity of the Atlantic. And between them and the latter they could see the ground which they had to cover to reach their hoped-for destination, a great tract of broken terrain, almost as much water as land, hillocks and lochans by the score, many miles of it.

Surveying it all, Neil pointed. "Men!" he said. "See there. Beyond that crescent-shaped loch. Not a mile off. A score of them, at least."

"*Ma foi*, yes! Will they see us? Up here?"

"I think not. Against these rocks and shelves. But I think that we should hide, Highness. Somewhere up here. Until darkness."

"Darkness!" O'Neill exclaimed. "Seek to cross all that in darkness!"

"There will be a moon tonight. All but full, I think. If the sky keeps clear, it should be none so ill. And safer."

It was windy up there, and they sought some sheltered spot where they could lie in their plaids secure. Not that they really expected any of the search-parties actually to climb to the top of this near-mountain, scarcely the place to look for their quarry. But they were very safety-conscious by now.

They found a cleft between rocks along a narrow ledge which could be approached only one at a time. They were becoming expert in finding clefts in rocks. Surely they would be safe there, and unseen. They huddled down to wait, wondering how their friends were faring.

By this time, the fugitives were as good at sleeping by day as by night.

In the early evening the prince awoke, and Neil pointed out to him a practically full moon rising palely to the east. They could move soon now, he judged.

They ate some of their small store of provisions, and set out in the half-dark, picking their way very carefully downhill amongst all those rocks and shelves, well aware of footwork dangers as well as all others. Neil said that it would actually be better as the night advanced, with the moonlight having brightened then, than in this gloaming. Haste, meanwhile, was inadvisable.

117

He need scarcely have warned his companions, with every step having to be prospected down that mountainside. And even on the lower ground it was difficult going, amongst all those shadowy, wet hollows and obstructing hummocks. And difficult not only in walking, but also in maintaining fairly consistent direction, with so much circling and avoiding to do. They had to use the moon itself, in its half-orbit to the south, to keep them on an approximately westerly course.

It made a strange, almost unreal progress, with much peering, stumbling, back-tracking and debating as to this way or that. Neil's aim was to keep well north of the inhabited lochside areas, which meant crossing the rougher country, to be sure, but where they were least likely to encounter their fellow-men. They did pass near one red glow of smouldering croft-house and sheds, but carefully kept their distance, while wondering where were the unfortunate tenants thereof, the prince keenly feeling that sense of guilt.

Neil had been right. The later into the night the better the moonlight and the less difficult the walking. But there was no means of guessing how far they had got on their way, or approximately where they were. They could only press on, hour after hour, in a westerly direction, and hope for the best.

Little as they relished this night-time tramping, the grey dawn came all too soon, the moonlight paling and the going again becoming more difficult. But as the new day grew towards brightness, mounting a rise, there ahead of them, some way off admittedly, was the sea, the Atlantic. They had all but crossed the waist of South Uist, in perhaps five hours. How many miles of walking that represented they did not know. But, cheered, they pressed on. Blessedly they had not seen a soul.

They were in no hurry to see one, even now, for this west coastal area would probably be just as carefully patrolled as was the east. Until they got to Milton of Kildonan they wanted no contacts with men. They did begin to see crofts dotted here and there, and avoided them.

Where were they approaching on the coast, then? Neil knew it all, to be sure, fairly well, but had never approached it thus, over the moors. The island's main road ran down this shoreline, about a mile inland; and somewhere hereabouts, he thought, they should be between Daliburgh on the south and Mingary on the north, two communities some four miles apart. Milton was just a little seawards of Mingary.

It would have eased their journeying to have proceeded up that road; but Neil saw that as dangerous, even at this hour of the morning. They would be safer down near the shore. Thither they worked their way, as the sun began to rise behind them.

This was, in fact, a vastly different coast from the eastern one, strange as this might be, with only some seven miles, as the eagle flew, separating them, with no sea lochs, few inlets and cliffs, no real hills close by, long strands of sandy beach and even tracts of sand-dunes. Because of this, Neil soon recognised one of the very few headlands projecting from it, the Point of Ardvule. He gauged this to be some four miles to the north. Which meant that they were rather further up than he had anticipated, within perhaps two miles of their destination. O'Neill thanked God.

They found walking up that sandy shore, by the now sparkling sea, so great an improvement of their previous progress as to be almost enjoyable, the larks singing, the waders scuttling and the gulls wheeling. Charles raised a song or two in appreciation.

They came to the house of Milton of Kildonan, set on a rise between two small lochans not far in from the beach, a fair-sized establishment and attached farmery, the present young tacksman holding it of Clanranald not Boisdale. Approaching it, they were a little concerned about arriving thus early in the morning. However, they could see smoke rising from two of its chimneys, so they might even be in time for breakfast! Neil said that Angus MacDonald was a cheerful and friendly young man, and his sister similar, moreover good-looking.

Their advance to the house produced a barking of dogs and then the opening of a door and the gazing out of a woman, but elderly, not young. She eyed their approach doubtfully and then disappeared within.

Quickly she was replaced by a tall young man, who also stared, but recognised Neil and held up a hand. They moved forward.

"Angus," Neil said, "I bring you guests, notable guests. One of them eminent indeed. I believe that you will not reject them!"

The other was gazing at Charles, whose looks were of course renowned. "Can it be . . . ? Do I see . . . ? Is it the Prince Charles Edward himself? His Highness?"

"I fear so," Charles said. "My sorrow if it is to your regret."

"I . . . no, no, sir! Save us – never that! It, it is an honour, whatever! Honour to my poor house."

"You are kind. This is Captain O'Neill of the French Dauphin's regiment of foot. We come begging a bite of breakfast! We have walked all night."

" 'Fore God, this is, this is . . ." That young man was wagging his head. "See you, come you in. If you will so favour me."

"Entertaining me, even for an hour, may not be to your advantage, sir. I would not have you suffer for it – as others have." Charles had not overlooked the fact that this MacDonald, tacksman as he was, had not served in Clanranald's regiment in the campaign, or he would have come across him.

They were led into a room where a table was set, but only for one, with a large bowl of porridge steaming on a sideboard, and the good smell of meat cooking emanating from a kitchen. The visitors were gestured to sit.

"We come, Angus, actually seeking your sister. Armadale, her step-father, tells us that she is here," Neil said.

"She is, yes. But not today." The other looked surprised. "What want you with Flora?"

"It is a long story. Armadale's suggestion. He is leading Sleat's men searching Benbecula, as you may know. Searching for the prince here. But . . . unwillingly. He would not have His Highness captured. Any more than any leal man, Sleat and MacLeod excepted! Nor you, I judge?"

"Of a surety, no! Never that. But . . . Flora?"

"He, Armadale, thinks that she might be prepared to take His Highness back to Skye with her. In, in disguise. With all the search here, in the Long Island, all the men and troops and ships, he would be safer in Skye meantime. Until he can gain ship for France."

"But . . ." Clearly astonished, the other remembered his host's duties. "See you, sit, Highness. There is porridge here, if you will stomach that. And cream, there. Steaks coming from the kitchen. I shall see to it . . ."

They eyed each other as he left them, and eyed that steaming porridge pot even more keenly.

"A pity that Flora is not here," Neil observed.

"He said not today. But . . . ?"

"She must still be somewhere nearby."

When Angus came back, with the elderly woman, bringing more food, Neil asked further about Flora.

"How can we see her?" he wondered. "We would wish to do so quickly."

The other smiled. "You were ever interested in Flora!" he said.

Charles glanced at Neil. Here was something he had not known about his friend.

"She is . . . worthy. Of esteem." That was stiff, for that young man. "But this is on His Highness's behalf."

"Yes. She is presently up at my summer sheiling on Sheaval. My cowherd is sick, and there are two cows at the calving. And I have to go to see Clanranald today."

"She is up there, on the mountain, alone? With all these wretched troops around!"

"They will not be up on Sheaval, I think, in their searchings. But she has Donnie with her, the herd's son. At the calving he is not so good. But come, eat you. Highness, if you do not eat porridge, here is the meat. And bread. And cream and cheese."

"Porridge, my friend, will gladden us. We have been supping oatmeal and cold water, sometimes not even the water!"

They sat down to an excellent meal, the first at a table for long.

Neil asked about Clanranald and where he was absenting himself from his principal home at Nunton on Benbecula, to avoid all this invasion of his lands. Angus said that he was presently at Dremisdale, some nine miles to the north. He had sent for Angus from there, he guessed, for him to visit Lady Clanranald, with his requirements and instructions. Twice he had had to do this recently. The militia did not seem to suspect him. This was why he had not gone up to the sheiling with Flora.

Neil asked if the young woman would be back here this day, to be told that this depended on the cows, how soon they actually calved. It could be today, yes, or tomorrow, or the next day, whatever. They could not time such matters.

What, then? It was important to see her soon. Could they wait for her here, if she returned this day? For they dared not risk going openly up there in daylight. And if she did not come, go to her at night? By the moonlight. Angus agreed with this, only regretting that he had to leave them meantime, on his chief's business. His house was theirs. None would look for them here.

So, when presently their host took his leave, saying that he might be back that night or he might not, depending on Clanranald's

121

orders, his three guests, better fed than for long, settled themselves to sleep, in comfort for once.

Thy did not sleep all day, but were glad enough to rest, for they might well have more night-walking to do. Glad also of more feeding from the housekeeper. They advisedly did not venture outside.

By nightfall there was no sign of Flora, nor of her brother. They decided not to wait. Angus had told them where the sheiling bothy was sited, up on the side of the quite high Sheaval. The sky was clear again and the moon would be bright. With thanks to their provider, and oatcakes and cheese in their pockets, they left the house. They had about three miles to go, apparently, but a number of lochans to circle before they reached the high ground. They blessed that full moon and more or less cloudless sky.

The better for full stomachs and rested muscles, they made good time of it, the dark loom of the quite prominent peak of Sheaval ensuring their direction. Once they were on the hill itself it was not difficult to find the bothy, for there was only the one corrie on this western face of the height, this actually the uppermost reaches of Kildonan Glen, and the cottage was set in the floor of that.

When they saw the shape of it dark ahead of them and drew near, a dog began to bark. The trio halted. They did not want to alarm the young woman unduly. She would have the youth Donnie nearby, of course, but strangers approaching in the middle of the night could startle, especially in present conditions. It was agreed that Neil should go forward alone, to reassure and warn her and her companion.

The others waited, the dog still barking.

It was a few minutes before a call summoned them to the door, where a youth, half-clad, was holding a growling dog in leash. The bothy was divided in two by a partition, and there was candlelight in one of the sections. Neil emerged from that one, to beckon them in.

"Flora is here. She is, she is prepared. To see Your Highness. I have told her who you are. Little more. Come, you."

They entered the apartment, it could scarcely be called a room, furnished only with a wooden bench for bed, plaiding heaped thereon, a rude chest on which women's clothes lay, shelving on which were platters, jugs and the like, and where two candles flickered, deerskins on the earthen floor. Beside the bed the young woman stood, wrapped fairly comprehensively in plaiding, but one shoulder, legs and feet bare. She was tall, well made, not exactly beautiful but with fine features, warm eyes and a firm mouth, her dark hair presently cascading partly to cover that white shoulder. She was gazing at Charles questioningly, searchingly, nowise with alarm despite the circumstances, but her doubts evident.

The prince bowed, baggage and all. "Can you forgive me, lady?" he asked. "Coming upon you thus. Arousing you in the middle of the night. Such invasion of your rest and privacy! But, they say, beggars may not choose, and I come a-begging, I fear!"

"Sir! Highness! You find me at, at a disadvantage! But . . . your servant."

"Scarcely that, Mistress Flora! Here is Captain O'Neill – Felix. Neil, Neil MacEachain, my friend and yours, I understand, will have told you that I come seeking your aid?"

"I only said a little. No details," Neil declared. "That you would go to Skye. Armadale's suggestion, her step-father."

"Yes, I am hunted, mistress. Have been for months. Now these Outer Isles will hold me no longer. Everywhere the searchers close in on me. I do not know MacDonald of Armadale, but he is kind. Although sent to hunt me down, he does not wish me to be taken. And makes suggestion that *you* might be prepared to help. To get me to Skye, where I may not be sought, meantime. If you would be so good, so kind."

"But . . . but how, Highness? How could *I* do this? I do not wish to see you captured, no, to be sure. I live on Skye now, yes. But . . ."

"He, Armadale, believes it possible. *Mon Dieu*, it is a great and extraordinary thing to ask of you. But there is sense in it. If you would do it. He says, if I could be dressed in woman's clothing and go as your serving-woman! Thus I could leave, in disguise. He would give you a note to pass his searchers. On the other island, Benbecula."

Those fine eyes stared now. "Dress! As a woman? With *me*! You, the prince! Do I hear aright?"

"It is much to ask, yes. But if you would, it could be the saving of me."

"Armadale says that it would be possible. And believes that you would not wish His Highness to be captured, despite Sleat's orders," Neil put in.

"No, I would not wish it. Not that. But this is . . . scarcely believable! Me!"

"You would be serving King James's cause greatly, mistress," O'Neill said. "To get us to Skye, until His Highness can get a ship for France."

"Me, I am not one for causes and intrigues, sir, Jacobite or Hanoverian. I am but a simple woman, a tacksman's daughter and sister. I fear that I could not consider this. With greatest respect and loyalty, Highness, I fear not!"

Charles spread his hands, but inclined his head.

Neil was less accepting of that. "Flora, do consider it, at least," he urged. "Think what it means. His Highness has been hunted and pursued and threatened for months. All over this Long Island. Through storms at sea. Marching trackless hills by night. All but starving frequently. He, the heir of our ancient House of Stewart, hunted like the vilest felon! Many who are not of the Jacobite cause have sought to aid him. None have betrayed him, none claimed the English gold offered for his apprehension. Are *you* the one to fail him in his need? You, of the kind heart and stout spirit? In this pass, something only you can do, I judge. Consider it, I say."

"I do not wish the lady to be troubled, distressed, Neil," Charles put in.

"Sir Alexander would be wrath," she said.

"He is not on Skye meantime, Armadale says. Away with the English, a plague on him!" Neil jerked. "Besides, you are of Clanranald, as am I. Not Sleat. And Clanranald supports the prince."

"I, I do not know. This is beyond all!"

"Your own brother took us into his house. Entertained us well. *He* had no qualms. He has gone to see Clanranald, but sent us up here to you. Believing, I think, that you would rescue us, kindly."

Drawing her plaiding closer around her, the young woman inclined her head. "I would not have you think me remiss, Highness, in my reception. This is a poor place, a sheiling shed, no more, with little of welcome to offer. But if you will give me a minute or two, I can provide a bowl of cream. And scones. I would not have you hungry, and me failing in hospitality."

"You are kind, Mistress Flora, to intruders who disturb your sleep. And trouble you with awkward requests." Charles glanced

124

at Neil. "We will be glad of your provision. But will wait outside . . ."

"In the other part, here." She pointed to the wooden barrier. "While I dress somewhat. Only minutes . . ."

The three men backed out, and into the other section of the bothy, where young Donnie had lit another candle, and stood, wondering.

"It was too much to ask of her," the prince said, low-voiced, for speech would probably be heard beyond the partition. "A dire proposal to throw at a young woman."

"I think that she might possibly be having second thoughts," Neil said. "You noted, she said that Sir Alexander would be wrath? That might mean some questioning of her refusal. She is a fine lass, and warm-hearted. I believe that she will come round to it."

"What could we offer her?" O'Neill wondered.

"Nothing. That is not the way."

It was not long before they were called back into the other apartment where, fully clad and hair dressed – and perhaps, in consequence, more herself – Flora MacDonald had her visitors sit on the bench, and presented them with a large bowl of whipped cream, thick and nourishing, with scones, somewhat stale but none the less acceptable, to eat with it.

As she watched the three of them share this unusual provision, the young woman said, "I am concerned for Lady Margaret, Sir Alexander's wife. She is my good friend. You think that, if I was to do this, Neil, take His Highness to Skye, her husband, and therefore herself, would not suffer? If it was discovered. *That* I would not have to happen. Myself, I am not over-fearful for. But the Lady Margaret – that is different."

Neil and Charles exchanged glances. "I see no hurt coming to her," the former assured her. "Sir Alexander has his clansmen here to aid the government forces. And your brother says that he is presently in the south, seeking Cumberland – why, I know not. Also to see Forbes of Culloden, the Lord President. Certainly he has nothing to fear from the Hanoverians, nor therefore his wife. Moreover, Lady Margaret is a good Jacobite, Catholic and royalist, daughter of the Earl of Eglinton – she would not disapprove. Nor do I see why you should fear for yourself, Flora. Armadale sees no danger in it, or he would not suggest it. Nor I, who am concerned for you, you may be sure. On a boat to Skye you could well have a maid with you. And, dressed as a woman, His Highness would pass as such well enough."

"I would shave most carefully!" the prince added, smiling.

That smile was such as to persuade, in itself.

"There could be talk. Afterwards. Gossip. About myself. My good name . . . ?"

"Suppose one of the party was offering marriage, Flora?" Neil mentioned significantly.

She shook her head at that, but turned to bring them more scones. "When would this be? If I was to do it. How soon?"

"The sooner the better, lass. They are closing in on us all the time. We dare not linger."

"I would have to go and consult my brother. And, if I could, my step-father. And to arrange for the boat."

"Yes. That is understood. Angus has gone to Dremisdale, to see Clanranald. You could follow him there, none so far from Milton, on a garron. As for Armadale, that might not be so simple. He is on Benbecula, not this Uist."

"And you, meantime?"

"We must go into further hiding. Some secure place. The most secure is Corradale. We were there before, for three weeks. It is very hard to approach. But none so far east of here. Eight miles, nine? Through empty country. We could go there. Now."

"Could Mistress Flora get a boat there?" Charles asked. "That most difficult landing, and climb. The ships seeing it, perhaps. It would look suspect, I fear."

"No, not there for the boat. It would not be sailing by night. Better if it could pick us up somewhere easier to reach. Also, in case it is observed. Wiay, perhaps. Behind Wiay. Or better, Rossinish, where you first landed, and which we know. The nearest for the crossing to Skye. If we could hide at Corradale. Then, on getting word that all is prepared, make our way to Rossinish on Benbecula? It would need a boat . . ."

"We would have to get across the narrows," O'Neill said. "How? How get from Corradale on South Uist to Rossinish?"

"Surely we could find a boat . . ."

"The boat which brought me from Skye landed me at Unasary, on Loch Eynort. Only a mile or so from here," Flora put in. "It will still be there, to take me back."

"Ha, that is good! Unasary. I know it. If we could get back to

126

there, near the head of Loch Eynort, unseen, when you sent us word, lass, that all was ready."

"Yes. The boatmen wait there. My step-father's boatmen."

Charles at least did not fail to recognise that the young woman was now speaking as though her co-operation was likely. Neil had known his Flora, it seemed.

A few more tentative arrangements were discussed and conditions envisaged. Then Neil was showing concern about the hour. If the trio were to get out of this comparatively populous area, and well on the way to remote Corradale before broad daylight, then it was time that they started out. Their plans could all be nullified if they were spotted hereabouts.

Flora MacDonald did not seek to delay them. Without promising to do all that had been suggested, she did say that, somehow, she would get word to them at Corradale as to the situation, probably send this Donnie over, on one of her brother's garrons. It might take a day or two . . .

So they said farewell, Charles repeating his apologies for all the trouble given, and gratitude for kindnesses displayed, without actually seeming to assume that all was settled as they desired. He kissed the young woman's hand, while Neil kissed her on the lips and O'Neill on the cheeks. Donnie and the dog saw them off on their way northwards, out of that corrie and over the shoulder of hill, to head down to the head of long Loch Eynort.

"That is a pleasing female!" O'Neill observed, when they were alone. "I was much taken with her."

"I also. Neil is to be congratulated on his taste, I say!" Charles added.

The moon was beginning to pale as they passed a scatter of lochans to reach the head of the great sea loch, and could turn north-eastwards. They could now make out the loom of lofty Ben More ahead a couple of miles. They were now making for the pass, the Beallach Crosgard, over the mountain's shoulder, which they now knew so well. Presently they could feel almost at home, for hereabouts they had done their deerstalking and grouse-shooting. It would be daylight before they reached Corradale itself, but the likelihood of any of their enemies being up on this high ground at that hour was remote indeed. In good heart they pressed on.

127

11

The cottage at Corradale was just as they had left it, with no evidence of anyone else having been there. They settled in, well aware that feeding would have to be thought about if they were to be here for a couple of days or more. Deer or grouse? They still carried one of the muskets, although they had not burdened themselves with much powder and shot.

As the day progressed, they saw warships beating up and down the Minch again. It was unlikely that Flora's boat would be able to cross to Skye, if that eventuated, without being investigated.

They wondered about Donald, O'Sullivan and Ned, with the boatmen. How were they faring?

The matter of food was pressing. They agreed that, with little ammunition, and one shot as able to kill a large deer or a small grouse, it must be venison. So, in the afternoon, leaving O'Neill, Charles and Neil set off together for the higher ground again, of necessity, rather than diversion now.

Fortunately there was no lack of deer amongst these mountains, and soon they spied a group in a minor corrie. Careful as they were, however, that stalk was unsuccessful, possibly a down-draught of wind from the heights warning the animals, for they were off well before the stalkers got within range.

So it was further prospecting, but not long before they saw a larger herd, up on the skyline. That could involve more difficult approach; but at least no down-draughts. Neil always said that the deer seemed to rely on their noses and ears more than on their eyes. Nevertheless, since one stalker was bound to be less evident than two, and the prince the less experienced stalker, he urged the other to take the musket and go on alone, while he hid. The meat was the vital matter, not the sport.

He had quite a long wait, there amongst the heather, indeed he all but fell asleep in the warm June sunshine, for Neil would have to make a very round-about approach to that skyline. But eventually he heard the crack of a shot, and was able to rise and start climbing. Soon he saw his friend waving up there on the ridge, a good sign.

Neil had indeed managed to shoot a young hind, which would provide them with tender meat for days. Part flaying, part detaching limbs, they cut up the carcase, practised as they now were; and, quite heavily loaded with bloody spoil, they picked their way downhill, well content.

Their eating was going to be ample, if monotonous.

That evening the fine weather broke, with heavy rain and the moon hidden.

In these Hebrides, conditions tended to be very fine and beautiful or else grim indeed. They had been fortunate with the good spell and its moonlight. Now it was otherwise; but at least they had cover, shelter, a fire and sustenance.

All the next day it rained, and they were glad to lie most of the time in their plaids, talking, Charles teaching the others songs and choruses, mainly French, dozing a lot, and declaring that all those search-parties would not be so blest. They took turns at roasting, braising and boiling the venison, even contriving a kind of soup, cranberry and blaeberry leaves added to the stock, which Neil said would do them no harm, at least.

But when the following day also was wet, and no messenger arrived from Flora MacDonald, they began to become restive. Charles wondered whether, in fact, that Donnie, or whoever was sent to inform them, was unable to find their refuge in this weather, hidden down in this hollow as they were. Perhaps, unpleasant as conditions were, they should go up on to some good viewpoint, possibly on the side of that mountain Hekla, and keep watch? Neil was doubtful, but said that there was no harm in it, save for the discomfort. And lying here in plaids day and night had indeed become wearisome.

So taking cold venison and those so useful plaids, they went to climb the southern spur of Hekla, only a mile or so off, where they could obtain an extensive view of the approaches from the west, as far as conditions allowed. Up there, in fact, they were not much more than five miles from the Atlantic coast, however tortuous those miles, and Dremisdale where Flora had gone to seek her brother and Clanranald.

They saw no sign of a messenger, in between rain-squalls, huddling under plaids draped between rocks.

129

With the evening, worried over the situation, it was agreed that Neil should go, alone, to Dremisdale, by night, unpleasant as that was going to be, to discover what was happening and whether the young woman had decided against involvement. They must know the position, and whether they had to make new plans.

So, while the others returned to the cottage in the hollow, Neil strode off downhill also, but westwards, declaring that he ought to be at Dremisdale, rain or none, by dawn.

It was good to get a fire going, dry themselves and sup their warm soup-substitute, sympathising as Charles did with Neil, before they slept.

All next day they waited, with no sign of Neil nor other messenger. Perhaps he was waiting to come back by night, militia in evidence? But by morning the pair were still alone, and worried indeed. Had he been captured? Was there any cause for searchers to suspect him, a lone local man? At midday they went back up to their outpost on Hekla. It was still raining, off and on.

With evening, cold and wet, just as they were about to make their descent to Corradale again, they caught sight of a single figure crossing a stretch of hillside below them. Gazing, they decided that it was indeed Neil, and thankfully, they moved down to meet him.

Neil it was, and after their relieved salutations, he had a story indeed to tell them. He had got to Dremisdale without trouble, but there had learned that Clanranald had departed for Nunton, his principal house, on Benbecula, being anxious for his wife in present circumstances. And Aeneas MacDonald had followed him thither. When his sister had arrived, and learned of this, she too had headed northwards for Nunton, hence the delay. Neil had to decide what to do then. He had borrowed a crofter's garron without difficulty, and headed northwards himself, after these others, reckoning that it was the only way to discover Flora's intentions and their consequent prospects.

Dremisdale was some seven miles from the northern tip of South Uist, where there was a ferry over to Benbecula. And this he found in the keeping of a platoon of the Skye MacDonalds. Despite declaring that he was of a MacDonald sept himself, and a friend of Clanranald, these Sleat men had taken him in charge and locked him up in a ferryman's cottage taken over by the guards, this on the Benbecula side. There he had been left to kick his heels.

Admittedly his captors shared their food with him, telling him that they had strict orders to detain all travellers, until their captain, Armadale, could interview them. Neil wondered about that; could this be some scheme of Armadale's possibly to help the prince? Anyway, he was kept all that day and the following night.

The same evening, with himself fretting, who should arrive at the cottage but Armadale himself. He apologised to Neil for this situation, but declared that in fact it was none so ill for the prince's cause. His step-daughter herself was here, detained also in another cottage, and she had told the guards that he, their commanding officer, was her step-father, and demanded to see him. So they had sent for him, from Nunton, where were Clanranald and Aeneas.

Astonished that he had been all this time within a few yards of Flora, Neil was taken to her cottage and a pleasing reunion. And there the three of them had held a conference. Flora had agreed to convey the prince to Skye, dressed as her maid. Armadale would take her, meantime, to Nunton, where she could get some suitable clothing from Lady Clanranald, and arrange for her to get to her boat thereafter at Unasary, on Loch Eynort. He would send a couple of his junior officers, who knew her, to act as escort. And he would make out written passes for her, her maid and Neil, to get them past any sea-searchers. They had had to invent a name for the maid's pass, and had chosen an Irish one, Burke, after Ned, but to account for her, or the prince's, accent should he have to speak to enquirers. So Charles was to be Betty Burke!

Intrigued indeed, his hearers listened to all this as they headed down to their cottage. All seemed to be working out for the best, after all, except that O'Neill found occasion to wonder whether Armadale had made out a passport for *him*? Neil said that, in all the discussion about clothing and a name for the prince, he had forgotten to ask for such; but probably Flora would see to it. Charles did wonder also; he had a notion that his two friends were not over-fond of each other.

So what was the procedure now, he asked? When did they move? And to where?

They were to make their way to Rossinish on Benbecula, they were told. That meant a boat, of course, to cross to the other island. But he was fairly sure that this could be arranged. The sea loch of Skiport was only five miles to the north, and on it Clanranald kept a boat, for the fishing, this being infinitely better on this east coast than on the west, sheltered inlets and bays by the score as against the open Atlantic beaches. Often he had fished, with his chief, from Horrogay, on Loch Skiport, and knew the men who crewed the boat. There could be troops there at the small ferry, admittedly, or shipmen; but if they arrived by night, and he went forward to inform the boat crew, they could probably set off to sea unobserved, and on up to Wiay, to hide behind that isle during the day, and on to Rossinish the next night. That would be much better than trying to get the boatmen to come here, unseen, to difficult Corradale Bay and the stiff cliff-climbing.

When to go, then? Tonight?

Neil thought the next night. It would take time for Flora to reach Lady Clanranald at Nunton, collect clothing and her escort, and go with them to her boat at Unasary on Loch Eynort, and so to Rossinish. Three days at the least. So, the following night. They were reasonably safe here at Corradale. Their venison ought just to last out.

The following night the weather had improved only a little, as they set out for Loch Skiport, over another shoulder of Hekla and northwards, down a deep corrie and over lochan-dotted lower ground, unpleasant going in thin rain, some three miles to salt water. Skiport was a long loch stretching far inland, and there was a ferry across at Horragay, to save the awkward journey up and round its head; and it was the ferrymen, who were also fishermen, who manned Clanranald's boat when required.

When they reached the lochside in the neighbourhood of the ferry jetty, in fitful moonlight, Neil left the others to go forward to the cottages cautiously, in case there were militia or sailors based there. He might be gone some time, for even though there were no enemies about, he would have to rouse the boatmen, four of them, explain, have them leave their families, collect food, and prepare their craft.

Wet and mud-spattered, Charles and O'Neill settled to wait. At least here, and elsewhere on these islands, there was no lack of rocks to use for shelter. Their life here seemed to entail a deal of waiting, these days. O'Neill was complaining of a bad back again.

At length Neil came back. All was in order, he reported. Seamen had been here, but they were gone these two days.

Sometimes ships sheltered overnight in the mouth of the loch, but there had been none yesterday. The boatmen had made no difficulties, he speaking in the name of Clanranald. They would be ready, with some provision, by the time they themselves got down to the jetty.

So, thus far no difficulties.

At the waterside they found the men waiting, two of middle years and two young, and these were presented to the prince, all MacDonalds apparently. They showed due respect for Charles, but scarcely awe, hardly to be wondered at in his present state of dress and appearance. They made no complaints about their rude awakening, and demands on them.

They all boarded the boat without delay and, oars out, they pulled away.

The rain continued.

They had about two miles to go eastwards to the mouth of Loch Skiport, and some five miles northwards thereafter to Wiay, ample time, even with these short June nights, to get to a hiding-place before daylight, especially as they could raise sail in the south-westerly breeze. However, rounding one of the many bends of that isle-dotted loch, quite near its mouth, they saw something which affected their situation – a gleam of light where no light should be. It could only be from a ship anchored there, a warship.

This worried the four boatmen. If it was still there in the morning, they would have to pass it on their return, and they would be seen. Fishermen did not spend the nights at sea here normally, they were not deep-sea fishers, and anyway they had brought no nets with them, and would have no fish to show. If they were stopped and investigated, what excuse could they offer? These minions of Captains Fergusson and Scott were not gentle in their questioning; and questioned they undoubtedly would be.

Charles recognised their situation and anxiety. They must not be endangered, he declared, Neil agreeing. So they must get back into their loch before daylight, that was clear. So the four of them must turn back at Wiay, not attempt to go on to Rossinish. It was only some five miles from the loch mouth, so they ought to be able to do it in time, especially with the grey wet weather delaying daylight. They could land the trio on the Benbecula side of the narrow Wiay kyle, whereafter these could make their way, by land, the remaining seven or eight miles to Rossinish.

That comforted the oarsmen.

Out in the Minch, with the breeze behind them, and the sail up, they took a bare hour to reach Wiay; and once into its narrow strait or channel they soon found a beach to put the passengers ashore on the landward, Benbecula shore. The turn-around was made quickly, and with thanks and a coin or two, the boatmen were pushed off. They ought to be able to pass that wretched ship well before dawn.

So now the travellers must press on their overland way, or find shelter meantime to hide, in case longboats from the frigate came searching. They had already had a difficult walk from Corradale, over Hekla to Horrogay, and O'Neill's back was paining him; so it was decided to lie up for much of the day. They searched for and found a clump of stunted hawthorn bushes, and pulling heather and shaking off the raindrops, contrived some sort of couch within their plaids, ate necessarily sparingly, and slept.

When Charles awoke it was well into the afternoon. He found only O'Neill beside him. On venturing cautiously out of their bushes, he saw no sign of Neil. He looked around. The isle of Wiay was only a few hundred yards off, and protecting them from the view of the Minch. Nothing alarming was to be seen, nor even Neil. He went to climb a little rise, to look for his friend.

It was on that hillock that he got something of a shock. They were on an islet, not on a peninsula of the main Benbecula, as they had thought. He could see a stretch of water to the west, cutting them off. They were stranded. These boatmen had put them on an islet! Fools! Much upset, he stared about him.

He saw Neil some distance off to the north, presumably prospecting. In his agitation he actually ran over the tussocks of heather to call to the other, pointing to the salt-water barrier.

"Neil, we are held, stranded!" he cried. "On an island. They have landed us on an island. With no boat! We are held!"

"Yes. But I have been looking. I think that it is tidal. By the seaweed and the shallows and the currents I think, when the tide ebbs, we will be able to get off. On foot."

"But . . . it is too wide. Hundreds of metres! Could we swim it? I can swim. But I do not know if Felix can."

"No need, Highness, I am sure. Look, it is shallow. No more

134

than four feet, I think. I have been along the shore of it. There are many such tidal islets, *orasa*, we call them in the Gaelic . . ."

"I pray that you are right! Even so, we will have to wait here until the tide goes out. A curse on those men!"

"I will swim across now, if you will. To reassure you."

"No, no. We will wait. I think that we will not be seen here. But it will delay us."

"That will not matter greatly. It is only another eight or nine miles to Rossinish, I would say. And best that we should not go in daylight, anyway. If Flora and her friends are there before us, they will wait."

Neil was proved right. By early evening it was apparent that the tide was ebbing fast, and that it was going to be possible to pick their way, on foot, across to the other shore. Thankfully they packed up, and did so.

Now it was a matter of heading north by west, in the dusk, over as wet and waterlogged an area as yet they had encountered, in order to work their way round the head of Loch Uskavagh, after which it would be only another three miles or so to Rossinish. The rain persisted, and it made no pleasant journey. But at least it was unlikely that they would meet with any enemies in these conditions.

It took them all night to cover those damp and exasperating miles, for many times they had to back-track and prospect different routes because of intervening lochans and bogs. But as a grey day dawned, Neil, topping a ridge, was able to point out to the others something to cheer them, a mere half-mile away, the farmery of Hakaidh, that first place where they had received help and sustenance in all these Outer Isles, and where they had purchased that heifer. It seemed a long two months ago.

They were glad to make their way to the farm, Neil going ahead. This, the nearest house to the Rossinish fishermen's bothy, was where Flora MacDonald and her escort would probably install themselves. But there was no sign of life about the place now, save for two milk-cows. Then there was a barking of dogs.

The door opened and young Hector MacDonald, pulling on clothing, recognised Neil, and hurried back inside, to bring out his father.

The MacDonalds scarcely looked pleased to see their visitors, despite their evident goodwill, esteem and deference. Quickly they urged the newcomers into the house nevertheless and shut the door; to explain that there was a patrol of a score of militiamen encamped in tents only a few hundred yards away behind a rise; and they had assumed that the barking of their dogs signalled the arrival of some of them for their morning's demand of eggs and milk. The fugitives exchanged glances. Troops! To have got thus far, within a mile of their destination, and then this! It was a heartbreak. What to do?

Neil asked, did the MacDonalds know the identity of these troops? If they were in tents, probably they would not be from the ships. And Benbecula was largely being searched by Sleat clansmen from Skye. They were told, yes, these were MacDonalds from Skye.

That was some relief, at least. For when Flora arrived – she had not come yet, it appeared – she was to have two of those Armadale's junior officers with her, and they presumably would be able to deal with this patrol. But meantime, they must be avoided, if possible.

Their involuntary hosts said that they should remain in the house for the present – the militia never came inside. And they were welcome to have some breakfast while they waited. The MacDonald clan was sorely and confusedly divided in its loyalties.

Soon they heard callers at the door for their daily provisions, their enemies within a few yards of them.

There followed some discussion as to whether they should try to go on to the Rossinish bothy. But the farmer advised not. The troops tended to haunt the beach area, for some reason; so they would be better to do their waiting elsewhere, he thought. He had a cattleman's shelter on the slope of a hill, Rueval, to the north. Hector would take them there, when he was sure that the way was clear.

So presently they were escorted, between showers, and by devious ways, on to a modest height, even though it was the highest in the area, where they were installed in a broken-down shed not unlike the one on Sheaval where they had found Flora, only in much poorer condition, Hector promising to come and inform them when the awaited visitors arrived.

More waiting.

After a sleep, they filled in the time with efforts at improving

136

to some extent this shack. Surely Flora and her escort would not be long in coming now? They were, after all, only some five miles from Nunton. Presumably she would arrive by boat from Loch Uskavagh, at Rossinish. It was a pity that they could not wait for her there. What would happen with those militiamen? If the young woman had two officers as escort, as proposed, then there ought to be no trouble, an odd situation indeed.

Night fell, and no sign of either Hector nor the awaited company. Fortunately no troops either, up here.

When, by noon next day, they were still unvisited, concern could not be banished. Had something gone wrong? Their project failing? By late afternoon, Charles said that Neil should go off to Nunton to discover the position. They could not go on like this, hungry again, and wet. Was that young woman a broken reed?

Neil counselled patience still. Flora would not fail them, he was sure. Nor her step-father. But nor would he, Neil, leave the prince again, in these circumstances. Let O'Neill go, if anyone did. Those militiamen would speak only Gaelic. If they did appear, searching up here, then it was essential that it was explained to them that their captain, Armadale, was sending two of his officers to deal with the situation. Neither of the other two could so tell them. They would be arrested and taken they knew not where. O'Neill could surely find his way the few miles to Nunton, on the west coast. There was a track all the way from Hakaidh.

Unexpectedly the Irishman was quite prepared to do this, tired of endless days hanging about. Indeed the prince wondered if he should not go also, but was dissuaded by Neil. If *he* was caught, that would be the end of it all, the Tower of London for him; whereas O'Neill, a French officer, would be treated as a prisoner-of-war and sent back to France. Charles did not think that this was behind Felix's preparedness to go to Nunton; but it did occur to him that O'Neill had a fancy for Flora, and saw opportunity here.

They took the Irishman on his way as far as the west side of this Rueval. He ought to reach the low west coast ground, less than eager walker as he was, well before nightfall, and head for Nunton in the security of the dusk.

Another night, and lacking food, for the pair left behind. The rain had ceased, but the midges had come to plague them instead.

But in the forenoon thereafter there was relief, not O'Neill returned but Hector from the farm, with bread, cold meat and milk, and the welcome news that the militia patrol had gone, tents and all, so they presumably would not be back. They all could go on down to the Rossinish bothy now, in safety, his father said.

Thankfully they set out, eating as they went. Hector, accompanying them, said that he would tell the Irishman where they were, for he had to pass Hakaidh on his way back from Nunton.

At the fishermen's bothy near the shore there was another surprise for them. They saw a fair-sized fishing-boat beached there, and four men carrying supplies up to the bothy. Charles and Neil hid at sight of them, but Hector went on to enquire – after all it was his father's bothy. Presently he came back to announce that these were Armadale's people, two of them officers. Greatly relieved, the hiders emerged and went on down.

Neil was pleasantly surprised thereafter to discover that he knew the two officers, friends indeed. They were the brothers John and Rory MacDonald, cousins of Flora. Armadale had arranged matters well. They had come with the boat from Loch Uskavagh, they said. Flora and Lady Clanranald would be coming soon to join them. This arrangement had been thought less likely to arouse awkward questionings, for unfortunately General Campbell had the day before landed fifteen hundred men on Benbecula, and the west coast was seething with the military, soldiers sent up from the south. The authorities were beginning to distrust the clans militia. It seemed that therefore they were just in time with this venture, for now Armadale would be superseded as commander on this island.

With the bothy thus occupied, Hector thought that the prince and Neil should come back to Hakaidh where they would be better quartered while they waited; and this was gratefully agreed to.

And wait they did, all the time expecting the coming of both O'Neill and Flora. But night fell, with no arrivals. With only the two bedrooms in the house, the visitors had to share Hector's apartment, that young man offering Charles his bed, with the prince assuring that he preferred the floor, where an old door was used to raise him a little off the stone flags.

The following forenoon, as they were about to go down to the bothy again to see if the Nunton party had arrived, one of Clanranald's men did appear, coming overland on a garron, and actually sent bearing a letter for the prince, and from O'Neill, a rather extraordinary circumstance. The missive declared that the delay was occasioned by his waiting upon Miss Flora and Lady Clanranald, as His Highness's representative, they being occupied with preparing suitable women's clothing for the prince. It was hoped, however, that they would be at Rossinish in a day or two, without fail.

Neil MacEachain, usually so equable, made unfavourable comments, whatever Charles thought of this. A day or two! And dancing attendance on Flora! With the Campbell military taking over, a day or two could be too late. This was folly! He would go himself to Nunton. He could be there in two hours, less, on the back of this messenger's garron. He would be back, hopefully, shortly with Flora.

So, for the first time in all this long saga, Charles was left on his own. At least he was sheltered and well fed. He did not know whether to be annoyed or amused over Felix O'Neill, a ladies' man most evidently.

It was late afternoon before there were any developments, with Neil coming back alone, and not from the west but from Rossinish beach. They were there, at last, a whole party of them, he announced. He had indeed managed to hasten matters; but instead of coming overland, with all the hundreds of new soldiery infesting the land, it had been decided to come by boat, round the northern tip of Benbecula, through the channel between it and Grimsay, the southern extremity of North Uist. They had achieved this without incident, a sail of only some ten or eleven miles, and all were now safely landed, and joined up with the four at the bothy. And by all, he *meant* all! For not only Flora and O'Neill were come. But, to see the young woman off, Lady Clanranald herself, her seven-year-old daughter, both eager to meet the prince, Flora's brother Angus, and another MacDonald officer representing Armadale, of the Glengarry sept this time, plus their boatmen.

Astonished at all this, Charles said his goodbyes, with fervent thanks to the Hakaidh household, and left for the beach, Hector coming with them to see them on their way.

Down at the Rossinish shore, the situation greeting them was so different from anything they had so far experienced as to be almost laughable. Instead of hiding, skulking, avoiding contact with others, here was quite a congregation waiting to receive Prince Charles Edward, fourteen of them no less. O'Neill, very much the gallant captain of the Dauphin's regiment, made the introductions, holding the two ladies by their arms as he led them forward, clearly in his element, Flora shaking her head over him and reaching out to the little girl who came shyly behind.

Lady Clanranald was a tall, handsome woman, a second wife to the chief, so not mother of Young Clanranald, younger than Charles had anticipated. She curtsied low and declared the great honour she felt in thus meeting His Royal Highness, the greatest moment of her life. Charles, clad all but in rags, and filthy rags at that, kissed her hand and announced that the honour was his. Then he did the same for Flora, asserting that he understood that he was from now on her maid, Betty Burke, and would endeavour to serve her faithfully, also seek to adopt an Irish accent. He patted the child's head, asked her name, and was told falteringly that it was Peggy. He was introduced to Flora's brother, and to the Glengarry officer who appeared to be named Rory MacDonald, confusing since one of Flora's cousins there already was called Rory – so one of them would have to be styled Roderick, of which Rory was a diminutive. The boatmen he waved to.

The Nunton party had brought supplies with them, roast fowl and cold beef, even kidneys and liver and, to be sure, brandy. So it was agreed that something of a feast was in order, part celebration, part farewell; a fire was lit and Charles himself insisted on roasting liver and kidneys on a spit over it, to present to the ladies, seeking to out-do O'Neill. Fortunately the rain had stopped although it was becoming misty, but that might be no disadvantage for their voyage. Improvised tables were formed, and they sat down outside, Flora on the prince's right, Lady Clanranald on his left, an occasion indeed.

But, sadly, the feasting was short-lived. Hector from Hakaidh suddenly reappeared with news. Their cattleman from Hacklett had come hastening over to tell them that a company of the new soldiers, Englishmen, had just landed from boats near his cottage, a bare three miles away, and were advancing southwards, this way.

Not exactly panic ensued, but distinct alarm and urgent reaction. They must be off, all of them, without delay, for it would have taken some time for these tidings to reach them and the military might well be very near now. So it was pack up and down to the boats. Where to go? Neil advised Loch Uskavagh, to the south, where their first boat had passed. It was not much more than two miles away, and with its innumerable inlets and islets made an ideal place to hide, Lady Clanranald agreeing, she remaining very calm, all things considered.

From celebrating then, they all were abruptly fugitives again. Embarking, the two boats were pulled away southwards. Pray that there were no warships on patrol nearby. It was nearly nine in the evening, so probably these would be anchoring for the night – let it be hoped not in the mouth of Loch Uskavagh.

Clinging close to the broken shoreline, they soon rounded the minor Meanish headland and entered the loch – and thankfully there were no ships in sight. The two younger officers called over that they might as well make for Scarilode, some way up on the north shore, where the prince's party had been before, and where there were two cottages where they might find shelter. Neil, knowing the place, agreed. Thither they pulled.

What the two fisherfolk families thought of this unexpected invasion of lofty folk, just as they were going to bed, was anybody's guess. But they were, like all others hereabouts, Clanranald's folk, and here was Lady Clanranald. So all was such hospitality as the households could produce, the group having to split up between the two cottages.

Over some resumption of their interrupted meal, Charles sharing a room with Flora, Lady Clanranald and the girl, this Roderick MacDonald and O'Neill, decisions had to be reached. Roderick, representing Armadale, more or less took charge, as clearly he had been sent to do. He had brought the passes made out for Flora, Betty Burke and Neil MacEachain as her manservant, which should ensure their freedom from any investigations. They should set out fairly soon, to gain the benefit of as much darkness as possible, he himself accompanying them. In the circumstances, he thought it wise for Lady Clanranald and her daughter, Aeneas and Captain O'Neill, also to depart without much delay, not by boat but overland the two miles back to Hakaidh, where-after there was that fair track all the way over to Nunton – if that was not too much for the small Peggy. They could pick up garrons at Hakaidh. Safer that than risking the boat again . . .

It was here that O'Neill broke in. "But *me*! Myself! To go thus.

141

I am with His Highness. I go to Skye with him. Not back to Nunton."

"I fear not." Roderick MacDonald spoke firmly, the voice of authority. It was clear to Charles now why he had been sent. "Armadale's orders. You, Captain, would be a danger to the prince. You are clearly no Highlander. You speak no Gaelic. How would Miss Flora account for you? A maid, yes, she could have. And a Highland manservant, MacEachain. But not a foreign man, with a foreign voice. Armadale has sent no passport for you, sir. You must go with Lady Clanranald back to Nunton. Perhaps, later, you may be able to rejoin His Highness in Skye."

Charles opened his mouth to speak, and then shut it again.

"But – but this is outrageous!" O'Neill cried. "You cannot do this, you and your Armadale! My place is with the prince. I am his friend, assistant, treasurer of his army. I represent the King of France. Where he goes, I go!"

"In normal circumstances, yes, sir. But these are not normal. Do you not see it? Your presence in that boat could endanger all. Endanger His Highness. Endanger Miss Flora. She is risking much in this. Her freedom, her good name and reputation. She could not account for you in her boat. You, Captain, must see it. Would you have all to fail? Have many, including Clanranald, Armadale and myself, all suffer arrest thereafter? Because of your presence!"

"I . . . I . . . it is intolerable!" O'Neill turned to Charles.

The prince drew a great breath. "I would have you with me, Felix. Perhaps, if you lay low in the boats? Covered by a sail, if we were stopped. Unseen . . . ?"

"It would not serve," Roderick declared. "These shipmen are thorough in their searches. He would be found."

"But I cannot leave him!" Charles insisted. "He has been with me all along. I cannot set foot in that boat without Felix O'Neill."

"You must, Highness, if you will forgive me so speaking! Your whole escape depends on this. Will you let it all fail now, endanger so many who seek to help you, for, for this Irishman?"

Neither of the women had spoken.

Charles turned to Flora. "Will you not take this risk?" he asked.

Silently she shook her head. And Lady Clanranald nodded her support.

The prince stared from one to the other. These people were all doing so much for him, risking all. He could not further endanger them than he was doing already. And he could not do without them, survive here. Silently he inclined his head.

Seeing the way things went, how the dice were cast, O'Neill had to make the best of it. With an accession of dignity, he bowed to the prince. "I will do as is said," he declared. "If *you* do not board the boat, Highness, I will go off on my own! Go you must. I will hope to see you again in Skye. Enough of this talk!"

The two friends eyed each other.

"I am sorry, Felix, sorry indeed. But if this is how it must be . . . ! *Ma foi*, we have been together for so long! But, it seems, for this sail over to Skye, we are to part. I do see the danger." Charles saw more than that, or thought that he did. He suspected that Neil MacEachain had been consulted, as had Armadale. Flora was sitting tight-lipped. This had been well rehearsed, he reckoned. Yet all was probably true, advisable, that they said.

"Felix, it seems that you must abide by this, my friend." That had to be final. "I hope that Clanranald and Armadale may be able to get you to Skye hereafter. I am sorry."

They left it at that.

It was raining again, and Lady Clanranald decided to put off departure until first light. So some adjustment of quarters for the night was necessary, the men all bedding down in sheds and outhouses, to leave the ladies and child the room for themselves.

At a misty dawn it was parting, an emotional one again, with so much at stake for them all. Charles clasped O'Neill to him, declaring that he hoped that they would be together again shortly; but that if he, Felix, found opportunity to obtain passage on a ship to France in the meantime, unlikely as this seemed, he was to take it. Lady Clanranald, after kissing Flora, gripped the prince wordlessly before turning away. With Aeneas as escort, and leaving the boatmen to come on when conditions were propitious, they set off for Hakaidh and the road to Nunton, with much waving and wondering. At least the rain had ceased.

The prince's party had the day to fill in. With Roderick MacDonald and Neil, Flora discussed the advisable route to Skye. The nearest area there was, unfortunately, the chief of MacLeod's territory, MacLeod an implacable opponent of the Jacobite cause, the north-west of that island, near Dunvegan

Castle, and, oddly, near Gualtergill, their faithful Donald's house. Flora wished to reach Monkstadt, considerably further off, where the Lady Margaret MacDonald, Sleat's wife, was presently living; and that would entail sailing round the tip of the long Vaternish peninsula, and so on round to Loch Snizort and the Trotternish district, which meant a voyage of almost fifty miles, Neil agreeing that this was necessary. Fortunately the wind was south-westerly, which should help. How long it would take them was anybody's guess, so much depending on the weather and sea conditions. But certainly it would be long after daylight.

Any idea that they might risk setting off before evening was banished when four longboats were spied being rowed, out in the loch, around noontide. These did not head in towards this Scarilode and its inlet; but the watchers were wary, for they must have come from a warship somewhere fairly nearby.

Concerned that a land-search of the vicinity might be forthcoming, Flora said that it was time that His Highness changed into his woman's garb, the which had him declaring that she must stop calling him Highness. It would have to be Betty, he supposed, if they were approached by enemies, or even strangers; but otherwise they were just to be Charles and Flora, she acceding. She led him into the room where she had spent the night, and produced a bundle of clothes.

"Here, then, Charles, is your new uniform," she said, smiling, and her smile was a very warm and lovely one, which he had not seen much of hitherto. "There is this blue-sprigged dress of white calico, with a coarser mantle of dun-coloured Camlet, of goat's hair, suitable for any serving-maid." She nodded at him. "These to be worn over a high-waisted quilted petticoat, with these stockings. And there is a cap, with flaps, to cover your head, very necessary in the circumstances. Shall I leave you to don them all?"

"*Ma foi*, no! I would not know which goes on first! And where! You will have to dress me, I fear, my good Flora. You will not be . . . discomposed?"

"I have seen men's persons, sir, many a time," she said simply. "When swimming, and the like."

"Good. I vow that I will be glad to shed these shamefully unclean clothes – even to don women's ones." And not pretending any undue modesty he stripped to his shirt.

She handed him the petticoat. "This first."

It was not unlike the kilts he had worn, but lighter. Too light for *his* requirement.

"This waistband is not strong enough," he objected. "I need my belt." And he reached for the leather belt he had discarded, with its pistol hooked on.

"No, no," Flora said. "That will not do. Too heavy. Not suitable. The petticoat will stay up well enough."

"It is not for that," he told her. "It is for my pistol. I keep it there, at my waist. I am never without it."

"You cannot do that – you cannot! Carrying a pistol there. No maid would possibly have one. It would give all away. If we are searched . . ."

"Indeed, Miss Flora, if we shall happen to meet with any who will go narrowly to work in searching me down there, as to what you mean, they will certainly discover me at any rate! The other . . . weapon!"

The young woman both frowned and smiled. "Sir, spare me!" she said, but less than censoriously. "No. Your pistol must remain hidden . . . elsewhere. Now, this dress. It can go on over your shirt. See, I will help you on with it. We had much choosing to do, seeking the right sizes for you. You are broader of shoulder than most women. But less, less below!"

"No, I fear that I cannot rival womankind in some respects!" he agreed. "But this fits well enough, does it not? Or shall we pad it out?"

"That will not be necessary, I think. Now, the apron. Maids usually wear aprons. Tie it around your waist. Over the dress."

"*That* would hide the pistol, would it not?"

"It would not. When you sat. Or stooped. No, no. Now, the mantle, on top. It is not beautiful, but will cover you in poor weather. You need not wear it all the time. And you can wrap a plaid when necessary, to be sure. We brought brogans, shoes, for you, but those you are wearing will serve well enough, I judge. Now this cap. We devised it with flaps which will in some measure hide your shaven cheeks."

"Yes. I must try to keep them lacking their stubble! Fortunately, I am fair of hair."

"So. You look – passable! Scarcely beautiful, beguiling, but we do not want that, do we! No close inspection sought!"

Thus clad, they emerged from the cottage – to cries of mirth from the rest of the party, all due regard for royalty for the moment forgotten. The prince bowed, produced a modest curtsy, but found that cap difficult to adjust and keep straight, the fit scarcely exact.

Flora showed him a letter which Armadale had given her, addressed to his wife, her mother. It read:

My dear Marion,
    I have sent your daughter from this country lest she should be in any way frightened with the troops lying here. She has got one Betty Burke, an Irish girl, who she tells me is a good spinster. If her spinning pleases you, you may keep her till she spins all her lint; or if you have any wool to spin you may employ her. I have sent Neil MacEachain along with your daughter and Betty Burke, to take care of them.
    I am your dutiful husband,
                    Hugh MacDonald

This was left open, to show to any investigator who might interrogate them.

Impatiently they awaited the dusk, and were not unduly displeased when once again the rain started, this and the lowering cloud helping to limit visibility. At length, around eight o'clock on the 18th of June, they decided that they could risk a start.

With farewells and gratitude to the cottagers, they went down to the boat, with their baggage, and pushed off, all thankful to be at long last leaving the Outer Isles. That is, so long as there was no warship anchored in the mouth of the loch.

There was not, to heartfelt relief.

12

Out of Loch Uskavagh they steered due northwards, concerned to keep as close inshore as might be for as long as possible. Not that they really anticipated any enemy vessels to be sailing up and down the Minch at this hour; but they could not be sure of it. And to be seen, stopped and investigated at this stage would be grievous indeed. Against a background of the rugged coast and offshore islets they would be unlikely to be spotted.

They made a strange crew, one woman, three Skye militia officers, four oarsmen, Neil, and the prince the only one of the original group which had left the mainland at Loch nan Uamh those months ago. Charles was very much aware of having left behind, at the various stages, Father Allan, John O'Sullivan, Ned Burke, Donald MacLeod and now Felix O'Neill. Was it a sort of desertion on his part? Or, in fact, were they all the safer without his dangerous presence? He did not know, but missed them all sorely.

With ten aboard, the boat, less than twenty feet long, was distinctly overcrowded and, not to get in the oarsmen's way, the passengers had to huddle close together, Neil finding much opportunity to keep an arm round Flora, for the wind was rising and the seas with it, so that there was much heaving and lurching. But they could hoist sail, and were able to make reasonably good progress. Charles sang to them, to the rhythm of the oars, and in time got almost all of them to join in the refrains and choruses, Flora's contralto adding a notable effect – that is, until she fell asleep, weary and rocked by the waves' rise and fall. Neil and he helped to ease her down into a recumbent position on extra sail-canvas; but there, in that very confined space, she was in danger of being kicked and trodden on by the others' feet, as they were jerked about by the craft's unpredictable motions. The pair took it in turn to lean over and try to protect her, a plaid covering her.

It would be just after midnight, it was reckoned, when they reached the tip of North Uist, some twenty miles, this becoming very evident by the different tidal action surging through the Sound of Harris from the Atlantic. And now, at last, they could turn eastwards and head for Skye, Vaternish Point, they calculated, some fifteen miles away. Now the boat's motion changed from rolling sideways to pitching fore and aft. This woke Flora, who made apology for the sleeping.

They had not glimpsed a ship or other craft so far.

Now they could make better time of it, wind and tide behind them. The rain had ceased. They were pleased about this, for they were anxious to get beyond the Vaternish MacLeod area before dawn. It was not likely that enemy ships would be waiting overnight thereabouts, but it was possible. And local folk, seeing a strange and overloaded craft skirting their shore, might become suspicious, and inform their chief's representatives.

Perhaps they miscalculated time, distance, and direction, lacking a compass, for in fact dawn broke before they reached Vaternish, and they could almost regret the clear sky and lack of rain. They could see the loom of land ahead. Not only that, but no break in the land. Which meant that they were further south than they had hoped. The Vaternish peninsula of Skye was a long one, fully ten miles, and they had to round the north tip. They had to swing more in that direction, then.

It was broad daylight, in fact, before they were able to pull round the cliff-girt headland of Vaternish Point, and into the comparatively sheltered waters of Loch Snizort beyond. So relieved were they all that they thought that they might risk a landing, briefly, for purposes of nature, for this loch was at least seven miles wide, and they had to avoid the chain of the Ascrib Isles in the middle. However, drawing in round a little promontory, they were alarmed to see men on the shore, near enough to wave and shout at them, whether local MacLeods or military they did not know, a most unfortunate occurrence. Hastily they pulled round and off – and promptly two shots rang out. No bullets came their way, but most evidently these were soldiers. A welcome to Skye, indeed!

It appeared that they had chosen quite the most unsuitable spot to land. So, instead, they continued on eastwards, to draw in to one of the uninhabited Ascrib Isles to make their necessary landing. There they did find the privacy they required, also a spring of fresh water, and ate something of a meal of stale bread and oatcakes. Charles actually managed to shave, a very necessary precaution. Their boat hidden in a little creek, they rested. They had still fully five miles to go, to a landing near Monkstadt House; and on the now sunlit day a ship might appear at any time, especially if these troops on Vaternish had been able to send a signal.

It looked as though the belief that Skye would be safer for the fugitive prince than the Long Island was less than accurate.

However, when no vessel had been spotted by midday, it was deemed that they could risk going on. Skye was all peninsulas, and the great Trotternish one lay ahead, MacDonald territory, not MacLeod, home indeed to Flora's two cousins. If the chief himself, Sleat, had been in residence, it would have been different, but so far as was known he was still in the south.

They headed for the rocky projection of Leachd Bhuidhe, just beyond which was the haven called Kilbride Port, the hidden landing-place for Monkstadt.

It was with major relief that all landed in the early afternoon. Here at least they would be safe meantime. There was a little community behind the harbour. Here they were known, although Charles was looked upon curiously, especially by some giggling children. Greetings were exchanged, in an air of normalcy which the prince found strangely affecting; it had been a long time since he had experienced normalcy.

Flora had to be assured that all was safe for them to take the prince to Monkstadt House, which was apparently a comparatively modern mansion replacing the ruined former stronghold of Duntulm Castle on its rock a few miles further north. Staunch Jacobite as the Lady Margaret was, there was always the possibility that Sir Alexander had returned. So with Neil and the three MacDonald officers, she left Charles in the care of the boatmen, sitting on a log washed up on the beach, clad as he was, feeling ridiculous and uncomfortable as he was eyed curiously by local folk. The boatmen were told to say, if anyone asked who this strange woman was, that she was Miss Flora's new maid, an ungainly jade from Ireland who was too lazy even to accompany her mistress on the mile-long walk to Monkstadt.

It was not long, however, before Neil came hurrying back, to inform the prince that he must be ready to embark again, at short notice if necessary. Apparently, near the mansion, Flora's party

149

had met Lady Margaret's maid, and she had told them that her mistress had callers that Sunday afternoon – not Sir Alexander himself, but a Lieutenant Alexander MacLeod of Balmeanach, of the Skye militia; also their chief's estate factor, MacDonald of Kingsburgh. So clearly Charles must not venture up to Monkstadt meantime. Flora and the others had gone on to see Lady Margaret and discover the full situation.

The prince was beginning to wonder why he had come to Skye, at all.

He could not continue to sit there on his log indefinitely, a target for all eyes. So, with Neil, he went some little way up above the beach to where, in a hollow amongst grazing sheep, he could wait unseen. The other left him to go back to the mansion, to help in the making of any decisions as to what to do now; also to tell the boatmen to be ready to take the prince off, if so commanded – just where to, remained to be seen.

Charles had quite a long wait, now, amongst the sheep. Fortunately nobody came near him. In time, he dozed in the afternoon sunshine.

It was sheep scampering off which roused him, to find a stranger approaching, a large, kilted figure clearly searching for him. Starting up, he grasped that cudgel. He was not going to be taken, at this late stage, without a fight.

He must have looked an odd figure indeed, dressed as he was and threatening resistance with a stick. But the newcomer called out not to fear, that he was Alexander MacDonald of Kingsburgh, factor here, and sent by Miss Flora. All would be well. He was come, concerned for His Highness's welfare.

Only partially reassured, Charles, however, lowered his cudgel. "Factor? Factor to Sir Alexander?" he said. "Then you are scarcely likely to be a friend!"

"I am, Highness, believe me!" The other patted a satchel slung over a tartan shoulder. "See, here I have brought you a bottle of wine and some bread, sir." He was a good-looking man of early middle age. "You are safe with me, I swear! We are not all Hanoverians here!"

The prince relaxed. "Pardon me, friend. But, what is to do? Where is Miss Flora? And Neil MacEachain? And the others?"

"They are keeping Balmeanach engaged. He is in charge of the MacLeod military hereabouts. He must not suspect that you are

150

here, Highness. So they are having to explain their arrival from Benbecula, the Lady Margaret aiding them."

"*Ma foi*, these MacLeods! The Uists are thick with them also! So what now?"

Kingsburgh got out and uncorked the bottle. "A mouthful of wine, sir, and you will feel the better! We have had to make hasty plans. Some bread? Balmeanach shows no sign of leaving the house. So you cannot go there, much as Lady Margaret would wish to entertain you, aid you. I suggested that you should come with me to my house. It is some seven miles to the south. Walk there, if you can do that, sir? Flora and MacEachain agree. He will join us, here, come with us. Flora will come on afterwards. We do not want to arouse Balmeanach's suspicions."

"I can walk, yes. I have done much walking. But, not the boat? Seven miles?"

"It would be less strange, arouse less talk we think, if we quietly made off over this hill and inland a little way, Highness. There is a good track in about a mile. If we got into the boat which brought you, and pushed off, the folk here would wonder. Without Flora and the others . . ."

"Yes, I see that. But, sir, do not call me Highness, of a mercy! Betty Burke I must be – if you can bring yourself so to name me!" Charles took another gulp of the wine.

"As you wish, sir . . . Betty! No, I cannot name you so! Impossible, whatever! I will endeavour not to name you at all."

The prince smiled. "I blame you not! You are risking much for me, I think. As so many another has done."

"Let us hope not overmuch. MacEachain should be here shortly. At first we thought of you crossing over all this Trotternish and down to Portree, and then get you over to the Isle of Raasay, where you would be secure, although it is a MacLeod place. MacLeod of Raasay served in your army. But that would be very long walking, almost a score of miles. Better to my house first. Then we shall see . . ."

"Raasay? Where is that?"

"It is an island to the east of this Skye. The north end of Skye. Quite large. Its laird is your man. Unlike his chief! Chiefs sometimes have their own views of what is right, best for them, and their clansfolk can think otherwise! As here. We do not all agree with Sir Alexander. His grandfather, Sir Donald, fought for *your* father, King James, in the rising of 1715. And lost greatly over it, in lands and favour. So now the grandson holds back. But many do not agree with this, my own self included. And those officers who came with you from Benbecula. Armadale likewise."

"I understand. And am grateful to those who risk their chief's wrath, for me."

"There is one such up here, at Monkstadt. Visiting Lady Margaret. Captain Donald Roy MacDonald of Baleshare. His island is off Benbecula. But he is over here receiving treatment for a wounded leg, from a physician. He was in your Clanranald regiment. He it was who suggested MacLeod of Raasay, a friend with whom he served. He is strong in your favour. He is prepared to come to my house, Kingsburgh. Then to take you to Raasay."

"*Mon Dieu*, you MacDonalds! So many, aiding me. I get confused with all your styles, your names. I have heard of Baleshare, yes. When I was over there. The sister of one who much aided me is wed to this Donald, I think. When I see him, I may well remember him, from the army . . ."

Neil MacEachain arrived, with some of the gear which had been left with the boatmen. They decided to set out right away. With sunset only an hour off, the evening church service would be apt to be keeping folk indoors, and so hopefully they would be spared much viewing and inspection, for Charles admittedly presented an eye-catching figure of a woman. They would go inland some way, to avoid the more populous coastal area; then turn southwards the seven miles to Kingsburgh.

Climbing over the rough ground, the prince hitched up his skirts, to the doubtful glances of his companions.

After about a mile of this heather-hopping, they came to the fair track Kingsburgh had mentioned, indeed the road to Monkstadt from the south. Charles asked how the odd name of Monkstadt came about, sounding scarcely Hebridean, to be told that it was a corruption of two old Norse words for a fort, this the site on which the present mansion was built, the local folk calling it Mugstot.

After something over another mile, their road passed the village of Uig. And this they could not avoid, for the Rivers Rha and Conan entered the Minch at the bay here, and had to be crossed by bridges, major streams. Unfortunately their passing coincided with the end of Sunday worship in the Uig church, and the congregation emerging were able to recognise Kingsburgh, who as their factor was well known to all. But it was at one of his companions that all tended to gaze, even if too polite to stare.

"For God's sake, sir, take care what you are doing! Or you will certainly discover yourself. Shorten your stride," Neil urged, low-voiced but urgent.

And Kingsburgh added, with a smile, "You are called the Pretender by some, are you not? So I fear that you are not the best at pretending! Now that you are a woman, I suggest that you lower your skirt somewhat!"

The prince laughed, shaking his head, but did as he was bidden.

Beyond Uig, another mile, they had to thread through a scattered crofting area called Earlish; and some of its people were amongst the worshippers at Uig; so the three travellers had some company before and behind. What these thought of the factor's present associates would have been interesting to learn.

After that, however, they were passing through fairly empty country, empty save for cattle and sheep, for almost four miles. They had just passed the deep dip of the entry to Glen Hinnisdale, with another river bridge, when the clatter of hooves turned their heads. No fewer than five garrons came trotting after them, bearing three women and two men – which at first concerned the walkers. But seeing that one of the riders was Flora, they relaxed.

Coming up with them, that young woman, dismounting, announced that here was Captain Donald Roy MacDonald, of the Clanranald regiment, and a kinswoman, Mistress John MacDonald of Kirkibost. She made that general, not specifically to the prince, on account of the two other riders who were, it seemed, Mrs MacDonald's maid and manservant, and who were evidently not to know of the identity of the prince. This produced a somewhat uncomfortable situation, for although the other lady had clearly been let into the secret, and kept glancing at Charles interestedly, he tended to turn away from her, remembering all the advice he had received on prudence. Perhaps he overdid it, for the elderly maid was overheard to say to the manservant, sniffing, that she had never seen so rude a creature, or a woman of such impudent appearance, and was in her opinion either Irish or a man in woman's dress.

Flora, at that, thought it wise to suggest that Mistress MacDonald should ride on ahead with her attendants, she and Captain Donald

Roy remaining with the walkers meantime, the latter limping as he led his mount.

"That was . . . difficult, Charles," Flora said, when they could speak openly. "I told Mistress MacDonald who you were, but she was not sure of her servants. It has been difficult, indeed, all along. This MacLeod of Balmeanach being at Monkstadt much upset my plans. Lady Margaret could not see you; she was much grieved, and sends her loyalest greetings. But these good friends, Kingsburgh and Captain Donald Roy, have greatly helped. We could not have managed without them. You have heard something of it all?"

"Yes. My sorrow that you should have been so troubled on my behalf. Ever this distresses me."

"It is little enough that such as I can do, Charles."

It was evident that Donald Roy's leg was paining him, and Flora said that he and she should ride on the remaining mile or two to Kingsburgh House, and await the others' arrival. It was now darkening.

Kingsburgh proved to be one more typical tacksman's house, long and whitewashed, of two storeys and an attic, with the usual farmery and outbuildings. The factor's somewhat flushed and disconcerted wife, who had obviously been asleep for it was less than an hour off midnight when they arrived, and was wearing a bedrobe, was hastily finding food and drink for her visitors. She did not fail to blink at the sight of the prince, although Flora clearly had warned her. Her young daughter, however, in her early teens, hearing the commotion, rose from her own bed to come and stare at her father's companions. She ran to her mother, and they all heard her comments.

"Oh, Mother, my father has brought a very odd, great, ill-shaken-up wife as ever I saw! I never saw the like of her, at all!"

Charles, listening, laughed. "There speaks an honest lass! Ill-shaken-up is very apt, I say! I make but a doubtful woman. Nor do I improve."

"I think that you will not require to practise it further," Flora told him. "We have brought you more suitable clothing, provided by the Lady Margaret. No need now, I judge, to dress you as a woman."

"*Dieu vous garde!* Your sex, my Flora, I greatly admire. But do not seek to rival!"

Soon they were all sitting down to an impromptu but very

154

adequate meal, although not Kingsburgh's wife herself, who, much impressed by the identity of their guest, if not her own appearance, refused to seat herself at table with royalty, as she declared, her goggling daughter sent back to bed. Royalty or none, Charles did hearty justice to the provision, saying that it was the best that he had eaten for long, drinking two bottles of ale in quick succession and finishing it off with a liberal dose of brandy.

Over that table, tongues perhaps loosed by the liquor, Donald Roy and Charles discussed the late campaign, the folly of turning back at Derby, and the mistake of making that stand at Culloden, when the army could and should have dispersed into the mountains and glens, to reassemble, intact, afterwards, and renew the struggle; all of which the MacDonald blamed on the Lord George Murray, whom he named a disaster as lieutenant-general and indeed a high-born rogue. The prince would not have that, declaring that Murray had misjudged, yes, but that he was honest enough and loyal. Flora and Neil listened but made no comments.

Charles produced his one remaining clay pipe-bowl, with its quill stem tied on with thread, and asked Kingsburgh whether he had any tobacco to serve his weakness? At sight of that pathetic object, their host got up and found a fine new pipe and a jar of the weed, requesting that he might be allowed to keep the broken one as a memento.

Presently Flora departed for bed, but the men remained at the table, passing round the bottle, for considerably longer, Charles greatly enjoying the leisurely and sociable occasion in conditions of well-being. It was the early hours of the morning before he was conducted to his room upstairs, and a comfortable bed.

As a consequence he slept late indeed next morning, his hosts reluctant to wake him. It was mid-forenoon before a knocking on his door roused him. When, sleepily, he answered, he heard his hostess's voice.

"Sir, it is I. With Miss Flora. It is past time for your breakfast. I can bring it to you here, if you wish. But I am imploring Miss Flora to come in to you, and get me a lock of your hair, your royal hair! To keep. To treasure, just. But she refuses to do it."

He sat up, yawning. "Ha, pray Miss Flora to come in," he called. "What would make her afraid to come where I am?"

The door opened and the two women entered, Flora looking not exactly embarrassed but shaking her head.

"Forgive this, I pray, Charles," she said. "It is an intrusion, a presumption. But the lady is most eager . . ."

"Say it not. Come, you. My hair is in need of some cutting, forby! Trim it, by all means." He swung himself down off the bed; fortunately he had slept in his shirt.

"Only a lock, sir, a single lock," Mrs MacDonald said, handing Flora a pair of scissors.

"Flora shall have a lock for herself!" Charles declared. "In token of future and more substantial favours!" And he waved a hand. "Come, sit here, my dear."

The younger woman, biting her lip doubtfully, took the bedside chair, removing Betty Burke's travel-stained clothing thereon, to lay on the floor. She sat.

Making an elaborate gesture of it all, the prince, bowing, got down on his bare knees, and putting both arms round Flora's waist, laid his head on her lap, the first time he had made any such intimate gesture, however often he had held and clutched her in their heaving boat.

She smoothed his fair head somewhat falteringly. "I have never done the like before . . ."

"I fear that it must be less clean than it should be," he murmured into her skirt. "But for me, this is a delight."

She did not comment on that, but snipped off a lock expertly enough. She handed it over to Mrs MacDonald.

"Now, another for yourself," he declared on to her warm knee. "Indeed, you can cut it all short, if you will!"

"I think not," she said. "As Betty Burke you will be the better of as much hair as possible."

"But I thought I was finished with that," he protested. "That you had brought me clothes from Sir Alexander's wife. Man's clothing. And no need for the other, now."

"We have decided not. Meantime," she told him. "The servants here. And people about the place. They have seen you come in as a woman, Charles. If a strange one! Better that they should not see you go as a man! Tongues to wag! You can change when we are on our way to Portree!"

"Ah, me! And I had hoped to be done with all that." He raised himself up, reluctantly. "But at least, while you are here, you can

156

help me don this wretched habit! I never get it all rightly. This petticoat in especial . . ."

"If you say so . . ."

To Mrs MacDonald's all but girlish giggles, Flora aided him to adjust that petticoat over his shirt, while he took the opportunity to hold her shoulders for support. Then the calico dress, a deal less fresh than when first presented, had to be put over his head and smoothed down.

"Where is the apron?" she demanded.

"Apron? Ah, I must have dropped it." He went round the bed, and there it was lying beside the tub of what had been hot water, in which he had washed himself before retiring. "Do I require this?"

"Oh, yes. It is the uniform of any maid."

"Tie it on for me, then." Once more he found it necessary to hold her as she draped it in front of him.

"I think that it is as well that Mistress MacDonald is here!" she mentioned, eyebrows raised. "Your cap, Charles, and you will be Betty Burke again."

The ladies led him downstairs for a belated breakfast.

He discovered that the company was one short. It seemed that Captain Donald Roy had ridden off for Portree, a dozen miles away, to discover the situation there as regards the military, and to try to contact some reliable boatmen who would put the prince over to the Isle of Raasay. It was thought that Charles should not risk the walk there in daylight, for there were crofting townships on the way.

So the rest of the day was spent at Kingsburgh, the prince remaining indoors so as not to arouse overmuch attention from the nearby cottagers. However, the Kingsburghs made excellent hosts. Charles learned that their son was presently serving as another of Armadale's officers over in Benbecula, and no more eager a searcher than that captain and his other colleagues.

With an early darkness forecasting more rain, it was time for departure. Charles made a grateful leave-taking of Mrs MacDonald and her still excited daughter, he urging the former to wash that lock of hair, whatever else she did with it, the lady now voluble in her praise, and less overawed by royalty. Her husband provided their guest with a young man called MacQueen, whose discretion he could trust, to act as guide for the night-time walking, and who would know the populous places to avoid. He then saw the four of them on their way, Flora and Neil leading their horses. His final salute and good wishes, at farewell, were heartfelt. The prince assured him that his services and good company would never be forgotten. He seemed to have said that to so many.

When, after a couple of miles, they reached one of the few clumps of trees which this part of Skye boasted, they drew in to their cover, and Flora said that here was as good a place and time as any to change his clothing. She produced from her saddle-bag a kilt and jacket which Kingsburgh had supplied, and no fewer than six fine silken shirts of Sir Alexander's, sent by Lady Margaret. Thankfully, there amongst the trees, the prince finally discarded his hated female garb and cap, also his own now ragged and less than clean shirt, and donned his new apparel, caring nothing for the watchers, completing the occasion by folding a clean plaid over one shoulder, to be held in place by a handsome silver buckle, he thus proving to have gained his own memento of a very memorable interlude.

They deposited Betty Burke's garb under a nearby bush, and moved on.

It began to rain, and heavily.

Presently, with still some seven miles to go to Portree, it was reckoned, Charles urged Flora to ride on, Neil with her. There was no point in them all getting soaked. She agreed to this, not so much on account of the rain as to enable her to contact Donald Roy in the town, discover what was being arranged, and where Charles was to be housed there until transport to Raasay could be provided.

Wrapped in their plaids, they parted company.

13

That was no pleasant walk for Charles Edward. The rain got worse rather than better; and the young man, MacQueen, could speak only in the Gaelic, save for a very few English words and, however trustworthy, made but an uninteresting companion. The prince did some singing, but stumbling along in mud and puddles scarcely lent itself to song, and most of those miles were passed in silence, apart from the odd curse.

They went by the east shore of Loch Snizort Beg, and thereafter sought to avoid the communities of Kensaleyre, another Borve and Achalean, although in almost midnight conditions and driving rain there seemed little likelihood of attracting unwelcome attention.

Something over two hours of this and they reached the outskirts of Portree, at the head of its own loch on the Sound of Raasay, this the largest community on Skye. There the arrangement had been that they should make for one of the inns of the place, run by somebody called MacNab, whom Donald Roy had judged could be trusted. But how to find this establishment in the wet dark? Charles guessed that, this being something of a port, the inns would tend to be down near the harbour. But which?

Thankfully, a figure emerged from shelter in the doorway of a shed, and this proved to be Neil MacEachain, on the lookout for them. He conducted them to a building, with sheds and stabling, just back from one of the piers, this one of the few premises where lights were showing that night. Here, in a side-room, they found Flora and Donald Roy awaiting them, with the innkeeper MacNab and a well-dressed, youngish man who greeted Charles respectfully and proved to be a cousin of MacLeod of Raasay, Captain Malcolm MacLeod of Brea, also from the Clanranald regiment, who, it transpired, had been wounded in the shoulder at Culloden. He was, he declared, honoured to be of some service to His Highness, and was in process of making arrangements to get the prince over the Sound of Raasay.

Charles, chilled and soaked to the skin, fortified with a glass of whisky, said without ado that he must get out of these wet clothes. Before a well-doing fire, he promptly divested himself, Flora by this time unconcerned over such matters, producing from her bag another shirt for him, and Donald Roy actually stripping himself of his own kilt and handing it over, while wrapping himself around in one of the ever-useful plaids; the prince had come to recognise all too clearly the need for these tartan shawls in these parts. The Captain MacLeod departed to see if the promised boat was ready, for it seemed that he had managed to contact the Raasay chieftain's two sons, who were in Portree on unspecified business, and they were readying their own craft and oarsmen.

So there before the fire the others waited, glad to put away a meal of roasted fish, cheese and bread and butter, the liquor clearly in plentiful supply. Charles asked if this was of Donald MacLeod of Gualtergill's supplying, to be assured that it was, although where the esteemed provider now was, these days, MacNab did not know; he had not seen him for long. He was not enlightened.

In their conversation it became clear to Charles that he was now at one more parting of the ways, and a sorrowful and moving one indeed it would be, for it was to be goodbye to both Neil and Flora. There was no point in them coming across to Raasay with him, only unnecessary danger, and nothing more that they could do for him in his efforts to get back to the mainland at Borrodale and Loch nan Uamh, the recognised calling-point for French ships concerned with the Jacobite cause. It made a depressing thought.

It was not long before Captain MacLeod came back, with two younger men, his second cousins, John and Murdoch MacLeod, Raasay's sons. These, much impressed by the company they were in and the importance of the present occasion, announced that the boat was ready, awaiting them, not at one of the piers where it could have been conspicuous, but at a beach nearby, two men with it.

So now it was to be farewell. After some argument about Charles using one of his few remaining golden guineas to pay their landlord for his services, and refusing the small change – Donald Roy asserting that this looked over-princely and therefore suspicious – Charles turned to Flora.

"My dear and good friend," he said. "Here we part meantime, it seems. It is . . . grievous. Grievous. After all that we have done

160

together, all that lies between us." He gripped her two arms, and their eyes met and held.

"Yes," she said simply.

"What am I to say? To do?" He shook his head, and all but shook her. "You have been so good, so kind, so giving. And I, I have given nothing. Only taken, taken!"

"Taken nothing that I was not glad to offer, Charles. To serve you, in a little way, has been an honour for me, and a pleasure. Yours the discomfort and problems. And we have been . . . our closeness has not been . . . any trial, difficult. Has had its . . . rewards." She also was having her problems now.

"Rewards, yes. *Ma foi*, the rewards have all been for *me*! But, one day, Flora MacDonald, it is my hope that we shall meet again. In St James's Palace mayhap. Where I shall reward you for all that you have done. One day!" He realised that he was still gripping her, and stepped back a little, to reach for her hand and raise it to his lips, bowing, although his eyes never left hers.

She inclined her head, finding no words.

Almost abruptly he turned from her to the watching Neil MacEachain. "You, faithful guide and good companion! Much do I owe to you also. Much! So much given, so much danger shared. My gratitude, Neil – but more than that. My great regard and fondness. How to thank you? Words are so poor, so lacking."

"None are necessary, Highness. We have what we have, without words."

"That is truth." Charles looked from one to the other. "You both have something of me, of myself. Always. And I, of you!"

"Yes. Always. And, and I have a lock of your hair!" Flora mustered a smile of a sort.

He nodded, and looking at her said, "Care for her, Neil."

The other reached out a hand to the young woman.

The prince sighed. "*Le bon Dieu* keep you both. And keep me, to show, one day, my caring for you and my gratitude." He swung round to the others there. "All my good and loyal friends! My indebtedness overwhelms me. And still you will endanger yourselves for me. You, Captain Donald Roy, will you accompany me to Raasay? As representing all the good MacDonalds who have so greatly cherished me? Despite their chief! Whose shirt I wear!" A lighter note was perhaps called for.

"With respect, no, Highness," that man said. "I would but

hamper you over there with my wretched leg. Serve you nothing. Better that I stay here. Let the MacLeods take over. Despite *their* chief!"

"And gladly," Captain Malcolm put in. "And, sir, time that we did so." He gestured. "In that regard, I think that we should be on our way. That we may be over the sound before daylight."

"As you will." Charles turned back to the pair behind him, silent, to search their faces. Then he stepped forward, to take Flora's hand again, and raise it, but this time to bring it palm upwards to his lips and kiss it thus, in a strangely moving fashion, before, without another word, he strode for the door.

Captain Malcolm and the two young MacLeods followed him out.

Almost as though in a hurry now, the prince set the pace along that waterfront, making for a little bay beyond the northernmost pier, Young Raasay guiding. Down on to the pebbly beach they went, in the driving rain, to find the two boatmen huddling under plaiding against the weather, beside the drawn-up boat.

Charles wondered how many such small craft he had sailed in now, as he climbed in – and how many more before he could board a larger vessel to take him to France and a new start?

They pushed off, the six of them, for one other Hebridean island.

14

That crossing, although of barely three miles, was a rough one, with a choppy sea and spume blown to add to the wetness. But at least it was soon over.

They made for the nearest bay on the Raasay shore, which his companions told the prince was the mouth of Glen Glam, where apparently there was a convenient shed or hut which had escaped the ravages of the Hanoverians. When Charles asked about this latter, Captain Malcolm confessed that it could all possibly be blamed on himself. He had been wounded at Culloden, captured, but had managed to escape – but not before Cumberland's people had learned his identity. Probably because MacLeod of MacLeod was known to be pro-government, and here was a MacLeod officer fighting against them, the enemy had taken careful note. The fact was, of course, that the MacLeods of Raasay were a sept of MacLeod of Lewis, a different branch of the clan from the Skye chiefs. At any rate, the enemy had picked out Raasay for especial dire reprisal, sending one of Captain Fergusson's ships, under a Lieutenant Dalrymple, to sack the island. Terrible had been the havoc. Three hundred homes had been destroyed, including the laird's own house. Seven hundred sheep and over two hundred and fifty cows had been slaughtered. All boats, over thirty of them, holed and sunk, and shameful violence wreaked on the people.

Much shocked, Charles heard all this, and not without his own sense of guilt, since all stemmed from his attempt to recover his father's throne. He said as much; not that the others would have it.

It was the first day of July, and dawn near enough for them to be able to pick out the gap of the glen mouth in the looming high barrier, for Raasay was a hilly isle although scarcely mountainous, some thirteen miles long, he was informed, but only two to three miles in width. They manoeuvred the boat into the inlet of the Glam Burn, and beached. Three ruined croft-houses were here, mute witnesses to devastation, further evidence of which was brought to the prince's notice when he stumbled over the carcase of a cow, and had pointed out to him, in the half-light, others lying scattered thereabouts. The invaders had slaughtered all that they could find, taken what they could use for meat, and left the rest of the hundreds of carcases to lie and rot.

The hut to which they were headed, perhaps half a mile up the deep, twisting glen, had escaped notice apparently, behind a thrusting shoulder, clearly one more cowherd's bothy. Fortunately its thatched roof was intact, so that it was dry inside, and there were even peats under a lean-to cover. So they were able to get a fire going and dry their clothing and warm themselves.

Young Raasay and his brother said that they would go off to obtain supplies with daylight increasing and the rain slackening, to their ruined home, Raasay House, which had been part demolished and burned like all the rest, their father and mother now having gone to Lewis for safety, while they themselves were living on Skye in various MacLeod houses, as indeed were most of the island's dispossessed inhabitants.

In these conditions, Charles wondered why he had come to Raasay. He was told by Captain Malcolm that it had been Donald Roy MacDonald's idea. He judged that, devastated as it was, the island would be unlikely to be searched again, and safer than Skye as a sanctuary in the interim – with the prince demurring that it was not a sanctuary that he sought but a means of getting away to the mainland and a ship to take him to France. He had had a sufficiency of lurking and hiding in secret places. He did not want to sound unappreciative, ungrateful for all that was being done for him, at grave risk for the doers, but it did seem to him that this Raasay would not greatly forward his purposes.

The other admitted that this thought had occurred to himself, that it was certainly no place to find a vessel to take the prince to the Borrodale–Moidart area where he wished to be. He had gone along with Donald Roy's suggestion because he recognised that some safe place was necessary while arrangements could be attempted for the onward journeying. That was all.

As they waited there, inevitably they discussed the campaign of the previous year, its early successes and ultimate failure, and again Charles found the Lord George Murray coming in for the principal criticism. His own attitude was that Murray, a conventional soldier, had been loyal enough and a capable commander in the field, but had lacked the understanding of the guerrilla type of warfare which could have changed all, and failed to perceive the political possibilities. MacLeod did not sound greatly impressed with that.

When, at nearly midday, the four others returned, laden with food, including dismembered portions of a lamb and a kid, these fresh-killed, they also brought word of a strange man said to be haunting the isle, allegedly a pedlar selling goods which he believed the surviving inhabitants would require, but thought by the said survivors to be most likely a government spy. They would have to watch out for this character.

They also brought more stories of the late terror, of a man from the north of the isle who had been beaten to death, of a blind girl being raped by many, of a cripple so maltreated that she would never walk again, and the like. Captain Malcolm agonised over his responsibility.

Hiding there, they ate well at least, Charles demonstrating his acquired skills at impromptu cookery.

Restless in the morning, the prince, against the advice of Captain Malcolm, went walking. Some way, and eyeing those burned and ravaged cottages, he vowed that, God willing, one day he would have them all restored and bettered, rebuilt in good stone. He would have gone further, examining the widespread havoc, but was persuaded to return to the hut, for if indeed that strange pedlar was a government spy, then, if he appeared, the sight of strangers, and well-clad ones, could possibly have him sending the word over to Skye and bringing troops for a capture. Acceding, Charles declared that he had suffered a deal of discomfort these months, but he would rather spend ten years of this than be captured by these cruel and unrelenting enemies. But, he trusted in Providence, who most surely did not design all this for nothing!

In the afternoon they were collecting branches for the fire from under some of the scattered and stunted trees of the glen, when one of the boatmen came hurrying from higher up to announce that a single figure, almost certainly the pedlar, was approaching downhill. Hastily they all returned to the shed and shut the door, thankful that they had not yet lit the fire, for its smoke would have given away that fact that it was occupied.

Peering through a space above that door, presently they saw a strange, bearded character, staff in hand, all but biblical-looking,

165

with a large canvas bag slung over one shoulder, pacing past on the other side of the burn. They noted that he looked over at their hut, but there was no easy crossing-place here, and if he wanted to investigate he would have to go further down, to cross a rough plank bridge. He moved on.

Young Raasay declared, "That man is an enemy, I swear it! What else could he be doing here but spying out the land? I say that we should go after him and get rid of him! He is a danger to Your Highness, to us all. And if he sees our boat . . . !"

"I agree," his brother, MacLeod of Rona, said. "That one could be the end of us!" And he produced a small pistol from an inner belt. "I have powder and shot here, not much but . . ."

"No, no!" Charles exclaimed. "God forbid that we should take any man's life while we can save our own! Put that away, friend. We have not yet reached such savagery as have our foes!"

They waited, but the stranger did not reappear.

Nevertheless, the presence of that man had its effect upon them. The prince asked if there was anything to be gained, in these circumstances, in waiting longer here on Raasay? He could see nothing in favour of it. If that pedlar was indeed a spy, and suspected the presence of strangers, then it might well quite soon result in another descent on the unhappy isle by the enemy, to the further misery of the remaining inhabitants, and no advantage to themselves. He thought that they should go back to Skye, and then his onward journey. And this before Donald Roy came over, as he had said that he might. Go that night.

Captain Malcolm nodded at that. Coming to Raasay had probably been a mistake. In which case, the sooner they were back on Skye the better. There they could plan the next stage, with Donald Roy MacDonald.

They awaited nightfall, deploring the fact that the wind was rising again, which would not help them. None of the MacLeods could remember so grim an early summer as this had been. Charles said that, since he believed that the good God was preserving him, however unworthy and however odd His methods, then the evil weather was probably hampering his foes even more than themselves.

Their boat, whether seen or not, was still beached there, its oars and sail intact, and in the windy dark they launched it and pulled out of the inlet. But with that gusty wind westerly, in the faces

166

of those not rowing, they soon realised that this was going to be no easy crossing, the waves already steep and their crests being whipped off in driving spray. The sail could not be raised, and the oarsmen had to work their hardest, prepared for down-draughts and overfalls in the narrow and fairly shallow sound, as well as the pitching and tossing of mere high rollers. It much reminded the prince of his first voyaging out to the Long Island from Loch nan Uamh. He, like Captain Malcolm, took his turn at the rowing, when they were not in fact baling out water, for the tops of many of the waves were coming inboard.

Their landing, at any rate, that wild night, should go unobserved.

In the circumstances they could not be very selective as to where they made a landfall, so long as it was a safe one, on a rocky, weed-hung coast. But when at length they did find a comparatively sheltered little bay to draw into, at least it was one the MacLeods could place, for nearby there soared up a great stack, known apparently as Nicholson's Rock, not far from the little community of Scorrybreck. And Young Raasay knew of an isolated cow byre nearby, one of the innumerable such scattered over the Hebrides, where they could hide and shelter while they discovered the situation prevailing here now, and sought to contact Donald Roy.

Hide and shelter, Charles said to himself, ever hide and shelter! Those seemed to have been his watchwords for these many months.

They effected a safe landing, and after a half-mile trudge, bent against the wind, they reached the promised cowshed. It was not as good as the hut they had left, but it would serve for the meantime. They ate cheese and oatcakes, all that they had now, and, wet as they were, settled to sleep, if they could, for what remained of the night.

When Charles awoke it was daylight, to find only Captain Malcolm with him, the others gone to Portree to gather information, food and to seek Donald Roy.

When the brothers got back it was with dire news. The boatmen, who had brought Flora, Neil and the prince from South Uist to Skye, had been arrested and put to the question. What they had confessed to, who knew? But the inquisitors' methods were not gentle, and the worst was feared. So now the authorities knew that Charles was on Skye, that for sure. Donald Roy, the innkeeper MacNab said, had gone back to Monkstadt after Flora and Neil, to inform them and Lady Margaret of the dangerous situation. The hunt for the prince would be transferred from the Outer to the Inner Isles, and Skye undoubtedly would be most thoroughly searched.

"Then I must be away from it, and at once!" Charles declared. "But where? Where is best? Much of this Skye is held by those against me, Sleat and your MacLeod chief. I must get back to the mainland. How? The warships will be based hereabouts now, watching for any boat."

"There is one part of Skye, to the south, Strathaird, where you would be welcomed and helped, Highness," Malcolm said. "The Mackinnon country. Beyond the Cuillin Mountains. I know it, for my sister lives there, married to Captain John Mackinnon, close kin to their chief, Mackinnon of Strathardal. He served in your army, with myself. If we could get to Strathaird, to Elgol, where they live. And from there it is not over-far to the mainland at Glenelg. Or better, Mallaig."

"Good! But you say *we*? Do you purpose to accompany me there, my friend?"

"What else? To be sure, I will take you there. Will our good boatmen be prepared to take us on that further voyage, John? Quite a lengthy one, this time?"

"They will do it, if we say so," Young Raasay asserted confidently. "It will have to be by night again. Can we get all that way, by the Inner Sound, Loch Alsh and the Sound of Sleat, in one night? I fear not . . ."

"No!" Charles said, definitely. "I will not have that. Those other boatmen arrested and held. No doubt ill-treated. Those warships will be all moved here, now, fifteen of them, at least. I will not have you all endangered. Better that I should walk there, since you say it is still in Skye."

"It is far, Highness," Malcolm pointed out. "Twenty-five to thirty miles, at least. More, for we would have to avoid populated parts, circle many lochs, cross mountain tracks. Better by boat. Short sailings, in darkness. And hiding by day . . ."

"No, I say! I have caused enough of sorrow and pain. These good friends are not to suffer. I go afoot. Alone, if need be."

"Never that! If walk you will, I walk with you. Far as it is," Malcolm asserted.

"We may walk our shoes off in the end, if it is so far and so rough! Have you ever walked barefoot? *I* have. I learned to do that in Italy. And all but did so again, on your Long Island! It is possible!"

"No, Highness, I have never attempted that. Nor wish to. Our brogans will serve . . ."

"We can walk also," Murdoch of Rona put in.

"No need. Four would attract the more notice, my friend, than would two. The captain and I will make for this Mackinnon country, Strath . . . what was it? And go at once, since the search will be on for me."

"Better to wait for darkness, sir."

"The sooner we move, the better. None so far from Portree, they might be here at any time. We go soon. Two men, walking apart, if need be . . ."

"We cannot disguise Your Highness as a woman again."

"God forbid!"

"But if you were to walk as my servant. Wear an old coat, carry some baggage, shameful as that would be, it might serve," Malcolm said. "Use some servant's name, not any clan one, in case your voice is heard and betrays you."

"Yes. Some name which sounds foreign to these parts. I have it – Lewie Caw! He was a young surgeon, who treated me, in the army. I thought it a strange name. That sounds sufficiently foreign. Irish perhaps? I will be Lewie Caw, servant to MacLeod of Brea! So, I throw myself entirely in your hands, my master, and leave you to do with me as you please! Sir!" Charles bowed low. "Better than being Betty Burke! Save for the company I kept then!"

Malcolm shook his head, while his cousins laughed.

"How do we go? We must avoid Portree at all costs."

"Yes. Go westwards from here. By Scorrybreck and on by Maligan, then south, passing well to the west of the town, and so into Glen Varrogill. That glen is ten miles long. Hide by day . . ."

"As you say. But, first, I have to get a message to Donald Roy. I owe it to him. Acquainting him with all. That he may tell the others. A letter. Have any of you paper?"

They had not. But Young Raasay said that he could go fetch

some from Torvaig, where he had friends, and sometimes stayed. No great distance off.

"Only a scrap I require. For I shall write no long epistle. And word it carefully, lest it fall into wrong hands . . ."

While the young man was gone, Malcolm told Charles about the Mackinnons, a comparatively small clan, but independent. They took their name from Fingon, a son or grandson of King Alpin of Dalriada, so they were of the same stock as the MacGregors, the Clan Alpin, who also descended from another son of that king, a brother of Kenneth MacAlpin, who united Picts and Scots. So they were of lofty lineage, the Mackinnons, and proud of it. The last Abbot of Iona was one of them. Their land of Strathaird and Strathardal was very close to Sleat, but they paid no service to the MacDonalds. Their chief was an old man, and a good Jacobite. Although they were not large enough to provide a regiment for the cause, they had sent a company to the prince's army, under this Captain John Mackinnon of Elgol, Malcolm's brother-in-law. His Highness would win help there, to get across the Sound of Sleat to the mainland.

When Young Raasay returned with a piece of paper, a quill and an inkhorn, Charles wrote thus:

Sir,
   I thank God I am in good health and have got off as designed. Remember me to all friends, and thank them for the trouble they have been at.
   I am, sir, your humble servant,
                         James Thomson

That should be sufficiently vague as to details not to incriminate anyone if seen by the wrong eyes; and it was to be hoped that the message would be passed on to Flora and Neil. Young Raasay promised to get it to Donald Roy even if he had to go with it to Monkstadt itself.

So, at around seven in the evening, it was once more farewell. Clad in one of the boatmen's old shaggy coats and carrying their baggage on his shoulder, the prince again expressed his gratitude and indebtedness, admitting that this was becoming a habit of his, but none the less sincere for that.

MacLeod of Brea and Lewie Caw set off westwards.

15

Knowing that part of Skye very well, Malcolm was able to lead
Charles by devious ways and unfrequented areas, round behind the
Portree vicinity, without encountering anyone, although whenever
they passed near any dwelling, the prince fell back, as suitably
humble servitor.

Two hours of walking, with the weather fortunately much
improved, brought them to the arm of Portree Loch well south
of the town where, with mountains rising ahead, the mouth of Glen
Varragill opened, a long, straight but narrow valley leading due
southwards towards the mighty and spectacular Cuillin Mountains,
the highest and most dramatic peaks of all that soaring seaboard.
Not that their drama was very evident now, for dusk was falling.

Malcolm said that they could walk less carefully now, at least as
far as required secrecy was concerned, for apart from a few houses
at the beginning, there was scarcely another in all this glen's ten
miles. But heedlessness did not apply to their footwork, for it made
for quite steep walking although there was a track of sorts all the
way, this being the main drove-road to the south and the mainland.
They went beside the rushing river, this fed by innumerable
waterfalls cascading down from the flanking heights, the roar of
these, after all the wet weather, providing the accompaniment to
their walking. It was not a route to hurry over in the dark.

They munched the usual cheese and oatcakes as they went.
Malcolm made a good companion.

He was concerned as to where daylight would find them, for they
were coming into Sleat's land now, indeed into what was known as
MacDonald's Forest, a deer forest rather than a tree one, although
the glen was becoming ever more wooded on its lower slopes, as
they progressed. They wanted no encounters hereabouts until they
could get through to the Mackinnon territory, still at least another
dozen miles ahead. They would have to pass the head of Loch
Sligachan, where there was a community which could scarcely be

avoided, and he feared that they would not get there before dawn. So it was a matter of trying to discover another hiding-place or shelter to lie up in for the day, this 3rd of July, a cave possibly, in one of the more rocky stretches of hillside.

Actually they did better than that, not far off Sligachan, with Malcolm becoming anxious. They found a pile of cut logs at the side of the track, and this led to the guess that there might well be a woodman's shed in the trees, not far off. Turning in, they found just that, in only a hundred yards or so, empty and not giving the impression of being recently used. They might risk settling down here for the day. If they were disturbed, they were, after all, just travellers resting.

Hungry, but not yet footsore, they lay down to sleep, plaids on the scattered bark of the floor.

They could scarcely sleep all day, to be sure, and they talked of many things, Charles particularly wondering, not for the first time, at the cruelty and heartless behaviour of the government troops, and of Cumberland himself, their commander. How could any prince behave so? For he was a son of the Elector, George the Second, of royal Germanic line, however wrongly on the British throne. And to his father's claimed subjects, with his flayings and tortures, his murdering of prisoners, his lack of all respect for womankind, his ordered burnings and brutal ravaging. It was scarcely believable, much less understandable. Malcolm wondered whether it might be some aspect of the man's German blood? They were a notable people and talented, but they had produced many fierce tyrants. Did unlimited power perhaps bring out the worst in them? Were not the Huns of old noted for their ferocity?

As they talked, the other noted the prince's frequent scratching of his person. On this being mentioned, Charles admitted that he seemed to have the itch, these days – not to be wondered at, perhaps, in the conditions he had been enduring, dwelling in cow byres, his clothing dirty. Somewhat diffidently Malcolm asked whether His Highness would wish him to search him for lice? To which he was told, if he was not off-put by the thought of it, that it would indeed be appreciated.

So there, in that woodman's hut, the heir to the ancient House of Stewart slipped off his clothing, and his companion made a careful and thorough examination of his person, with as much delicacy as was possible, and ended up by removing no fewer than eighty

172

nits from the royal body, surely, as he declared, an almost unique experience.

When, gratefully, Charles re-dressed, he took the opportunity to exchange his fine scarlet tartan waistcoat, with the gold buttons, for the other's plainer one, remarking that one day he would present his friend with a still better one, the day that he walked the streets of London town in his philabeg or kilt!

Restless with all the lying and sitting about, Charles, in the late afternoon, ventured outside and cautiously went down to the edge of the woodland and the track, looking around to ensure that their area was still clear of folk. That is what he set out to look for; but swiftly his gaze was drawn otherwhere. They were almost at a branching of the glen, and consequent widening of prospect; and beyond this, to front and right, was the most stupendous, arresting vista which he had ever seen. He knew the mountains of north Italy, of course, magnificent as these could be. But here before him soared a dark array of mighty, jagged peaks and dizzy pinnacles, with yawning gaps between, linked by sheer naked rock precipices and savage escarpments, to form a daunting barrier of all but overhanging height, threatening in its strange, majestic dominance. Dark, all but black, that is, on their right hand; but ahead, only slightly less challenging, the clustered summits were reddish, the corries and chasms between strangely, smokily blue by contrast, the whole a quite extraordinary and all but overwhelming scene. Nothing of this had been apparent, of course, in the half-dark of their arrival.

Charles, staring all but askance at it all, found Malcolm at his side.

"No unwelcome callers?" he observed. "We are fortunate. I see that you are struck by what we have before us! The Cuillins. The Black and the Red. Fierce, are they not, the Black menacing, the Red burning. That is MacDonald's Forest."

"I, I have never seen the like! *Mon Dieu*, they, they appal!"

"They could be scarcely our friends, these mountains, but could aid us nevertheless. For amongst them no man lingers. And they cut off Mackinnon's land from the rest."

"These are the Cuillins, yes?"

"Cuillin. More correctly Cuchullins, the mountains of the Fell Hound, the chief of the demons, who brews great storms up there! You have not heard the ancient story? Cu-Chulinn, *cu* meaning

173

hound in our tongue. Culand, the old druids' smith, who hammered out the earth from the Sun God, had his hound, which he left to guard this his chosen abode, up there, while he went to forge new worlds in the sky, the stars! You can hear the Fell Hound's howling of a night. Perhaps we shall this night, as we journey on!"

"Spare us that! Do we have to go there? Over that!"

"Through it, rather. Between the Black and the Red. There are ways through. We have to thread the Red Cuillins later, by passes, to reach Strathaird. Now you know why I would have gone by boat! But we will do it. Your Providence, Highness, will see us through, Fell Hound or none!"

They went back to their shed, Charles silent. He was of an impressionable nature.

They had to wait late, for real darkness, for they had no option but to pass close to the little community of Sligachan ahead, and they wanted all therein to be abed. A more unlikely place for any community the prince could not envisage. Presumably the woodcutter whose hut they were using haled from there. Malcolm had heard that Sir Alexander kept a permanent guard there, at the northern gateway as it were, to his main territory of the Sleat peninsula.

When, presently, they did pass within a few hundred yards of the houses, no light showed. Admittedly a dog barked briefly, but that was all. Malcolm was relieved to be past Sligachan.

Now the glen of the same name opened before them, south-wards, if glen it could be called, more of a deep and narrow chasm slashed between the two towering masses of mountains, Black and Red. Even in the darkness, the jaws of this seemed to yawn. Into them the walkers headed, not unaffected by the strange feeling of menace of it all, the menace not of men but of the mighty hostile terrain itself.

For a mile or two the going was not particularly difficult, although they had to wade across a number of incoming burns rushing to join the Sligachan River. But the cataracts and waterfalls of the river itself warned them that they were going to be climbing now. Picking their way over another upheaved mile or so, Malcolm kept peering to his left, eastwards. Sometime soon, he said, they would have to turn off, and then really face their challenge. For his part, Charles found his present going challenge enough.

It was soon that, at a stretch where the river was not making so much noise with its cascading, he heard another sound, a weird and

174

distant howling and moaning, which rose and fell, coming from he knew not where.

"You get it?" Malcolm asked. "The Fell Hound! I wondered if we would hear it."

"What – where is it coming from? It sounds . . . all around!"

"It is from up on the summits of the Black Cuillins. The highest tops. On our right. The winds there, they say . . ."

"But there are no great winds tonight."

"These mountains make their own winds. As the Rhum mountains make their own clouds. Have you seen those? Up there is a different world. Let us be thankful that it is not up yonder that we turn!"

"We turn?"

"Aye. Any time now. Left-handed. Up into the Reds. Demanding enough, I think, but . . ."

Shortly thereafter, they reached one more incoming burn, but this was wilder, and even in the darkness its white water raced to contribute to the river. But they did not have to cross this. Malcolm pointed eastwards and made an upward gesture. He did not have to elaborate.

Up the steep side of this torrent, more waterfall than burn, they turned and started to climb, really climb now. It was difficult to tell whether there was a track or not, amongst all the rocks and bends and obstacles, but Malcolm seemed to know his way approximately, keeping fairly close to the splashing water as he slowly mounted, edging this way and that, often having to use hands and bare knees to surmount obstructions. If this was a pass, as had been indicated, over to Strathaird, then small wonder that the Mackinnons remained detached from other clans.

Charles was too breathless to make comment.

That seemed an endless ascent, in which they paused many times to regain breath. But in time the burn did narrow, which was a hopeful sign, less and less water. So they must be nearing where it rose, a watershed.

At length the ground began to level out, and their toiling blessedly eased off. Charles was vaguely aware of great landmasses rearing on either side still, so they were entering some sort of valley, however lofty. And although there had been almost no breeze down in Glen Sligachan, a wind whistled through here. Drawing in behind a great rock fallen from above, Malcolm suggested a rest.

"This is the beallach, the pass," he panted. "We are between the tops of Ben Dearg, that one, and Marsco, the higher, behind us. That is the worst over. Half a mile of this and then it is downhill, towards Loch Ainort. Much longer, but less steep and rocky a descent."

"Praise the good Lord! That was a sore road to travel, indeed! Are your shoes, your brogans, still holding together? Mine do, I think, under all the mud. We are not barefoot yet!"

They moved on, the going infinitely easier here in the pass, that local wind at their backs. They could no longer hear the odd howling from the other range.

Presently they began to lose height, and a new burn developed at their side, going in the other direction. This would take them down a quite lengthy corrie, right to sea-level, Malcolm said. Three miles or so. Better going. But he was concerned about timing again. It had taken them longer to get this far than he had hoped. And there were two small communities down there at the Loch Ainort shore. They did not want to be seen, not yet.

"But is not this the Mackinnon land? Where we will be secure?"

"Scarcely yet. We have another, but lesser, crossing to make. Hereabouts there will be MacDonalds still, as well as Mackinnons. And even so, when we are in Strathaird itself, it would be wise not to reveal your identity, Highness. Safer that there be no talk. Mackinnon tongues could wag, loyal as they are, and others hear of it. However friendly, the word could get around."

"Am I so evident?" Charles demanded. "Lewie Caw, your servant!"

"I fear that you are, sir. Unmistakable, if I may say so!"

"Then I must disguise myself the more. Shall I blacken my face? Mud on it? Part cover it with my old kerchief, sufficiently dirty!"

"I doubt if that would serve. It is not only your features and hair. It is your whole bearing. You always carry yourself like the prince you are. All remark on it."

"*Ma foi*, you make me sound a prideful wretch! What am I to do? Crouch and creep!"

"Better that we go only by darkness. Until we reach my sister's house at Elgol."

Down that long corrie they were heading eastwards and, sure enough, before they were much more than halfway down, the dawn was beginning to lighten the sky before them. Soon they would see

176

the waters of Loch Ainort ahead, leaden but still wide and evident. They must now look out for a hiding-place, Malcolm asserted.

This time they did find a cave of sorts, amongst the crags near the mouth of the corrie, no convenient bothy or shed in evidence. But it gave them cover and made an excellent viewpoint, looking out over a farflung vista of the Inner Sound and its islands towards the mainland Lochs Carron and Alsh. They settled down to pass a hungry day after an energetic night. This matter of food supply remained as difficult as ever.

After adequate sleep, Charles entertained his companion with stories of his youth in Italy, of his father James the Eighth and Third, who had married an Italian wife, Mary of Modena, and of his brother Henry Benedict, who had entered the Church, who was indeed already a bishop, although aged only a score of years. Although reared a Catholic himself, the prince admitted that he was not a perfervid one, and he indeed deplored his grandfather's rigid attitudes, which had resulted in his banishment from mainly Protestant England. Had James the Second and Seventh been less entrenched in his religion, there would have been no need for this Jacobite movement and these campaigns, and his own father would have been sitting on his throne at London. Malcolm asked, what of Scotland? The Stewarts had been Kings of Scots only, until 1603. Would the prince and his father be prepared to return to that status, breaking up James the Sixth and First's United Kingdom, if England still rejected him or them? King of Scots again only? Charles said that he could not speak for his father, for that question had never come up, to his knowledge; but for himself, he would consider it.

In the late evening they made a move, not going right down to the loch shore where the houses were but keeping well up on the slopes for a couple of rough miles. Quite a major hill, if scarcely a mountain such as they had left, called Glas Ben, was soaring on their right, and they had to work their way round this, without touching Luib, a fair-sized community below its northern slopes, and so into the major valley of Strath Mor, running due southwards, which cut off the whole peninsula of Strathaird and gave it its name. Once through that, and they could go less warily.

The crossing of the high shoulder of Glas Ben did involve more climbing, for it was rocky and cliff-girt, but nothing to compare with the previous night's efforts. And once they were able to descend into the four-mile-long valley, the going was easier, a track of sorts all the way. Dawn saw them facing another sea loch, that of Slapin, but this opening due southwards and not into the Inner Sound. Now they were in Strathaird proper, and once they were round the bend of this loch, a mere two miles would bring them across the peninsula to their destination at Elgol. They could risk it in daylight, if the prince was not weary?

Charles was all for doing that.

That remaining walk was again dominated by the Black Cuillins, which now reared on their right, to the west, six or so miles off, another aspect of them but just as awesome and ominous, with a vast horseshoe indenture visible, which could scarcely be called a valley or a corrie, more of a daunting cauldron, opening into the grim heart of them, with its walls thousands of feet high towering on all sides save this to seawards; a dark and louring place indeed, even in midday sunlight. Malcolm said that within it was confined what he judged was the dourest sheet of water in all the Highlands and Isles, Loch Coruisk, secret and bleak under the encircling array of peaks. That was the Fell Hound's washbasin, he averred, no place for mankind.

They were glad to be able to turn their backs on that prospect, draw the eye as it did.

Soon they were into lower-lying and populated country, even though scarcely populous, Mackinnons', with scattered crofts and some fair-sized farmeries. Charles remarked on the difficulties there must be in living in such a cut-off and isolated place, and was told that practically all communications and links were by boat, across the sea lochs of Scavaig, Slapin and Eishort, allowing access to the Sound of Sleat and the mainland as well as the Minch. The Mackinnons were great boat-people, necessarily. But it was to be doubted indeed whether the warships would be patrolling *these* waters. This was why His Highness had been brought here.

Even so, they avoided houses and people, at this stage, as far as was possible, by holding to the higher ground of two comparatively modest hills, Bens Meabost and Cleatt. They did see folk, but at a distance.

But in mid-afternoon, with the community of Elgol in sight ahead at the shore of Loch Scavaig, they came, round a shoulder, on three men repairing the stonework of a sheep-fank, of use for lambing, dipping and shearing. There was no way that they could avoid these, without actually turning back, which was unthinkable. Charles hastily tied that kerchief, which had been round his neck, partly to cover head and brow. Also he dropped behind his companion, servant-like, with the baggage.

Malcolm, coming up with them, greeted the trio civilly, mentioned that he was MacLeod of Brea come to visit his sister, Mistress Mackinnon of Elgol, and hoping that she was at home? He was told, respectfully, that she was, but that the captain, her husband, was away visiting the chief at Kilmane. But while they answered him thus, the three men's eyes were more on Charles, although he stood well back. Indeed they stared.

The prince turned away. But he was near enough to hear their voices. They spoke in the Gaelic of course; but certain words registered, *Tearlach* which he knew meant Charles, *prionnsa*, which was prince, *ban*, which in Doric would be bonny; and he knew that the troops of his army had called him Bonny Prince Charlie. So, there it was. He was known, recognised. These men must have been in the Mackinnon company, and seen him many times. He turned back, and moved over to greet them.

The men's reactions were varied, with obvious doubts as to how they should behave, but all showed wonder and distress at his plight, almost disbelief, head-shaking, one actually with tears in his eyes. Charles smiled and waved a hand reassuringly, saying, "*Failt' ort! La math duit.*" Which was as far as his Gaelic went.

They bobbed heads and made suitable remarks, unintelligible to their hearer.

Malcolm, waving, led the way onward.

They were down to the levels of the loch shore soon. On a mound, where a burn reached salt water, a larger house was set, overlooking all. Malcolm, ever cautious, did not approach it directly, but led the prince around, inland a little way, to cross the burn by a plank bridge, and go on down to the beach behind the house. He would go forward alone, to prospect, and ensure that there was no one with his sister who might constitute a danger.

Alone on the shore, eyeing those fierce mountains across the water, Charles had not long to wait. His friend came back to say that all was clear. He had told his sister whom he had brought; but to the servants there the prince was still to be Lewie Caw, for safety's sake.

179

They went back to Elgol House, where Charles was greeted by a comely young woman who started to curtsy, recollected that this was vetoed, and shook her head instead, flushing, unable to seem to pay little attention to her brother's attendant. She quite hastily turned to lead them into a private room, and shut the door.

"Sir! Your Royal Highness, this is beyond all belief!" she exclaimed, and performed her curtsy now, but still head ashake. "I could not . . . my brother said not to . . . Oh, what can I say, Highness?"

"Say that you will not allow my coming unduly to trouble you, lady," she was told. "I fear that I cause much upset, whilst wishing only good, well-being. Your good brother has helped me greatly. My sorrow that I endanger all, in my misfortunes."

"Some food, Meg, of a mercy!" Malcolm put in. "We have not eaten for long. And we would wash, mud-covered as we are. We have ploughed through bogs a-many, in the darkness . . ."

"Yes – oh, yes. Katie will bring hot water. I will see to the providing." She hurried off, much flustered.

"Living here, Meg sees but few visitors, especially highborn ones," her brother explained.

A maid quickly appeared, with a pail of steaming water. She giggled. "I am to wash your legs, sir," she announced. "Where have you been to get in such a slouster!"

"We have walked far to get here. Lacking horses," she was told.

Ignoring Charles, she went to kneel at the table where Malcolm sat, and when he began to draw off his brogans and short hose, coated in peat mud, she insisted on doing it for him, clearly much tickled and enjoying herself. She went on very thoroughly to wash his bare legs, by no means stopping at his knees. He grinned over at the prince.

But when she was satisfied, all but reluctantly she picked up her pail, and made for the door.

"Katie, not so fast!" Malcolm said. "There are two of us. You see this poor man there, Lewie Caw. He needs your washing also."

"No such thing!" the girl exclaimed. "Although I'll wash his master, it's not for me to wash his servant!"

"Oh, but you must. He needs it equally."

"Not from me! He's nothing but a lowborn countrywoman's

180

son! I will leave the water, if you say so. He can wash himself."

"I insist!" Malcolm said. "Do as you are told."

"Heed not," Charles laughed. "This young woman has her own standards!"

"She will do as I say, whatever."

The maid, sulky now, came back to the prince, set down her pail jerkily so that the water slopped over, pulled off his brogans roughly, making faces, then his half-hose, and began to splash his legs in slapdash style, and, to express her feelings further, went dabbing and poking well above the knees, pushing his kilt up.

"Save us, Captain, I would you desire this girl not to go so far up!" Charles exclaimed, making his own face at her, brows raised, and crossing his legs.

With a sniff and a flick back of her hair, Katie got up, deliberately spilt some more water, and flounced out of the room.

"I see that I have much to learn as a servant!" Charles said. "An education, indeed!"

"I am sorry. A minx, that one!"

"Blame her not. She teaches me my place!"

Meg Mackinnon returned to tell them that a cold meal was laid out for them in another room, and later something hot would follow. The men did not complain about her maid's behaviour.

They ate heartily thereafter, in between yawns, for they had not slept for over twenty-four hours. Noting this, their hostess said that she would prepare couches for them, weary as they must be. Her husband ought to be back shortly from Kilmane, from seeking the Mackinnon; but let them sleep meantime.

Thankfully they did as she said.

Charles was a sound sleeper, as he had proved ere this, and did not awake when Meg came in to announce that her husband was back. Malcolm rose and went out with her.

Roused later by his friend, the prince was told that Captain John Mackinnon had arrived and was happy to co-operate in efforts to get them over to the mainland. Unfortunately Malcolm had been proved wrong in his belief that warships would not be appearing hereabouts as yet, for in fact three frigates were now visible out at the mouth of Loch Scavaig. Unhappy as he was to see these, indication that the government forces believed that their quarry was now in these parts, he had used the sight of these vessels to introduce his testing subject of the prince's presence, asking his brother-in-law what he would think if the royal fugitive had been captured and was held aboard one of the ships. To which John Mackinnon had said God forbid that there could be any such thing! Then he had been asked whether, if the prince arrived here at Elgol, would he seek to preserve his safety, John declaring strongly that His Highness would be safe with him, indeed he wished that he might so serve him. So, that commitment ensured, he had been told the facts.

Charles went out to meet Mackinnon, but on the way, in the next room, came across instead a child, the small son of the house. Fond of children, he picked the little boy up, and tossing him about in his arms, and singing a song to him, entirely forgot his servant's role; and then Mackinnon was brought to him. Presenting his son to him, Charles declared that one day, who knew, this child might be as good a captain in his service as had been his father!

Much moved by this confrontation and greeting, the other had difficulty in controlling his feelings. He had seen the prince frequently before, but never had had any personal contact. When he could gather his thoughts and emotions, he assured that he would be proud to serve His Highness, and with his life, if need be.

Soon they were discussing how and where to arrange for a boat to take the prince over to the mainland. In view of those three ships seen off this Loch Scavaig, Malcolm thought that the effort should be made from the other, eastern, side of the Strathaird peninsula, to row southwards to round the Point of Sleat, and so across the sound to the nearest place on the mainland Morar shore, Mallaig. The Chief of Mackinnon's house of Kilmane was on that east coast, some five miles away. No doubt they could arrange for a boat and oarsmen to be readied.

Captain John agreed, but said that the chief was old and getting infirm, although an honest, stout and good man. Better, probably, that he himself should ride across and seek to make the arrangements, in the chief's name. He would go at once, and, who knew, they might be able to sail that night.

Charles went back to playing with the child, to the delight of the mother, while her husband returned whence he had just come, from Kilmane.

He was back sooner than was expected. For, part-way there, he had met old Mackinnon himself, not so infirm it seemed, for he had been riding to see one of his tenants who was sick. And when told of the prince's presence on his land, nothing would do but that he must see him and pay his respects. Not only that, but he insisted that he himself would take His Highness over to Mallaig, the least that he could do. He would have a boat prepared, and manned, and bring it round to the west coast here. Evidently a determined and forceful character, as befitted a clan chief, old as he might be, he said that the prince should not remain at Elgol House meantime, in case those damnable shipmen sent search-parties ashore. Better that he went to hide in a cave a mile or so to the south, near the Strathaird headland, beside the little haven of Port an Luib, where the boat could put in and collect him in the darkening.

Clearly, in Strathaird the chief's decisions were not to be argued with. So, after another meal, and given more food to take with them in the boat, Charles took leave of his hostess and her child, and with the two captains set off on the short walk to the rendezvous, this as the sun was setting. Out at the loch mouth, wide as it was, they could see a ship outlined against the golden brilliance.

The coast near the headland was typically cliff-bound, and at a deep inlet therein they were led to a shallow cave halfway down. Evidently it was used by local fishermen, for there were nets and lobster-creels stored in it.

Captain John left the two others there, to go down to the haven and await the boat. There were no houses nor indeed other boats there.

As they waited, Malcolm announced that he was thankful to be leaving the prince in good hands, for he himself would be turning back now. At Charles's voiced regret, he pointed out that there was nothing now that he might contribute usefully, the Mackinnons to be trusted to take him to the mainland; also his own absence from home might arouse suspicions, and he had his family to think of. There might already be enemy searching for him. Anyway, if he knew old Mackinnon, he would wish to be in full charge, and not want MacLeod assistance!

When Charles saw that his friend was determined in this, he told him how greatly indebted to him he was and how much he had appreciated his good company. He would not forget the Black and Red Cuillins and the Fell Hound; and one day hoped to welcome him to his court in London, or possibly in Edinburgh if that was how matters fell out and his father became only King of Scots. He gave him a grateful message for his cousins, John and Murdoch MacLeod.

Actually, from the cave mouth, they saw their boat arriving, clinging close to the shore as it came. Why it did this was clear, for the ship out there had been rejoined by the other two, and although they were perhaps almost two miles off, they represented menace.

Captain John came for them and they went down to the shore, where Charles was introduced to the Mackinnon, a heavily built elderly man with a limp but no lack of authority, who asserted his allegiance and loyalty but promptly made no secret of the fact that he judged the recent campaign and rising to have been but poorly led, the inference being that if *he* had been able to have been with his Mackinnon company, things might well have been different. Again the Lord George Murray was blamed.

John MacInnes, a Skyeman, and his boatmen stood beside their drawn-up craft, and were presented.

It was nearly nine o'clock, but not yet really dark, and there was some discussion as to whether to wait for a while or to push off forthwith. Malcolm advised waiting, because of those ships, but the old man said that if they kept in close to the land at first, they would not be evident from out there. And Charles, testing the air with a wet finger upraised, said that the wind was changing into the north, and those frigates would be likely to use it to sail southwards. Let them get off in the boat, round the headland, and so eastwards, drawing away from them.

As they were about to step into the boat, Charles drew his clay pipe, again with a broken stem, such being very apt to snap off when carried about. Malcolm made something of a little farewell ceremony of it, by pulling out his pistol and some tow from a pocket and by snapping the hammer once or twice against the flint, managed to create the necessary sparks which, in the tow, and blown upon, duly caught fire, to enable the tobacco to be lit, all but scorching the princely cheek in the doing of it.

Both laughing, this was as good a way of parting as any, Charles handing over a silver buckle as a keepsake, and clasping the other to him, patting his back.

Wordless now, Malcolm could only shake his head.

The travellers climbed aboard and pushed off, leaving the lone figure on the shore amongst the shadows.

16

It was not much more than a mile to the southern point of Strathaird, and this was protected, seawards, by a scatter of small isles. Once they were within the cover of these, there was no risk of them being seen from those ships. Moreover, they would hide them for sufficiently long as they turned eastwards.

The Mackinnon, who it transpired had taken part in the earlier Jacobite Rising of 1715, was strong on tactics and matters military, declaring that King James was unfortunate in his choices of field commanders then also, Bobbing John, Earl of Mar, having been as incompetent as Murray on this later occasion. Charles had to admit that mistakes had been made, some no doubt by himself. But that on the next attempt, he would ensure that proven strategists were put in charge. And he himself had learned a little, he thought.

It was some four miles across from Strathaird to the great Sleat peninsula, and after two miles of east-going, they decided that it was sufficiently dark for them to venture due southwards, for they had to go fully eight miles in that direction before they could round the Point of Sleat and head across the sound thereof for the mainland. Fortunately the now northerly wind aided them and they were able to hoist sail and to cover the distance in good time.

Mackinnon unburdened himself also as to his opinions of Sir Alexander MacDonald of Sleat. His father and two uncles had been out in the rising of thirty years before, and the cost of this for his clan had seemingly been sufficient to deter him on this occasion. The same applied to MacLeod of MacLeod, good blood turned weak, sour!

It was well after midnight before they rounded the Point of Sleat, to face the final crossing, another eight miles, Captain John said. The sea was roughening, with this rising north wind, but by tacking this way and that they could still use the sail.

The Mackinnon had brought a compass with him, so they were able to keep approximately in the right direction despite the darkness. Not that they could possibly miss the mainland shore; but they were anxious to reach, not Mallaig itself, which was a sizeable community and large harbour, the largest in Morar, but Mallaigbeg, a small haven a mile or so to the north, at the entry to the wide Loch Nevis. Their ultimate objective, of course, was to get down southwards to the Loch nan Uamh area of Arisaig, Young Clanranald's country; but they realised that this might well now be occupied by the military, and they must go warily. In the Loch Nevis and Knoydart country they must gain what information they could.

In the event, they became aware of land ahead around three a.m., and as they drew closer, reckoned that they must be too far to the south, for the loom of the land stretched unbroken before them, no wide loch mouth evident. So they turned north, and now had to row strongly against the wind, sail no longer of use. How far south of their mark they did not know, although the Mackinnon thought that they were probably off the Glasnacardoch vicinity.

His judgment was proved fairly accurate, for after an hour's northwards pulling the land faded away before them and they realised that they were facing Loch Nevis. So they had passed Mallaig itself on the way. Their chosen destination, Mallaigbeg, lay only a mile or so into the loch on its south and rocky shore, the first sizeable inlet there. A faint lightening of the sky ahead of them helped. They reckoned that sunrise would be in about an hour.

Presently they were able to perceive a distinct opening in the cliff-girt shore, and pulled into it. There were only two or three cottages at this Mallaigbeg, these to be avoided at this stage. So they beached at the far side of the little bay, in a sort of cove. Charles jumped out first, to set foot on mainland Scotland again after twelve weeks hiding in the Outer and Inner Hebrides, evading capture. Thankfully he stamped his feet on the pebbly beach, before turning to aid old Mackinnon out of the boat.

With sunrise, Captain John and one of the boatmen went off to discover what they could of the situation here, at the three cottages. They were soon back, to inform that two of the houses were empty and only an elderly fisherman occupying the third. He had been up and about, but exceedingly suspicious of visitors at this hour of the morning. On being reassured however that they represented no threat to him, he had declared that the land was ridden by evil strangers, all seeking that accursed Charles Edward Stuart who had brought this plague on all honest men, these sailors and militia ravaging, stealing, raping and taking men's boats. There was a great camp of them at Mallaigmore, where one of their ships was based; and a smaller group eastwards along this loch shore at Earnsaig, four miles away. The sooner they caught that wretched prince and left the country and decent folk in peace, he had added, the better!

This was scarcely the sort of news that they had hoped for. Clearly Mallaigbeg was no place to linger in. They decided to move further along this Loch Nevis shoreline at once, but not too far or they would get over-near this Earnsaig encampment, and in daylight, be seen. The old chief, who knew this coast better than his kinsman John did, said that there was quite a major hill, with corries in its sides, perhaps a couple of miles eastwards, and coming down quite close to the shore. Somewhere there they might land and hide.

So it was afloat again, and pulling away into the loch, new problems to worry them.

Quickly now they saw the high hill soaring out of lower ones, a jagged ridge not far ahead, its sides seamed with corries. With something of an internal groan, Charles recognised that he was back to hiding and skulking on mountainsides. This was not what he had returned to the mainland for.

They saw a tiny islet off a shallow bay at the foot of that hill, and reckoned that this would be as good a place to draw in and go to ground as any, cover for the boat, and with a burn descending in waterfalls from one of the corries, thus giving access to the high ground. But the Mackinnon eyed those steep slopes more than doubtfully. Not for him climbing and clambering, they all could understand.

Fortunately, landed, they found a sheltered hollow not far from the beach and beside a pool below the first of the waterfalls, with much broken rock around. Here they could settle meantime, and with scrub birch around, be able to light a fire and cook some of the oatmeal they had brought, smoke unlikely to be evident in these circumstances. Now it fell to the prince to demonstrate the techniques of building shelters out of stones, turf, branches and their plaiding, he the experienced practitioner.

187

They built, ate and slept, that 5th day of July, one always on watch.

It was on Captain John's turn at this duty that, in the early evening, he came to rouse the others, declaring that there was a warship out on the loch, presumably the one based at Mallaig. Alarmed, they all went out on to a nearby hummock where they could peer lochwards without being obvious. There the frigate lay, perhaps halfway between them and the Knoydart shore to the north, apparently at anchor.

What could be the reason for this? Did it mean that there were suspicions as to the prince's presence? Already? Had somebody, somewhere, talked? Or was it something to do with the militiamen camped at this Earnsaig?

They left one of the boatmen to keep watch, in case of a boat being sent ashore from that ship.

They did not risk a fire that evening. Charles and the old chief talked late into the night. Fortunately the weather remained fine, so their shelter did not leak.

In the morning that frigate was still there. What were they to do? They could not risk launching their boat before darkness. And anyway, in these circumstances, where were they to sail to? Without better information. They needed to know what the position was in the south, where they wanted to be, in Morar, Arisaig and Moidart, before they might venture thither, if at all. Loch nan Uamh, the recognised calling-place for French ships, was the prince's goal. He explained to his companions the peculiar situation regarding this of the ships. Britain and France not being officially at war, French vessels, warships at least, could come and go without being attacked, although they might be put to question. So the *Mars* and the *Bellona* had been able to bring, and land, all that French gold to Loch nan Uamh, which Donald MacLeod had told him about, two weeks too late to be of any real use.

They decided that there was nothing for it but to wait where they were until either the frigate moved off, or they could get reliable news as to conditions further south.

Unable to lie about idly all day, Charles and John did climb up their corrie and into the safety of the hills behind, hoping to get within pistol-shot of grouse or other wildfowl, but with no success. The muskets had long been left behind. Food, with seven of them to supply, was again becoming a problem.

Next morning, with the frigate gone, the chief declared that he would go over to Mallaig itself, not by boat which might arouse questioning but cross-country, less than three miles. He was quite capable of such walking; it was the climbing which he could not face. He was not known personally in Mallaig and, an old man, would not be likely to be suspected. He would take only one of the boatmen with him, and they would make discreet enquiries as to the situation hereabouts and in the south. Charles and John protested that this was unsuitable, the latter saying that *he* should go; but the old chief was determined. He was perfectly capable of it, and a younger man might well be suspected. They would bring back some provisions, much needed.

Dutifully, if doubtfully, the others saw them off.

Time thereafter hanging heavily, Charles suggested that, the warship gone, they might risk taking the boat some little way eastwards along the loch shore, to see if they could find a croft or fisherman's house where they might obtain food, hunger the spur. The chief and his companion would not be able to carry much back with them, all the way from Mallaig; and seven men required quite a deal of feeding. They must not go so far east as this place Earnsaig, of course.

It was agreed, and the five of them set off in the boat.

That coast consisted of a series of small headlands and shallow bays. Keeping close in, they examined the first two, but saw no houses, the hillsides behind becoming ever more wooded, they noted. Thereafter there was a longish stretch of plain shoreline and then a larger promontory with an islet beyond. Rounding the quite sharp bend of this, they were suddenly confronted with the unexpected.

It was not a house or croft that they came upon but another boat, beached quite close round that corner; and on the shore, five men standing. These were near enough to have visible on their bonnets the red crosses of government-supporting militia, the English equivalent of the Scottish saltire.

Much alarmed, the rowers hastily backed-water, to turn and away, but not before a call came across to them demanding who they were and where they had come from.

"We are from Sleat," John, at one of the four oars, shouted back, hoping that they would be taken for pro-government MacDonalds. And he urged the prince to lie down flat on the floorboards and to cover himself with a plaid, not to be seen. He and the other three did not halt in their rowing.

His reply obviously did not satisfy the militiamen. Not one hundred yards away, they ordered the boat to turn and beach, waving muskets.

The effect of that was to make the oarsmen row harder than ever, back to round that headland.

More shouts from behind sped them on.

Before they were able to turn the promontory they saw the other boat putting off after them. Charles, rising to gaze, was curtly ordered to keep down.

There was no need for other instructions, nor breath therefor, the oarsmen pulling at their hardest. And to good effect, for when, well past the headland, they saw the other craft appearing round it, they judged that they were making the better time of it, the militiamen being presumably less expert with oars than the three fishermen islanders and John.

As they reached that wider stretch, westwards, John panted that this was all very well but what now? They could not just go on and on, the other craft following, even though they were gaining on it. They would still be in sight if they turned into their own bay and shelter. That would give all away.

Charles, still lying prostrate, suggested that they turn into the next bay, this backed by the woodland, leaving the boat, and disappear into the trees. These soldiers would never find them there.

"But that would lose us the boat," John objected. "And we must have it. They would either take it or sink it."

"Better that than being caught. Taken. The woodland would save us."

"We could land, yes. Hide. But not far back. Within pistol-shot. And if they began to take our boat, shoot! We have two pistols, yours and mine. Prime them."

"No, no – no shooting!" the prince exclaimed. "No needless bloodshed."

"Better that than being captured, or to lose our boat, for we need it."

"Ye-e-es." Charles was doubtful. He had vowed to himself that there should be no more killing in his cause if it could be helped.

"You would not yield yourself, Highness?"

190

"No. Not that. Indeed I had rather fight for my life than be taken, yes. Taken prisoner," he admitted. "Fight, yes, but not shoot men in cold blood! There are but five of them, and five of us. We could rush them . . ."

"They have muskets . . ."

Covering that stretch of open coastline, and gaining obviously on the other boat, round the next headland they turned sharply in, under cover of it, and rowed hard for the shore with its woodland, Charles upright again now. There were one or two little coves at the head of the bay, where burns entered, and making for one of these, with rock-strewn jaws which might help to hide their boat, they beached, pulled the craft up, and headed for the cover of the trees. Their boat would not be seen from any distance, but would not remain undiscovered if there was any search.

They did not go far but waited, hidden, to watch for developments, ready either to fight for their boat or, if muskets were going to be used against them, to flee uphill through the woods.

Presently they saw the enemy craft appear out at the mouth of the bay. But it did not turn in after them, and continued to be rowed across. These were small bays, of course, and the next headland only some three hundred yards further. No doubt the militiamen thought that their quarry had already got that far and out of sight behind it. With sighs of relief, the watchers saw their foes themselves disappear around the point.

They waited. And as time passed and the other boat did not reappear, John asked whether this was the closest contact that the prince had made to the enemy searching for him? And what he thought would be the result if they indeed captured him? Would he be sent prisoner to London? And there held? Or . . . even executed?

"I do not think that they would execute me, not openly, in public," he was told. "But these Hanoverians might well arrange to get rid of me secretly. They would not wish to offend and displeasure the other monarchs of Christendom. But I might be disposed of in some devious fashion. But God spare the king, my father, and my brother from such . . . affliction!"

"Amen to that!" John said.

They had quite some time to wait before they saw the other boat come back into view. Whether it had been searching the other bays in the meantime they did not know, but if so, the foe seemed to have given up the chase, for the craft did not turn in towards them but continued on across, to pass out of sight beyond this eastern headland.

Thankfully the watchers praised God. The pistols could be unprimed.

They still waited there, however, for some time, just in case a watch was being kept out there on the open water. But, after perhaps an hour, they esteemed themselves safe to venture forth.

They saw nothing to alarm them as they left that bay, but they kept close inshore westwards thereafter nevertheless.

Back safely to their shelter, they found the Mackinnon already returned from Mallaig. And he had news. The prince was suspected to be on the mainland now, and in this neighbourhood, and the search was being concentrated hereabouts and down to Moidart, nearly all the warships come from the outer waters, and General Campbell himself now in Mallaig – grim tidings. But there was some rather better news also. Clanranald was said to be none so far off, indeed just across this Loch Nevis. He had left Benbecula after his wife had been put in house arrest; and his brother, Boisdale, had been sent south a prisoner, and was now thought to be staying with his daughter at the house of Scotus in Knoydart. She had been married to MacDonald of Scotus, who had been killed leading a charge at Culloden.

This information at least gave the fugitives some hope of assistance and guidance. Clanranald ought to know the situation of his son Young Clanranald, and what went on at Arisaig and Loch nan Uamh.

It was decided that, in the darkness of the night, Captain John and Charles should be rowed across the loch the five miles or so to Scotus. Old Mackinnon would remain at Mallaigbeg with his one boatman until they returned, when they would be able to make further plans.

One more night-time sailing, then. The chief said that there was an island a little way off the Knoydart coast near Scotus. Probably it would be wise to leave the prince on that while John went to see what was the position at the house and whether Clanranald was indeed there.

They waited until quite late before sailing, with only five miles to go. No point in John arriving at Scotus in the middle of the night.

There was no difficulty encountered in their sail, for the wind was back in the south-west, not strong but sufficient to help them on their way. They did have something of a problem in finding the right isle, however, in the darkness, for there proved to be three or four small ones off this Knoydart shore. But eventually they found one distinctly larger than the others, and they took this to be the one the chief had meant. They pulled in, landed, just before dawn, and wrapping themselves in their plaids, slept.

Daylight proved them to be a bare quarter-mile off one more cliff-bound coast, with a major waterfall cascading down close enough for them to hear the noise of it. And less than a mile to the north-east they could see a level stretch of grassland, and on it a large whitewashed house, Scotus without a doubt.

John informed Charles about this Knoydart. It was a large, mountainous and comparatively empty land, hardly a peninsula but bounded on three sides by sea lochs and sound, MacDonald territory again but of the Glengarry branch of the great clan, Scotus having been a chieftain of a sept thereof. It was understood that he had left a small son, who would be Clanranald's grandson. There was a senior chieftain, MacDonald of Knoydart itself; but he lived at Inverie, further to the east.

There was no sign of any ships out in the loch behind them; and in the early forenoon John and the boatmen set off for Scotus, leaving the prince alone on the isle, to resume his sleeping. He was becoming almost more used to sleeping by day than by night.

He was awakened by the return of his friends, John in an angry mood. They had seen Clanranald, yes, but he had proved a grave disappointment, a soured man, wanting apparently nothing more to do with the prince. He had actually called His Highness a muckle devil, for bringing down all this trouble on the Highlands and Islands; and if he was now hereabouts, then he, Clanranald, wanted nothing more to do with him. He and his had suffered sufficiently. Here he was himself all but a hunted fugitive, exiled from his own Outer Isles to this Knoydart, his brother a prisoner, his wife confined to her house, his kinsman, MacDonald of Borrodale, formerly the prince's host down in Arisaig, living in a bothy, his house having been burned down. As to Young Clanranald, the father did not know where he was nor how he fared.

John had apparently told the other what he thought of him for adopting this attitude, and there had been words between them.

Clanranald's only advice to the Mackinnon was to take Charles back to Raasay or Rona, which, having been already searched, would probably give him refuge for a time. His daughter, however, like others of the womenfolk, had been more helpful, despite the loss of her husband in the royal cause, suggesting that they should head south to MacDonald of Morar, whom she understood was at home, and loyal. He might help them on their way.

Charles was much upset over this of Clanranald. Ever distressed that his needs caused so much trouble and danger for others, he felt unhappy indeed, declaring his sorrow at the pain his plight was bringing to others; but adding that there was no help for it – they must do the best they could for themselves, not rely on others. That is, if the good Mackinnons were still prepared to aid him?

John's response to that was almost violently positive.

They had to wait again for darkness to make the crossing back to Mallaigbeg, a slower progress this time, with the wind now in their faces.

When they wakened old Mackinnon, in due course, to tell him what had transpired, he was as critical of Clanranald as was John, and as vehement as to his continued support and help for the prince. He agreed that they should strike south for Morar, but not in daylight. It would have to be done overland, none so far, perhaps eight miles. Going by boat it would be more than double that, and having to pass Mallaig itself, they could not risk it with all these warships about. He knew this MacDonald of Morar, a man almost as old as himself, and he reckoned that they could rely on him. But they could not go by daylight, with so much searching being concentrated in the area – although remaining even here, the more dangerous it became. They would leave the boatmen and their craft here meantime.

That day, as they waited, there developed a long discussion on the clan system and the responsibilities of chiefs and chieftains, to their people as well as to their monarch. Which had priority, when lives and homes were at stake? The Mackinnons had no doubts, declaring that the clansfolk had themselves the duty of loyalty to their rightful king, in line with their chief's; but Charles said that there could be another point of view, he recognised, such as Sleat, MacLeod of MacLeod and now Clanranald were adopting, that loyalty could bear too harshly on their people, in defeat, and that the chief's responsibility was to cherish and protect. Was

194

he, therefore, the transgressor in continuing to bring down hurt on his father's subjects? Yet, he could not just yield himself up, to save them.

His hearers shook their heads over such doubts.

Evening saw them saying farewell to the boatmen, and on their way.

17

Their walk across the moors and hillocks behind Mallaig and Glasnacardoch, averaging a mile inland from the coast, was not particularly difficult, save in that there were two longish lochs to be avoided, which involved some marshy circling. And they had to go more slowly than the younger men would have done, on account of the chief. But no complaints were forthcoming, even when the eastern sky was lightening well before they reached Morar. This area had its claims to distinction, other than over the activities of its MacDonald owners; for it contained two especial features: what was probably the shortest river in Scotland, and one of the largest freshwater lochs to lie within half a mile of the sea, the River Morar crossing that same brief distance and into a deep bay, the loch probing inland for a dozen miles, and one of the deepest in the land, said to give refuge to some strange water creature similar to that reputed to inhabit Loch Ness in the Great Glen. Morar House and community necessarily had to be clustered there at the only crossing-place in the dozen miles. Not that the travellers had to cross that strategic bridge, for their destination was on the northern side; but they did have to ford a lesser though longer stream, which issued from the second of the lochs they had had to circle. And approaching this, despite the early hour of the morning, they fell in with a small party from the scatter of crofts called Beoraidbeg, heading in the same direction, these seeing them and waiting, not to be avoided. Charles hastily resumed the role of Lewie Caw, limping behind the Mackinnons and taking the luggage, also wrapping that kerchief round his head again.

Oddly, this produced a rather similar incident to the foot-washing situation at Elgol, for John, wishing to emphasise that the third member of the trio *was* only a servant, perhaps overdid it by declaring that the man Lewie was sickly, unfortunately, and when they came to the said ford suggested that a strapping young man in the party might take the poor fellow across the water, pick-a-back, to have his request rejected outright with scorn, the other saying that he was certainly not going to carry any servant on his back, but would indeed give the old gentleman a lift gladly. The chief came to the rescue then by announcing that, if their servant must wade, he would wade with him, and taking Charles's arm, stepped stoutly into the fast-running water, John hastily taking the other arm. The prince was certainly learning something about Highland pride.

But such thoughts were quickly superseded when, at Morar itself, this side of the short river and the bridge, they found the mansion-house a burned-out shell, along with sundry of the cottages. They were told by local folk that the laird and his wife were presently biding in a bothy in woodland nearby. The English sailors had been here.

The three of them made their way, as directed, and duly found MacDonald of Morar and his lady, who proved to be a sister of the Cameron chief, Lochiel, one of the prince's most prominent supporters, making the best of conditions in a secluded herd's cottage.

On learning the identity of their visitors, husband and wife could not have been more welcoming, whilst apologising for the standard of hospitality they had to offer, proud to be hosts, even so, to His Royal Highness. It seemed that the notorious Captain Fergusson had brought his ship into Morar Bay, and with this result. Charles had to express his sorrow and distress at what his cause was costing once again.

Over a meal, the situation was discussed. Morar said that he was uncertain as to conditions south in the Arisaig area, and had heard nothing of any French ships coming to Loch nan Uamh; but he believed that Young Clanranald was none so far off, he having visited them only two days previously, on his way to see his father at Scotus. If the prince could contact him . . .

Charles was both enheartened and vexed by this news, vexed that they had apparently missed his most valued adherent, at Scotus, by only a day or two, but hopeful that Young Clanranald would be able to help now, if he could be reached. Morar said that while his wife would endeavour to arrange as comfortable sleeping accommodation for the visitors as present circumstances allowed, for rest after their night's walking, he himself would ride to Scotus in Knoydart – he could cover the less than twenty miles or so, by Tarbet, on a garron in three hours

– and either bring back Young Clanranald, or his advice and guidance.

This was gratefully received, and the three travellers were glad to repair to a nearby cave, where they were able to couch down on plaids laid on straw, feeling fed and encouraged.

However, when in the evening MacDonald of Morar returned, it was an altogether different story. Seldom had the prince seen such a change in a man in such short interval. Obviously uncomfortable and embarrassed, the other avoided Charles's eye, and indeed his wife's also, and spoke in jerks. He had not seen Young Clanranald, and apparently there was nothing further which he, or others, could usefully do. He could only suggest that the prince went on down to Borrodale, whatever the conditions might be there. Most evidently he had been told by Clanranald not to get further involved with the royal fugitive.

Disappointed over the hopes of aid from Young Clanranald, Charles was unable to disguise his feelings, and when Morar left the cave, turned to the Mackinnons.

"I hope, Captain John, that you will not desert me also, and leave me in the lurch, but that still you will do what you can for me and the furtherance of my father's cause?"

It was the old chief who answered, tears starting to his eyes. "I never will leave Your Royal Highness in the day of danger, but will, under God, do all that I can for you, and go with you wherever you order me."

John added, "With the help of the Almighty, I will also go through the wide world with Your Highness, if you desire me."

Charles grasped both their arms, much moved.

The Mackinnons decided that clearly Morar had been given hostile counsel by old Clanranald, and that they could look for no more help from that direction. Whether *Young* Clanranald was now so inclined remained to be seen, but the prince thought that unlikely. Where he was Morar had not indicated.

Charles was now eager only to get away from Morar and on to Arisaig and Borrodale, another dozen miles by the coastal road but less by the more direct inland route over the high ground. The latter was advisable for security reasons, but it would involve rough going, apparently, and the prince was adamant that the old chief, already showing signs of fatigue, should not attempt it. He and John would go on alone.

Morar's wife, as befitted Lochiel's sister, behaved quite differently from her husband, bringing food to the cave, wishing the prince well, and assuring that she would look after the Mackinnon as well as she was able until his son returned for him. She declared that his long riding had apparently been too much for her elderly spouse, but that he would undoubtedly feel and behave better after he had rested. She said that her younger son would act guide to take them to Borrodale.

With that assurance, and dusk falling, Charles took one more emotional leave of a good friend in need, the old chief all but overcome. Morar redeemed himself somewhat, no doubt at his lady's urging, by agreeing that their son should act guide.

The journey to Arisaig was no better and no worse than so many that Charles had undertaken and, without the old man to delay their progress, the dozen miles were covered in better time; indeed they arrived at the Borrodale house before dawn, to find it another burned-out shell. Much concerned, this being the first house on the mainland to welcome him when first the prince had come to Scotland, they found a cowherd to tell them that the chieftain and his family were now, like Morar's, having to live in huts further up the Borrodale valley a mile. It seemed that this destruction of lairds' houses was the policy of the government forces, as warning for none to give help or shelter for the prince. It also indicated that their enemies knew that their quarry was somewhere in this neighbourhood now.

When they arrived at the bothy and hutments up the glen, just as the sun was rising, as usual Charles stood discreetly well back behind a shed while John went forward to knock on the closed door.

Aeneas MacDonald himself came to open, a plaid wrapped around him, obviously roused from his bed. When after introducing himself, John asked what the other would do if Prince Charles Edward was to be brought to him here, he hesitated and then said that he would provide a hearty bottle, reduced to this state as he was, to see the prince safe. And he eyed the caller questioningly.

"Well then, I have brought him here," he was told. "And I come to commit him to your charge. I have done *my* duty. Do you yours, sir!"

The other, of middle age and heavy build, with florid features, drew a long breath. "I am glad of it," he said eventually, nodding. "I shall not fail to take care of him. Where is he? I shall lodge him so secure that all the forces in Britain shall not find him!"

Thankfully, from round the back, Charles emerged, to be respectfully but warmly greeted by the man who had, almost exactly a year before, been his first host.

Greatly cheered by his reception here, and declaring his sorrow for the price paid in advance for Borrodale's loyalty, the prince and John were taken over to another shed where the chieftain's two sons were sleeping, and there left while their father went to inform his wife in the first bothy of what transpired, and to find refreshment for the travellers.

So, in due course, adequately fed, it was time to say goodbye to John Mackinnon, and to Morar's son. As in all these partings, Charles was much affected and distressed. He had almost lost count of all the occasions, but would never forget the persons involved, or their help and caring. O'Sullivan and O'Neill apart, there was Ned Burke, and Father Allan, Donald Campbell, Donald MacLeod, Boisdale, Flora MacDonald, Neil MacEachain, Donald Roy, Malcolm MacLeod and his two cousins, the Mackinnon and now this John, as well as others less prominent in his affairs. Passed from one to the other, it seemed to be his fate to be ever making inadequate but heartfelt farewells. And promising, promising . . . Would he ever be in a position to redeem those promises?

No French ships had appeared as yet in Loch nan Uamh since those bringing the belated gold *louis* treasure.

18

In the event, Charles remained for three days at Glen Borrodale, while Aeneas sent on one of his sons to glean information as to warships, enemy search-parties, and the whereabouts of possibly useful friends, particularly Young Clanranald. And the news which in due course came in was dire. The entire coastline was infested with frigates under Captains Fergusson and Scott, with their longboats and crews probing everywhere, General Campbell's military painstakingly combing the land, deep into the hills, communities and crofts being savaged and burned, as in the Outer Isles, with cattle and sheep slaughtered. But more personal than this, the word was that old Mackinnon had been captured at Cross of Morar, and was now a prisoner in HMS *Furnace*. Charles all but wept for the chief, and prayed that his son would escape a similar fate.

There was one more cheering development. Alexander MacDonald of Glenaladale, summoned, arrived to help. He was a bold and able man, a major in the Clanranald regiment, whom the prince knew well. He had been wounded at Culloden, but had made his escape, and was now sufficiently recovered to leave his wife and young children to come and take over the task of trying to lead the prince to safety.

He it was who strongly advised that, with troops very close at hand, Charles should move to a cave they knew of, halfway up a high precipice some four miles up this glen, all but inaccessible save to those in the know. His uncle, Aeneas, agreed, and with his sons John and Ranald, both former lieutenants in the regiment, and Glenaladale, the move was made, the ascent to the cave proving to be a dizzy business indeed, reminding Charles of the cliff-ascent at Corradale in South Uist.

This retreat, when actually reached distinctly precariously from above, proved to be a deep cavity, with a bend in it, but dry, with extensive views, and, whatever else, provided a great sense of security. But it had no water, which meant that constant supplies had to be fetched from the hillside above the cliff, a handicap. They could not stay here for long.

Glenaladale was a very practical character, and said that since the enemy clearly knew that His Highness was in this vicinity, no doubt waiting for a French ship to call at Loch nan Uamh, their best course was to get right away from the area meantime, to somewhere further east, possibly into the central Highlands, where word could be sent to him without too much difficulty when such ship did arrive. He suggested north-eastwards, first, to Lochiel's country around Loch Arkaig, where the French gold had been taken to the remnants of the loyalist army. Lochiel was utterly reliable and effective, and his clan wide-scattered enough to be able to hide the fugitive in many different localities.

It was agreed that they should set out on the first stage of this quite lengthy journey on the morrow, Borrodale's two sons going back down to the low ground, in the darkness, to collect the necessary food and drink to take with them.

Their first stop, next day, should be Meoble, due northwards on the shore of Loch Morar, where Borrodale's son-in-law, another MacEachain, Angus by name, had his house, some nine miles. Through those empty mountains they could risk walking in daylight.

With food duly brought back, also the word that two warships, English not French, were now lying in the vital Loch nan Uamh, Borrodale himself insisting on accompanying the three others, but sending his younger son Ranald back to look after his mother, they made a move from their cave.

It proved to be an arduous but uneventful tramp over high passes and down deep corries, and they duly reached Angus MacEachain's house of Meoble before darkness, not having seen a soul on the way. There they were well received into a young family; and that night Charles was able to sleep in a comfortable bed, after much-needed bathing in hot water, a luxury these days indeed. Upper Loch Morar so far seemed to have escaped search, they were told. Although its foot was so near salt water, ships could not reach it, nor their boats, because that brief river was little more than a series of rapids.

According to MacEachain, Young Clanranald was not far away, at Tarbet, the narrow neck of land which lay between Morar and

202

the sea loch of Nevis to the north. He, Angus, would go and inform him of the prince's presence. He kept a boat at the lochside, and would cross the mile of water and walk the remaining mile to Tarbet.

When he returned in the late afternoon, however, it was with tidings which again grievously affected the hopes and approximate plans of his visitors. General Campbell had arrived with six ships in Loch Nevis, and made this Tarbet his base. Young Clanranald had disappeared, which was not to be wondered at, where none knew. And the Tarbet locals said that a long line of camps had been established to the north-east, from the head of Loch Arkaig of the Camerons, to Loch Morar, so that the nearest was only some five miles away. In other words, the Clanranald country was entirely surrounded; and if the fugitives did not get out of it quickly they would be trapped.

A hasty conference came to the conclusion that the prince should now go on eastwards by *south*, to the Glenfinnan area, where he had first raised his standard a year before, this at the head of Loch Sheil. But in the circumstances, the smaller his party the less chance of detection. So they would leave Borrodale and MacEachain. Glenaladale would go with Charles to Glenfinnan, but the two Johns MacDonald, son of Borrodale and brother of Glenaladale, would go on separately, the latter ahead to scout out the Glenfinnan area, the former to seek out Donald Cameron of Glenpean, a kinsman of Lochiel, who had sheltered the prince for a while after Culloden. Glen Pean lay nine miles to the north-east from Glenfinnan and ought to provide a safe haven meantime. The four of them would meet up again on the summit of a high and readily recognisable hill called Fraoch Bheinn, just north of Glenfinnan, ten miles distant from Meoble through a mass of trackless mountains.

That country could not be hurried through, a jumble of soaring peaks and yawning valleys, so that their circuitous, clambering walking involved nearer twenty miles than the ten which the eagle might fly, and daylight saw the pair only halfway. However, utterly empty as this territory was, they could continue on in daylight safely enough. It was two in the afternoon in fact before, weary and hungry, they reached their Fraoch Bheinn rendezvous. There was no sign of Glenaladale's brother, and they wondered how he fared, as they settled down to wait. Charles slept.

He was awakened presently, not because of their scout's arrival, but with his companion, on the watch, pointing downhill into the glen of the River Finnan, a mile or so north of the head of Loch Shiel. There was to be seen a large herd of cattle being driven northwards. This was highly unusual, to say the least, and Glenaladale said that he would risk going down to investigate, His Highness to stay where he was.

It was a good hour before he came back, sweating from his climb, for it was a notably hot day, also unusual in these windswept parts. He announced that the cattle were being driven by some of their own Clanranald people, to escape the ravages of the military further south. They had been heading for the Cameron country around Loch Eil, but had almost reached that loch's head when they had met folk fleeing therefrom also, with the news that six hundred soldiers had arrived there from the east, from the Great Glen area and Fort Augustus. So now they were making northwards for Loch Arkaig and Glen Pean, more and hopefully safer Cameron territory.

So now what for the prince? Glenaladale thought that, in the circumstances, they might be wise to go down and join the cattle-herders. At least, if troops did appear, they would scarcely look for their quarry thus engaged. After all, the herders were heading for the same area as were they.

So down they went, Charles to play the servant again.

That herd was inevitably slow-moving, and proved to have more than a score of men, women and children trailing on with it. Charles agreed that this would provide good cover against identification; but the progress was tardy in the extreme – indeed sufficiently for one of the women to milk a cow and give Glenaladale and his servant a drink to sustain them.

The prince asked about his companion's brother. He would be looking for them on top of that Fraoch Bheinn. He was told confidently that John would find them.

In fact, going slowly up Glen Finnan, the brother caught up with them before long, with the news that they had had a lucky escape, for there had been over one hundred of the Argyll militia camped only one mile down Loch Shiel-side.

When the cattle-herders halted, with the darkening, for the night, the trio bade them farewell and went on up the glen. And about an hour later, well before midnight, rounding a bend, there was a single man, just visible in the half-dark, walking towards them, staff in hand. There was no avoiding meeting, however warily they approached each other.

It was Charles who first recognised the newcomer. "Glenpean!" he cried. "It is *you*, Donald Cameron! *Ma foi,* yourself! We were coming to seek you."

It took the other longer to recognise the prince, clad as he was, although Glenaladale was known to Glenpean. When he did perceive who greeted him, he was quite overcome. A middle-aged man, he had been a major in the Lochiel regiment.

It was a fortunate meeting indeed, which might so easily have been missed. Borrodale's son had reached the Cameron at Glenpean House, and told him that the prince needed him. They had set out together for the rendezvous on Fraoch Bheinn, but just before this meeting the younger man had left him to walk on down the glen while he climbed uphill to the arranged meeting-place; no need for both to climb the mountain.

Glenaladale's John offered to go back up to the hilltop to inform the other, but his brother thought that this would not be necessary; young Borrodale, when he found no one on the mountain, would come down into the glen, and the cattle-herders would tell him that Glenaladale and his servant had gone on ahead. He would realise that they would meet Glenpean, in that narrow valley, and would come on after them.

They explained to Donald Cameron how all the Clanranald country was encircled, and that they had decided that the only course for the prince was to head, first northwards through the Cameron land and then eastwards for the Great Glen and Badenoch. The other agreed with this, but said that *his* country was also now being watched, and that there was this line of camps, small as they were, each only half a mile apart, stretching between the head of Loch Arkaig and Glen Pean. To get north, they would somehow have to win through this barrier.

But now, at least, they had a guide who knew every yard of the land, his own. He would take them to the Braes of Arkaig, above the head of that loch, and there rest during the day, to attempt the penetration of the enemy line by night.

So, from the head of Glen Finnan, they were led north-eastwards to climb over a high pass below the mountain of Streap, and down Glen a'Chaoruinn beyond, which in fact was how Cameron had just come, and led into Glen Pean. But they did not risk going that far, turning to climb right-handed eastwards, along a secondary ridge, part of the Braes of Arkaig. That brought them, as the sun was rising ahead of them, to a hollow in the ridge, where Glenpean said that they ought to be safe to lie up. Looking down to the loch-head, less than two miles below, they could see two of the small military camps. If, by any chance, troops were to come searching up here, they would have ample warning and could escape back into the trackless hills behind.

This was satisfactory. But hunger was now afflicting them, or three of the four, who had had nothing to swallow but some milk in thirty-six hours. Donald Cameron, sympathetic, said that he knew of a croft down near the shore of the loch, which he thought that he could approach unseen, and where he might be able to procure something to eat, at least. He left the others there in the hollow, two to sleep and one to watch.

It was some time before he returned, this because, after collecting a couple of cheeses, all that the crofter could spare, he had seen a familiar figure crossing the hillside above and realised it was Young Borrodale. He had joined him and together they had made their round-about way up to the others.

The party was complete again, and glad to be. The cheeses were demolished promptly, however inadequate fare for five men. They discussed their further progress, once they got through that line of encampments.

Glenpean said that they could only go northwards for quite some distance, past Loch Quoich to the head of the great and long sea loch of Hourn, wild country indeed. Thereafter it might be safe to turn eastwards, through the Cluanie district to Glen Moriston, and so down to the Great Glen itself, the mightiest valley in all Scotland, which divided Badenoch from all the West Highlands, and wherein was Loch Ness. That would amount to almost one hundred miles of walking. Was His Highness able for it?

Charles declared that he did not mind the walking; he had become adept at it. So long as they could avoid the military. At least they would be spared the warships and savage seamen on this long overland journey.

Around nine o'clock, with the dusk settling, they made a move. Donald Cameron thought that he knew the best place to seek to penetrate the enemy line. The two rivers, Pean and Dessary, joined just half a mile from the head of Loch Arkaig, and formed another kind of barrier which they could *not* cross. But there were fords on each, just before they joined, and there were camps beside these. So he advised that they should go down to the wider river, creep along its bank, and reach the first ford thus, below its camp, and get across in the dark without being seen. That was the Pean one. That of the Dessary, half a mile on, would be less difficult, for the camp there was well back, because of marshy ground. They could thread that marsh.

Following the cleft of a burn down, they duly came to the river near the loch-head, moving right to its quite steep bank, to work cautiously along this, in single file, sometimes knee-high in the water. Soon, ahead of them, they saw the gleam of a camp-fire.

It seemed strange, actually to be heading directly for an enemy position thus, but essential if they were to cross that ford. Cameron leading, they edged along.

Presently they were near enough that fire to hear men's voices, as the speakers lounged round it. Charles all but held his breath. Fortunately the River Pean had carved quite a trench for itself, so that they could remain hidden until the ford itself; moreover the noise of the water was a help.

Two posts identified the crossing-place, and there could be no hiding here. But at ten o'clock at night there was little likelihood of men being on watch there. Glenpean was first into the river to cross, stepping carefully and high. There was an underwater causeway of stone slabs, but these could be slippery and they wanted no falling and splashings.

They crossed without incident.

The second ford, over the Dessary, was a lesser problem, save for the ploutering over its marshy approach, which kept the encampment far back.

After that it was just walking, clambering, climbing, through mountainous country, a dozen miles westwards, up to the head of Glen Kingie, over a pass to the Corrie nan Gall, and down towards the head of Loch Quoich. But there they saw a red gleam ahead, which almost certainly represented a camp-fire. So they did not risk going down, with daylight approaching, and holed up for that day amongst rocks on the side of the steep ravine, this Corrie nan Gall.

Glenaladale's brother went in search of possible food. In time he brought more cheese from a croft, plus the news that one hundred militiamen were strung out on the other side of the hill, An t'Sail, but, fortunately, heading southwards.

Evening saw them on their way again, still northwards, to cross Glen Cosaidh, making for the head of Loch Hourn, seven miles. It was about two in the morning, up on the precipitous side of Sgurr Dubh, near the head of the fourteen-mile-long sea loch of Hourn that, weary with climbing and dizzy with hunger, Charles slipped on the deer track at the lip of a cliff, and would have fallen to his death down hundreds of feet had not Cameron and Glenaladale managed to grasp him by the ankles and pull him back. Much shaken, they proceeded the more cautiously, occasionally taking the prince's arm.

But not for long, for as the ground fell away before them northwards, they saw a string of camp-fires agleam down by the loch shore. Hourn, being a sea loch, ships could sail up it, and no doubt these were sailors or troops put ashore from frigates. So another day had to be spent, hungry, on the high ground, before they might venture down to cross this next valley.

That night once again they had to work their way through an encampment line and ford a stream; but this time it was not so difficult, for these enemies, presumably seamen, were not so efficient, and had not set their tents close to a fording-place. And it was a hot night of thundery rain, and if sentries were indeed posted, they were sheltering. The wayfarers could not afford that luxury. They crossed, and went on northwards still, towards another Glen Shiel, confusing but scarcely to be wondered at, since shiel just meant a summer pasture with hutments. This was seven miles on; and Charles had the notion that, since this valley led down to the head of Loch Duich, one more sea loch, from which the port of Poolewe could be reached, it might be worth going there to see if he could find a vessel to take him, by sea, down south to Loch nan Uamh. Duncan Cameron was very doubtful about this, but gave in to the prince's urging. If friendly shipping could be at Poolewe, so could enemy ones; yes, and up Loch Duich also.

Eventually they did reach Glen Shiel and crossed its river just before dawn, by a deep ford which soaked them to the waist, but they were already wet from the thunder-showers. There was a farm near the far side of the ford, dark, which the Cameron named Achnangart; but avoiding this meantime, they proceeded up the dell of a burn some way, to find a hiding-place.

In daylight, Glenaladale's brother went back down to the farm to try to obtain provisions. When he came back, he was not alone, having with him a young man whom he had found hiding at the farm. He proved to be a Donald MacDonald, one more of them, who had served in the Glengarry regiment, and was now himself on the run. He was able to tell them that both sides of Loch Duich were overrun with soldiers, ships based on Poolewe, and no way out for the prince in that direction. His Highness would have to go eastwards, by Cluanie to Glen Moriston. His father had recently been slain by the seamen in his efforts to effect his son's escape.

Charles, once more, was considerably distressed.

But at least the pair had brought food, more than they had seen for some time, much cheese and butter, some cold meat and fish and a bottle of goat's milk.

Donald Cameron announced that he would leave them now, since they would be hereafter turning eastwards into country he did not know, his usefulness past. The new Donald did know Cluanie and Glen Moriston well, and would act guide hereafter.

So that evening it was one more parting. Glenpean had been an excellent companion and a great help, able and confident. These farewells did not become any easier for the prince on account of their frequency, indeed the reverse. He felt that he was endlessly leaving behind him, and to their dangerous fate, friends to whom he owed so much and was unlikely ever to repay fully. Loyalty to his father's cause was costing dear indeed.

At nightfall the goodbyes were said, Donald Cameron making back for the ford by himself, the five others to head up the dozen miles of Glen Shiel to Loch Cluanie. This was Glengarry country now, and their new guide familiar with it all. The shameful killing of his father seemed to have made him eager to avenge him by serving the prince. As far as he knew, there were no troops east of here until they reached Glen Moriston.

All young men now, they walked the faster and further. More-over, at this stage they were merely making their way up a glen, long as it was, not climbing hillsides and over passes, although they were ready at short notice to dart up the flanking slopes should need arise. In consequence of this, and their improved feeding, they were able to carry on all night and well into the forenoon and they were seeing Loch Cluanie ahead of them. Here they were three-quarters of the way from west coast salt water to Glen Albyn or the Great Glen, and Loch Ness, the very centre of the West Highlands. Now they had left all those sea lochs far behind, which was a comfort in a way, although Charles, with Loch nan Uamh as his ultimate goal, could not but be aware that he was getting further and further away from it. He had had pointed out to him, on the way, the very dorsal ridge of the land, where the Shiel River had flowed westwards to the Atlantic and the Cluanie eastwards to Ness and the Norse Sea. And here a battle had been fought in the second Jacobite Rising, of 1719, with Spanish involvement and indefinite results.

They halted on a hillside above Loch Cluanie; and here their guide, offering to go in search of food, informed them that, after Culloden, he had made his way homewards by devious ways and stages, in company with six others of the prince's common soldiers from these parts. They had had to live off the land as best they might, while dodging Cumberland's pursuing forces, and ended up at the head of Glen Moriston, to which area two of them belonged. These were all very tough and resourceful characters, Donald MacDonald said, and he expected that they would still be thereabouts, as remote and secure a haven as any; at least, they had been when he left them a week before to go down and seek his father. These might well be useful to His Highness. Should he go on ahead and seek them out?

Charles was not anxious to embroil more men in trouble on his behalf; but Glenaladale thought that these men might be of considerable help in the new conditions into which the prince was now entering, to form a sort of bodyguard in the more populous, open country of the Great Glen and Badenoch.

Their guide went off. It was not far down Loch Cluanie to where the River Moriston flowed out of it.

When he returned, in the afternoon, he brought a companion with him, one more MacDonald, one of his six friends, both carrying supplies of cooked venison. They announced that they and their companions would be glad and proud to serve the prince in any and every way possible; and that meantime they would welcome him to their base, a secure cave above the glen-head, which they had made reasonably comfortable, the cottages and crofts below all having been burned. Somewhat alarmed over this

210

last, Glenaladale asked whether the military, whom they were so urgently seeking to get away from, were now in this vicinity also? He was told that, not so very far from Fort Augustus as they were, Glen Moriston had been one of the first areas to be raided and punished – for this was where the Glengarry regiment had been partly raised – but that thereafter, the glen desolated and its people driven out, there had been little further in military presence.

Sustained by the venison, the party of six set off for the foot of Loch Cluanie and the head of Glen Moriston. Charles recognised that this was probably the beginning of a new chapter in his prolonged adventures.

19

The cave to which their guides led them was indeed almost palatial as caves went, long and deep, with offshoots to provide extra accommodation and storage. There was even a stream gurgling through one of these, providing excellent water. Also cracks in the rock of the roofing where smoke from the fires would disperse without attracting attention. All the flooring had been covered liberally with heather and dried grasses, and ample supplies of peat and wood stocked. Charles had become a habitué of caves, but had experienced none so fine as this.

Only one man was therein to welcome them, on the cliffside below a great escarpment of sheer rock, presented to the prince as Patrick Grant, the others of the group apparently out foraging. Despite his Strathspey origins in Badenoch, this man had served in the Glengarry regiment as a sergeant; and they gathered that he was the leader of the party. He declared how grieved he was to see His Highness in such state and circumstances, saying that they all had wondered what had become of him after the Culloden disaster; but he assured that while he was in their company he would be safe and supported with all that they had, their very lives.

He went on to inform of their state here, and way of life. They were all originally crofters or the sons thereof, and all their homes had been destroyed and their families slain or scattered. They were now in the nature of outlaws, living as best they could off the land, visiting colonies of refugees from devastated glens in their remote hiding-places amongst the mountains, helping these, especially where there were old folk and women and children, where they could. They were strong enough, as a group, on occasion to seek out small patrols of the military in their encampments, by night, to attack and kill, and so to win arms and ammunition, gear and food. They had been making something of a campaign of this, in revenge for what had been done to their own homes and families, and so far had been not unsuccessful in their endeavours. Apart from the two MacDonalds from this glen, there were three Chisholms from Strathglass to the north, two of them brothers, and also a wild MacGregor who had escaped with them by chance from the battle.

Charles was much impressed by this Patrick Grant and his attitudes and initiatives, and said how grieved he was that he and his friends' services, on his father King James's behalf, had resulted in this state of affairs. But he hoped and believed that one day not too far distant he would be in a position to show his appreciation in more than words, with his father on the throne of Great Britain, or at the least King of Scots. How often had he said that, over the months?

He was correspondingly impressed with the four others when they in due course arrived at the cave, the three Chisholms, Alexander, Donald and Hugh, and Gregor MacGregor, from the Inversnaid detachment of that clan, the latter bringing much of a deer which he had managed to stalk and shoot, the others with food and clothing from some unspecified source. They certainly seemed to form a sturdy and determined band, who seemed to know just what they were doing, anything but flight-conscious refugees these, more of an aggressive and punitive gang bound on vengeance. The prince had not come across anything like this hitherto, and was much stimulated. He wondered how many others of the rank and file of his now scattered army might be similarly operating. After all, despite the great casualty numbers, some thousands of his people must have escaped, and found their homes and families the objects of Cumberland's savage retribution.

After a substantial meal, with Charles given a little branch-cavern to himself, with even a bed contrived out of planking from a ravaged croft-house, and ample plaiding, Grant brought his six friends to the prince, to make something of a formal declaration, an odd but moving little occasion. He announced that, in traditional Highland fashion, they were going to swear their allegiance to His Highness.

He intoned thus: "Our backs shall be to God, and our faces to the Devil. All the curses the Scriptures pronounce come upon us and all our posterity if we do not stand firm to help Your Highness in your great danger!"

Shaking his head in wonder and gratitude, tears coming to

213

his eyes, Charles stood and shook hands with each of them, Glenaladale and the others watching.

Thereafter there was a discussion on advisable procedure. The prince still had hopes over Poolewe port. Ships from there were known to carry hides and wool, the principal exports from these parts, not only to Lowland ports like Glasgow but to France and the Low Countries. If he could win secretly aboard one of these, for France preferably, where he could pass as a French sailor, but even one which could drop him at Loch nan Uamh, this would get him out of danger. The others, as Glenpean had been, were very dubious about this, pointing out again that enemy shipping was sure to be using Poolewe; but it was agreed that, since they were now going north anyway, they should send two of their men to make enquiries. If they found it inadvisable, then the Great Glen and Badenoch for the prince.

Charles spent three days at that cave while his new guardians ranged the area, prospecting for the enemy, seeking news and also searching for the necessary food. It was good for the others to rest.

Then the word was brought that a certain Captain Campbell, factor for the Seaforth estates, had raised a band of irregular militia, had come into this Glen Moriston from Fort Augustus, and was searching the glen's eastern parts. So far, this company remained some ten miles off; but it was considered that a move northwards now would be wise.

Thereafter, for some time, Charles at least became utterly confused over their comings and goings, his new bodyguard moving him and his friends on, ever approximately northwards, by stages long and short and seldom direct, this through the Lochgarry and Bunloin mountains. They met with occasional little groups of local folk in various hiding-places in lonely glens, sympathising with them; and in one of these they were joined voluntarily by another former Glengarry regiment sergeant who had served with the seven, Hugh Macmillan by name, he declaring that he would do better with His Highness than idling here. Always two or three of their number were off scouting, watching for the enemy, especially this Captain Campbell's company. But eventually, on the second day of August, they reached Strathglass, Chisholm country. And here they risked calling on the son of the chief, Young Chisholm, at his House of Comar, and learned that so far there was no word

214

of the military in this area. So Charles was able to accept the hospitality of the young chieftain, with its blessings of civilised living, comfort and good fare, while two of their party went off north-westwards to try to discover the situation at Poolewe. This was facilitated by them being provided with garrons for the forty-mile journey. Much as the prince appreciated the help of his Glen Moriston friends, it was good to be spared the endless trudging, and to enjoy Comar House.

But this interval did not last long, for in three days the messengers were back from Poolewe with the word that a French ship had indeed been there, actually sent to look for the prince, but had sailed off again a week earlier, leaving two officers to try to find the fugitive. Where the Frenchmen were now was uncertain, but the rumour was that they were also wishing to contact Lochiel. There was no other sea-going vessel at the port save for an English frigate.

Downcast indeed by this news, and declaring that he *should* have gone to Poolewe as he had wanted to do, Charles now began to suffer a rather prolonged bout of low spirits, scarcely to be wondered at. And these were not uplifted when Young Chisholm came to announce that some of his people were reporting troops entering Strathglass from the Urquhart area of Loch Ness. It was time to move on, it seemed, the 6th of August. Surely, the prince felt, the government authorities must be beginning to despair of ever catching their quarry by now, thinking of giving up their quest? Glenaladale, for one, did not think so. Nor did Patrick Grant and Hugh Macmillan. This coming of troops up Glen Urquhart seemed to indicate otherwise, did it not? This was the furthest north they had heard of enemy penetration. It looked as though the belief was that the prince was indeed in this vicinity, and heading in a northerly direction.

What now, then? All the land to the south and west was overrun. They desired to go eastwards – but there lay the Great Glen, and at this level, the vast barrier of Loch Ness to cross. Before, they had hoped to win over below the head of the twenty-three-mile-long loch, but that route appeared to be closed to them. Would it be possible to get round the *foot* of Ness, none so far from Inverness itself, and so into Badenoch that way? It would make a long journey, and latterly through populous country, but it might be the answer. The authorities would hardly look for them there.

215

Charles had all but given up speculating. But the others decided for him. Westwards, then.

On they went, as far as Glen Cannich. And, infuriatingly, there they learned that a body of soldiers had arrived only the day before, from the Beauly area, north-west of Inverness, Fraser country, and were, so far, up to Struy. These tidings were sufficient to rule out any crossing of the Great Glen north of Loch Ness. Clearly there was nothing for it but to turn back and work southwards again. They would not go the same way as they had come, but go up Glen Cannich and over by Fasnakyle to Glen Affric, and so southwards to Glen Moriston again, making for Lochiel's main seat of Achnacarry at the foot of Loch Arkaig, in the hope that they might find those French officers there. But, would that do them any good?

The prince's spirits did not rise.

A journey of at least sixty miles was involved. But it seemed that they had to go in that general direction anyway, back past Glen Moriston to the Cameron country. Charles remained quite the least hopeful of the company of thirteen, which was not like him.

It took them six days of continuous trudging, climbing, circling and back-tracking to reach the Loch Arkaig area, for the prince an ordeal indeed, and this after so much of frustration, months and months of it. Somehow the heart seemed to have gone out of him. There were occasions in fact when he was so reluctant to move on, in the prevailing wet weather, after sleeping, that his seven men of Glen Moriston – he thought of them as that although there were now eight of them – had threatened to tie him up and carry him onward, even though this was pronounced with smiles.

Ashamed of himself, later, he told them, "Kings and princes must be ruled by their privy councils. But I believe there is not in all the world a more absolute privy council than what I have at present!"

The laughter helped.

When at length they neared Loch Arkaig, two men were sent ahead to spy the land and seek out Lochiel, or, if he was not to be found, some Cameron chieftain, to gain information and help.

With still some ten miles to go, they had to cross a ford of the River Garry. This, swollen by the rains, the swirling water came more than waist-high, and the prince was almost swept away. He told those who grasped and aided him to the southern bank that perhaps they should have let him drown, since it seemed that he was a curse to himself and everyone else. Clearly he had not fully recovered his spirits.

They had arranged with their two messengers to wait for them at a wood Grant knew of, not far back from Loch Arkaig, near the tacksman's house of Achnacaul, and here they settled. The pair, Young Borrodale and Hugh Macmillan, presently returned, and with them a newcomer, MacDonell of Lochgarry, who it seemed had been visiting Cameron of Clunes near Achnacarry.

They had news, some of it heartening. First of all, Lochiel himself was not available. Wounded at Culloden, he had been poorly since, but had recently recovered sufficiently to go over secretly to Badenoch to visit his friend and fellow-chief Cluny Macpherson, to discover what might yet be done for the royal cause. There was some point in this, for it transpired that the deplorable Duke of Cumberland had finally departed for London, disappointed in his efforts to capture Charles Edward, and leaving the Earl of Loudoun, a Campbell, as commander-in-chief in Scotland, with the Lord Albemarle in charge at Fort Augustus. And that moderate and sensible individual had promptly begun withdrawing all the troops he commanded in this area back to the fort. So although all was by no means yet clear of danger, hereabouts the situation was greatly improving. There was as yet no sign of the French officers. Young Borrodale had seen Cameron of Clunes, and he would come to visit His Highness next day.

Lochgarry, who had been a captain in the Glengarry regiment, was a personable man in his thirties, and an enthusiast. Kissing the prince's hand on introduction, although staring almost unbelievingly, he announced that he was overjoyed thus to meet His Highness, whom he had seen often to be sure but never had the honour of speaking to directly. Now it would be his privilege to seek to alleviate the royal misfortunes in any and every way possible.

Much taken with this immediate and forthright declaration, Charles agreed that he was in need of some assistance in these circumstances. But the news just brought, of Cumberland's departure and the withdrawing of troops back to Fort Augustus, was in itself a great encouragement and advance in his fortunes. He was grateful.

The other shook his head, glancing from the prince to Glenaladale and the others, and then back again, eyeing the royal person.

"Highness!" he exclaimed. "The state you are in! It is scarce believable. A, a sorry sight!" At the others he jerked, "Is this the best that you can do for the heir to the throne! In your care?"

Admittedly Charles presented no very princely impression despite his habitual fine bearing. He was actually, at this stage, barefooted, having lost one of his tattered brogans at that fording of the Garry, and kicked the other away thereafter as useless, more holes than leather. He was unshaven and had sprouted what almost amounted to a reddish beard. His coat and kilt were stained and ragged, his shirt torn and filthy. He was long past concerning himself with his appearance. He smiled, and raised a foot.

"See you, my friend, I grow my own leather now! I have been footing it for months on end, and I have grown such thick soles to my feet as to rival any cow's hide! And what does a man's garb signify in my circumstances, *mon Dieu!*"

Glenaladale, who was himself in little better state, was frowning. "If you, Lochgarry, can do better for His Highness, clad as you are, do so! We have been six weeks on the run and have had more to do than consider our dress!"

There were murmurs of agreement from the others.

The MacDonell stiffened. "My house is a dozen miles off. But I will send for at least decent clothing for His Highness. I do not, sir . . ."

Fortunately at this juncture the two Glen Moriston Chisholms arrived, dragging between them a young stag which they had managed to shoot – for they all had muskets – and Lochgarry was further educated in the state and priorities of the prince's party by seeing the satisfaction with which this presentation of fresh meat was greeted, dirks quickly being unsheathed to gralloch and dismember the carcase, with praise to the slayers. Recognising the realities of the situation, he said that he would go to Achnasaul farmery and bring back some more suitable provision.

So, experts as they were at it, the Glen Moriston men set up a shelter there in the wood, and got a fire lit to cook that venison. When Lochgarry in due course returned, with his servant and the Achnasaul farmer's son, bearing more food and drink than had been seen since Comar, better relations were established, and the subsequent meal wolfed down, with praises. There were still, however, some doubtful looks when the MacDonell announced that he intended to spend the night with them all.

That evening, the group, sitting around the fire, and with no fears of its light attracting enemy attention, the rain blessedly having ceased, inevitably perhaps discussion reverted to the Culloden débâcle, a subject never far from those men's minds, for all except Young Borrodale had been present, in the Clanranald, Glengarry and Lochiel regiments. Once again the prince felt bound to stand up in some measure for his lieutenant-general, the Lord George Murray, son of the Duke of Atholl, whom all others seemed to blame. They declared that the battle should not have been fought at all, at that stage, and in those circumstances, on an open moor and not using the land to fight for them as was the Highland expertise. But when action *was* decided upon, part of the disaster was caused by the refusal of Murray to put the MacDonald regiments in their accepted position on the right of the line, placing his own Atholl brigades there instead. Always it had been Clan Donald's privilege, down the centuries, in any Highland battle, to occupy that proud position, stemming from the ancient Lords of the Isles' eminence. Lochgarry himself had been with his chief, old Glengarry, and his son, later captured, along with Young Clanranald, Keppoch and others, when they had gone to charge the Lord George with the folly of this, but to none effect. And undoubtedly the MacDonald regiments had fought less effectively, on the left wing, as a consequence.

Charles, at the time, had not realised quite how much Highland pride mattered in warfare.

Before settling to sleep in their shelter, the prince, sensing that Lochgarry and Glenaladale tended to rub each other the wrong way, proposed a short walk with the former, through the woods, allegedly to show how bare feet, duly calloused, could be no handicap to a man. And as they went, the MacDonell reverted to the subject of warfare, and in no back-looking fashion this time. He declared that, given, say, forty-eight hours or so, he thought that he could muster up to two thousand Glengarry and Cameron men, eager for the fight, for there was fury all over this land at the atrocities perpetrated on the inhabitants of the glens by Cumberland's forces. What did His Highness say to an assault, by such a force, on the reduced garrison and soldiery under this Lord Albemarle at Fort Augustus? The word was that there were only some eight hundred men there now, some of the enemy brigades having been sent south-west to Fort William. If they took and demolished Fort Augustus, would not that be a dire blow to the devilish Cumberland, and a great enheartenment to all loyal men, a spur to resume the campaign?

Charles, all but astonished by this proposal, so utterly unexpected, wondered whether it was indeed possible. Would all those men rise? Flock to Lochgarry's banner after all the misery and loss they had experienced? And thereafter? Even though they did win at Fort Augustus, what then? Could it, would it, spark off a rising again, all over the Highlands?

The other was strong in the belief that it would. Not one half of the loyalist army had in fact been engaged at Culloden, so much of it dispersed beforehand to their glens and isles, after the long campaign in the south. Such a move as he proposed should encourage and embolden the chiefs and their people all over the land, a challenge to resume the fight, and make the Hanoverians pay for their misdeeds and savageries.

The prince, pondering, said that before such an attempt was put in hand, he would have to consult his senior supporters and advisers, the chiefs readily available, especially the Camerons. This was a major matter for decision. What of his own chief, Glengarry? He had heard that he had attempted to submit himself to Cumberland after the defeat, in an effort to save his clan and lands.

Lochgarry declared that the behaviour of his chief was despicable. But the old man had lost one son at the Battle of Falkirk and his heir, Young Glengarry, was captured at Culloden; so he was much disheartened. But that was not to say that the clan itself was. He believed that it would rise, given the leadership and this opportunity. And he would lead them.

Very much in two minds over it all, but his spirits much uplifted by this man's loyal fervour and enthusiasm, Charles said not to speak of it meantime to the others, until he had opportunity to seek the advice of Lochiel and the other Cameron leaders. The other agreed.

"And there is the matter of the French gold, buried not far from here, at the side of Loch Arkaig," Lochgarry added. "It is important, but not to be spoken of to all. Sufficient trouble with it, and enough of it stolen already!"

"You mean . . . ?"

"Aye, Highness, stolen! The shame of it. When it came, too late for your army's use and aid, it was grasped and taken over, and by those who should have cherished it for your continuing cause. I have never seen the like. Proud chiefs bickering over French gold pieces, claiming that they were owed them to recoup their losses in the warfare and to pay their men, all but fighting each other for it. Much was taken. But much also was saved, saved and hidden – I know where. But, best that word of it be kept close. Thousands of gold *louis*. It could be used, now, to help renew Your Highness's campaign."

"M'mm. Here is something to think deeply on. I must consider," Charles said. "How many know just where it is? What is left?"

"Lochiel and his Camerons, or some of them. It is in their land, to be sure. Murray of Broughton, the secretary, but he is now none knows where. And has no little of the gold with him, they say. Others, but not many, I think."

They were nearly back at the shelter, and no more was to be said meantime.

Next morning Cameron of Clunes, with his son Sandy, duly arrived, no stranger to the prince for he had been senior in the Lochiel regiment, a stern-seeming man but reliable and effective. He made no comments about the royal appearance, but declared that he had been having a better and more secure place prepared for His Highness to lodge in the meantime. With Lochiel's Achnacarry and his own House of Clunes burned down, he and his family living in a croft-house nearby, there was no room for the prince's party there. The refuge he had chosen was an abandoned bothy in woodland a couple of miles to the east, which had escaped the troops' attentions because of its hidden situation and empty state. He had had his men repairing it and making it reasonably comfortable. It was at Torr a Mhuilt, near where the short River Arkaig ran into Loch Lochy in the Great Glen. From there it should be possible for the prince to move, in due course, by night, up Lochy-side, to cross over to the other side of the vast natural barrier at a ford, admittedly only a couple of miles south of Fort Augustus, but because so near probably unguarded by a picket. The last two times he had been there it had been free of any surveillance, the garrison soldiery themselves using it frequently. He understood that His Highness was intending

221

to make for Badenoch, where Lochiel was hiding presently with Cluny Macpherson. This arrangement would set him on his way.

All accepted that this was probably the best way forward. They would wait here until darkness, when Clunes would come back and escort them to this Torr a Mhuilt bothy. So comparatively close to the principal military base of the enemy, there was no sense in taking risks by day.

So idle hours were spent, welcome enough. But at least Charles had recovered his spirits, thanks to Lochgarry's enthusiasm and dedication, whether anything came of it or not, meantime. That, and Clunes's evident confidence.

It was mid-August now, and already the darkness was falling earlier. Clunes came, and they all went with him down Loch Arkaig-side for a mile, to its foot and the start of its outflowing river, like that of Morar only a mile long, and a rushing torrent with wooded banks in something of a pass. Halfway down this they were led off left-handed to climb a quite steep and rocky hill, the torr, or hill of the red berries, still wooded, where, on a shoulder but well hidden, perched their bothy, larger than most they had seen and reasonably entire. A light gleamed when its door was opened, and there were some of Clunes's men to welcome them, with a fire lit and a meal prepared. All were cheered.

Clunes pointed out that on the steeper, northern side of this hill, threading its own short pass, was the only road to the west in scores of miles, this pass known as the Mil Dorcha or Dark Mile. They had not come that way for fear of encountering other travellers, military or otherwise. He also said that he had sent up-loch for Dr Archibald Cameron, Lochiel's brother, and the Reverend John Cameron, a kinsman and Church of Scotland parish minister, who were presently staying in a farmhouse which had escaped ravagement, some eight miles up. They should be down on the morrow. Glenpean, of course, was considerably further away, but he could be sent for if required.

Compared with most of the prince's temporary refuges, this bothy was comfortable indeed and sufficiently large for the quite numerous party.

Clunes and his son spent the night with them. Charles managed to speak with the older man alone, and put to him the proposal of Lochgarry for an attack on Fort Augustus. The other was highly doubtful, concerned with its after-effects even though the actual assault could be organised and was successful. They should speak to Dr Archie and the Reverend John on the matter when they came.

That pair arrived sooner in the morning than anticipated, indeed while breakfast was being prepared on the central hearth of the bothy, this because they had ridden the eight miles on garrons, and starting in the half-dark for security reasons. The horses, sturdy as they were, could not climb this steep and craggy hill, so they had left them at the foot, with their servant. The prince knew Dr Archie, who had been with the army, but not the elderly minister. Like Lochgarry, they were both much concerned over the prince's state.

Their attitude towards the raising of an armed force and a descent on Fort Augustus was the same as Clunes's. It might succeed; but it would almost certainly provoke great and wholesale reaction from the government, Cumberland coming north again with increased numbers of troops and intent on still more dire retribution than hitherto. To muster a large enough Jacobite army to counter this would take time, and meanwhile the Highlands would suffer indeed. They certainly were not against a revival of the campaign; but it should not start off at half-cock, as would be the case with this over-bold project. They were sure that Lochiel and Macpherson would agree with them.

There was something of a false alarm that forenoon. The servant left with the Cameron garrons came hurrying up to the bothy to announce that a party of troops had come marching along the riverside, and had turned off on to the little track which led up here. He thought that they had probably seen the new horse tracks in the mud, and considered them suspicious. He had observed this from higher, and had quickly led the beasts into some thick bushes where they would not be obvious, tethered them, and come on to give warning.

This, needless to say, caused considerable apprehension. Were these soldiers likely to come right up to the bothy, well hidden as it was? Charles asked how many there might be in the company, and was told about fifty. Lochgarry said that amongst these crags, if they did come, they could ambush them; after all, the Glen Moriston men had muskets and so had Glenaladale and his brother and the prince. But Clunes was strongly against this. Even if they managed to drive off any attack, some would get back to Fort

Augustus with the news and a major hunt would follow. Much better that they should make their escape, while there was time, down the north side of this hill and across the Dark Mile, and climb into the empty hills behind, there to lie up until the danger was past.

This was probably wise, but it did mean that their group would have to split up. The doctor was fairly fit, but the Reverend John somewhat frail. They would not be able to descend that abrupt and precipitous hillside, nor climb the further edge.

Dr Archie and his kinsman were much upset that they were thus proving a nuisance, and their horses seemingly the cause of it all. They said that they would go and hide somewhere in the deep undergrowth, and hope to regain their garrons in due course. Clunes's son Sandy and two of the Chisholms volunteered to go down towards the river to keep watch on the enemy, and join the others later.

So move was made from their comfortable quarters, in three directions, the main party due northwards.

Descending that drop into the Dark Mile was all that Clunes had warned of, often necessarily a hands-and-knees progress; but at least it probably precluded any immediate military pursuit, Charles emphasising the benefits of bare feet. Crossing the road below, after careful scouting up and down, was no problem; and with the climb beyond, most of them found the mounting, however toilsome, easier than the descent. Up on the heights behind they presently found a cave; this land was well provided with such, thanks to the basic rock being everywhere near if not on the surface. It had begun to rain again, heavily, and they were glad of the cover; but this again would probably inhibit any search and pursuit – not that Clunes anticipated any such up here. This was all his own land, and he knew it well.

He suggested that, while the others should stay there overnight before venturing back to their bothy, he himself would leave them to go and discover how the older men were faring. He was concerned for them, especially for the minister. Even if their garrons had been found and taken, he could supply them with others from Achnasaul and escort them back up Loch Arkaig-side. That mention of Loch Arkaig reminded Charles. Taking the other aside, he asked if *he* knew where all that gold was hidden, to be informed that Clunes did; he had helped to bury it. Then, the prince asked, would it be possible to dig up a small collection of the gold *louis* and bring them to him? He was now practically devoid of moneys, and he had certain debts to pay, or to make gesture towards repayment. When asked how much he wanted he was told that fifty of the coins would serve. Gold was heavy to carry. He felt almost apologetic about asking for this but, after all, the great treasure of forty thousand pieces had been sent for *him*.

Clunes left with his son who had rejoined them, and all settled down, but with a watch being kept.

Next day a move back to Torr a Mhuilt was made, scouts ahead, to find that nothing at the bothy showed signs of interference. And there, in the afternoon, they were presented with a surprise, for Dr Archie came back, this time on foot, and with him brought two strangers, none other than the pair of French officers landed at Poolewe, an extraordinary development. These, Captains Desforges and Dumont, had apparently been advised to try to find Lochiel, as one of the prince's foremost supporters, and had somehow managed to work their way across the land to Loch Arkaig, heading for Achnacarry. They had found Dr Archie, and here they were.

Their consternation at the state of the royal fugitive was all but comic to see, all dramatic gestures and exclamations. Their accounts of their travels and experiences amidst these barbarous mountains were also highly sensational, but at least they had achieved what they were sent to do. It took some little time for Charles to discover just what *was* the object of their visit; but it proved to be that Kings Louis and James had not forgotten the hunted refugee, and would continue to send ships to bring him back to France. They had heard from some of the other Jacobite escapers who had reached the safety of France that the prince had now returned to mainland Scotland and headed northwards. So their ship had made for Poolewe, not Loch nan Uamh. With no word of him there, they had decided to land and seek to find and reach him, to learn *where* he would wish ships to try to pick him up.

Grateful, enheartened, Charles said that Loch nan Uamh was probably still the best haven to seek, being so very difficult for the enemy forces to reach by land, and with its so numerous offshore islands and protective headlands giving covered approach from sea; also its local folk there entirely reliable. The visitors, thus informed, saw their duty as done, and declared that they themselves would try to get back to that strangely-named place to await passage back to their own country, since it seemed to be the recognised calling-port for their navy. But how to get there? How to find it, in all these desolate hills, valleys and lakes?

The problem was solved by Glenaladale. He pointed out that since his usefulness to His Highness was now all but over, until a new campaign was started, for he did not know the country at the other side of the Great Glen, and there were here ample Camerons and MacDonells who did, to escort him therein, he could at least offer his final service. He would take the Frenchmen to Loch nan Uamh, he and his brother and Young Borrodale, since they all came from approximately that area. So that was decided.

Clunes arrived again in the evening with the fifty gold *louis* Charles had besought, declaring that the remainder of the treasure remained obviously undiscovered and secure.

Now it was a question of when and how to set the prince on his way to Badenoch. Dr Archie said that he knew the way to the Macpherson country well, and wanted to see his brother anyway to ensure that he was recovering satisfactorily from his wound. Probably Lochiel had seen no physician since leaving Loch Arkaig-side. So he would take His Highness. And Lochgarry announced that he would do so also. If they would give him two days to get back up to his own territory, he would come back with a couple of score of armed men to act as guards for the party on the fifty-mile walk through to Badenoch by the lengthy Corrieyairack Pass. The word was that these central Highlands were not nearly so closely patrolled as were the western areas – at least, not as yet; but when it became rumoured that His Highness had entered them, as no doubt it would, then conditions might be different. Two days . . .

Lochgarry was obviously a great advocate of militant reaction.

The decision was made. Two days, or three, and it would be movement, parting again, more farewells. Meanwhile Clunes would bring Charles better clothing, good footwear and of course food and drink. All were aware of change ahead. Till then, assuming that no further search-parties came their way, it would be a spell of ease, comparative comfort and good company.

Two evenings later Lochgarry arrived back with no fewer than fifty MacDonell clansmen, proving that he could indeed raise large numbers if required. All were armed with muskets, pistols, swords and dirks. Fortunately they brought adequate provisions with them. They camped on another part of the hill lest their presence was spotted and drew attention to the bothy refuge.

Clunes, who visited the prince each day, sent for Dr Archie. Lochgarry was somewhat doubtful about an elderly man accompanying them, however physically fit, and possibly holding them up; but Charles insisted that he should go. He was wise and able, knew the country intimately, and had given service as physician to him during the late campaign. They would move with the darkening.

This time the farewells were as moving as ever but more prolonged, for the numbers were larger; not only Glenaladale and his brother, Young Borrodale, the Glen Moriston eight, Grant, the three Chisholms and two MacGregors and Hugh Macmillan; also Clunes himself and his son, his men, and of course the two Frenchmen. It all made a notably poignant and, for Charles, trying occasion, as he sought to suppress his surges of feeling, for he was admittedly an emotional man. And he had trouble, too, in persuading, indeed commanding, Patrick Grant to accept twenty-five gold pieces from the bagful Clunes had brought, for the Glen Moriston group. What was to happen to these stalwarts hereafter, he preferred not to speculate. That indeed applied to almost all his helpers. Glenaladale, who had been with him the longest of all this company, in tears himself, tapped all the resources of the royal composure.

But at length it was done, or at least an end made of it all, while the prince could still partly control himself. He told the Frenchmen that he would hope to get to Loch nan Uamh within, say, six weeks, in the quest of finding a ship there. Then, with Dr Archie and Lochgarry, he all but ran from that bothy. It was the 28th of August.

20

They picked up the MacDonell escort, and moved down into the eastern end of the Dark Mile again, the doctor managing the difficult descent very well. Then they started on the long journey northwards up the steep side of Loch Lochy, through forest almost all the way. It would have been much simpler and quicker just to cross the River Lochy flowing out at the southern end of the loch; but the ford here was known to be permanently guarded, as strategically important; and although Lochgarry's fifty might well have been able to overcome this enemy group, that would have been to advertise the prince's crossing, and undoubtedly instigate a large-scale hunt and pursuit. So it was up that lengthy journey, of fully twenty miles, along Lochy-side to its head, at Laggan, then further on still up the west side of the adjoining Loch Oich to Invergarry, where the Glengarry chief's castle had been partly demolished, fifteen miles. They managed that before dawn. Here Lochgarry knew the ground intimately, indeed where some of his men had come from. Crossing the Garry ford, they settled for the day near Portmacdonell, a mile to the north, in a ravine-like glen, where even their numbers could remain hidden, well back from the lochside. They were well pleased over this first stage of their lengthy march.

The next stint would be the crucial one, where they had to make the crossing of the main valley, before the vast length of Loch Ness was reached, this so near to Fort Augustus itself. But both Lochgarry and Dr Archie were fairly confident that they could win over the River Oich there without any real trouble, partly because it was normally left unguarded, in the fort's backyard as it were, but also because the country at the other side was all but impassable, a succession of high and jagged escarpments, rearing trackless and forbidding. So this ford was used merely for the troops to gain access to Marshal Wade's military road, built ten years before, after the previous Jacobite rising, to help control the area, but little used at this stage of the occupation. That military road, an engineering feat indeed, was to be *their* road, ironical as it might seem.

The MacDonell men all around acting as scouts, and in their own country, the prince and his two companions passed a peaceful day, mist low on the hills but not raining.

They waited until well into the night before making the vital move. Now they were actually crossing the watershed between the eastern and western Highlands, for the River Lochy ran westwards, eventually to reach the Atlantic, and the River Oich eastwards to Ness and the North Sea. Not that this was very obvious to the travellers in that steep, uninhabited valley. They saw no one on the way.

The Oich was in fact a broad but shallow river, and when they came to the crossing-place, it proved to consist of two fords, for the watercourse was here divided by something of an elongated pebbly island. But the fords proved to be easy enough to cross, not deep, and unguarded, scouts ahead making sure that they were so. They crossed with no least problem, water only up to their knees, this near Coiltry. It was remarkable for Charles to think that Fort Augustus, that dread and ominous location, where so many had been executed, was only two miles away.

Now they were on territory which the busy Marshal Wade had been so greatly concerned with in 1735, where his two roads met. They had to cross the north–south road almost at once, to reach his other one, which probed south-eastwards, up the narrow Glen Tarff, making for the strategically important Corrieyairack Pass, which was to be their route. Now Lochgarry's men spread out back and front and on either side, to ensure no intervention. Not that such was likely in the circumstances.

Crossing from one road to the other entailed quite a climb, a sharp descent, a detour to avoid a large waterfall, then another climb. In the darkness, those not knowing the land would never have found their way. Then they were into Glen Tarff and on the famous Corrieyairack track which, if all went well, would bring them, some twenty miles on, to the headwaters of the River Spey, in Badenoch, still on that military road. Whereafter they would head south for the Macpherson country around Lochs Laggan and Ericht.

This all represented very different progress from any of the prince's previous wanderings, although it was not actually new ground for him, for his army had marched over the Corrieyairack a year before, after the raising of the standard at Glen Finnan. It was straightforward, long-distance walking on a recognisable route. They might have to do some dodging and hiding, to avoid meeting other travellers, although with fifty of a bodyguard they would be very well able to protect themselves. They would have to climb over very high ground at the summit of the pass; but they would not see a single community until Kinlochlaggan. There could be few stretches of mainland Scotland quite so empty and devoid of people. Charles could not get over the fact that the Hanoverian soldier-engineer Wade had spent so much time and labour in surveying this road, to aid the government subdue the Jacobite Highlands; and now to have it serve as an escape-route for the much-hunted Jacobite heir.

The first part of the night's journey, then, was the most demanding. Once they were on that second road it was just a matter of onward trudging until weariness overtook them.

In the event they were, according to Lochgarry, nearing the summit of the pass at almost three thousand feet, higher than many of the major mountain-tops of the land, when they decided to rest, for Dr Archie was beginning to lag although nowise complaining. Up in the jaws of the pass itself it would be bleak in the extreme, so they found a reasonably sheltered hollow where there was a well to give them water, obviously of Wade's construction, to mix with their oatmeal, uncooked, and wash down their cheese. Scouts out, they slept, but only for a few hours. There seemed to be no good reason not to proceed in daylight on this desolate part of their journey.

They crossed the Corrieyairack summit before noon, and began the downward progress into Badenoch, reaching the headwaters of Spey in the Drummin area in mid-afternoon, well pleased with themselves. Not a soul had they seen, only deer, grouse and circling eagles. They had to cross Spey eventually, which they did at the Garva ford, and here they did encounter humanity, in the shape of two shepherds who, seeing such numbers of musket-carrying men, prudently kept their distance.

Now they were into Macpherson country. But it was a vast area. Where were they to find the chief, Cluny, and Lochiel? They certainly would not be at Cluny Castle, down Spey near to Newtonmore, in the prevailing conditions; it was probably burned, like other chieftains' houses. Lochgarry said that they should make for Aberarder, at the head of Loch Laggan. It so happened that the tacksman there was a far-out kinsman of his own, one Ranald Mac-Donell, an odd circumstance so far from MacDonell country; but this Ranald had maternal links with the Macphersons. He would probably know where Cluny was based. Aberarder was none so far off, some seven or eight miles southwards down Glen Shirra. Dr Archie thought that he could manage another seven miles.

They pressed on, over lower ground now, and into the small wooden glen of Shirra, still on Wade's road leading down to Loch Laggan, a major water of Badenoch, which presently they could see stretching westwards for many miles. And at the head of it was this Aberarder, quite a large house, with nearby the little community of Kinlochlaggan, with its church, the first they had seen for long.

Charles was concerned that so large a company as this should descend on what amounted to a village, sure to attract much attention, and word of it spread around in consequence. The bold Lochgarry did not seem worried by this; but he agreed that his men should wait behind, hidden in the woodland, while the trio went on to the tacksman's house. It was evening, and Ranald MacDonell should be at home.

He was, and with his wife and large young family, received the prince with great excitement and acclaim. He had been an officer in the Macpherson regiment. Hospitality was the order of the day. He could scarcely entertain Lochgarry's fifty, MacDonells as they were; but he would send a sack of oatmeal and some butter and cheese, the best that he could do.

Aberarder proved to be valuable in more than just liberality. He was a source of important information. Cluny Macpherson, it seemed, had been hiding in the Ben Alder vicinity about fifteen miles to the south, where he was actually building an elaborate shelter which he was calling his Cage, linked with a cave on the mountainside. But he was not there at present, having in fact gone north himself to seek out the prince, whom he had heard was in the Cameron country, this news having reached him via Lochiel. That chief, being still frail from his wounds, had not returned to his own country with Cluny, but was presently living in a sheiling called Corrienieur, near the small Loch Pattack, nearer this Aberarder. He, Ranald MacDonell, would take His Highness there on the morrow.

231

It seemed, therefore, that this journey of theirs had been not exactly in vain but scarcely necessary. If they had waited with Clunes at Torr a Mhuilt the Macpherson would have come to *them*. But at least they could see Lochiel. And this Badenoch area appeared to be much less troop-ridden than the westerly lands which they had left.

They spent the night in comfort, whatever the state of the fifty in the wood.

Next day Aberarder took them all southwards from Loch Laggan, over rising ground to the source of the modest River Pattack, and down its six miles of glen to near the equally modest Loch Pattack, under the shadow of the mighty Ben Alder, one of the highest as well as the most extensive summits in all Badenoch at not far off four thousand feet. Here they turned aside to climb the twisting valley of one of the other entering burns, towards a fairly lofty corrie overlooking the greater Loch Ericht, which Ranald MacDonell called Mealan Odhar, their destination. This was all new country for the prince. At this stage Aberarder halted the company, declaring that once so large a column was sighted from the sheiling up there, major alarm would be created and possible flight. He would go forward alone and inform them. They knew him; indeed he had visited them only three days before, with food.

In due course he returned, and not alone, bringing with him Macpherson Younger of Breakachie and Allan Cameron, Lochiel's brother-in-law, who came in haste and surprised delight to greet the prince. When these could produce coherent words, they announced that Lochiel was upby waiting to pay his duty to His Highness. But they looked somewhat askance at the large escort of MacDonells. Perceiving this, Charles told Lochgarry that his fifty should remain where they were meantime, as hidden as was possible.

So, with Dr Archie, Aberarder and Lochgarry, he was led up to a quite substantial sheiling bothy on a shelf of the corrie, hidden by rock shoulders, where they found Lochiel and two servants awaiting them.

Charles was quite shocked at the appearance of Ewan Cameron, who came hastening to meet them. A slender and handsome man in his fifties, he had become thin and drawn, indeed emaciated and stooping, seeming to have aged by years in those months since

Culloden. But his reaction to the prince's presence lacked nothing in spirit and ardour. First holding out both hands, arms wide, he then bowed low and would have got down on his knees had not Charles stopped him.

"Highness, my dear and royal master, God has preserved you! I have prayed for this day! I, who have been of no aid to you in it all. I . . ."

The prince grasped those outstretched arms and forcibly held the other upright. "Say it not, my good friend," he commanded. "And do not kneel, I pray, my dear Lochiel." This with a smile. "You do not know who may be looking from the tops of your hills; and if they see any such motions, they will conclude that I am here. Which may prove of ill consequence!"

Lochiel shook his head, at a loss for words, while his brother Archie patted his shoulder.

Ushered into the bothy, the visitors were offered a remarkable variety of provision to be found in such a place, much outdoing anything hitherto encountered in any refuge, an anker of whisky, no less, that is a score of Scots pints, roasted mutton, fresh-killed not salted, an almost complete ham, collops of venison, as well as the usual meal, oatcakes, butter and cheese. Remarking on all this, Charles was told that Cluny kept them well supplied, for they were in the heart of the Macpherson country and, compared with the Western Highlands and Isles, it was a rich territory.

Accepting a generous dram of whisky, and a dish of steaming collops, with even a silver spoon with which to eat it, Charles raised his beaker high.

"Now I live like a prince indeed!" he declared. "Your healths and well-being, my good friends. Here's to us all! And to my father's cause!"

They drank to that, with acclaim.

All were concerned that Cluny himself had gone seeking the prince, to the Cameron country; but no doubt he would quickly learn the true position there and would not be long in returning. They must have passed near him at some stage, no doubt both travelling in the darkness.

Meanwhile Lochiel and Breakachie were worried about those fifty MacDonells left down in the corrie. Such large party would be apt to be very evident; and even though not spotted by enemy troops, would certainly attract attention from the local folk and be talked about. Lochgarry was urged to send them back to their own country, with thanks for their escorting services. Aberarder said that he would see them on their way, and would arrange for them to pick up supplies at Kinlochlaggan.

Before these two MacDonells went off, Charles had a private word with Lochiel regarding Lochgarry's suggestion of an assault on Fort Augustus, again to be strongly urged against anything such at this juncture. The Cameron chief agreed with his brother, as with Clunes, that the Hanoverian repercussions would be drastic; and that, even if the attack was successful, instead of encouraging a revival of the royal cause in due course, it would almost certainly have the reverse effect, wholesale devastation and savageries perpetrated all over the Highlands, arrests and killings, ensuring lowering of morale. The loyal clans needed a breathing-space.

Lochgarry had to accept that, combatively-minded as he was. He would send his men back, but himself remain with the prince's Highness meantime; he might be of some small service.

The others, all save Aberarder, settled in to await Cluny's return, in fair comfort, and with stomachs better filled than for long.

21

Two restful and uneventful days later, Ewan Macpherson of Cluny duly arrived, a well-built man in his early forties, thankful to have found the prince at last, and blaming himself for having managed to miss him on his journey.

He, like Lochiel, had to be restrained from kneeling to kiss the royal hand, and instead was himself kissed heartily on both cheeks, and told how greatly he and his were esteemed; and how grieved Charles was that he, and the Lord George, had not realised how comparatively close the Macpherson regiment had been before the Battle of Culloden, what a mistake that premature confrontation had been, and how, fought a couple of days later on a better field, and with the Macphersons coming up behind Cumberland's army, all would almost certainly have turned out differently.

No use weeping over spilled milk, Cluny averred; but they would prepare for a renewal of hostilities in due course. He also was not in favour of any immediate gesture against Fort Augustus. The clans would rise again; but that must be properly timed and organised, with due French help in arms and ammunition.

Cluny said that, despite their comparative comfort here on Mealan Odhar, he advised a move. He had learned, on his way back, at Kinlochlaggan, that an enemy column was coming up Loch Laggan-side from Fort William, presumably making for Inverness or Fort George, and was sending out patrols as it marched; and quite possibly these would learn of the comings and goings of strangers up and down this Glen Pattack, especially those fifty MacDonells, and might send down the glen below them here one of the patrols. In the circumstances, it would be wise to leave for an alternative hiding-place in more remote country. He knew of one, indeed had used it earlier, at Uiskchilra, south-westwards into the trackless mountains between Lochs Ericht and nan Earba, where they surely would be safe, another sheiling, although it was less comfortable than this one.

In the darkening, if His Highness approved, they should move.

It was a pity to have to leave this agreeable retreat, but clearly wise. At least they could take their supplies with them, nine of them now, including Cluny's two servants, so able to carry it all, the prince insisting on bearing his share. It was, fortunately, no lengthy journey, however rough going, with two quite deep valleys to cross and sundry lochans to avoid. Charles assured that, compared with the Outer Isles and Skye, this was child's-play.

They were none of them greatly enamoured with the new bothy above the stream called Uiskchilra, which apparently meant Water of the Great Surprise, cramped and with a leaking roof and, when a fire was lit, filled with smoke. But it was sufficiently hidden and secure, the dawn revealed. Cluny had no idea why the river, it was more than any burn, should be so called. He apologised for these premises, but announced that he was having a notable shelter built up on the side of great Ben Alder, only another couple of miles away, which he was calling his Cage. It must be nearly ready by this time. He would go and see how it went, and they could all move thither shortly. It ought to be almost as comfortable as any house, and as sure a refuge as they would find in all Badenoch.

They discussed the situation with regard to the two French officers, and the hoped-for appearance of rescue ships. Would vessels keep coming from France to try to pick him up, Charles wondered? Presumably to Loch nan Uamh. Or would those two emissaries somehow have to get back to their own country and then send a ship? In which case it would all be apt to take a long time. It was now the first day of September. He wondered what he ought to do. Stay here with Cluny and Lochiel until they could get word of a ship's arrival? Or make his way back over to Borrodale and Loch nan Uamh, and be there ready for when one did arrive?

Both chiefs were strongly of the opinion that His Highness should do his waiting here in Badenoch, infinitely safer than on the west coast. That was the principal search-area. Those English frigates would still be patrolling there, ever on the watch, and landing parties ashore. Here they were spared ships; and the enemy would not know where to look for him, even though they might suspect that he had crossed the Great Glen. Cluny indeed had heard that one, Francis Grant, had actually engaged a ship at Crail, down in far-away Fife, to take the royal fugitive to

France. Why Fife, he did not know; but if true, it was a significant attempt. Whether the vessel and this Grant were still waiting there was unclear. Certainly embarkation from Fife, with no Jacobite connections, would be far safer than anywhere in the north.

Cluny, who had no lack of supporters available to do his bidding, said that he would send messengers to both Crail and Loch nan Uamh, to try to discover the situation at each place; and when they heard, they could decide on preferences. On horseback, one of his young lairds could get down to Fife, by Perth and Kinross, in three days; so could be back in just over a week's time probably. Charles suggested that whoever went westwards for Borrodale and Loch nan Uamh should try to contact Glenaladale, who lived thereabouts, and was reliable and with initiative. Young Borrodale also, needless to say.

So Cluny went off to select and despatch his messengers, and to inspect his Cage, the others making the best of their present awkward and smoky quarters.

In two days Cluny was back, to announce that both couriers were off, and that the shelter was ready for occupation. He vowed that His Highness would find it extraordinary.

Next day, the 5th of September, the move was made, two more of the Macpherson's servants coming to help carry the baggage. For this was going to be a strenuous transfer, however brief in mileage, mainly uphill, and steep hill at that, in fact all but mountaineering. Cluny's chosen refuge was up the south-west side of Ben Alder overlooking Loch Ericht, and the slopes on that side of the ben were all but precipitous. Picking the least difficult way possible, round-about and back-and-forth, even so it was a major test for Lochiel, others aiding him as they did. They took their time to it, Charles, after his months of practice, probably the most spry, the youngest also, to be sure.

They climbed parallel with a burn, which was a succession of waterfalls, and eventually reached a hollow, less than a corrie, and, surprisingly in that position, quite thickly wooded. And here, on an upper shelf they found Cluny's Cage – although found is scarcely apposite, for even close up it had to be pointed out to the visitors, so well hidden was it.

Astonished, they inspected. It was in, indeed part of, a dense clump of woodland, birch, scrub oak, even holly, made partly of the living trees themselves, still growing uprights to form the walls, with interlacing branches, the roof-ridge a single tall birch bent over and down, with its own boughs, plus others, forming the joists and rafters, all bound together with ropes made of twisted green creepers and twigs. It was thatched with greenery of brushwood and reeds. It was roughly oval as to shape, and large enough to be termed commodious, indeed larger than the viewers even thought, at first, for when they entered by a screened side access they found that it actually contained two storeys, this made possible by the steep slope of the hillside, so that the rear and higher portion had been used to bear a sort of wide shelf. The lower and main flooring was of levelled logs, filled in smooth with soil and gravel. There was a ladder up to the shelf at one end; and at the other, where there was a projection of naked rock, a fireplace had been contrived, using the crevice therein to form a flue or chimney for the escape and diffusal of the smoke, which would disappear amongst the trees and bushes above. Altogether it was a most extraordinary and ingenious creation, and clearly Cluny was proud of it. His guests were loud in their wonder, admiration and congratulation. Not only was its position highly secure up there, concealed and difficult to access, but even when reached indistinguishable from its surroundings. Here fugitives could roost in utter safety, surely, and in comparative ease.

So here the seven of them settled in to await the return of Cluny's messengers, and the advice they would bring, four Macpherson servants helping to attend to their needs effectively, keeping them well supplied with food and drink – and more than that, for they brought clean clothing, including new shirts for the prince from Cluny's three sisters, all living none so far off, one of them Breakachie's wife. Charles declared that all his previous hardships and deprivations had been worth it, just to prepare him to enjoy present luxury.

The weather also was kind, and although they did not venture far over the steeps of Ben Alder, they did often sit out on ledges of the precipices admiring the magnificent views to south and west, all Macpherson country with mountain and loch, but somehow all so different from those of the western areas and isles. They talked a lot, inevitably of the past campaign and mistakes made, but also of hoped-for future ones and better strategies and tactics; also of the Loch Arkaig gold, and of all the good and kind services of so many loyal friends, and the remarkable fact that Cumberland's

238

thirty thousand pounds had never been claimed, even by those who had failed to support the royal cause, Charles asserting that it spoke volumes for Highland character and pride. They played cards frequently, and experimented with a variety of cooking, the prince proud to show off his acquired expertise.

When, after five days, no word came from the west, they sent Breakachie off thither, with two of his men, to make his own enquiries, in case some mishap had overtaken the earlier messenger. Were they impatient?

It seemed that they were, for in only two days Breakachie returned, with their previous courier whom he had met on the way, and with another companion, not Glenaladale, whom the latter had failed to contact, but none other than Colonel John Roy Stewart, whom he had found at Borrodale. Charles, sitting on a lofty ledge, with Lochiel, saw the little party approaching up that difficult ascent, recognised at a distance his friend from the French army, whom he playfully called "his Body", and who had frequently acted as a sort of aide-de-camp during the campaign. In his present relaxed and euphoric state he chose to play a trick on the colonel. He hurried back to the Cage, telling Lochiel not to declare his presence, and wrapping himself in his plaid, head and face covered, lay on their sleeping-shelf to await the new arrivals, hidden. Presumably John Roy knew that he was somewhere about, but when he eventually came up on to the shelf and saw the body, he gained a shock indeed when Charles reared up, throwing off the plaid, and revealed himself. The colonel gasped, all but staggered back in danger of falling off that platform, and then came to kneel and grasp the prince in his arms, gabbling disjointed exclamations.

It was all something of a childish display, but had its own significance undoubtedly.

That odd reunion's excitement was quickly superseded by the news John Roy brought. Two French privateers, *L'Heureux* and the *Prince de Conti,* were in fact presently anchored in a small hidden bay off Loch nan Uamh, and, learning of the prince's present whereabouts, were prepared to wait there for him. They were of thirty-four and thirty guns respectively, and if meantime discovered and assailed by one or more enemy vessels, would give a good account of themselves. But it was hoped that the present precarious peace between the English and French governments would prevent any actual assault, as had proved the case hitherto. But haste on the royal part was advised and urged.

All at the Cage agreed that no time was to be lost. They would not wait for the return of the messenger to Fife, whatever his findings. Better the certainty which they now knew of than the possibly somewhat safer option which might or might not be available.

They would move, then, and forthwith.

After eight days at the Cage, it was pack up and go. All would join in the progress, although not all would aim to sail with the prince.

With the darkening they set out, Lochiel declaring that he was fit for the journey. He would endeavour not to hold them up. Cluny offered to find him a garron to ride, but he pointed out that this would make them conspicuous. It was refused.

22

They went, not as Charles had come, but by a shorter, more direct route known to the Macphersons, by the valley of the Allt Cam over to the foot of Loch Laggan, not its head, a saving of many miles, as the Corrieyairack military road was not to be used, this by a drove-road for cattle being sent to the Speyside markets of Kingussie and Grantown. By dawn they had covered a dozen of these miles, and were overlooking Lagganfoot. Here they would have to cross a ford, and since it was on the main east–west road down to Glen Spean and Fort William, and might well be watched or guarded, they decided to rest up and await the dusk. No doubt Lochiel was grateful, even if he did not say so.

In the evening, the days getting noticeably shorter, they moved on, in early moonlight. They found no one at the Laggan ford, and crossed safely, to turn left-handed down Glen Spean. But not for long, for this could be a dangerous road. They struck off to the north over a shoulder of hill to reach Glen Roy, the moonlight much helping. They went another ten miles, and halted for the day on the west side of that lonely valley, none so far now from the Great Glen itself, Lochiel still managing remarkably well.

Here they risked sending Breakachie ahead again, in daylight, to try to contact Clunes, at Torr a Mhuilt, whom John Roy had seen earlier and who was aware that the prince would probably be coming this way.

By moonlight again, it was on almost due westwards, to where the River Lochy emerged from its great loch, near Gairlochy. This was a wide and swift-flowing river, and again the ford could very well be guarded. This was why Clunes's help was being sought.

Fortunately Breakachie had managed to find him, and the pair of them were waiting for the party near the riverside. And they had a boat. This was an unexpected blessing, for one of the first things that Cumberland's forces had done, in their searchings for Charles Edward, was to sink or destroy all small boats whatsoever, and

241

whoever they belonged to. This one had survived merely because its timbers were rotten and leaked, not worth the trouble of destroying. Clunes had managed to patch it up somewhat, but he admitted that it was still less than watertight. But it ought to serve to get them across the river without using the ford. He and Breakachie had just done so.

He had more than the boat for them, six bottles of brandy, no less. These, Charles suggested, were to give them all courage to risk the crossing! Whatever for, they were much appreciated, and three of them were emptied there and then.

With a dozen bodies to be transported, and the craft small as well as leaky, it was decided that three crossings were necessary, Clunes taking the first three men over himself, to demonstrate confidence, Lochgarry, Dr Archie and one servant going with him, baling as they went, advisedly.

Clunes duly returned, rowing strongly and having to; and the prince, Lochiel and Cluny went next, jugs at the ready, and Charles volunteering to take an oar. Unfortunately the servant dumping the three still full bottles of brandy inboard with them stumbled as he did so, in the shallows, and, crashing, all the bottles broke. So they rowed over to the strong smell of liquor emanating from the floorboards. It made quite a lengthy and slantwise passage, for a strong current tended to drag the craft downstream, however hard they pulled against it. There was quite a lot of richly scented water at their feet before they made a landing reasonably near the previous trio.

When, presently, Clunes brought Allan Cameron, Breakachie and the remaining servants over, the latter were in high spirits, declaring that as well as baling they had scooped up some of the brandied water from the bilge, to drink, fresh from Loch Lochy as it was!

An enlivened party proceeded on, by moonlight, up Lochy-side to the incoming River Arkaig, familiar ground now to Charles, just under the hill of Torr a Mhuilt.

They continued on up the Arkaig to Lochiel's ruined house of Achnacarry, where dawn found them. All estimated that they would be safe enough hiding in the basements of the roofless and ravaged building during daylight, grieved as they felt for Lochiel thus having to act refugee in his own desolate home.

Here they were only some sixty-odd miles from their destination, and it was reckoned that they could cover these in three more nights' walking, plus a little daytime travel in the emptier stretches, Charles finding himself almost the best walker of them all now. They would go up Loch Arkaig-side for some ten miles, to Glen Camgharaidh, and turn up that, southwards, to take them over the passes below the mountain of Streep to Glen Finnan, and thereafter westwards again along Lochs Eilt and Ailort to Borrodale and Loch nan Uamh.

In the early evening Cluny and Dr Archie and servants went ahead along Arkaig, to ensure that all was safe, and to try to obtain provisions for the long mountain stretch southwards; for once they left the loch they would not see another dwelling until they reached Glen Finnan. There was a tacksman's house at Camgar, on the waterside, the name a corruption of Camgharaidh, and there food ought to be available, on Lochiel's orders.

This, in due course, proved to be the case, a young heifer having been slain and cut up for them, and even fresh-baked bannocks ready, with the usual oatmeal, butter and cheese. Thus well supplied, they headed on up the glen, and over two passes, to where Charles had raised his standard those thirteen months before at Glen Finnan. They saw not a soul on the way; and although they approached the head of Loch Shiel with caution, they learned at a croft there that no enemy troops nor sailors had been seen thereabouts for many days. They were gaining the impression that this new commander-in-chief, the Lord Albemarle, was a considerably less determined anti-Jacobite and searcher than had been his predecessor.

They rested only until noon the next day before commencing the last lap of their journey, and the longest; but it would be the least difficult as far as walking conditions went, no hills and passes to surmount, comparatively easy going along the deep valley which contained the lochs of Eilt and Ailort, until they struck off over higher ground, into Borrodale itself.

Nearing, eventually, that surely most dangerous area, salt water ahead, and where enemy ships were probably still patrolling, they went warily indeed, with scouts well ahead prospecting the way. But no alarms were raised, and they reached Borrodale bothy which replaced the house which had suffered the fate of so many chieftains' houses; but they delayed approaching it until dark, just in case . . .

There they found Young Borrodale, who had been hopefully awaiting them, on tenterhooks lest the prince did not arrive before the French ships might be forced to leave. Thankfully he kissed Charles's hand, declaring that all was prepared for him to get to the ships, secretly, with some other refugees already aboard. He had tried to inform Glenaladale of the royal coming, but had failed to reach him; he was somewhere down in Moidart, apparently. As was his own father, Aeneas.

There was no lingering at the house, save for a hasty bite and drink for the travellers.

Young Borrodale took them by his own hidden ways to the coast, saying how anxious for His Highness they all had been these last days, although the anxiety had been theirs for months, to be sure, before that; but it was rumoured that the enemy commanders had a fear that the prince had indeed already escaped to France, and therefore were slackening their efforts; but recently the whisper of the country was that he was still here, on the run, and making for Loch nan Uamh. If this got to the ears of the English captains . . . !

Charles said that he was sorry not to be seeing Glenaladale and his brother, as had been hoped for. He owed them all so much.

Strangely, now, their guide seemed more in awe of the great chiefs, Lochiel and Cluny Macpherson, than of the prince, this no doubt because of the intimate weeks he had shared with the latter on their wanderings.

They had about three circuitous miles to go, by a secret route, towards the head of the loch, if that loch could be said to have a head, rounding little capes, forelands and bays innumerable. Here it became very obvious why this Loch nan Uamh had been chosen as the principal destination for the French ships, for surely, of all the hundreds of major sea lochs of the Highlands and Isles, few if any could be so apt for hiding even quite large vessels, so full was it of creeks and coves, inlets and straits, and all littered with islets, large and small. The most careful navigation was necessary, admittedly, but given that, no better retreat for ships requiring concealment could have been selected.

Although the harvest moon was waning now, something of all this was evident – but not the two ships themselves, against that background of rocky prominences, until suddenly there they were around a sharp headland. A few hundred yards offshore they lay, the most blessed sight which Charles Edward had ached to see for so long. All the party exclaimed with relief, satisfaction, elation.

Young Borrodale had brought a lamp, which he now lit and swung to and fro, there on the shingle, as sign and summons. Watch was set on the ships undoubtedly, for they had only minutes to wait before the rhythmic splash of oars heralded the arrival of a couple of longboats, which beached and landed two men, armed with muskets at the ready, to await the advance of the would-be passengers, young ship's officers clearly. Calls of reassurance greeted them.

No time was lost, all piling aboard amidst greetings and praise. They distinctly crowded the boats, probably a larger party than expected, but none had to be left on shore. Out they were rowed, the craft pitching noticeably, for it was a windy night and the water fairly rough.

They came to the nearest of the ships, which proved to be the smaller, the *Prince de Conti*. One of the officers climbed up a rope-ladder hanging there, on to the deck, concerned that the newcomers, especially the prince, should follow suit carefully, all others holding back to allow Charles to go up first. Gaily demonstrating his agility and proficiency in such clamberings, he mounted swiftly, to be met at the top by a familiar figure, who proved to be Captain Michael Sheridan, son of old Sir Thomas, whom Charles had last seen on Culloden field, and now, shouting acclaim, sank on knee to greet him. Lochiel came up next, much more slowly, helped by Lochgarry behind him on the swaying ladder.

Soon they were all aboard, greetings and congratulations the order of the night, much French being spoken. But, all but apologising, young Sheridan said that, in fact, the prince and his closer friends should descend that ladder again, to go over to the larger ship, *L'Heureux,* anchored a little way off in slightly deeper water, for on board that was Colonel Richard Warren, in charge of the expedition, with some other Jacobite refugees who had arrived earlier.

Nothing loth, Charles followed Sheridan down and into the longboat again, Lochiel less cheerfully, with Cluny and the others, to be rowed over to the larger vessel. As they went, Sheridan asked whether MacDonald of Glenaladale was not with them. Surprised, when hearing that he was not, he said that he and Colonel Warren

245

had managed to contact Glenaladale on first arrival, and sent him off to find His Highness, to bring him. The royal party must have missed him, in passing, sad as Charles was to hear it.

More ladder-climbing. At the top there was surprise and joy indeed, for the hands ready to help him over the rail proved to belong to none other than Neil MacEachain. Astonished as he was delighted, the prince clasped the other to him, shaking him, no need for words. They continued to hold each other, however unsuitable the watchers may have deemed this.

Warren, who had been aide-de-camp to the Duke of Atholl, Lord George Murray's elder brother, greeted the royal refugee more formally, as did MacDonald of Keppoch, another senior chieftain of the Clan Donald, who had lost an arm at Culloden. Lochiel, coming up, was glad to see Cameron of Torcastle, whose fate had been unknown after the battle. Greetings, thankfulness and salutation were expressed on all hands, with brandy to celebrate.

At turned midnight, Warren anxious to be off through the difficult navigational waters of the loch and into the Hebridean Sea before daylight, it was time for farewells, this in a forward cabin.

Charles turned to Cluny Macpherson who had thought of coming to France also, but had been persuaded otherwise. "My dear and good friend," he said, gripping a shoulder. "What am I to say to you? What would I have done without you? Leaving you is a sorrow. Yet you will probably fare well enough here, back in your Cage. Be able to serve my sire's cause better than you could do in France or Italy. No?"

"What I can do, Highness, I shall, to be sure. But I grieve at parting."

"It will not be for long, I hope, good Cluny. For I shall return, to do better than I have done so far, *le bon Dieu* willing! Stronger, wiser, more able. And meantime, there is much for you to do, in preparation, in keeping the clans informed, in readiness to rise again. Much, and none could do it better than you, my Ewan. Work with Young Clanranald, with Glenaladale, with Mackinnon, with Borrodale and Glenpean and the rest. See you, there is the matter of the gold, the *louis d'or*, at Loch Arkaig. You know where all is buried?"

"I do, yes."

"Then use it. Do not leave it lying there. I give you charge. What is left of it. Use to help forward the cause. And also to repay some of my great indebtedness to those who have paid a great price in supporting me. Some to the Glengarry MacDonells. To the seven of Glen Moriston, or eight, indeed. If you can find them! To Kingsburgh. To Miss Flora MacDonald. To Donald MacLeod of Gualtergill. To Clunes and Glenaladale. To others I have told you of. Some small acknowledgment. There are still thousands of the gold pieces. Use them mainly to forward the cause. For when I return."

"Can I *do* this, Highness? Handle the treasure? It is not mine to use."

"I will give you the authority. Write you a letter." He moved over to Colonel Warren, to ask for paper, a pen and ink.

"I fear over this, Highness," Cluny said, shaking his head. "That gold has already been the cause of much trouble, disunity, men squabbling over it. If I go handing it out, there will be more. Disputes over who gets what. How much. Some will claim who deserve none. I see it all as difficulty, a cause of discord and conflict. I would wish no hand in it."

"Somone has to see to it, Cluny. And you I trust. None better. Lochiel, do you not agree? The money lies hidden on *your* land. It should be used, was sent to be used, *ma foi!* Who better than Cluny Macpherson. Glenpean will help him. *He* knows. Their judgment right, wise, honourable."

Lochiel nodded. "His Highness is right, Cluny. This is something that you can do and which needs to be done. Who else remains to do it? You know who deserves the money. And who will make best use of it. Do it, Ewan."

Warren brought paper, pen and an inkhorn. Charles sat to scribble a note authorising Ewan Macpherson of Cluny to disperse funds, to be given upon receipts which he was to keep as record, and signed it *Charles P.R.*

Cluny took it reluctantly.

Farewells to Macpherson of Breakachie and Young Borrodale followed, with the prince's commands to them to pass on to others of his helpers, not present, his gratitude, concern for them, and hopes for the future, he naming not a few. But, with the ship's captain becoming agitated about the problem of getting through those isle-strewn and skerry-littered waters safely, in time to be well out to sea by dawn, this to lessen any possibility of enemy interception and demands for inspection, Warren adding his urgings, these leave-takings had to be cut short. The departing friends, varied in their displays of emotion and concern, climbed over the side and down the ladder to the waiting sailors, to be rowed ashore amidst cries of goodwill. It was an affecting moment, Charles considerably stirred, gripping the rail beside one of the ranked cannon, and staring after the departing craft, a lump in his throat.

That lump was still very much there when, presently, anchors were clankingly raised, sails hoisted, and *L'Heureux* slowly swung round, to commence the cautious navigational challenge of Loch nan Uamh, crewmen lining the foreparts and shouting instructions and warnings to the bridge, the *Prince de Conti* following close behind.

Charles, however, went otherwise, to the stern of the ship, to gaze back to the land he was leaving, none of the others thinking to go with him just then, that land he had come to love, despite all the trials it had laid upon him, and leaving it from the very same spot as he had reached it a year before. Not that, despite the intermittent moonlight, he saw much of its loom, for his eyes were filled with tears.

Charles Edward Stuart was saying a different sort of farewell, and without words.

Epilogue

Sadly, of course, Charles Edward never came back to Scotland, desperately as he wished and sought to do so. Urgently as he worked and planned to muster a second armed attempt, he was badly and consistently let down by a weak father and brother, and by King Louis of France, who found other and more pressing demands on his resources of men and money and munitions of war. Long Charles fought for his and the royal cause, without success, to become, in time, an embittered man, soured and all but degenerate, as some claimed, a sorry fate for one born with so many talents and heir to the most ancient throne in Christendom, as was that of the Scots. And one for whom so many sacrifices had been made.

For those who supported him in those months after Culloden, fate was apt to be even less kind, some executed, some forfeited of possessions, some exiled, few escaping punishment – save perhaps Ned Burke, who managed to return to obscurity in Edinburgh, and resumed his profession as sedan chair man; and John O'Sullivan did reach France unscathed.

Of the long list of adherents and abettors, the cost to some may be indicated. Donald MacLeod, the pilot, was captured on Benbecula, ill-treated, and sent to London, where he was imprisoned at Tilbury. He was released, like others, after a year. Clanranald was arrested, also his wife, and his step-brother, MacDonald of Boisdale. Felix O'Neill was captured and imprisoned in Edinburgh Castle. Eventually released on parole. Flora MacDonald was arrested, sent to London and imprisoned in the Tower. She also was released the following year. She later married, not Neil MacEachain but Kingsburgh's son Allan MacDonald, emigrated to North Carolina, but returned to Skye in 1779. MacDonald of Kingsburgh himself was arrested and, like O'Neill, imprisoned in Edinburgh Castle for a year. Captain Malcolm MacLeod was captured on Raasay and sent to London. Released at the same time as Flora MacDonald and returned to Scotland with her, this under the Act of Indemnity of 1747. Mackinnon of Mackinnon was captured, imprisoned for a year in the notorious hulks at Tilbury, but survived and died at a good old age at his home in Strath, Skye. Captain John Mackinnon of Elgol was less fortunate, in that, arrested, he was so maltreated that he became a cripple and died comparatively young. John MacInnes, boatman, of Skye, lashed with cat-of-nine-tails and imprisoned at Tilbury. Dr Archibald Cameron reached France safely with the prince, but returned to Scotland to try to prepare the clans for a further rising, was captured and hanged at Tyburn. Cluny Macpherson remained in hiding for nine years, astonishingly, then eventually escaped to France, but his estates were forfeited. Lochiel died in exile in 1748. Lochgarry became an officer in the French army.

Neil MacEachain's fate was very different. He remained in France, changed his name to the clan name of MacDonald, and married a French bride. They had a son Etienne, who in due course entered the French army and rose high, high enough to be made Marshal of France and Duke of Taranto.

The list could go on and on . . .